Victoria Routledge
before her first novel, FRIENDS LIKE THESE, was
published. She was born in the Lake District and now
lives in London, where she writes full time as a novelist and
a journalist. She is the author of FRIENDS LIKE THESE,
KISS HIM GOODBYE and . . . AND FOR STARTERS.

Swansong

Victoria Routledge

BCA

LONDON   NEW YORK   SYDNEY   TORONTO

Acknowledgements

All events in the book are the product of a feverish imagination and too much time listening to Led Zeppelin; any glaring inaccuracies are entirely my fault. I'm very grateful to Linda Kenis for humouring me so patiently and telling me better stories about life on the road than you ever could pass off as fiction. Thank you, too, to Redmond and Sheila Morris for lending me their haven of peace and quiet; and to Hulya for the best pre-Christmas Holi-Dazzle ever.

Thanks to Suzanne Baboneau, Jane Holland & everyone at Simon and Schuster for their endless enthusiasm and encouragement, and particularly to Nigel Stoneman: a phenomenal publicist, not to mention a brave man for undertaking a publicity tour with an author who now knows the correct way to chuck a television out of a hotel window.

I'm also indebted to Wendy Kyrle-Pope, not just for making everything work out and add up, but for the intriguing ideas that drop out of nowhere.

Most of all, thank you, Dillon, for making me feel lucky every day.

With love to James Hale,
who makes everything happen.

Chapter One

Chelsea, 2001

'*Rosetta* ...' The little muffled laugh, followed by the rustle of music or chairs, or maybe newspapers, then the bass twiddling, John Lennon explaining something to someone, something about a pick-up, *a pick-up with the fingers, man* ...

Greg shuffled around in the depths of his chair and slid a glance at Flora, Barney's latest girlfriend, who was perched like the confident white Aristocat among the fat velvet cushions on Rosetta's harem sofa. If she looked like she was at an interview, it was because to all intents and purposes, she was. Obviously Flora hadn't done the necessary interview preparation because she didn't seem that nervous. In fact, she probably thought she was going for an entirely different job.

Greg had been watching her all evening with his photographer's eye trained for the unguarded moment when the cute Sloaney mask might slip, and so far it hadn't. Now she caught Barney's eye from beneath long dark lashes and smiled, as if she imagined that his presence offered some kind of guarantee of approval. Flora obviously hadn't met Rosetta before.

Nor had Barney – not entirely without reason – exactly filled her in about their mother.

'Rosetta,' Paul McCartney murmured again through the

expensive speakers, and Greg flinched as Rosetta's expression, slightly hooded as she served the coffee in Flora's direction, registered Flora's lack of response. Greg then knew that he – not Barney – would be driving Flora home in . . . he looked at his watch, ooh, about twenty minutes, probably.

Taking her home as in dropping her off at her front door, rather than *taking her home* in the way Barney would, if, of course, he was still interested once she'd failed to impress their mother.

Miserably, Greg helped himself to another ricciarelli from the crystal dish in front of him, discreetly rubbed in the icing sugar he'd dropped on the red velvet of his squashy armchair and wondered whether there was room in the car for Flora's endless racehorse legs, along with all the new lighting gear he'd borrowed for tomorrow's job. She had informed them, as an opening gambit that probably impressed most people, that she was a model, so she ought to be used to sharing space with lights and equipment in the backs of vans.

Greg frowned. There was a joke in there somewhere.

Barney, happily accepting his third brandy from Rosetta, looked as though he was settling in for the night, with or without Flora.

Flora was not the first, and probably not the last, girl to fail at the Rosetta hurdle with one of the four Mulligan boys. It was one of Rosetta's little tests for her sons' potential girl-friends, to invite them round for some elaborate supper in her gorgeous house in Cheyne Walk, ply them with good wine, ask about their jobs and their flats and their lovely clothes. Then, once they were lulled into a false sense of security about the Demon Ageless Mother from Rock Hell, she would hit them with the Get Back Test.

Under the pretext of serving the very strong Turkish coffee, Rosetta would get up, affect to rifle through her records, and slip *Let It Be* on to her turntable, dropping the needle on the thin band of vinyl with the loving precision of a junkie hitting a vein. Then, when 'Get Back' started, with its gentle rustle of studio chat, if the potential girlfriend was still sufficiently alert to ask whether *she* was the Rosetta whose name Paul McCartney murmured with such amused affection as he tuned his guitar – well, she was in.

Or at least, in with a chance.

If they didn't notice, foolishly imagining they were on the home straight by the friendly way Rosetta had asked them about their fabulous shoes, they were generally amazed to find themselves saying goodbye on the stairs before the record finished, unable to tell exactly what they'd done wrong and wondering whether Rosetta really was some kind of drug casualty or just imperially arsey.

Greg Mulligan, third son, total non-event, as he'd worked out from an early age, watched as Flora, only the latest in a long line of Barney's girlfriends, compounded her error by putting too much sugar in her coffee and failed even to recognize The Beatles. He'd tried to help her out before the critical track came round, deliberately jiggling his eyebrows at the stereo, and asking who was her favourite Beatle, but she'd looked scared and muttered, 'Mick Jagger?' with all the confidence of someone guessing the fifth president of the United States on *The Weakest Link*.

As Flora havered about where to put her used coffee-spoon once she'd stirred the viscous coffee, Rosetta continued to prowl around the darkened sitting-room, rearranging the teams of photographs which crowded the bookshelves in hammered silver frames. 'Get Back' carried on playing, each bar sweeping off Flora's remaining seconds in the warm, lily-scented sitting-room like a giant metronome.

Greg couldn't see Rosetta but he could hear the familiar heavy swish of her wide-legged silk trousers as she moved about somewhere behind him. This was her favourite room, the one where she usually held court, and the wine-red walls were lined with gilt mirrors, making the room feel like a giant musical box – done, Greg reckoned, so Rosetta could keep an eye on everyone from every angle. Typically, of course, she knew where to stand and not be seen. But Greg had a sense of where she was: he had grown up listening to Rosetta moving silently round darkened hotel rooms, checking on her boys, hoping they were all asleep as the party raged on downstairs, then slipping away again, while he lay wakefully next to Robert and Patrick, both of whom could have been put to bed on the Glastonbury main stage and still snored all night. Greg always lay awake, waiting for her to come back.

Barney, being four years younger still than Greg and effectively a whole generation younger than Patrick and Robert, had missed all this. Patrick and Robert had been born when The End, the band their father Brian managed, were still laboriously scaling the heights to their own private jet. By the time Barney was old enough to remember things, The End had imploded dramatically, Rosetta had put her foot down about the endless touring, Brian had more or less moved out, Patrick was spending his boarding-school holidays hitching alone round Europe with his sketchbooks, and Robert . . .

Greg caught his lip curling involuntarily in the mirror which reflected his own chair back at him. It was really hard to remember what Robert had been like as a child, because he'd been in training to be thirty-two most of his life.

'Barney, do you think you could pass me some water?' asked Flora, raising her voice to be heard over the guitar solo.

Greg flinched. Another *faux pas*. Never talk through guitar solos unless you have swallowed something untoward and require help, or unless someone's hair is on fire and they haven't noticed.

There was a clunk behind him, and he knew that Rosetta would be moving the news picture of her and George Harrison drinking rum and coke at the Bag O'Nails to the front of the shelf, just to rub it in.

Barney poured some water from the blue jug into a glass

and handed it to Flora. He dropped a kiss on her pin-sharp centre-parting as he did so and she looked pathetically grateful. It looked a lot like a kiss goodbye to Greg. He also murmured something in her ear that Greg didn't catch but he hoped, really hoped it was something useful.

It was a bit of a mystery why Barney had brought Flora round to see Rosetta anyway. Greg had never met Flora before himself, although meeting all of Barney's girlfriends would be like trying to count the individual rivets on the Forth Road Bridge. It really annoyed Greg that despite all the stupid magazine surveys he kept reading about, having a great sense of humour and an artistic job might be great *in theory* but when it came down to it, what girls *really* went for were huge brown eyes, longish brown hair, tight black jeans, and a grin that confirmed all their worst suspicions.

Most of the time Barney appeared to be dating the Cheltenham Ladies' College netball team, in strict rotation, of course. Like Rosetta, if family lore was anything to go by, he had generously eclectic taste and didn't limit his attentions to one kind of woman in particular; blonde, brunette, dark, Gothic, curvy or emaciated, they all seemed to wear a badge of similarity: the haunted expression born of being kept in a state of nervous tension by the constant street-auditions Barney conducted for their replacements.

Flora was blonde and fragile and very SW3, with a shadowy mark on her nose that might have been a hastily removed nose-ring, or a spot. She looked all right, if a bit flaky, and that might have cut it on the King's Road, but it was a bit invidious, Greg decided, to have to assess her in the context of Rosetta on her home turf.

A bit like taking a remote control Mini along to *Robot Wars*.

He heard the clicking of his mother's Indian tension balls behind him. They didn't relieve tension so much as indicate it. Rosetta was bored, and that was a dangerous time to be around her if you didn't know the tactical moves necessary to outflank a sudden personal attack. Especially when she was serving hot beverages.

'Coffee, Gregory?' she asked, suddenly and carelessly waving the enamel coffee-pot inches above his head. A tension ball clacked in the other ear.

'Please.' He extended his cup and trusted her not to pour it on to his shoulder.

On the other side of the room, reflected in the huge picture mirror with silver fish leaping around it, Greg saw Barney flash a quick smile at Flora, and look at his watch meaningfully. In return, she looked worried and fiddled with the single pearl strung around her white neck.

The guitar solo arched and finished (pop fact: lead guitar by John Lennon, noted Greg automatically). With only one more chorus and half a bridge to go, Flora had one more chance to spot – or pretend to spot, if Barney had been bothered to brief her – Rosetta's voice in the studio chatter at the end, but it didn't look likely. Greg looked around for his camera bag while he sipped quickly at his scalding coffee. He felt very tired all of a sudden and very mindful of his job in the morning. One of them, he felt like pointing out, had to work round here.

As if by telepathy, there was a thud behind him and Rosetta's hand grabbed the back of the chair, right next to his ear. Dangerously, the coffee-pot appeared by the other ear. 'Oh, for fuck's sake!' she snapped. 'Bloody photographers!'

At this, Flora's ears pricked up and one hand went to her cheek. 'Really? Where?'

Rosetta stood up, holding a tell-tale film canister in her hand, a pained expression on her face.

'Sorry, Rosetta,' said Greg hastily, 'I thought I'd left it by the –'

'Why are all you photographers the same?' she demanded. 'An hour to set up, two hours to clear up and only ten minutes actually doing anything? That's men for you.' She gave him a familiar beady look.

Greg scowled. He hadn't exactly volunteered to do this afternoon's pictures. He'd been summoned, found a cowering make-up artist in attendance, and an explanation had been summarily refused, even though he hadn't asked for one. For the next two hours, Rosetta had ordered them both around without mercy, then, as an afterthought, invited Greg to stay for supper, since Barney was coming over. She had even specified the type of film she required him to use.

He stifled an exhausted yawn, surprised at how worn out he was. But, he had to admit, Rosetta was still the easiest person ever to photograph. All you had to do was close the shutter. Flora might claim to be a model, but next to Rosetta she was just a clothes-hanger.

According to the scrapbooks which someone (or someone's secretary) had devotedly compiled of Rosetta's press-cuttings, Greg knew that by the time she was Flora's age Rosetta had already been photographed for five years, traipsing around London in a variety of glamorous outfits with Brian and The End: Red Fearon (drums), John O'Hara (lead guitar), Simon Parr (bass) and Glynn Masterson (tight trousers). The initial addition of an infant accessory in the shape of Patrick, Greg and Barney's oldest brother, didn't diminish her resemblance to a fairy queen at all, at least not on the inner sleeve of The End's first album, where she lay on a rock, with Patrick over her stomach and a rope of scarves over the rest of her.

Rosetta, in those high days of seventies excess, most resembled a ghost queen slumming it with rock musicians. She had been one of the most beautiful girls in London. And unlike Flora's delicate, flower-like prettiness, which Greg knew would fade away after a few years of school runs and ski trips, the strong features that had made Rosetta a stunning girl made her equally stunning even now. Her eyes were still deep green and still wide-spaced above round, high cheekbones. Her hair, which had once been thick and deep red, was now thick and pale gold, twisted up into a bun at the nape of her neck which, rather than looking a bit Princess Anne, only invited thoughts of how it would look tumbling free of its tortoiseshell pins. Rosetta's hands remained young and smooth, with just the one heavy platinum band on her wedding finger to remind herself and her sons of Brian, now living in Geneva, where he ran his empire of tour transportation and collected antique chessboards. The wedding band that linked the current Rosetta to the old Rosetta.

And that was the thing, thought Greg, watching his mother with resigned admiration. Like Mick Jagger, Rosetta existed in a sort of hologram version of herself: the real-life, current Rosetta, drifting inexorably past fifty, but becoming more mysterious and sexy the older she got, overlaid with the luminous myth of the proto-rock-chick twenty-year-old glaring out of all the black and white prints pinned round Brian's old darkroom in the cellar, as if time was just another nosy reporter she could charm or dismiss.

As the clock downstairs chimed twelve, Greg reflected that it probably wasn't healthy, in the scheme of things, to know your mother via a press-cuttings agency.

He drained his coffee-cup.

'Right, I'm off, then,' he said, unable to wait for the end of the album. It was late, he needed to be up early and he couldn't bear to see Flora's eyes all confused like that. Even if there was about as much chance of him pulling her as there was of him levitating her. 'Where are you going, Flora? Can I give you a lift?'

'Uh . . .' Her eyes automatically rose to Barney, now beating up the cushions in the manner of one settling in for the duration, and looking about him for the remote control. She bit her lip. 'Uhm, I don't know, I thought, uhm, Barney . . .'

Barney looked up, surprised. 'What? Oh, yeah, no, I'd go with Greg, actually, Flo – I thought I'd stop over here for the night. Had a bit too much of that wine at supper, you know? Don't want to get stopped by the police. And you live in, er,

Putney, don't you? Greg's not too far away. He'll drop you off. Or get you a cab, or something.'

She wasn't yet old enough to hide her feelings properly, despite her expensive clothes.

'I –' she began, but Rosetta held out her hand – to be shaken, although through long practice it was also just at the right height to be kissed.

'Flora. What a lovely evening,' she said with a smile. The silver filigree bracelets on her slender wrist jingled as she shook Flora's limp hand. Rosetta had a firm grip. Flora didn't.

'Thank you for having me,' said Flora, politely.

'It was my pleasure entirely. I so love meeting all Barney's girlfriends.' Rosetta gave her a chilly smile. 'You're such a sweet bunch of girls.'

Flora looked up at her in dismay, unable to see quite where things had gone wrong. 'Thank you, I . . .'

'Night, Barney,' said Greg. Since Barney was currently dossing in his spare room, it was unusual to say the least that he didn't want a lift back. Then again, his wasn't a big house and it would be nice not to have to be an unappreciative audience to Barney's nocturnal gymnastics for a change. He frowned at his younger brother, meaning, 'Get up and take her home,' or, at the very minimum, 'Get up!' but Barney had long ago ceased to take any shit from Greg, living as he did under the protective canopy of Rosetta's favouritism.

'Night, night, then.' Barney lifted a hand and gave his brother a lazy smile, crinkling up his brown eyes at the edges. Rosetta's brown eyes. Lucky Barney had every single attractive family trait distilled into a potent ninety per cent proof sex appeal, and – bonus time – none of Brian's manifold genetic disadvantages. No wonder he didn't have a job – who could fit one in, with the amount of female attention he had to fight off?

Greg turned away before he saw his own creased brow in the mirror. He felt lacking in ornamentation in this room, in a family where even being a photographer didn't give him glamour points.

'Good night, Gregory,' said Rosetta, suddenly affectionate. Greg frowned deeper as his feelings churned up, as they inevitably did when his unmaternal mother did something maternal. She was always much nicer to her children when they were leaving. She touched his cheek tenderly with a cool hand as he kissed her forehead, and despite himself, he felt touched by her affection.

'You'll send me the contacts, won't you?' she murmured. 'Don't print anything until I've seen them. Nothing at all, OK? And don't show them to anyone. Very *secret*.' She winked conspiratorially at him, but Greg had had enough exposure to her charm to remember it was *him* doing *her* a favour.

'Yeah, yeah,' he muttered. Everything was very secret with her. Except the stuff she told interviewers.

He looked at his watch. Ten past twelve. He had to be in Richmond for eight the next morning, and Putney wasn't exactly on his way, no matter what Barney said. Greg wondered half-heartedly why Barney didn't want a lift home.

So did Flora, by the look of things. Having failed to rouse Barney to his feet, she was disconsolately shrugging her way back into a cardigan which looked so scruffy even Greg had to assume it had been extortionately expensive. She seemed to be having trouble getting into it, going by the shoulder-rolling and stretching.

'Um, Flora,' he started, 'can I, er . . . help you into . . .'

She looked up with an expression of bewilderment, instinctively stepping away from his outstretched hand, and Greg felt himself flush.

Barney gave him a 'Go for it!' wink, which Greg didn't appreciate.

Flora wriggled herself into her cardigan at high speed so it stretched over one shoulder, making her look hump-backed. 'No, I'm fine, really.'

Greg jingled his car keys in his pocket. Maybe if he had a girlfriend of his own women wouldn't be such a closed book. Maybe if he had a girl next to him like a security stamp, he would stop looking like some kind of pervert every time he tried to be nice to one.

'Right, let's go,' he said. 'Night, Barney. Night, Rosetta.' Without waiting, he picked his way around the sofa and floor cushions and headed for the stairs, breathing through his mouth to avoid the onset of the mild hayfever he seemed to get in Cheyne Walk. Greg hated the heavy scent of lilies in warm, enclosed spaces – these days they reminded him of wedding marquees and stress.

He jogged down the wide staircase and, above him, heard the sounds of polite goodbyes. With a guilty feeling of relief Greg opened the front door and felt the evening air chill his face. The Beetle was parked on the opposite side of the road, under a street lamp, which lit it flatteringly and disguised the new dent on the offside wing. Greg didn't feel like getting it repaired – it added to the general effect of ramshackle artistry. He crossed the road, pausing in the middle to let some madman on a weekend Harley Davidson speed by, presumably on his way to a contract killing or an audition for *Grease*, and unlocked his door, using the special 'twist and shove' technique designed to confuse would-be thieves.

'Nice car.' Flora appeared at his side in her now complete wraith outfit. The street light gave her skin a faint blue cast, and set against the backdrop of the Embankment, out of the carefully subdued lighting of Rosetta's house, she did look as if she was in a fashion shoot. The setting was everything with these girls, thought Greg. Half the models he'd met you wouldn't give a second glance to in Sainsburys, but as soon as you saw them through a viewfinder, they transformed.

'Thanks. I got a crap one so no one would nick it.' Greg got in and opened her side. Flora looked down at the passenger seat and gingerly moved a couple of old contact sheets and a handful of empty film canisters, then slid her narrow body into the seat.

It started first time. Greg smiled into the rear-view mirror. At least he had a way with technology.

'Wow!' Flora covered her mouth with a hand. 'I mean, not being rude or anything but I didn't think . . .'

'Yeah, well.' He shrugged. 'It doesn't exactly have a conventional VW engine.' In demonstration of this, Greg put his foot down, hauled the wheel round and shot off towards the river.

Once Flora had informed him of a quick taxi shortcut way to get to her flat they drove for a while in silence. In an ideal world, Greg would have liked to have charmed her with fascinating chat and celebrity gossip, but his small talk was either so small it was bizarre ('Do you like rain?') or he over-compensated so much he sounded like a serial killer ('Are people hollow inside, do you think?'). Besides which, he was drearily running through the timetable for tomorrow: although it was just a straightforward Friday morning register office job, the bride's mother had insisted he do black and white reportage of the pre-wedding preparations, presumably to get as much of her newly redecorated house in as possible. Greg hated pre-wedding shots. They involved women in an ambiguous state of undress, and without the whole veil thing it was often hard to spot the bride – which of course could result in some fast talking. Shame Barney couldn't hold a camera.

'Are the other two like you and Barney?' asked Flora, out of nowhere.

Greg, for whom embarrassments lived on internally like viruses, didn't hear her, as he was still riding out a hot flush of embarrassment at the memory of his last reportage disaster, when he had mistaken a bathroom for a cloakroom and shocked a bridesmaid into hysterics. His hands went suddenly slippery on the steering-wheel. He had never seen a naked seventeen-year-old before. Even when he was seventeen.

'Greg? Are the others like you two?' she repeated.

'Sorry? Sorry . . . Are what?'

'Your other brothers, Patrick and Robert. Are they like you two?'

'Barney and I aren't alike. None of us are anything like each other *at all*,' said Greg emphatically. 'Not even vaguely.'

There was an awkward silence.

'Sorry!' sniffed Flora. 'I didn't realize it was such a sore point.'

Greg took a corner a bit faster than he should have done and clipped one wheel on the kerb. 'No, I'm sorry. Didn't mean to snap. It's just that . . .' He trailed off. 'We're so *not* alike we never believed we could all be related.'

Actually, Greg thought too late, she didn't need to know that.

'I mean,' he backtracked, trying to make it sound like a joke. 'I don't understand how I could have had the same dad as Barney, if Rosetta's genes cancel themselves out.'

Flora made a noise of agreement, which for the sake of his ego Greg tried to ignore.

'I haven't seen Patrick in ages,' he went on. 'Patrick's the real looker. I'm not exactly sure where he is – Ireland, I think. Or Scotland. Somewhere with stones. He travels around a lot. He does those big stone sculptures, the ones you have to photograph from above. Sheep pens. He doesn't really keep in touch with us.'

'Mmm.' Flora didn't sound convinced. She had obviously hoped for something along Barney's lines of glamorous semi-employment.

'And Robert is an accountant. He lives in Clerkenwell.'

'Accountancy? Phew, rock 'n' roll,' Flora observed drily. She scrabbled in her Indian bag and pulled out a tiny purse. Greg hoped it wasn't drugs. Not in his car.

'No, actually,' he added, seizing on the only interesting

fact he could produce about Rob, 'he lives with Patrick's ex-girlfriend. Tanith. She's a casting agent, for films and television, you know.'

'For real?' Flora's attention was abruptly distracted from the contents of the bag – which was, to Greg's relief, her nose ring, in the shape of a tiny lilac pansy. 'What happened? Was there a fight?'

'No, no, I don't think so . . .' Having divulged this much, Greg felt his clam instinct return. He hated talking about his family to outsiders. No one really understood them – either they *wanted* to hear Jerry Springer stories of freak show behaviour, just because Dad and Rosetta had hung out with famous people, or they got all censorious because, well, things that the boys thought were normal apparently weren't. Finding out, in English class, that What I Did on My Summer Holidays was meant to be "My Gite Holiday in Provence", and not "My Holiday on Mustique with The Stones Which Was Actually Dead Dull Because There Wasn't a McDonald's" had made Greg defensive from an early age. He wasn't a show-off. He was possibly even less rock 'n' roll than Robert.

As for Tanith . . . Greg's stomach lurched with uncomfortable desire, as it always did at the thought of independent, dynamic, sexy Tanith.

'I don't think Tanith realized Robert was Patrick's brother when they met,' he said. 'Like I said, we're all very different.'

Flora pushed her finger up her nose to check the security of the stud and arched an eyebrow at him. 'Oh, yeah? Sounds like she's trying you all out for size. Sensible girl. Suppose you're next, are you?'

'No!' Greg frowned so hard his eyes almost shut, which wasn't a great driving tactic on a road comprised entirely of speed humps.

As if. Greg didn't know why someone like Tanith would be with Rob, but he knew for certain that she wouldn't be with him. Even if she did take a sisterly interest in his clothes. And lack of girlfriend.

'So, anyway . . . Barney,' he said. At least Barney had no chance with Tanith. That was some consolation. She was far too clever to be taken in by charming winks and shameless flattery. 'Have you known him long?'

'About six weeks.'

Greg resisted the temptation to say, in that case, she had about another ten days to go. He just thought it, with a throwaway tone in his mental voice that he couldn't ever get right in real life. Besides, Flora might be different, and now she was out of the house, she seemed to have taken on much more definite personality traits. She didn't seem half so obliging, or half so fragile. In fact, Greg was starting to feel a bit nervous.

'And where did you meet?'

'Crazy Larry's.'

'Oh. Right.' He paused. 'Larry the Scouse guy who used to have the bar in Pimlico?'

'No.' She sucked her teeth. Long pause while she assessed whether he was being cute or just stupid. 'Crazy Larry's the *club*. Off the New Kings Road.'

'Oh right! Right, yeah, course.' Greg flushed with a new strain of dormant embarrassment. He'd only ever been there once, for Barney's birthday. He hadn't wanted to go back. Not without training. 'I didn't realize . . . I mean, I thought that was just where you went to pick up fifteen-year-old girls . . . Oh fuck, not that you're . . .' He trailed off and bit his upper lip. *Duurrrh*. He wondered whether Rosetta slipped him truth drugs whenever he had tea there. He wouldn't put it past her.

Flora removed her disposable lenses and flicked them into the footwell. Greg didn't see much point in asking her not to, since it was already full of rubbish. She rummaged again in her bag and pulled out a pair of lemon-tinted, black-rimmed picture editor glasses, possibly, Greg thought as he checked his mirrors, for the sole purpose of staring dismissively at him over the top.

'You don't get out much, do you.' He recognized this as a statement, not a question.

'No. I have a job. Do you have one?'

Flora slumped back in her seat without bothering to reply, and rubbed her eyes under the specs.

'Just drop me at the end of the road, will you? My flat-mates are expecting me back.'

Greg suspected this was coded in some way, but he didn't know enough to translate. He just felt pissed off, and more pissed off that he couldn't shout at her.

Once he had dropped Flora off, at a huge house with four separate dustbins and four Polos in varying states of decay outside, Greg turned on the radio and drove home in a simmering bad mood.

More and more these days he had the distinct feeling that his entire life was spent being summoned and dispatched back and forth by women, usually without so much as an explanation or thanks. Or even any recognition that he was a single, available bloke, most of the time. The more helpful he was, the more they smiled and treated him like an honorary girl. No one, not even Barney, met as many single girls in the course of a normal day as Greg did (all, as Barney pointed out, in an agreeable state of panic at the marriage of yet another of their mates), and yet Greg hadn't had a girlfriend since . . . since . . .

I'm just waiting for the right woman, he told himself and winced at how unconvincing it sounded, even in his own head.

Greg's eye was caught by a stray, half-finished Yorkie which emerged from under a pile of negs as he went round a corner too quickly, and eating it cheered him up considerably, the downside being that it opened up a new hunger hole in his stomach. The roads were quiet and he put his foot down, suddenly wanting to get home. There was some kind of pasta sauce thing in the fridge that Tanith had made him take home last time he'd eaten at Rob's. Four days ago – that should still be OK, shouldn't it? To stop himself thinking about food, Tanith's maternal instincts, and, more disturbingly, what Rosetta wanted those new photographs for, he retuned the radio to Classic FM, so no lyrics could add to his growing sense of unease.

There was a space about two hundred metres from his house – some kind of record. He steered the car into the gap, and sat for a few moments and listened to the ticking of the engine cooling down in the silence of the street. There was a long stray blonde hair where Flora had leaned back in her seat; Greg reached out to flick it away, then hesitated, and left it.

With an effort he got all the lighting gear out and dragged it inside in one go. He had perfected a system of balancing himself so he could move slowly forward while weighed down with inordinate amounts of stuff. It didn't do to leave things lying around at weddings. Not for the criminal element – they would be far too distracted by the table full of white goods from John Lewis – but for the simple reason that tipsy mothers had a habit of falling over things, and it was amazing how many of them were addicted to daytime TV and had learned the numbers for 'no win, no fee' solicitors who could get you eight grand for stubbing your toe in B & Q.

Greg let himself in, with some juggling of bags, and was surprised not to feel the door catch against a pile of junk mail. He dumped the lights in a pile and was more surprised to hear the distant sound of soft music, and to discern the faint trace of burning hair and candle wax and camomile tea in the air.

A young woman barely concealed by a precarious white towel put her head round the bathroom door and breathed, 'Hi, Barney, I thought you'd never . . . aaargh!'

And seeing not Barney but Greg, she shot back behind the door.

'Oh . . . fuck,' he breathed, not too loud in case she heard him and took it as a threat.

At least it explained why Barney had stayed at Rosetta's. It didn't make the lingering sting of Flora's dismissiveness go away.

Rosetta drained the last of her cooling coffee and looked at her youngest son, who had dozed off at some point during her explanation of why Gram Parsons was so important to the modern singer-songwriter. It would be easy to be annoyed – he was the rudest of four very rude boys, and knew it – but luckily for Barney, it was equally easy to feel an indulgent sense of pride.

Barney's beauty stirred up both relief and panic in Rosetta. He was a kind of proof that she had once been as beautiful as that, and yet a reproach that she wasn't any more. Of all her children, Barney looked the most like her: with his high, strong cheekbones and pale skin, and the confident, wide-eyed stare that would have tipped him over into prettiness if he hadn't had the attitude to go with it.

Barney was the one she had been so sure would be a girl, sure enough to have bought and hidden all the little dresses and hats. Brian had bought clothes secretly too; she found a tiny pair of butter-soft leather bootees tucked inside his sock drawer. He hadn't said anything in case he upset her, which was like him, but Rosetta knew he really wanted a little girl and had done since Patrick was born. Rosetta wanted Brian to be happy, of course she did, but by 1980, that had been the state of their marriage in a nutshell; two business-like friends, who didn't want to inconvenience each other too much.

Rosetta sighed. Barney had been a surprise. Was it so odd to have hoped for a little girl who would understand her moods, who could be dressed up and taken to see her friends, and not give out those impenetrable freaky male glares that her sons could silence a restaurant with. Yet when Barney was born, a calm and creaseless baby boy amidst the falling debris of her life and her family and the band's career, she couldn't help feeling a terrible guilty kind of relief that here was another tiny man to charm and love.

She watched him sleeping in the huge velvet chair. Barney's lashes, as long as hers, fluttered against his cheek, and the soft duck-egg cashmere of his jumper rose and fell peacefully as he dozed. He was like a sleek cat, Barney, and he didn't snore. More than one nymphet on similar evenings had confided that to her with wide-eyed delirium – as if she wouldn't know. Barney's childhood was tangled up so much with the final days of the band, of her old life, that sometimes Rosetta's breath caught, thinking about it, and her heart felt heavy in her chest. Barney had felt like her last chance to get it right, but Rosetta wasn't sure if she hadn't screwed it all up royally even before he was born.

She shook herself and put down her coffee-cup.

Absolutely no point getting maudlin now, she thought sternly, and checked her watch against the clock. It was ten past one, though it felt later. She looked at her son for a moment, then decided against waking him up. He was twenty-two, after all, and he knew where his bedroom was.

Rosetta walked up close to the big gold mirror hanging over the fireplace and stretched the delicate skin around her eyes until the green lids closed of their own accord. She tried to summon up a vision of Barney as a child – one appeared immediately like a photograph: four years old on the King's Road, wearing his little pedal-pushers, and her in a tight black skirt and batwing jumper. They had just been to some vintage clothing shop, where she'd seen a Mary Quant pinafore exactly like one she'd rushed out and bought herself before Patrick came along. In a vintage shop!

'Mummy, why are you crying?' Barney had cooed with concern, stroking her leg with infinite tenderness, learned from she didn't want to know where.

Thirty-four years old, with four children, and already she was vintage.

She opened her eyes, looked at him, and couldn't transpose the image of the child on to his adult cheekbones and flopping hair. It was hard to see, in these adults, the children she had brought up and fought with and fought for. Which was funny, because despite the four lads she'd never seen herself as a mother; it hadn't exactly been top of her to-do list.

Rosetta sighed and pushed her fingers into her hair. No time for messing around any more. There was so much to arrange and she always had had her best ideas just before bed. She got up silently, padded to the door, and turned down the lights on the dimmer switch so only the orangey street light filtered into the room, making the gilt on the mirrors glimmer dully. Barney dozed on, the image of tranquil manhood unsullied by snores or dribbles, looking as though he was only posing there momentarily for a cashmere catalogue shoot. To Flora he would probably have looked vulnerable, but to Rosetta he didn't. She could see too much of herself there. He was merely refreshing himself before another charm offensive.

She shut the door, and turned to go up the stairs. As she passed her study, the one room in the house with a lock on the door, where she could sit and write letters to people and read books in peace, her eye fell on her diary for the rest of the week. It was empty. On a whim Rosetta went in, without bothering to switch on the light, and sat at her desk. As she breathed the familiar smell of old leather and ink, she could hear her own voice in her head, turning over the old 'Do Not Disturb' sign, telling the boys to go away and play in the road while she locked herself in to make her phone-calls and sort out her week into lunches, drinks and escape-time. She always did far more than they imagined.

The light from the street gave the room a faded glow, with the colours only shadows. On the desk next to her was a vase of purple tulips that Greg had brought for her the previous week. He was thoughtful like that. They had carried on growing, and were now leggy and curling, stretched out of their original arrangement, with the petals splaying into papery tongues where they once had a glossy uniformity. Rosetta liked tulips in the final stages of decrepitude. They looked more interesting, twisting out towards the window for the final rays of light.

For a moment, she supported her head with the tips of her fingers, and let the silence of the house flood her mind, smoothing and arranging all the arguments bubbling up in her head. She wanted to push her whole life away, like a fractious, wriggling child, but without letting go. Then she took out a notecard from the rosewood stationery drawer.

Once she began to write, absently admiring the glossy wetness of the black ink on the creamy matt paper, it all seemed perfectly obvious.

'Dear Sue,' Rosetta wrote in her looping cursive hand, the d's like musical notes and o's curled in like Chelsea buns, 'it was such a treat to see you last week – thank you for a marvellous lunch. I've been thinking about the project you suggested, and after much soul searching, I think you're so right. It would be a wonderful idea . . .'

Chapter Two

Interview number one, 1967

It took Rosetta about three hours to get the flat exactly right for Sue's interview, even though the place was so small that, lying down, head to toe, she, Brian, Red and Glynn, the drummer and the lead singer from The End respectively, could touch each wall. They'd done that one evening. Brian had insisted that that was how fields were measured in medieval times. Well, they'd been stoned, Brian had done A-level History.

It had taken her three hours because she was determined to make the right impression for her first ever magazine interview.

Her first ever interview! she added to herself, and immediately battened down her excitement.

Rosetta was desperately keen to make the right impression, even if the interview was with Sue – a friend from school who'd left the same time as she had and somehow talked her way into a job on the very fashionable *Pop Miss!* magazine. Sue had spent five years kicking her heels mutinously in the shadow of her more out-going popular friend, but she famously wasn't easy to impress.

Rosetta knew that she had quite a strong card to play in terms of the flat Brian had just rented; she'd heard a pleasing intake of breath from Sue when she dictated the Cheyne Walk address to her. The challenge now, though, was to make the interior live up to the trendy location, given that their remaining income barely kept her in mascara.

Being a well-informed girl, Rosetta knew every last detail of the Rolling Stones' groovy pop palaces, and their heady mélange of glamour and squalor, but she couldn't quite bring herself to mess up her own flat with real filth, even to impress Sue's readers. What glamorous squalor there was in Brian and Rosetta's flat was discreetly detachable – peacock feathers in distressed silver vases, random Indian receptacles that might or might not contain exotic drugs, glittery swags of material from an Indian warehouse in Chiswick rather than Marrakech. Rosetta had doubled it all prior to Sue's interview, until the flat looked like some kind of harem, albeit one with a kitchenette and a small black and white television.

But even with all the magpie glamour stripped right back, her mother would still have hated the place – *if*, of course, she'd ever been invited round to pass an opinion. Not that that was likely, given that both of them had sworn vehemently not to have the other darken their doorsteps *ever again*, the night Rosetta announced that she wouldn't be going back for her A-levels or trying for Oxbridge or fulfilling *any* of her mother's plans, since she was moving out of her mother's house and in with Brian, 'that dirty, long-haired cradle-snatcher!'

Brian Mulligan was twenty-two and had four A-levels, and under any other circumstances would have been welcomed with open arms, since he had a good job, his very own car and horn-rimmed reading glasses.

It shouldn't have been a surprise to anyone. To the despair of her mother, Rosetta had never fancied a semi in Sheen with a garden for kiddies to play in. As long as she could lean over her balcony rails and look out on to the wedding-cake houses of Chelsea, she didn't really notice the smallness of the flat, or the damp and prehistoric bathroom. All the really important things were right: it was near the river, it was light and airy (ish), and, more to the point, it was three seconds from the King's Road, where her best friend Anita had opened a boutique selling hand-embroidered shirts and tie-dyed sheets. There were other parts of London that Rosetta liked, but when it had come down to it, she hadn't really been given a choice: Brian, who had a sharp instinct for the right thing, had insisted that they got a flat as near to Cheyne Walk as possible, even if it meant living in a wardrobe.

Which was pretty much what they did anyway, seeing as Rosetta's clothes and Brian's papers had quickly filled up any storage space and now every picture-rail in the tiny studio was filled with Anita's velvet psychedelic drapey gowns on hangers, or the latest batch of The End's cheese-cloth stage shirts, freshly laundered by Rosetta.

She threw a couple of the dresses over the chairs to add colour and texture, and decided to leave the shirts up. Washing for husband = bad. Washing for rock group = good.

She checked her watch again and her heart fluttered with uncharacteristic nerves. Four minutes to eleven. Sue had always been dead on time at school. Quickly Rosetta did one last scan for anything unbefitting an up-and-coming pop manager, dumped her knitting and Brian's sheepskin slippers into a box, threw a sari over it and shoved it into a corner. As an afterthought, she put a lamp on top to give it more of a deliberately 'table' look.

If her mother could see the carpet she would probably have some form of spasmodic speech failure. Rosetta had painstakingly gone round all the insanely swirly carpet with a sweeper, and put rag rugs over the most worn sections, then beaten the curtains to try to get rid of the smell of dope and curries. As she hammered away at the long drapes with a cricket bat, like a deranged housemaid, it occurred to her that maybe dope and curry was exactly the impression she should be leaving *in* the flat, but a lingering sense of propriety still just about had the upper hand.

What was it Brian had said before he went out to meet the bank manager? She stopped hammering. Oh yes, don't forget to offer Sue some coffee and biscuits.

Coffee. Rosetta rocked back on her stacked heels and contemplated the tiny kitchenette. Sue was a journalist now, she was bound to want that strong Turkish coffee everyone was drinking. Brian had bought some kind of percolator contraption, but since they always went out on to the King's Road for coffee, Rosetta had never even worked out how it switched on. And the one time she'd heard Brian use it, it had sounded like it was about to explode. She grabbed her *Good Housekeeping* book to see if there was anything in there about where you put the water.

The intercom buzzed before Rosetta could ascertain whether she'd even bought the right kind of beans, and in a panic she slammed the book shut and hid it in a big carved (bread) box. The stairs weren't all that easy to negotiate in her clumpy shoes and her feet overlapped the narrow treads in a worrying fashion.

From now on, she instructed herself, smoothing down her skirt, imagine you're reading about yourself in a magazine.

Downstairs, Rosetta could see Sue's dumpy outline through the frosted glass of the grand front door. Mini-skirts hadn't been any kinder to Sue than gym-skirts had been, but the newer maxi-skirts at least allowed her to hide a substantial pair of heels underneath and lever her up from stumpy to statuesque. The downside of platforms was that Sue now frowned with concentration when she walked and moved as if she was on casters.

OK, Rosetta thought to herself, pulling the band off her hair and smoothing it down into a long amber wave, tweaking strands in front of her eyes. Remember to be cool. Remember, don't talk about school or curtains. The End. The End. You are a rock girlfriend. Think Anita Pallenberg, not Jane Asher. Think *cool*.

'Hello there, Sue!' Rosetta beamed, opening the door wide.

Sue, second best at English at school after Rosetta, was wearing a long red skirt and a red plastic mac. She looked like a postbox, especially since every other accessory – panda eyes, plastic handbag, clunking Lucite jewellery, Cher curtain haircut – was jet-black.

'Rosemarie!' she said and kissed her cheek.

'Ah, it's Rosetta now, actually,' said Rosetta firmly.

'Oh, really? OK,' said Sue with an ambiguous smile, which Rosetta ignored for the time being. There wasn't anything wrong with a touch of self-reinvention. She would have to check, but presumably Sue wasn't writing pop features under the byline Susannah Morton-Thomas.

'Come on in,' she said, trying to be expansive and casual, while not making enough noise to wake up the mad old dowager who lived in the downstairs flat and who still hadn't totally forgiven Rosetta for a late party the previous week. 'Brian's out at the moment, but he said he might be back for lunch.'

'Well, it is you I've come to interview, not Brian,' said Sue. She was puffing a little going up the stairs, which Rosetta was surreptitiously pleased to note. The fact was that both of them were having to go up virtually facing the wall, in order to get enough purchase on the narrow treads.

It had been half Brian's idea to get Sue over as part of his masterplan to launch The End on their stellar career. He might be the manager, but they'd both come to the conclusion that since Rosetta was a good deal more photogenic than his acne-ravaged band, it might be an idea to approach publicity from a more roundabout angle. It had only taken one artful phone-call to persuade Sue to come round and interview 'Rosetta, the new girl-about-town who's seen with all the new bands, in the company of pop's Brian Mulligan.' Naturally, both of them had had to pretend to check diaries first and so on – because it wasn't just Rosetta who was angling for publicity. Sue had a sharp nose for gossip, but she was in rabid competition with the sudden new crop of cool girl-journalists who filled the pages of all the papers, as though Lucie Clayton was now running a course in pop-picking.

That's the thing about London, thought Rosetta, as she let them into the little flat, suddenly seeing it from a new, critical perspective and being pleasantly surprised. You can be whoever you want, but you have to be convincing about it.

'What lovely curtains!' exclaimed Sue and immediately looked cross with herself. 'I mean, fab view! You must be ten seconds from the King's Road.'

'Oh, we are,' Rosetta agreed. She was pleased to note that she wasn't the only one fighting *Good Housekeeping* instincts, and it reminded her to go straight into her interview technique. Rosetta had taken the precaution, the previous night, of sketching out the interview the way she wanted it to go, with Brian's help, to be sure of getting in all the appropriate answers, whether Sue remembered to ask the appropriate questions or not.

'When we're in London, it's really convenient. Brian's all over the place at the moment, up and down the country. The lads are always on the road, you know, touring, so I'm hoping we'll be . . .'

'Hang on,' said Sue, holding up her hand, so the black bracelets clattered down and stuck on her brawny lower arm. She put on a huge pair of round glasses and hauled a tape recorder out of her shiny black bag. Rosetta swallowed hard, as Sue looked round for somewhere to put it, and she quickly dragged over another orange box, this one covered with one of Anita's mad op-art batik shawls. She had to drag it carefully, so as not to reveal the orange box beneath. Maybe she *should* reveal the orange box beneath, she thought feverishly. Would that make her look cooler? More bohemian? Hmm. Maybe if the interview started going badly she could whip it off.

'What a fab lamp!' cooed Sue, running her fingers over the printer's block. It was a capital R. 'Is it from Heal's?'

That rang a bell somewhere in the back of Rosetta's mind. Damn. Where was it from? She should have kept the packaging.

'Mm-hm. Brian gave it to me,' she said. OK, *casual*. 'For passing my . . .'

No, not her driving test. Too suburban.

'For when the band, uhm . . .'

One of Sue's pencilled eyebrows lifted in enquiry.

'You know, it was just one of those spur-of-the-moment mad gifts,' said Rosetta airily. 'Brian's a very generous man. Come and see the balcony.'

'Are these clothes from Granny Takes a Trip?' asked Sue, fingering one of the dresses from Anita's shop, currently doubling as a chaise longue spread.

Rosetta wondered if Sue wasn't allowed a photographer and therefore had to remember the flat and draw an illustration from memory. 'No, darling, they're from Anita's. You know, Anita's Boutique? It's down the road from World's End.' With about three items currently left on the shelves, if the stock currently 'on loan' in the flat for the purposes of this interview was anything to go by.

Sue's over-kohled eyes widened behind the glasses.

Those glasses, on top of the handbag and the eyeliner, really were a bit last year, thought Rosetta. A bit too plastic fantastic. Maybe she should say something? As a friend?

'Not Anita *Crowther*?' exclaimed Sue. 'Anita owns Anita's Boutique?'

Rosetta nodded and smiled. This was good. Good that she was getting some publicity for Anita, who would now maybe give her the blue silk smock she'd been after, good that she was one step ahead of Sue, who was, after all, meant to be a journalist, and *very* good that Sue had been at school with both of them and would therefore feel some kind of moral obligation to do them justice, if only to boost her own connections.

'Oh, well . . .' murmured Sue. The quick brown eyes behind the glasses also seemed to be putting two and two together and coming up with a couple of new outfits. 'Well, she always was very good at Domestic Science, wasn't she?'

'Anyway . . .' Rosetta casually cleared a space on the chaise longue and sat down delicately in the middle of the green velvet. She looked like a mermaid on a lilypad. 'Shall we get on with it? You must be so busy with your deadlines and everything.'

Sue snapped out of her mental calculations and her face resumed the expression of a busy professional journalist. Now she could see it was an expression, rather than any-thing more threatening, like experience, for instance, Rosetta was beginning to feel more confident that she could take this interview wherever she wanted.

It wasn't that different from school, really.

'Oh, er, yes. Absolutely,' said Sue. 'Is it OK to . . .?' She gestured at the tape recorder and Rosetta nodded dismis-sively, as if she had been interviewed about a million times before.

'OK,' said Sue. She bit her lips, pushed her hair behind her ears and produced a notebook from her pocket. 'Hello, Rosetta!' she said suddenly.

'Hello, Sue.'

'Thank you so much for letting us come in and talk to you in your lovely home.'

'Um, that's my pleasure,' said Rosetta, and then added, 'It's cool,' for good measure. Her mind slid back to the per-colator. What if she made instant and just poured it out?

'Your husband, Brian Mulligan is closely associated with The End, who are one of London's most talked-about new bands,' Sue informed her, reading from her notes. 'Perhaps you can tell us how you met your fiancé, Brian?' There was a pause. 'I mean, your fiancé, who *is* Brian.'

Rosetta stared at Sue, then stared at the tape recorder. *Fiancé*, Brian? Was this the right moment to say that she

and Brian weren't actually engaged? Surely Sue knew that?
Her mother would go insane with embarrassment. But then
did her mother actually bother to read all this stuff?

Rosetta's mind spun rapidly and she fiddled with a button
on the dress. The reality was that she'd been desperate to
move away from home, and Brian, with his swift decisive-
ness and intoxicating confidence, had swept her off her feet
and into their own little flat, which she somehow found herself in charge of. Naturally, whether she wanted Sue to know
the *reality* was a whole other issue.

While she was considering this at lightning speed, she could
see Sue picking up the most recent framed picture of them
together, taken at quite a trendy party at the Scotch of St
James. She didn't exactly know how they'd got there, but
Brian, packaged neatly in a sharp suit and black square-
framed glasses, was looking as though he was the founder
member, while she sat on his lap in a pair of white patent
leather knee-high boots, taking care to keep the knees together.
It was a very cool picture. That was why Brian had bought a
frame for it and made sure it was constantly in one's line of
sight. Those glasses literally followed you round the room.

He was pretty cute, she thought indulgently. Like a very
sexy English teacher.

'Oh, Brian and I aren't *engaged*,' she heard herself say,
with a kind of breathless insouciance she realized she was
copying from Marianne Faithfull. 'All that marriage baggage is such a head-trip, don't you think?'

On the other side of the tape recorder, there was a slight
intake of breath from Sue.

So much for the unshockable face of Fleet Street, thought
Rosetta.

'That's very . . . modern of you,' said Sue, with a hint of
something in her voice that Rosetta couldn't quite make out.
Was it disapproval? Or just jealousy? Anyway, plough on . . .

'Shall I . . . tell you how we met?' she suggested, sensing
Sue had lost her place in her questions.

'But I know . . . Oh, er, yeah, that would be great,' said Sue.

'Brian and I met at the Crawdaddy Club you know, in Richmond,' said Rosetta dreamily. 'We both used to go a lot, but the first time we met was at a gig in 1965 . . .'

'You must have been very young,' said Sue, sharply.

'Er, yes,' said Rosetta, then added quickly, 'He'd heard about this new group who were opening for The Yardbirds, and I was there with my brother, Neil, who was the drummer in a group called The Pick-Ups . . .' Rosetta gave Sue an inclusive, 'You know my brother Neil, don't you?' wink, in the hope that it might soften her up a bit.

'I know Neil, yes.' Sue's face was steely.

Rosetta remembered too late that she'd tried and failed to set the two of them up at Christmas. It hadn't worked out: Neil had made Sue pay for the drinks then escaped through a toilet window. Oh damn, she thought, how can I turn this one round?

'And are The Pick-Ups still successful?' Sue enquired, obviously hoping that they would have changed their names and gone on to be the Pink Floyd or similar.

'Er, not really *here* . . .' Rosetta debated internally. To lie or to be deliberately obscure? Something just appeared in her head and she heard herself say it. 'They're quite big in . . . Spain at the moment,' she said and flicked up a shy glance from under her sparkly eyeliner.

Sue's thin eyebrows twitched again and she made a few notes on her pad. It was typical of Sue to be taping the interview and taking notes at the same time. Rosetta could see the sentence, 'Brother No. 1 in Spain!' form upside down as if by magic.

God, she thought with a rush of exhilaration, *interviews are easy!*

'Do carry on,' said Sue. Rosetta noticed Sue's manner was now swinging erratically between coffee-bar cool and Home Counties politeness under the mixed influences of her seraglio sitting-room, the tape recorder in front of them and the fact that they'd been doing O-level Chemistry together a matter of months ago.

'Oh, well, our eyes met at the bar' – mainly because Rosetta had needed someone to buy her a drink, since, though she looked about twenty-one and had been sneaking out to R 'n' B nights since she was twelve, the barman knew she was only fifteen – 'and that was it, really.' She paused to share a soppy smile with Sue, and, realizing that soppy smiles wouldn't show up on the tape or the notepad, added, 'I was just swept off my feet by his dynamic personality and the fact that he obviously dug the music as much as I did. And we've been blissful ever since.'

That much was true. Rosetta firmly believed there was no aphrodisiac like rhythm 'n' blues, and Brian – the sexiest older man she'd ever met – agreed.

The *only* older man she'd ever met, she corrected herself. Rosetta had scornfully rebuffed all male approaches beyond cinema dates and mild necking until Brian. But it had been worth saving herself. Oh yes.

'How charming!' said Sue. 'I mean, wow, what a cool scene.'

Rosetta started to plait a thin section of amber hair and wondered who on earth had commissioned Susannah Morton-Thomas to write about rock music when she probably thought R 'n' B was some kind of new cocktail. What was the point of the interview anyway – to check out her curtains?

A cold finger of doubt traced down Rosetta's spine. She wasn't the kind of girl to have doubts often, but when she did, she took notice of them.

She stopped plaiting for a moment, and considered the possibility that Susannah Morton-Thomas was planning some huge intellectual stitch-up. 'Rock Stars Stole My Youth, says Latin scholar' and all that. Was Sue up to that? Was she really working for *Pop Miss!* and not, say, *The Tablet*?

'Can you tell us a bit more about this place in ... Richmond?' Sue looked over the top of her glasses. 'For those readers that haven't actually been to the, er, Crawdaddy Club?' She pulled a face which was meant to say, 'Poor old uncool them!' but it didn't fool Rosetta.

Or maybe Sue's minimal knowledge of R 'n' B was an advantage ...

Rosetta took a deep breath, and tried to imagine what she would want to read about herself, were she poring over this in a magazine. The photos and text floated up in front of her mind's eye – they were more familiar to her than German verb tables: Marianne lounging ambiguously on cushions with Anita Pallenberg, Julie Christie, Paul McCartney in his Aston Martin ...

'Well, it was the most exciting night of my life,' Rosetta elaborated earnestly. 'It's a very exciting place, you know. Or it was a little while back, anyway. The night we met, one of the local bands had just got back from touring, and the crowd was just leaping up and down, focusing everything, all their energy at the band, and even though the place was going wild, the guys were completely cool, like they didn't even care about all the madness going on at their feet, and that just made the crowd scream even louder.'

Her eyes drifted away, just thinking about it. It had been the best gig she'd ever, ever been to. It had made her feel ...

'Anyway?' Sue prompted, peering at the spinning reels of her dictaphone.

'Oh, anyway, I was dancing at the front with Anita – one of my friends from school,' she added for the benefit of the tape, noticing too late the sudden, 'why-didn't-you-pick-me' frown that appeared over Sue's owlish plastic specs, 'when I saw this man standing at the side of the stage in a really sharp brown suit. He had a pair of glasses just like Andrew Loog Oldham. I didn't know whether he was with the band, but he just had that look about him, that he knew what was going on. I like that in a man, it's a real turn-on, don't you think? He saw me too, and I knew immediately that I'd be with him. It was exactly like something from a song.'

Rosetta believed strongly in life turning out like songs. That was why people wrote them in the first place, wasn't it?

'Really?' asked Sue. 'Which song? Like, "I Saw Her Standing There"?'

'Yes,' Rosetta agreed. 'Or "Da Do Ron Ron".' She realized a little too late that first, neither of these songs would make her look particularly hip, and second, she couldn't think of hipper ones off the top of her head. There weren't a lot of blues standards about having a couple of Black Velvets and meeting the love of your life at a dance. Most blues songs seemed to be about being ditched by a fourteen-year-old child-bride, hauling them off to Rosedale, wherever that was, and then topping yourself.

And, given the circumstances of their meeting, fourteen-year-old child brides was a topic she'd rather stay off.

'Anyway,' she said quickly, falling back into the teen queen summary she'd prepared for Sue's ease of reporting, 'Brian was at that time a logistics manager for one of the South-East's top commercial transport outfits, but was looking for an opportunity to combine his great passion for rhythm 'n' blues –' Rosetta enunciated this carefully for the benefit of Sue's tape '– with an independent business venture of his own. And now of course he coordinates tours for some of the country's leading pop acts.'

With the press-release veneer scraped off, what Rosetta meant was that Brian had been the most competent logistics manager Knott and Cram Removals had ever known. It helped, of course, that his dad owned it. Name a client and Brian could reel off number of pieces, delivery addresses, times of availability, men assigned to the job and, in some cases, phone numbers and descriptions of the furniture. Brian was brilliant at keeping a hundred different facts in his head at the same time. He was also a very sweet bloke, with an HGV licence and a grammar-school voice that made him sound posher than he really was.

That was why his original plan had been to combine his hobby and his trade in one musical logistics firm: lots of managers preferred to hand over the increasingly tiresome business of dovetailing bands, equipment, hotel rooms and venues to Brian while they got on with maximizing the profits on other stuff and keeping the drummer's wife and three kids out the picture. And Brian had liked it too, keeping out of the messy band politics and concentrating on the pure logistics.

Until he saw The End at the Crawdaddy Club. Then he'd reintroduced himself as a freelance manager.

'So are there any plans for marriage, now you're living together?' asked Sue, pointedly. She paused the tape and added, 'Didn't your mum go *nuts*?'

Rosetta pulled a very descriptive, unrecordable face to demonstrate her mother's rage, then said, for the tape, 'Oh no, no. No, I don't think we need to get married just yet.'

Much as she loved Brian, she wasn't sure that was totally necessary. It would spoil that lovely feeling of total romance – this older man, sweeping her off her feet, giving her everything she wanted and letting her go to as many gigs as she could stay awake at. It wasn't as if she wanted to play around anyway; her mother's ingrained guilt trips about What Happened to Unfaithful Women took care of that. Besides, getting married was so square and it made you look so paranoid. No matter what the little Richmond voice in the back of her mind still had to say on that topic.

'God, no,' she elaborated for Sue in a suitably bored tone, winking over the tape recorder, 'we're having far too much fun being young and single, running around without any ties to lay any of that heavy marriage stuff down.'

'And children?'

'Sue! I'm seventeen!' A bubbling laugh broke through Rosetta's glacial expression and she covered her wide mouth with her hand, pulling an expression of total disbelief. '*Oh my God*, no! What kind of woman wants to saddle herself with kids just yet?'

'I'll take that as a no, then,' said Sue tartly.

Rosetta remembered too late that Sue's professed ambition in French had been '*se marier et avoir les enfants*'. She had had the names picked out since they were eleven, revising them each year. Rosetta's ambition in French, on the other hand, had been '*s'amuser*'.

'I mean,' she added quickly, in case it made her look too hard-faced, 'obviously I'd *love* to have a family with Brian, but it's such a terrible responsibility having children, and I don't always think that I'm the sort of person I'd like to *have* as a mother. If you know what I mean.'

Sue coughed and made some notes on her pad. 'I understand that you have embarked on a career as a model?' Either she'd perfected the journalistic technique of asking questions as if they were really accusations or she hadn't forgiven Rosetta for some school misdemeanour Rosetta had forgotten about. Their friendship had always been odd. 'I suppose that's why you don't want to lose your figure?'

'Oh, that, yes, well, I have, I suppose.' Rosetta widened her green cat's eyes and gave Sue a big smile, full of healthy square teeth. 'My mate Anita – well, *our* mate Anita, isn't she? – sometimes asks me to model her clothes for her when she has her in-house evenings.' Rosetta pretended not to notice the black look Sue was giving her. Anita never had had much time for Sue and her desperate competitiveness; Sue hadn't exactly been a fan of Anita's casual adaptation of school uniform, and indeed, school rules.

But as the mutual friend of both, Rosetta did feel an ongoing responsibility to build bridges – for the challenge, if nothing else. So she flashed her most conspiratorial grin and added, 'Anita's always looking for victims, you know. Come round one evening and . . . try some stuff on,' she finished, as upbeat as she could in the face of the blackest glare she had ever seen.

Whatever she had done to Sue, it must have been really bad from the expression on her face. In very clipped tones, Sue said, 'So it all seems to be jolly exciting for you then.' There was a loaded pause. 'Rosetta.' She rolled the R, making it sound like a Spanish holiday resort.

Rosetta broadened her smile and crossed her fingers. 'I'm really very lucky,' she said, demurely. 'But it's all karma, isn't it?'

'Oh, er, yes, I suppose so.'

Sue rubbed her eyes again, and the thick black lines smudged.

Rosetta frowned at herself and hunted about in her mind for something really nice to say to Sue, before it was too late.

As the tape whirred from one reel to another, and Sue fiddled with her pencil, Rosetta wondered whether she should prompt her to switch it off. She couldn't tell whether the interview was over, or going somewhere else or what. For one thing it had always been quite hard to tell where she was with Sue. And now they weren't in school, she couldn't charm her like she did the boys in the band, with pop knowledge and flattery and London gossip, because Sue knew her in netball skirts and pottery classes. And she had no intention of charming her with home-made biscuits, because what was the point of doing an interview that talked all about her baking and said nothing about her life with London's coolest guitar band? Besides, Rosetta couldn't cook to save her life. The best they could settle on was some kind of uneasy truce, and agree not to reveal each other's flower-arranging abilities.

'You know what I'd love now?' said Sue. Her eyes glittered like little pieces of coal in all the black liner.

'What's that?' Rosetta got up from the sofa and touched her arm in a friendly fashion. Sue's skin was very cold, and there were black ink stains on her left hand, where Rosetta wore a couple of turquoise rings and a silver bangle.

For a second or two, she felt a real rush of power coursing through her. Sue had come to *her flat* to interview *her* about *her life* and *her cool boyfriend*! So what if Sue envied her? What was there in this flat that any woman *wouldn't* envy?

'I'd *love* a cup of coffee.' The eyebrows again, flicking up and down in triumph. 'God knows, I drink so much, I must be addicted to the stuff,' Sue added casually.

Rosetta hoped her hand hadn't frozen noticeably on Sue's forearm as she caught the third-form triumph in that smile. At least she hadn't asked for hash. That would really have caught her out. Sue might be wearing what she imagined were cool clothes, but underneath, she was still pure St Mary's, just like her mother, and this to her was just a coffee-morning one-upmanship gala, but with incense and a tape recorder.

The next single in the stack dropped on to the turntable of Rosetta's little Dansette and at that exact moment, Rosetta knew with a crushing certainty that if she was going to be a real part of this life of music and coolness and dilettante pop-stars, and not some day tripper that everyone laughed at while she was out making the tea, she could never even give so much as a hint that she had ever been anything else. She just had to pretend she didn't understand the petty games, much less play them. It was like being an astronaut, going up into space: you couldn't take anyone with you. *Everyone* in Brian's world was self-invented. They all had parents in Deptford and brothers who worked for the gas board, but from what you saw on *Ready Steady Go!* they had been born in a different century, a different continent.

And under no circumstances was she going to look like Sue Morton-Thomas, who dangled her Lucite Biba bangles off her wrist in exactly the same way her mother wore her handbag.

If Sue had had a moment of triumph it was very short-lived.

'Oh, darling, what a good idea!' Rosetta exclaimed,

clasping the chunky wrist in a life-saving gesture. 'I would just love an espresso! I just need waking up after the night we had last night! Listen, why don't we go down to this fab little coffee bar near Anita's shop and kill two birds with one stone? They get all the pre-release singles in there. Brian told me to go in and talk loudly about The End.'

But even as Rosetta led the way down the stairs, groovily 'forgetting' to lock her front door, she should have sensed that perhaps there was something she was missing about Sue. That maybe someone who had doggedly insisted on wearing mini-skirts when her legs were like something you'd throw on a barbecue, someone who had swotted her way to the top in RE so she could get at least one prize on Parents' Day, might not be crushed quite so easily.

But Flood Street was washed with sunlight, the shops were full of brand new clothes and everywhere seemed to smell of lilac, even though Rosetta couldn't see any trees. At that moment, the thrill of being someone you read about in the papers blotted out a single drop of doubt in her mind.

Chapter Three

Clerkenwell, 2001

'Are you listening to me?' demanded Robert. He paused in his systematic lining up of several multi-coloured vitamins, ordered by size from breath-freshener to horse-pill.

'Of course I am,' lied Tanith automatically, because in a sense she was. She could hear his voice above the radio and she knew he was going on about his mother because he'd reminded her about ten minutes ago that she had invited them all over for supper on Saturday. Robert could go on about his bloody mother for days at a time without repetition or hesitation. Contradiction was another matter, but then since Rosetta contradicted herself continually it wasn't fair to level that one exclusively at Robert.

'What did I just say then?'

Tanith sighed. That was Robert's most irritating characteristic: a complete inability to let things go. He was like one of those terriers you could swing round your head before they'd let go of the bone. 'You were saying about your mother's dinner party thing at the weekend and ...' She allowed the clatter of plates going in the dishwasher to disguise the specifics.

'Your mother' was a disturbingly frequently used phrase in their house, so much so that in the year that Tanith had been living with Robert it had taken on capital letters in her mind. In fact, she thought, Rosetta's subtle domination of her sons would be like something by Alan Bennett, except that none of them were allowed to call her 'Mother'. It had been 'Rosetta' since birth. With anyone else that would have seemed weird, or laughably seventies, but Rosetta clearly was never a Mum, and almost not even a Mother figure, except in a faintly malign Greek way. From what Tanith had pieced together from Robert's grudging revelations, she should just ask to be called Jocasta and be done with it.

Brian, Robert's dad, on the other hand, was a reasonable man, who Tanith could only think had had a personality transplant after all the rock 'n' roll madness which had left such an indelible impression on the rest of them. Or maybe he had always been a small-ish, normal-ish business-type man with a dodgy back. Tanith suspected the latter. It was where Robert got the other side of his personality from: the normal, nit-picking side that remembered to book taxis in advance. She fervently wished Brian would move back to London, but could quite understand why Geneva now seemed so inviting.

There was a pause, which she hoped indicated that Robert was mollified. Sometimes he fell just short of asking her to take notes and setting a short test afterwards. But as Tanith raised her head from the dishwasher, she saw he had only paused to take his morning vitamin dose – a handful of pills which he was stuffing into his mouth in the frenzied manner that over-made-up housewives used to tranquillize themselves to death in made-for-TV movies. He then poured her own fresh orange juice into his tumbler and swilled them all down with a grimace similar to the one Sue Ellen used to pull after drinking her own body weight in JR's finest single malt.

There was the usual dramatic pause in which he appeared to have stopped breathing and then he shook his head as if trying to dislodge the pills from his throat.

Tanith had seen this often enough not to be concerned, and returned to checking the contents of her work-bag.

'Where are you going to be today?' he asked, massaging his neck.

'Schools in north London. I'm looking for a young Amber.'

'Still?'

'Still.'

'Isn't she going to be adolescent Amber now?'

Tanith had been trying to cast the lead in a film about a sixties pop starlet for three months now; a young version, an ingénue one, and a grown-up one. It was very hard, because she didn't have a complete script – although every day it seemed that another factor emerged to make her life even more difficult.

Her boss, Frances, had agreed to break her own house rule and take on an unfinished script *purely* as a personal favour to the director; not that she was having to deal with it, of course. Only sheer bloody-mindedness and a determination to impress Frances was keeping Tanith going through another round of fifteen-year-old kids who all sang like Emma Bunton and wanted to look twenty-five, when she needed a gauche, late-1950s-style teenager. Or at least one who could pretend to be gauche. There weren't many teenagers left in London she hadn't seen. Tanith was beginning to feel like King Herod.

She sighed and started packing things she would need to see her through the day: instamatic camera, tape recorder, mobile phone, banana. Magic wand.

'Never mind,' said Robert. 'Soon be over.'

'Every time I hear a vibrato version of "Baby One More Time" with accompanying dance steps, I understand why teenage boys go berserk with guns in American schools,' said Tanith, through gritted teeth. She sighed again, and put some Anadin in the bag's mobile phone pocket. 'I'm just amazed it's not the teachers too.'

'But surely, by sheer process of elimination, you must be close to finding someone,' persisted Robert. 'What did they do before stage schools – breed midget actors in ranches behind Hollywood?'

Tanith fixed him with a baleful glare. Try as she might, she just couldn't explain the whole casting process to a man who accepted right answers, and only right answers. 'Look, do you know any small, ginger, fourteen-year-old girls who can convincingly act as though they've never seen a boy or a gramophone before and don't mind hanging around a film set for most of their summer holiday?'

Robert shook his head and began to plaster a thick layer of butter on to his cooling toast. 'Barney might, though.'

'Oh, yeah,' said Tanith, remembering. 'That reminds me. I said I'd take Greg late-night shopping after work. You don't need anything, do you?'

'You're taking him shopping again? You were only out with him last month.'

'He needs clothes. Last time it was shoes.'

Robert frowned. 'Can't you tell him you've got more important things to do with your afternoons than drag him round Gap explaining that grunge died in 1992 and isn't due for a comeback in our lifetimes?'

'Yes, of course I have.' Tanith stopped rearranging the bags within her bag, and looked at him. It saddened her that Robert couldn't be nicer to his own family; picking faults with them seemed to give him fresh energy, like an ego-vampire. 'I've got *loads* of more important things to do with my time. But if you want Greg to stop coming round here for supper all the time, then he needs to get a girlfriend and, let me tell you, he isn't going to get a girlfriend with shoes like that.'

'I thought you'd sorted out his shoes.'

'I have. But there's no point having the right shoes when his trousers look like he stole them from a tramp. No, when they look like the tramp *gave* them to him.'

Robert snorted derisively and bit into his toast. His even white teeth made a little half-moon in the butter.

'I thank God every day that I don't have to talk to people unless they make an appointment,' he said through a mouthful of organic wheatmeal.

Robert was an entertainment accountant, specializing in unpicking the books of 'creative' clients and then knotting them back up again in complicated tax-proof arrangements. Despite the fact that most of his clients were international actors, or musicians, Robert liked to dress as though he represented an obscure eighteenth-century city bank.

Tanith picked up her A–Z and stuffed it into a front pocket, making a mental note to try Greg in a suit for a change, see if it might change his personality into something more streamlined.

Despite what she'd said, she didn't actually mind Greg coming round to the house: unlike his other brothers, he didn't radiate intensity like a sunbed, and he could talk about television programmes without giving you a hard time about not watching the ones that got reviewed. He was unusually light relief for the Mulligan family. But, to be fair, the sooner he got a girlfriend, the better for everyone. There was a very fine line between cute singledom and 'Was he traumatized as a child?'

Opposite her, Robert carefully replaced the lid on the marmalade, taking care not to get any on his cuffs.

Robert's neatness set him aside from his brothers even more than his sensible job. Whereas Patrick carried off Byronic dishevelment, Greg was post-grunge scruffiness, Barney was King's Road casual, only Robert was *neat* in a way normally only achievable with staff. The only man Tanith knew with his own home trouser press. He was eating his toast neatly, keeping his sleeves out of the crumbs, while his beady brown eyes scanned back and forth across the stocks section of the paper from behind tortoiseshell glasses. Greg had once observed that, first thing in the morning, when his toilette was at its peak, Robert was straight out of one of those picture library catalogues, illustrating Young Businessman, or Modern Man at Breakfast. By supper, though, as the voluble, dramatic side of his personality was coaxed out by the irritating stupidity of other people, his thick gingery hair had thrown off the controlling wax and gone into tufts where he'd run his hands through it in horror at someone's badly kept accounts, and his cuffs had coffee stains on the pristine white cotton.

Tanith didn't wash his shirts. They went to the laundry round the corner.

She looked at her watch. If she was going to make it to the first round of would-be Ambers before ten, she'd have to get a move on, and Tanith didn't like being the last one in the house. She wasn't sure why – maybe because it still felt very much like it was Robert's house and being there after him gave her an uncomfortably, wifey sensation.

Suddenly she was filled with a desire to be out in the open.

'I've got to go,' she said. That usually hurried him up. Robert also liked to get out of the door first. Some kind of male ritual thing. My job's more urgent than your job. My suit means my job needs me more than your jeans and boots.

How Patrick would laugh.

Tanith was suddenly aware of a quick throb in her chest, like a missed breath, which always seemed to flicker when she thought about Patrick. Though much less so recently than it had done for a long while, she had to admit. Finally.

'See you later then,' she said. 'Mind you put that plate in the dishwasher.'

'I'll come with you,' he said, stuffing the toast into his mouth and grabbing his jacket off the back of the chair. 'How are you getting there?'

'Tube.'

'I'll drop you at the station, yeah?'

'I can walk.'

'I can drop you.'

'Robert, I really don't mind walking. I'm a big girl.'

Robert's chin set. 'I'll drop you at the station. Now, come on, you're making me late.'

Tanith bit her lip and picked up her bag.

Tanith really liked Robert a *lot*, for all his odd ways. But it seemed that some short time after she'd moved in, Robert had decided that she was The One (or rather, that she Would Do), and had put their relationship on to a dizzying fast track, which meant that he was now quite obviously contemplating marriage while she was still wondering whether she could live long-term with a man who fully supported traffic wardens and clamping. She knew in her heart – and from doing quizzes in magazines – that she should probably move out before things went horribly wrong, but she honestly didn't want to: Robert was funny, and kind, and perfectly good company.

Tanith just found it rather troubling that he was effectively asking her to decide whether she wanted him for the rest of her life or not, when she didn't even know how she wanted that life to turn out yet.

And of course, she would vehemently deny that she was still recovering from her relationship with his brother.

Greg's version for Flora's benefit of how Tanith came to move in with Robert was sketchy, but actually contained about as much of the facts as the family knew. Patrick wasn't around to tell them, and Tanith certainly wasn't about to fill them in on the full details.

In truth, the chain of events was all so weird that, from the safety of a few years, even Tanith had trouble believing it had ever happened. Essentially, it had begun normally enough: Tanith and Patrick met at university – she was an undergraduate, he had gone back to college after a couple of years' travelling. Within hours of meeting in the college bar, they'd formed the sort of deep, scary, burning bond that only students can form without any lingering sense of embarrassment. The trouble was, as Tanith found out to her cost, that Patrick could keep up deep, scary and burning indefinitely.

After two years, while her side of the relationship started to mature into shaving her legs in front of him and the occasional fart in bed, he remained at the fever pitch level of writing songs about her, and waking her up in the middle of the night to demand to know what she was dreaming about. Once or twice he had made her drop acid with him, to find out if they could make their minds merge into one giant bubble of thought, like a Roy Lichtenstein cartoon.

Tanith, though a bit freaked out by all this, didn't mind to begin with, because even without his very hip background (Rosetta had started to appear on late night review programmes, talking about women in rock music, and even Brian had achieved some sort of status as having made millions out of being professionally uncool) Patrick looked like something out of a Jane Austen novel. In her mind now, whenever she was casting a romantic hero, she couldn't help but think of him – with his liquid, brooding eyes, and curly dark hair, and strapping thighs that came in handy for spontaneous al fresco passion. Since he was forever instigating walks over wild and dramatic areas of the National Park, it was just as well. But that kind of passion was fine when you were watching it on the screen, with your popcorn; living with a man who would stay up for three days and nights trying to find five rhymes for your name so he could write a Petrarchan sonnet about you was another.

And nothing very mainstream rhymed with Tanith.

It wasn't that she didn't love Patrick – she did love him, *very much* – but after a while the pressure of it started to kill her. Little bits of her at a time. He demanded continuous spontaneity. He could take offence at the wrong word. He freaked her out regularly by admiring personality traits she didn't even know she had. Eventually Tanith started to become paranoid that she wasn't living up to some fictional version of herself that existed only in his head.

She knew it was time to get out when being scared of Patrick being in love with her overtook being scared at how much she was in love with Patrick. But by then, Tanith knew that it wouldn't just be as simple as shuffling around awkwardly and muttering something about needing more space and it being her, not him.

If going out with Patrick made her feel isolated, then trying to split up with him was even worse. It was a bit like wanting to pack in a job as a luxury holiday tester: none of her friends could possibly feel sorry for her, or indeed understand why they should. But it was hard to explain how genuine terror inched up her spine some nights, when Patrick was telling her how much he loved her in terms that she last heard in A-level Latin poetry, and how scary it was, bearing the weight of responsibility for his Olympic happiness on her shoulders.

And at the back of her mind, Tanith was uncomfortably aware that it was never really just him and her in Patrick's spooky world. It was him, her and thirty years of history that even he didn't seem to understand properly. Every time she tried to cool things down by wailing, 'I'm only nineteen!' he would cup her head in his big, strong hands, and murmur, 'But my mother was seventeen when she met the love of her life! It doesn't matter when you meet if you're meant to be together!'

Then Tanith would bury her head in his chest, because she didn't know what to say when, from what little he'd told her, his mother clearly wasn't an example she wished to emulate, and he would make love to her, skilfully and slowly, and she would wonder how she'd got herself into this whole mess and whether she could deal with the head-wreck when the sex was so incredible.

Then Patrick brought matters to a head for her by asking her to marry him.

So Tanith ran away, and Patrick ran after her.

It never occurred to Tanith that people could have real-life confrontations on beaches, but she was minding her own business on the beach near her parents' house, where she'd gone to get herself together, when Patrick came charging down the sands, flapping his long black coat like wings behind him.

As usual, she struggled between hunted horror and desperate attraction.

'I love you, Tanith!' he yelled, while the seagulls circled overhead, thinking there was some kind of fishing excitement about to happen. 'You have to be with me! It's meant to be! We can't ignore destiny like this – it ruins lives when you don't go along with what's meant to be!'

'Patrick,' hissed Tanith, squinting along the beach at the various dog-walking neighbours. 'Why do you always behave as if you're in a film?'

Patrick had looked disproportionately stunned by this. His dark eyes welled up with manly tears. 'What? I don't know what you mean.'

'All this drama and declaration!' she said, losing her patience. 'I can't cope with it! It's not *normal*!'

She looked at him as his face winced with hurt, and it dawned on her that this kind of behaviour probably *was* normal to him, after a lifetime of nomadic living, and rock-star hissy fits and attention-seeking from a mother who had more photographs of her clothes than she did of them (apparently). Poor Patrick had no idea what 'normal' was. And, if his mother was any template, the more she ignored him, the more he would carry on charging around, waving his Big Love at her.

Tanith put a hand up to her mouth as her heart melted with tenderness and pity.

But then came the crashing realization that if she took this man on, great sex or not, it would be a restoration job to put Battersea power station to shame. And she knew she just wasn't strong enough to do it, in case she failed and made it all much, much worse. How many family therapists had tried and failed?

Maybe the only woman who could set Patrick back on the rails was this selfish, butterfly mother of his. No, not maybe, *definitely*.

She bit her finger.

'Patrick, please go home and talk to your mother,' she said. 'You need to sort things out with her first.'

'Talk to her about what?' he demanded. 'Are you *crazy*? I don't consult Rosetta about relationships. I don't even consult her about *Christmas* lists.'

Tanith put her arms around him, unable to look into his wounded eyes. 'I don't know exactly what you have to talk to her about, but . . .' She squeezed him tightly. 'I love you very much, but I can't give you what she can. I can't put this right.'

There was a long pause, as Tanith miserably contemplated the fact that she was kissing goodbye to the most gorgeous man she was ever likely to go out with, for the sake of her sanity.

Maturity was not as satisfying as she'd hoped.

'I'm never going to see that bloody woman again,' said Patrick violently over her shoulder. 'This is all her fault.'

And with one last passionate, engulfing, hair-tangling kiss – by now neither of them were able to resist the cheap lure of the filmic Heathcliff departure – Patrick turned and stomped back up the beach, hair and coat-tails flying.

He didn't come back for his final year, but Tanith found a whole sheaf of poetry in her pigeonhole at college and all of it made her want to take opium and hide under her duvet.

After she graduated Tanith ended up in London, knowing no one, which she actually didn't mind, partly because no one in London seemed to know anyone either, and after the frenzy of Patrick's departure she quite enjoyed the peace and quiet.

She lived in a grim house-share in Shepherd's Bush, where she liked to freak out the South Africans by *adding* milk to the marked cartons, and she found herself a job doing administration for a theatre company. It wasn't exactly taxing, but at least it made her laugh twice a day and provided her with free theatre tickets and access to people weirder than Patrick.

Meanwhile Patrick wrote long and very syntactically complicated letters to her mother's address, and her mother forwarded them, until Tanith begged her not to. And after a while, she assumed he'd stopped.

Weeks stacked up into months, and Tanith was promoted to Production Manager since she managed to combine charm and ruthless efficiency (and no one else applied for the post). She moved into a more expensive but equally annoying flatshare in the back end of Highbury with a publicist and a trainee director. She grew her hair long again. She bought a small car that broke down a lot. Soon after, she met a very charming casting director called Frances Wainwright who decided she was perfect trainee material and poached her to join her agency. Then, just as she was beginning to feel her life had returned to normal and she was finally holding the reins again, Tanith met Robert in a bar.

At the time she hadn't the faintest idea who Robert was. It was only later that she freaked out at the billion-to-one coincidence of it. But as she explained to a disbelieving Greg, she wasn't to know what Robert looked like; Patrick had only introduced her to his mother once, very, very briefly and very, very reluctantly in her Chelsea flat, while they were *en route* to the London Dungeon, and though she knew he had brothers, Patrick wasn't exactly the photoframe type. Given the determination with which he steered the conversation away from his family in general, she hadn't asked.

The night they met wouldn't have rated particularly highly

on Patrick's romance-o-meter. It barely registered on Greg's when she told him. It was a dark, wet winter night – the only factor of which Patrick would have approved – and Tanith was waiting on her own in the corner of a crowded City bar with a glass of corked red wine, doing the *Evening Standard* crossword and getting pretty pissed off. She was meant to be meeting Natalie, her flatmate-the-publicist, who was auditioning a couple of single men for a skiing holiday, although they didn't know that, and Natalie wanted to borrow Tanith's piercing appraisal skills before allocating the last space in the chalet.

Natalie was forty minutes late already, and Tanith had been forced to use scaremongering tactics to hang on to the three seats and the table she was saving. To add to her irritation with the bar and its braying contents – all men who seemed to be competing in a Loud Tomato Impersonation contest – Tanith was even more annoyed with herself for bothering to arrive on time.

Quite why people went to bars to pull was beyond her.

She sensed a presence around the chair next to her and said, 'Don't sit there, I've got diarrhoea,' without bothering to look up.

The man took no notice of her, and with irritation throbbing at the back of her skull, Tanith put her paper down and wriggled meaningfully in her seat.

'I said . . .' she began again.

'Don't be ridiculous,' he said, taking out a paper of his own and folding it round to do the crossword. It was *The Times*. 'You're wearing a white skirt.'

Tanith looked round, ready to whiplash him with a seriously sarcastic comment, and stopped abruptly when she saw his face. It gave her a mild shock of partial recognition. Her mind raced through a photo library of people, trying to work out why he looked so familiar. Tall-ish but solid, dark round eyes behind glasses, not much older than her – as far as she could tell in a suit that was designed for a fifty-year-old – but with mad gingery hair that she would surely have remembered if she'd woken up next to it.

'I really do have terrible diarrhoea,' she said as sweetly as she could, and realized that Natalie and her interviewees turning up wasn't going to be much of an improvement. God, London was depressing. She dropped her eyes to the *Evening Standard* quick crossword and felt a gust of mental inferiority blow in from the left.

The man pulled a Mont Blanc pen out of his inside pocket, clicked it and filled in the first three clues of his crossword, marking off the clues with a dismissive flick. He didn't seem to feel it was that necessary to talk to her.

'And I've just moved from that chair,' Tanith went on, less confidently. There wasn't much further she could take this particular one, without actually showing him a prescription.

He looked up at her, over his glasses. 'Look,' he said impatiently. 'We both know you don't have diarrhoea. But I don't like to see a woman sitting on her own in a bar like this, so if it's OK with you, and doesn't offend your feminist principles, I'll just sit here and do my crossword until whoever it is you're waiting for turns up.'

Tanith was taken aback so much that for a couple of seconds she had absolutely no idea how to respond.

'And what's wrong with this bar?' she managed eventually.

'It's full of idiots.' He rattled off four more clues.

'So?'

'So, do you want to talk to the idiots when they lurch over and try to pick you up? Or would you rather be left alone because they think you're with me?'

Tanith stared at him in amazement, and taking her dumbfounded lack of response for polite acquiescence, he carried on with his crossword. From a distance, she could see in the mirror behind the bar, they did look exactly like a couple who had been together for about ten years.

When they had been sitting there for twenty minutes,

Robert testily introduced himself and insisted on ordering some wine, which they shared in intermittent silence, as the icy wall of her irritation melted with curiosity and a much better Merlot than she would have ordered on her own.

When Natalie failed to turn up, Robert insisted on making sure Tanith got home safely in his taxi. He didn't so much as put a hand on her knee but he did give the driver £30 and told him to wait until she'd opened the door and gone in.

Three dates later, in very expensive restaurants, Tanith agreed to come back to his house for coffee, and as soon as she walked into Robert's elegant sitting-room and saw his neat array of family pictures she realized why his eyes were so familiar.

Two months after that, when Natalie moved to Fulham and Tanith was effectively homeless again, she gave in to Robert's arguments and moved in with him.

Although she didn't tell her mother his surname straight away.

Tanith took her bag to a coffee shop near her office and ordered herself a large cappuccino while she went through her diary for the day. There were things she had to collect from the office in Duke Street before she could set off in search of Ambers, but she knew her boss Frances had an accountant coming round first thing and as Frances hadn't told her what it was in aid of, she deduced it must be covert. Therefore, rather than have them slope off into another office to discuss things 'in private', leaving her feeling like a lemon in the open-plan office, she wanted to give them both a clear berth.

Not that she didn't want to find out what was going on. Any salient details, she would, of course, winkle out of Lily-Jo, Frances's enchantingly indiscreet assistant, later, with dextrous use of a copy of *Heat* magazine and a mocha frappuccino. Lily-Jo's deep jealousy of actors was second only in terms of passion to her own twisted, secret determination to be discovered by a major Hollywood producer, preferably in a muse-type capacity so she wouldn't actually have to go through the tiresome casting process.

Frances, of course, was aware of this but didn't care unduly. Some people might have considered personal acting ambition a disadvantage in an assistant, but Frances knew that the longer Lily-Jo spent in casting, the less she would want to act. And besides, she knew Lily-Jo loved the power games too much to give up her advantage. This was Frances's management style all over, to Tanith's mind. Interesting, instinctive, impossible to predict.

In the time that she'd been working with Frances, Tanith had learned the ropes of casting, plus three hundred other life skills from emergency first aid to graphology, and the more crises she took in her stride, the more crises Frances cheerfully threw at her. It amazed her to have found a job she loved doing and was really good at. Tanith's great skill, according to Frances, was her ability to see a problem, sort it out and then calmly walk away from it before it had a chance to bite her on the arse. Tanith hadn't deemed it necessary to fill Frances in on the astounding amount of training she had received in this from Patrick – or how off-beam her judgement had been there.

She sipped her double-strength, whole milk coffee and felt it start to trickle through her veins, returning her to the full-on dynamism necessary for dealing with teenage actresses and her hyperactive boss first thing on Monday. Not to mention Lily-Jo, who had spent the weekend on location with her film student boyfriend, criticizing the low-budget horror movie he was directing, from the comfort of his camper van.

They were an odd combination, the women in her office, but they made a very good team: Frances was professional and enthusiastic, Lily-Jo presented an unchanging front of near despair and Tanith was somewhere in between. Maybe that was why Frances had taken her on: to provide a semblance of normality.

She frowned into her mug. Their strength was their ability to be very honest with each other. Recently, though, Frances had taken a lot of calls in her office, something she never normally did, and she'd left her to get on with this project all on her own, for the first time ever. Tanith knew when Frances had been going through her office diary after hours because she left flakes of pearly nail varnish behind, from her incessant nervous picking and peeling. Her diary had been flake-free for days now, although Lily-Jo was complaining incessantly about having to Dirt-Devil Frances's own office. And Warren, Frances's dodgy boyfriend, had been floating around a lot, making the office reek of Gucci Rush for Men and St Tropez fake tan.

There was a definite quiver in the office vibrations and Tanith needed a little time to unfocus her brain and try to tune in to what it was. And that was another reason she hadn't really wanted Robert to drop her off – she wanted time to think about work *in silence*. Living with Robert was mentally stimulating, but didn't really afford her much independent thinking time, and convenient as it was to have a live-in plumber, builder, chef, accountant and paralegal, sometimes Tanith felt she would happily swop it all for half an hour's complete and utter unforced tranquillity.

She drained the rest of her coffee and pushed away the negative thoughts about Robert. Not charitable, this early in the morning, even if it was – according to Lily-Jo – a good sign when you felt safe enough in your relationship to criticize your partner.

It was nice to think that maybe Frances had started to trust her a bit more – that was the positive, upbeat way of looking at this new development – but she was getting the distinct impression that this Amber project was some kind of test, and Tanith didn't like jumping through hoops without having at least a rough idea where the hoop actually was. That wasn't fair. She tried not to think about the possibility of Frances having found someone more experienced. Being sacked would be a real disaster now she'd got to the point where she could finally keep all thirty-three plates spinning at the same time while arranging travel tickets and viewing show reels and keeping Lily-Jo from annotating the files with disparaging Post-it notes.

Although having said that, Robert would march Frances through the High Courts if she did try anything legally dubious.

She checked her watch. Time to go back to 1967 again.

Chapter Four

The Kingston Poly Student Union was heaving with kids. Rosetta did a rough head count and reckoned that, for the first time ever, there were more people there now than there had been at the start. The End were thrashing their way through their blues-ed up version of 'Roll Over Beethoven' – a bit old as a standard, sure, but the only one they knew that was guaranteed to tear up the hall if things had got a bit slow. They mostly did covers anyway, because none of them could really write songs, and the stuff Glynn came up with tended to be thinly disguised versions of Rolling Stones numbers, only with lyrics that dealt exclusively with the stress of having too many girlfriends all at once. Tonight, though, she noted admiringly, if they stoked this crowd up much more, the hall would burst into flames.

Rosetta was leaning on an amp at the side of the stage. It was her favourite place to be: half in the darkness, half in the light, where she could catch the little nods and mutters of communication between the band as they adjusted the set to suit the mood, and where she could see the pushing and shoving of the audience at the same time. She liked being balanced between the two sides of the stage; a fan *and* an insider. And, of course, she loved being where the audience could just catch a glimpse of her, watching enigmatically in the shadows, the light glinting off the buckles on her Biba pirate boots, and wonder who she was as

The End gradually melted away the cool from their student audience and pushed them to embarrassingly unrestrained dancing.

Or she assumed it was dancing. The five lads nearest her could easily have been stamping out a small fire.

Rosetta closed her eyes slowly to check that her long false eyelashes were still in place and, once sure they were, she fluttered them luxuriously. She was *with the band*, and most importantly, she had *arrived* with them, not been swept up afterwards, lingering hopefully round the back door, and taken home because the pubs had closed and there wasn't much else to do.

Brian turned to Rosetta with a look of smug pride flooding his round face and bellowed, 'They're good tonight, aren't they?'

He put his arm round her and hugged her paternally. Rosetta could smell the musky aroma of honest male sweat coming off him, and wondered why he didn't take off his jacket, when everyone knew he was the manager and he already had the cash off the booker. It made him look very . . . out of place. But Brian, she knew, intended that effect. Unlike her, he didn't want to look as if he was with the band – he wanted to give off the impression that the band were with *him*.

'Yeah, they're very good,' she shrieked, cupping her hands round his ear to make herself heard over Red's frenetic drumming.

They both grinned back at each other, knowing that that 'good' was an understatement. Tonight was special. Something was finally happening to The End to turn them from a bunch of competent art school part-timers into a genuinely exciting – proper – band. Rosetta wasn't sure what it was – Brian liked to say that it was down to his carefully arranged programme of small club dates and bigger student venues – but to Rosetta's more intuitive eye, it seemed to have something, possibly everything, to do with John

O'Hara, the lead guitarist they were trying out this evening. She didn't know much about him, only that he was Irish and a mate of Red's, but she knew instinctively that he could turn the band around.

She also knew, with a shiver of guilty excitement, that he was doing something weird to her head.

Regardless of the fact that her boyfriend was standing next to her.

Rosetta had never had much time for the previous lead guitarist, Ian. He could only play solos he'd learned off sheet music, and refused to let his hair grow over his collar, because his mother gave him hell about it. Three weeks ago, Ian had announced at the end of an agonizingly pedestrian gig in Richmond (half-way through which the local WI bingo-nighters had come in and demanded their hall back – and got it) that he was leaving to spend more time studying for his actuary exams. Brian had seen this coming for weeks, but instead of sacking him, he'd cannily elected to wait for the inevitable resignation, rather than risk the rest of the lads siding with a sacked and wounded Ian, undermining his authority. So Brian kept a straight face as Ian delivered his news, then, with the pub door still swinging shut, he cheerfully got the drinks in for the rest of the evening and they'd celebrated until Red passed out under a table and Rosetta drove the van home.

No one was distressed at Ian's departure, though they slapped him manfully on the shoulder when he came to pick up his Chuck Berry LPs – but they *were* concerned about who they could get to replace him. It wasn't that he was so spectacular no one short of Peter Green could step into his shoes: the unspoken consensus among the others was that Glynn had only let Ian play in the first place because he didn't draw any attention from his strutting and yelling at the front, as was the danger with a good lead guitarist. Simon, the bass player, was pathologically shy, and Red, the true exhibitionist in the band, was safely hidden behind a drum-kit. Although the spectre of Keith Moon hovered constantly at the back of Glynn's suspicious mind and he would gesture threateningly towards Red at the slightest hint of a drum-kit being kicked over.

The trouble was that most competent lead guitarists in London were spoken for, Brian knew that they still weren't getting enough regular work to lure anyone good away from an established band, and Glynn refused even to consider anyone who had better hair than him.

All in all then, John O'Hara was something of a gift from the gods.

'Red's going for it tonight, isn't he?' Brian yelled in Rosetta's ear.

She nodded, knowing she couldn't make herself heard over the thumping rhythm section anyway. The basics of the band were there – the rhythm section was tight, even if the vocals were erratic – but in the past they'd tended to be a bit, well, solid. Red was all right – he had his moments, but he also had a tendency to speed up as the evening went on and his bladder became more strained under his considerable beer consumption. Sometimes they licked through 'Little Red Rooster', their second-to-last number, in under two minutes, which usually annoyed those in the crowd who relied on it as their smoochy last dance in The End's otherwise pretty smooch-free set of flailing R 'n' B.

However, Red's generous commitment to drinking in all the pubs in London meant that he knew every part-time musician in the south west, including this John O'Hara, who he claimed was 'criminally wasted' in an otherwise unremarkable little blues group of Dublin ex-pats that gigged sporadically round South London. John could also take his whisky, and beat Red at pool. And so John had come for a try-out at a rehearsal that Rosetta had missed, being out with Anita and Sue at some crummy gallery first night. But the others had liked him, he'd known all the set-list backwards, including the solos to everything by The Yardbirds

(Clapton, Beck *and* Page), and consequently this was John's official first night.

On the strict proviso that if Glynn didn't feel he could work with him, it was all off. Nothing signed, and no guarantee of the takings.

Rosetta watched John improvise a little riff over the bridge between verses and suspected that he hadn't played like this at that rehearsal or there would have been no way Glynn would have allowed him in the Transit. He had a glossy sunburst red Gibson Les Paul, the first she'd ever seen in real life, and new riffs and clever little fills seemed to trickle out of his fingers. The lacquer gleamed and shone in the cheap lights like a shiny red apple, all juicy and fresh. Every so often, Rosetta noticed John looking down at his fingers in amazement and then looking over at Red with a dazed grin on his face, as if for confirmation that he really was making those sounds.

Red grinned back, looked over at Glynn, and winked at Rosetta.

She winked back.

Simon, as usual, was oblivious to everything other than the safety of the van in the car-park.

So far John hadn't done anything in particular to upstage Glynn but Rosetta could tell that the rhythms were tighter and there was a definite sense of when the songs actually finished, a factor that was usually missing and often led to half the audience sloping out before the end of the set, for fear of missing their bus home. Right from the start of the evening, she felt a buzz of excitement building in her chest. They *really could* be good. They *really could* make it.

Rosetta couldn't stop a wide, wide smile stretching her face in sheer exhilaration as the sound rose and swelled to the bridge of the song. She had a feeling about John, and her feelings were usually spot on.

OK, so she'd agreed with all the mad ambitious plans Brian had for the band, and she'd talked them up to Sue for the paper, so that they were in her column most weeks, listing their favourite colours and favourite Underground stations, but there were so many bands in London, and so few deals, and everyone knew half of it was how you talked the talk. The End had always been entertaining, but never essential. Not until now. Now – God!

John shifted key and Rosetta sucked her lower lip and hammered out the rhythm on the top of the amp with her flat palms as Red, elevated by the moment, started drumming on and off the beat. She was getting the same sort of hysterical buzz that used to make her see white inside her eyelids when she queued to see the Stones at the Marquee, as if she'd drunk far too much coffee and her legs needed to sprint away.

And, it had to be said, as well as playing the kind of rock 'n' roll that went straight to her pants, John was also very attractive.

Rosetta blinked sternly. She was trying to ignore the rising tide of adrenalin that rushed up her chest every time she looked at him and his gleaming guitar. OK, so she'd had cheap thrills from music before, and she'd had flushes of I'll-die-if-I-don't-have-him desire when she first met Brian, but never all rolled into one pale, inspired package.

She hammered encouragingly on the amp some more, and forced herself to look at the rest of the band. It was hard – without even trying, John had the kind of stage presence that Glynn would kill for. And indeed probably would, as soon as the gig was over. Rosetta made herself assess Simon's stage outfit, which had plumbed new shallows of mediocrity, even for him. Granted, it wasn't cool for the bass-player to look too good, but it was surely time to haul him off to Anita's boutique before someone mistook him for Glynn's dad.

Her attention slid back to John and she bit her lip in irritation at herself. Rosetta hadn't *ever* fancied anyone in the band. It was completely against the rules, especially now she was dating the man at the top, the man sweating slightly in his suit and emitting Proud Father vibes like a two bar electric heater next to her. It had been a pretty easy rule to keep though, when she'd known Red and Glynn for years, being footie mates of her brother Neil, and more like brothers to her too.

But she didn't know John like a brother, and he had a guitar that was the sexiest thing she'd ever seen, in all the years she'd been idolizing guitarists and pressing herself up to the front of the stage to hear the tiny sounds before they were amplified to everyone else.

If he's cute, then that's great for the band, she thought severely, shuffling on her seat. Finally, someone will want to photograph them. It's a good professional attitude to have. Good that you can see it like that.

You can find someone attractive without it turning into a problem, she thought, even more severely, as John shut his eyes, leaned back and ground his guitar into the crotch of his tight jeans. That's cool. I'm a modern girl. I can handle it.

Right.

'Is that –' she began and then stopped in mid-sentence as Glynn came to the end of the chorus, stopped singing, pushed his hands through his hair and let the microphone sway on its stand, pointing to his left for the guitar solo, whereupon John rocked back on his heels and let a peal of triplets slice through the air like twirling electric ribbons.

Normally Glynn affected an air of total disinterest during Ian's solos, as befitted a lead singer, but even his head spun round and stared. Behind the kit, Red beamed at Brian and upped the tempo in tribute. John's fingers didn't plait, as Ian's normally did, slopping through 'Roll Over Beethoven', but pushed and hit the strings with something approaching demonic possession.

'Is that *what*?' Brian yelled in her ear.

Rosetta didn't even hear him. She couldn't hear anything except John O'Hara. Suddenly, her heart was racing as if she'd been electrocuted, she wasn't breathing and her fingernails were white beneath her French manicure, gripping the side of the amp. This was *more* than rock 'n' roll. It was more like *taking drugs*.

'Good, isn't he?' Brian bellowed again, taking her silence for approval.

John stood swaying in the middle of the stage, illuminated by the only fully working light in the place, half the audience going crazy and the other half staring at him, in a dazed and seduced stupor. He had a half-smile on his face, as if he were loving the round pure sound of his guitar as much as the audience.

Rosetta stared at John, his head shaking slowly from side to side, dark fringe sticking to his forehead, and wanted to hold the moment in her head so she could come back to it for ever. She had a terrible feeling that this was some kind of big moment in her life, and that she wasn't properly ready for it. It was like falling from the top of a building in slow motion, knowing that this man, this John O'Hara, was leading her heart around with his guitar like the Pied Piper making the rats dance cheerfully off the end of the pier. Knowing that John O'Hara was pulling together all the strands of talent in The End and making them into something real. Something that they might finally have to live up to.

'Oh, wow,' she breathed aloud and bit her lip. 'That's more than good. That's . . . chemical.'

'Has Red given him purple hearts?' Brian demanded, and grabbed one of Red's mates who helped them lug the gear around for a couple of quid and three bottles of light ale. 'Here, Nev, is John on something tonight?'

Nev shrugged. 'Dunno. Now, Red is. He's got this –'

'I don't want to know about Red.' As long as Red didn't fall off his drum-stool, there wasn't much Brian could do about him anyway. 'Just tell me – is John on something tonight? I don't want some junkie in the band, not if . . .'

'Shut up!' said Rosetta. She had a terrible feeling that if

she let go of the amp she would walk on to the stage and lie down at his feet.

Glynn was back at the centre of the stage now, clearly waiting for John to finish so he could come in with the last verse and chorus. But John appeared to be under the spell of the solo he was playing, which looped around and repeated itself and sounded so brilliant that Rosetta was sure she'd heard it before somewhere. He was playing like Eric Clapton doing a Carl Perkins doing a Scotty Moore, but without ripping off any of them.

The crowd didn't seem to want him to stop either, and Rosetta noticed that the five lads at the front of the stage had vanished, swamped by a thick tide of black-eyed teenage girls, pushing and shoving each other to get a fraction nearer.

'He couldn't play like that if he were on summat,' said Nev authoritatively. 'If 'e were on speed it would sound more like a shredder.'

Glynn stopped prowling around like Mick Jagger, unable to look cool with the situation any more, and stood with his hands on his hips, glowering at John through his shades. The crowd were going berserk at his feet and it had nothing *at all* to do with him.

'Do you think there's going to be a punch-up?' asked Nev, gleefully. 'It's been ages since Glynn smacked someone.'

Rosetta doubted whether Glynn would risk wrecking his hairdo, but there was definitely some interesting tension in the air between them and that only added to the feeling that this was like a whole new band.

All, apparently, because of John and his new Gibson Les Paul.

He'd seemed so quiet on the way over, thought Rosetta, unable to stop gazing longingly at the pale skin on the back of his neck where the black curls were sticking to him with sweat. He'd barely spoken a word to anyone in the van, just listened while Glynn did his usual rant about 'blues credibility' and 'performance values' and rubbed the joints of his long fingers, circling his knotted silver ring up and down his thumb. She'd watched him curiously from her privileged position in the front passenger seat. Through the rear-view mirror, he reminded her of the clever scholarship lads at the boys school opposite theirs, the ones who'd done Latin or Greek or something.

But onstage . . .

Rosetta took a deep breath, trying to make her heart beat more slowly. It wouldn't. All she could think of was what it would be like to snake her fingers into his hair, pull him closer, have him play just for her. She bit her lower lip.

Abruptly, John wound up the solo (with such efficiency that he didn't even have to signal to the others that he was about to finish, as Ian did most nights) and Glynn, still glowering with jealous outrage, missed the first line of the chorus and had to pretend he was scatting. It didn't help that John then slid over to Simon's mike for the harmonies, came in at exactly the right time, and at exactly the right pitch.

The girls at the front squealed with delight.

'Good lad,' said Nev appreciatively. 'He's just what the lads need, eh?'

'Er, yes,' said Brian. He too was transfixed by John's lanky figure, now rocking back and forth to the beat. 'Well, yes, of course he is.'

Glynn was now simultaneously trying to dominate the lead vocal line over John's harmonies, dance more provocatively, catch Brian's eye to register his annoyance and persuade some of the girls in the front row to rip his trousers off.

'He's *just* what the band needs,' beamed Brian. 'Jolly good.'

Rosetta smiled. This was far more like it.

Red did a triumphant series of triplet fills, crashed through to the end of the song and slid happily off his drum-stool.

*

'I am *telling* you, man, if you *ever*, and I mean *ever*, do *any-thing* like that *again* I will rip off *each* of your fucking *fingers* and you can use them like . . . like . . . like those things you play slide guitar with!' yelled Glynn, punctuating himself with jabs to John's sturdy shoulder.

'Ah, for God's sake. Do *what* again?' demanded John. 'Play guitar solos? Is that not what I'm meant to do, as lead guitarist, like?'

Glynn scowled, aware that admitting that John had stolen his thunder would put him in a weak position, but still unwilling to let it go without a fight. Then again, though it was his prerogative to demand a fight as unofficial founder member, taking on John, who certainly hadn't developed muscles like that just from lifting a guitar case, probably wasn't going to do his pretty face any good.

Brian coughed. He was looking flushed in his heavy suit and the air in the minute dressing-room was fetid as it was. With Glynn's ego in full force, there was scarcely room to breathe.

'Now, come on, lads, let's not get aerated here,' said Brian. He finally took off his jacket and hung it carefully over the back of a chair.

Rosetta noted his new tactic of using phrases he'd heard on *Coronation Street* in an effort to give himself the common touch. It didn't work. She felt mildly irritated that he wasn't stamping on this pointless insurrection, but bit her tongue.

'I'm not getting aerated!' spluttered Glynn, without break-ing his mean stare at John, who was quietly wiping down his Gibson and putting it away in its velvet-lined vampire case. 'I'm the lead singer, aren't I? The focus is meant to be on me, isn't it? And how am I meant to keep any sort of control over the gig when he's . . . he's . . .'

'What's your problem, man? John was bloody *amazing* tonight,' said Red unexpectedly, cracking open a bottle of ale from the crate in the corner. Nev, in between dismantling the kit and removing the last of the female fans had revived Red expertly and he had reached a simmering state of restrained manicness. 'I'm not surprised all those birds were trying to get on stage.' He tilted his bottle towards John and grinned, showing the cheeky gap in his teeth. 'There'll be some laundry goin' on tonight in Kingston, ah'm tellin' ya.'

'How charmingly put,' snarled Glynn. 'Exactly what you'd expect from a *drummer*.'

Rosetta saw John and Red exchange a conspiratorial wink as Red flicked the top of the beer bottle off on the edge of the table and handed it to him. The incessant mind games were the only serious downer about this lot. She hoped Red wouldn't wind Glynn up too much – and give him a reason not to let his mate in the band.

'It was a great gig all round,' said Brian in his most conciliatory tones. 'Just marvellous. Everyone played really . . . well.'

'Well, you must admit that the crowd were going bloody mad out there,' said Red, as innocently as he could. 'And normally you have to take your shirt off to get that many girls yelling up at the front, don't you, Glynn? Or are those just gigs where you've a lot of local exes?'

'Right, that's it! Brian, I want a word with you!' hissed Glynn and dragged Brian outside, slamming the door shut.

There was silence in the dressing-room, broken only by a loud and melodic burp from Red as he reached the end of his ale.

'What a bloody arse that lad is,' he said, conversationally.

The door was flung open again. 'And you, you foul-mouthed Geordie prick,' said Glynn, grabbing Red's arm and dragging him outside.

Rosetta watched John from the top of the filing cabinet she was perched on. She couldn't shake off the feeling of being drunk, even though she hadn't touched a drop all evening. She tried to feel guilty, being so disloyal to Brian, but she couldn't. It wasn't like fancying someone else, it was just like falling obediently under a spell. And everyone else in the audience was doing it, weren't they?

The funny thing was, John seemed to be under some kind of dream too, but Rosetta, ever the pragmatist, knew that he was probably thinking about the next gig, working out how to make his solo better. It always was with the real musicians.

'I've never heard anyone play better than that, and I must have heard them do that number a thousand times,' she said and frowned to herself. She felt really gauche. Not like the manager's girlfriend at all. Easy complimentary words that would normally have flowed out of her mouth in an unstoppable stream evaporated out of her brain, and she struggled for something to say that could convey half of what she felt. 'That guitar of yours – it's just . . . wow.'

John pushed his hair back out of his eyes. It was starting to dry off into damp black ringlets. Rosetta could see why Nev and Brian might have thought he was on drugs – there was a micro-second delay in his speech, and his wide eyes were dark and spaced.

'Thanks. I, er . . . I just don't know what was happening out there,' he said with a little gasping laugh. 'Sometimes it's like . . . someone else is playing, and I'm just listening. You know what I mean?'

Rosetta nodded. His voice was heart-stopping all on its own: melodic and Irish. Shy.

He finished wiping down the guitar, leaned over and said, confidentially, 'Fair play, though, I think there's some kind of spell on this thing. I think I must have sold my soul without knowing it in a pub in Kilburn.'

She tilted her head nearer him, and said, very seriously, 'You mean you've got ten years of playing like a genius – then an eternal lifetime of building sites?'

He laughed and looked up at her, as if noticing her properly for the first time. His eyes were searching, and without thinking, she smoothed down her mini-skirt as far as it would go. Which wasn't very far.

'So, Rosetta. You're Brian's wife?'

'Girlfriend,' Rosetta corrected him, and flinched. 'We live together.'

No need to say how long for. Got to be mysterious. Don't have to tell everyone everything.

You big liar.

'I see.'

Rosetta felt another part of herself melt at the slow lilt of his accent, and angrily shook herself inside. How pathetic was this going to look? Was this how an embryonic style icon and cool girl-about-town acted?

She pulled a long strand of hair from behind her ear and began twisting it round her finger. She knew from photographs and the way it irritated Brian that this made her look utterly disinterested, and a bit like Brigitte Bardot. 'Have you been in London long?' she asked.

John fiddled with the locks on his guitar case. 'Oh, about two or three years. I've been working short-term contracts, doing some gigs now and again, when I can, different people, depending who's around. You know how it is. A day's honest toil and all that.'

Rosetta couldn't imagine John doing anything else other than standing on a stage playing like a possessed man, but then again none of the musicians she knew were full-time. Even Glynn, who acted as if he were internationally famous, did five day-time bar-shifts a week in Soho. A day job was fine. She just didn't want to hear that John was an actuary, like Ian. That would be killing.

Although, having said that, a bell did ring in a distant part of her Richmond brain that it was nice that he didn't just slob around all day, getting stoned and never changing his socks.

Like some she could mention.

In the continuous broadcast of the conversation, running

in her head, Rosetta raised an eyebrow and looked cool, but somewhere along the line, it got mixed up and she smiled broadly at him and let the hair slide off her finger in a perfect long ringlet.

Maybe it went wrong because John was smiling back at her.

'Do you write yourself?' she asked. 'You know, songs?'

'I do,' he said proudly. 'I've written quite a few since I've been in London even . . .'

'Oh, that's just serendipity!' she exclaimed. 'Wonderful! They really *need* someone who can write original material right now. I mean, they're never going to get a record deal unless they can demo some of their own songs, and Glynn's just hopeless at –' She stopped herself, conscious that she was being rather disloyal. 'But, no, that's really great. Can I hear them? I mean, you will play some for us?'

'If you want to.'

She nodded. This just got better and better. 'So what do you do when you're not doing all this?'

He tilted his head. 'Well, I meant it about the Kilburn devil pact. I'm a builder. Our national occupation, you know? Carpenter, decorator, bit of everything, really.'

Rosetta flushed with embarrassment. 'Oh, God! Before . . . I didn't mean . . .'

John grinned wryly. 'Ah, don't worry about it. It's a bit of a cliché, really – the old Irish builder thing . . .'

'That's not a cliché,' said Rosetta. 'No more than Glynn's three paternity suits.'

'I'm quite good with my hands, as it goes,' he said. A faint blush appeared round his ears, but it made him look more appealing. He was quiet, thought Rosetta, and now she looked more closely, there wasn't a hint of swotty schoolboy about him. But he was a nice lad, nicer than most men that talented would be.

John snapped the locks on his guitar case shut and flashed her a warm smile. Rosetta noted that he looked like he needed a decent meal – not that she could cook to save her life, or even Brian's, but something about him made her want to whip out a steak and kidney pie.

She was about to suggest that he came back with her and Brian and took his chances with one of her omelettes, but at that moment the door burst open and Glynn stormed back in, now in full-on rock star mode, leavened with just a hint of pissed-off barman.

Brian and Red followed. Brian looked weary and Red looked distinctly mischievous. Whatever they'd been talking about seemed to have drained Brian of all his diplomatic powers.

Rosetta noticed John brace himself, carefully running the flat of his hand over his guitar case as if he didn't want it to get involved. The fluttering muscles in her stomach tensed, and she realized that even without knowing what Glynn was going to say, she was already itching to defend John against him.

Glynn waited for Red and Brian to come fully into the room, satisfied himself that he had everyone's undivided attention, and then pushed his fingers through his hair, shook his head, and adopted his 'groin out, shoulders back' stance that he had devised to draw attention from his incipient pot belly.

Rosetta huffed crossly down her nose and thought – *again* – that it was a real shame for everyone that Glynn wasn't half as sexy as he thought he was. She really hoped Brian was going to take charge, before Glynn got comfortable with the erroneous idea that he was running the show.

'Right,' he said, affecting the posh Estuary voice that went with the pose. 'We've had a band meeting and we think that –'

The door creaked open and Simon slunk into the room. He looked aggrieved to see everyone all together. 'Oh, right, is *this* where you all are?' he whined. 'I've been sitting in the Transit waiting for you for the last twenty minutes.' He shook his asthma inhaler accusingly at Red. 'Red, have you been at my inhaler again? I warned you about that.'

'Shut it, Simon,' said Red. 'Glynn's going off on one and you're in'erruptin'.'

'Give it a rest, Red,' said Brian, evenly. His eyes were darting between them all, trying to see where the balance was. 'Let's get this over –' He stopped himself and raised his hands diplomatically before anyone else could leap in. 'I mean, let's hear what Glynn has to say, shall we?'

'Well, then.' Glynn turned to face John, and gave him a very obvious up-and-down look. 'We've had a very frank discussion of the way you fit into the band, and taking into account our new direction –'

'We'd like you to come in with us, man,' finished Red. He grinned and extended a sweaty palm, which John took and shook heartily.

Rosetta felt her heart skip again. This time it almost hurt. Her chest seemed black and cavernous and she hadn't felt this close to having a heart attack since the one time she'd allowed Red to persuade her to try Dexadrine at a club.

Externally, she only let a tiny Mona Lisa smile flick across her pale face, and glanced over at Brian, willing him to push himself forward more. She just couldn't understand how he could be so impressive with promoters and the like, but not in front of his own band.

She saw John look up at her and it took a Herculean effort not to extend the smile further.

'Oh, fine, cheers,' said Simon through a mouthful of curling ham sandwich. 'Thanks for asking *me* again. Thanks for getting *my* opinion on this. Thanks for . . .'

Rosetta couldn't contain herself any longer. 'Simon,' she said sweetly, touching his shoulder. 'Would you like John to come into the band? Or do you *want* to go back to sounding like the runners-up in the Streatham High School Pretty Things Soundalike Competition? Hmm? Just say. It's your scene, too, you know.'

Simon's baleful little eyes swung from Red to Glynn to Brian to John. He looked like a King Charles spaniel suddenly offered an entirely new brand of dog food. When his gaze went round the whole circle and reached Rosetta, her long legs swinging against the filing cabinet like a King's Road rag dolly, the little eyes narrowed. 'Hey, don't you start criticizing what you don't dig, young –'

'I think you'll find Rosetta knows more about this than any of us,' said Brian pompously.

'Yeah, specially since she's the same *age* as most of the audience,' Glynn interjected with a nasty leer. 'Or do I mean, the same *under*age?'

Red simply shot out a hand and shoved Glynn in the chest, sending him sprawling back against the desk with the plate of sandwiches on it. The dish of ready-salted crisps turned over and spilled into Red's kitbag like crispy confetti.

'Oh, shit,' breathed Simon and flinched into the corner.

Glynn lay looking up from the debris of the meagre buffet for one menacing moment and then sprang to his feet with surprising agility for a man in such tight trousers, his arms stretched out in a pretend kung fu stance, and his even white teeth bared. 'Come here, you little Geordie nonce!'

Red rarely turned his back on an opportunity to give Glynn a good smack, but before he could put his beer down, Rosetta angrily slipped off the filing cabinet and stood between them. In her stacked heels, she was taller than Simon but still only level with Glynn and Red's shoulders. She put a hand on each chest, not flinching at the clammy sweat, and glared around the room. All the men fell silent and stared at her with surprise and fear registering equally in their faces.

'*Stop* that right *now*!' she yelled, giving Glynn and Red a shove for emphasis. 'John's in and that's *it*. I will *not* let you screw this all up because one of you's a big kid and the

other's a raging egomaniac!' She paused to let this sink in
and to get her breath back. Glynn tried to protest, but she
gave him another shove and he shut up.

'You've never played better than you did tonight,' she
went on, in a marginally quieter but no less authoritative
voice, 'and I mean *all of you*. You were really doing something special, and they all knew it out there. Just don't ruin
everything by acting like a bunch of big kids.'

Glynn cut Red a pointed glare, to which Red responded
by balling his fist, behind his back so Rosetta couldn't see.

Once she'd released the torrent of words, Rosetta suddenly felt self-conscious, and worried that she'd made herself
look hysterical in front of John. But that concern went as
quickly as it came, to be replaced by the strong sensation
that she'd actually stepped into a void in the group – and
filled it better than Brian had.

She looked between Glynn, who was staring mutinously
down at his buckled shoes, and Red, who was grinning
cheekily at her, as if he'd enjoyed her yelling at them. With a
final shove, she let them go and returned to the filing cabinet,
still glaring. No one spoke.

Brian discreetly peeled a cheese and Branston sandwich
off the back of Glynn's velvet jacket. 'You *were* great
tonight,' he said soothingly. 'The president of the union was
asking about their summer ball . . .'

'Look, Red's the bloody retarded adolescent round here.
And I don't see how I can be expected to –' Glynn began in
his familiar 'I need a dressing-room of my own' whine. Not
that he ever expected to get a dressing-room, but after a
year he felt he should be asking for one.

'It's not *about* you any more, it's about the *band*. Can't
you see that?' Rosetta interrupted him impatiently. She let
the issue of Brian not decking Glynn go for the moment.

Glynn looked as if he was about to say something else and
then changed his mind as he caught her eye. But his expression was that of a meercat fomenting serious unrest, and

Rosetta felt a chill run down her back, although she showed no reflection of it on her face.

'Listen, darling,' she said to John, taking a tiny thrill from the easy social boundaries that let her flirt without appearing to flirt. Somehow it was easier with them all there; it was expected of her. 'We all need to celebrate! Someone gave me some champagne tonight – it's in my car somewhere. Brian? Would you?' She threw him the keys to her Mini and he fumbled them, catching them by the key-ring. 'It's in the side pocket.'

'I'll get the glasses,' said Simon, and went to the bar.

'Who needs glasses?' said Red, winking at Rosetta.

Chapter Five

Chelsea, 2001

Rosetta didn't often host family dinners, outside of Christmas and her birthday, and she preferred to be taken out for those. Having everyone back to the house usually sparked off some argument over nothing, as the familiar smell and feel of the place merely served to illustrate how far they'd all gone since it had been a family home – or perhaps not as far as they'd like, as the squabbling suggested. Robert had a particularly inflammatory habit of wandering round, picking up Rosetta's beloved artefacts and assessing them under his breath, as if he were on *Antiques Roadshow*, and Greg's attempts to jolly up the mood invariably began with, 'Do you remember when . . .?' which Rosetta would take as an assault on her age, and Barney and Robert would take as the opening gambit in a long argument about factual inaccuracies.

Recently, Greg had noticed, on the occasions he had been summoned round on some errand, Rosetta had started talking wistfully about how other people got together on Sundays with their families, and walked dogs and stuff like that. Tempting as it was, he'd refrained from sarcastic comment, because Rosetta occasionally went through phases of seeing things on television and imagining that they could be recreated in real life, and besides, he didn't really feel able to offer her any genuine encouragement, since twice a year was about the maximum for civilities to be maintained between the four of them.

Patrick, of course, hadn't been home properly for over five years. This diminished the row quotient accordingly, and his continuing absence had provided the other three with some form of temporary emergency defence when their mother launched a general assault on their familial short-comings.

Rosetta liked to rotate her sons' attendance and Greg, Barney and Robert hadn't been round to Cheyne Walk simultaneously since last Christmas. So though Greg was a little bemused when Rosetta called him and announced that she wanted to see them all for dinner at the weekend, Robert wasn't. He'd guessed something was up when, at the start of the week, Brian had phoned his second son from his new ice palace in Geneva to say that he'd be making over some more music publishing shares to the trust set up in 1975 to avoid taxes.

Well, partly to avoid taxes, and partly because it had initially amused Brian that a four-year-old boy would be making more money off the songs than the drummer.

If Dad was moving money around, then it followed that Rosetta would want to see him, Robert thought. She had a second sense about things like that, even if she and Brian rarely spoke.

'Why does she want us *all* to go over for supper?' asked Tanith. She was struggling with her only expensive outfit: a black wrap-over dress that had wrapped over just fine a month ago and now revealed a bit more of her knee than she really wanted to. In principle Tanith refused to be intimidated by Rosetta, but even she couldn't help picking up on externally transmitted panic vibes.

'There has to be a reason for us to go over?' he said evasively.

'Robert, in the year we've been living together, I've seen Rosetta once. And you've been round there every time she needs a jar opening, even though you bitch about it *every time* and come back with a new problem and a headache.' Tanith bounced a dark look off the mirror, towards the dressing-table where Robert was deliberating over three equally boring ties. 'There's always a reason with your mother.'

'Funny that, because reason isn't a word I freely associate with Rosetta.' He held a charcoal grey silk tie beneath his chin.

Tanith ignored the cheap jibe. Robert was an angry man, but he seemed to reserve a special bile for his mother. He kept a drum-kit in the cellar and often thrashed away on it for hours after a visit to Cheyne Walk. Soundproofing had been expensive, but he claimed it was cheaper than therapy. 'I mean, is it something to do with the house?' she went on. 'Barney was only there last week, and so was Greg. So it can't just be something run-of-the-mill.'

'You have no idea what Rosetta considers run-of-the-mill,' said Robert. He selected the navy tie with the silver stripes meandering across it like snail's tracks. 'She's modelled her entire family life on the Borgias. Anyway, why would I know? She's probably been watching *Dallas* again on cable and thinks it's time we had some kind of high-impact bonding session.' Robert knotted the tie with quick, confident strokes. 'Having systematically ignored all concepts of parenting while we were actually children, she seems to be taking a rather belated interest in the whole thing, if you ask me. God knows she's been trying to get Greg to come out over the cheeseboard for years. She dragged him round clothes shops for years and now she thinks if she sets up enough tender family conferences, homosexuality will just spill out of him. But only so she won't have to blame herself for him not having a girlfriend because she's screwed him up so comprehensively.'

Tanith stopped tugging at her dress and let it fall in defeat. She studied Robert's face in the wardrobe mirror. 'I don't know why she should assume that. It's a very repressed sixties attitude, you realize,' she said reprovingly. There was a long pause, in which she tried to feign disinterest. Then she added, despite herself, 'You don't think Greg's gay?'

Robert shrugged and looked for matching cufflinks in his cufflink organizer. 'Maybe. Wouldn't bother me if he was. Might explain why he spends all his time hanging out at wedding receptions.'

Tanith processed this thought. Professionally, her mind worked like a Rolodex, storing little facts and snippets about actors, assessing what felt right about them, what could be changed, and what would be totally out of character. And though she was alive to the very distant possibility of fourteen-year-old white girls playing Othello, for some reason, Greg being gay hadn't even occurred to her, not convincingly. Or maybe it had and she'd dismissed it. 'I don't think he can be gay. No, I'm willing to bet he's not.' She searched her mind for the reason. 'Have you seen his shoes?'

'What about them?'

'They're just . . .' Tanith gazed at Robert's shoes, smart lace-ups, black and polished like glass. Men's shoes. The antithesis of Greg's. '. . . Inept. Oh, I don't know.' She went back to the wardrobe and pushed back hanger after hanger. Tanith didn't normally go through wardrobe panics like this – she wasn't a fussy girls' girl, and normally gave little more thought to her clothes than what wouldn't show up the dirt too much, but she had a weird feeling about tonight. It was never 'just supper'. Something about the way in which Rosetta issued summonses, rather than invitations, got her back up.

Or maybe it was more to do with the way in which her sons whined endlessly about Rosetta, and yet came scrambling back as if on retractable leads, the moment she folded her hands on that red sofa and assumed her Madonna and Children expression.

'Anyway, I said we'd pick him up on the way,' said

Robert. 'Though not literally, of course. I fear that may be out of his sphere of experience. He's in town, at . . . Joe's Basement?' He squinted at the text message on his mobile phone. 'Do we know Joe? Is he a friend?'

'It's a processing shop,' said Tanith heavily. She pulled her black jeans out of the drawer and hauled them on. 'He'll be dropping his films in. He did a wedding today, at Arsenal, I think.'

'Very stylish.' Robert stood up and began to brush his suit jacket. 'Would you like to get married in a football ground, darling? Or somewhere more tasteful. Harrods Food Hall, maybe?'

Tanith looked at herself sideways in the mirror and tried to pretend she hadn't heard what Robert had just said. 'We don't have to get that dressed up, do we?' she asked hopefully, picking a silk V-neck jumper off the top of the laundry pile. It was the colour of Caramac, and had a small hole on the arm. Tanith hoped that would help pass it off as vintage. 'It's not . . . formal?'

'That depends what kind of wedding you want it to be.'

Rather than meet Robert's eye, she turned back to consider her reflection which, she noted objectively, was looking as if it had been freshly punched in the stomach. Tanith ran her tongue over the sharp edges of her teeth and tried to keep her voice light and level. 'I meant tonight. It's just a quiet dinner? Not one of Rosetta's fancy dress evenings?'

Robert said nothing but carried on staring at her shoulder blades, until she was forced to look round. It was one of his best tricks and she hated herself every time she fell for it. Greg and Patrick had independently informed her that Robert had been the sort of child who held his breath until he got what he wanted. They'd only had to call a doctor the once, too.

'Tanith. Don't try and change the subject like that.'

She sighed at her reflection, and it pulled a sympathetic

face back. There was no point trying to change the subject with Robert. He refused to drop his eye contact until he got what he wanted. Which would have made him a fantastic highwayman, with or without flintlocks.

She hauled the jumper over her head, ruffled up her hair again until it stood up in blonde chunks, and turned to look at him, standing there by the dressing-table in his suit, looking for all the world like her dad on his way to parents' evening. Only Robert was thirty-one, not fifty-one. And he had a dressing-table, for God's sake. It was almost incredible, even for a woman raised on Brookside and AIDS adverts, how unromantic Robert could make the whole concept of marriage.

'Come on, Tan. We are going to discuss this, aren't we?'

Before Tanith could say, 'Discuss what? My dowry?' the phone rang downstairs and she ran downstairs to get it, hating herself more with each step, and knowing that he would be staring at her from exactly the same spot when she went upstairs again.

'Just run through *why* you agreed to pick up Barney *as well as Greg* one more time,' said Robert. 'See if I can make sense of it this time round.' He was breathing heavily through his nose and staring at the Audi in front. Tanith hoped the driver wasn't looking in his rear-view mirror. There could be a crash.

She turned the radio on in the hope of lightening the mood in the car, which was bordering on toxic, and cleared her throat. 'Well, because he asked if we were driving to Rosetta's and I said yes, then he asked if you minded picking him up and I said I didn't think so. It's not that hard, is it?'

'Apart from the fact that it seems a little pointless, seeing as he is in a coffee-bar about three minutes' walk from her house. Idle little waster.'

Tanith snapped. Suddenly it felt like a very long time since

Robert had spoken to her in the manner of a boyfriend, rather than either a fractious child or a thundering husband. 'Oh, right! So *that* was what you were trying to signal to me when I was on the phone to Barney! I thought you were trying to mime climbing up an invisible wall.'

'Ho ho ho.'

'Do you *appreciate* how hard it is to say no to that boy? I don't think he understands the term. Did your mother ever *explain* the concept of not getting his own way?'

'She doesn't understand it herself.' Robert threw his mobile phone at her. 'Call Greg and tell him to be on the corner of Shaftesbury Avenue and Wardour Street in three minutes.'

Tanith flung him an evil look, but he had resumed staring at the man in front, as if willing him to stall so he could really start an argument.

Greg sat in the back of Robert's BMW, clutching his plastic envelope of mounted slides in one hand and a crumpled packet of Nurofen in the other, with an Oddbins bag between his feet. His headache was so bad he couldn't let go of either. He had wanted to take three Nurofen as soon as possible, to alleviate the banging in his temples, but Robert had taken a perverse pleasure in refusing to allow him to open his can of Coke in the car.

Supper at his mother's was exactly what Greg didn't need to round off a pretty lousy day. Or maybe it was. Maybe it would get all the bad stuff out of the way all at once for the next few weeks. The last thing he wanted to deal with was another bloody dysfunctional family pretending to get on with each other, not after the day he'd had, doing a wedding at Highbury football ground.

He had known it wouldn't be an easy one from the start, which had given his migraine a forty-eight-hour run-up: the groom wanted the pictures in the communal bath and the bride's brother had been a Spurs supporter. And while they were setting up the lighting for the family shots, Maggie, his allegedly psychic assistant, had gleefully predicted a divorce in three years – which the bride's father had overheard. But rather than go spare at her, as Greg had expected, he'd corrected it to two years, with costs to be paid voluntarily by himself. The wife already had an ISA set up to cover it, apparently. And the wedding presents (season tickets) were in his name, so at least the wedding wouldn't be a total write-off.

'Why are we picking Barney up?' he whined. 'If he's in Starbucks he's just down the road from Rosetta.'

Tanith opened her mouth to explain, but before she could speak, Robert barked, 'Because if I pick *you* up, then I have to pick *him* up. You idle little waster. For crying out loud. What do you think I am, some kind of taxi service?'

'You didn't have –'

'Yes, I bloody well did. I'm not sitting there fielding Rosetta's Church of the Sacred Heart routine on my own, waiting for you two to slope in, just in time for pudding and recriminations.'

'Robert, *stop* it!' said Tanith.

'Have you brought any wine?' he went on, ignoring her.

Tanith turned up the radio, but that just made them shout louder.

'Of course I've brought wine.' Greg didn't ever go to Rosetta's without wine. That would just be stupid.

'What kind of wine?'

'Strong red wine.'

'How much?'

'Two bottles.'

'Good.'

'Do you know what it's about?' Tanith twisted round in her seat and, throwing her eyes towards Robert's rigid driving position, pulled a face of apology, for which Greg smiled gratefully.

'I have no idea,' said Greg honestly. 'I thought it might be

about Patrick. That he's finally dropped off the edge and
taken holy orders or someth—'

He ground to an embarrassed halt and blushed. It was
easy to forget that Tanith was actually Patrick's ex-
girlfriend – no one had really seen them as a couple, so there
was no reproachful mental picture to stop him putting his
foot in things. Besides which, it was hard enough accepting
the fact that someone as Premier Division as Tanith would
want to sleep with *Robert,* without bringing *Patrick* into the
picture too.

'Sorry,' he mumbled. 'Didn't mean to, um . . .'

Tanith gave him a sympathetic shrug, then bit her lip.
Greg was impressed to see that the cherry red lipstick didn't
smudge. He looked more closely. *Was* that lipstick? Did girls
have lips that colour naturally?

'Is that lipstick?' he said. 'What colour is it?'

Robert rolled his eyes in the driving mirror. 'Explain to me
again how we're related? Were we some kind of job lot at the
orphanage?'

'No, I don't think Pat's up for holy orders just yet,' Tanith
said. 'Robert, on the other hand, is going in for some kind of
living sainthood.'

'What did you just say?' demanded Robert from the front,
before an Audi in front distracted his attention by swerving
in front of him. 'God! Did you see the way she just crossed
those diagonal lines? Don't people *read* the Highway Code
any more?'

'You're such a policeman, Rob. Why can't you be more
Zen?' demanded Tanith. 'I mean, *you're* Zen in London,
aren't you, Greg? You don't drive like you're trying to escape
from nuclear fallout?'

The driver of the Audi was now attempting to line her
car up for an illegal U-turn, despite being too near a pedestrian crossing and causing mayhem with the oncoming
traffic.

Robert buzzed his window down and yelled, 'That's three

points on your licence automatically if you get caught doing that!'

The driver's boyfriend started to mouth obscenities through his window.

'What?' demanded Robert. 'Did you just say what I think you did?'

The boyfriend confirmed that he did, with a descriptive gesture.

Tanith was horrified to see Robert lean out of his window to continue the discussion. She and Greg simultaneously slid down in their seats, as far as they could go.

'Well, maybe if she took those sunglasses off she might be able to see where she's going!' he yelled. 'Oh fine, I'm just stopping you from killing someone else! There are *reasons* why you're not allowed to cross those lines!'

'St Robert of Clerkenwell,' observed Greg, breaking open his Nurofen to swallow them without water. 'The world's first traffic martyr.'

They were halfway down the King's Road when Greg caught sight of Barney ambling past Waitrose with some blonde woman who, he noticed immediately, wasn't quite Flora, but wasn't far off.

Robert screeched to a halt and leaned across Tanith to bellow, 'Get in the fucking car!'

'Would you excuse me, schweetie?' said Barney to the girl, pushing up the sleeves of his dove-grey jumper and shrugging apologetically. 'I'm being kidnapped by the IRA.'

'Shut up and get in!' roared Robert.

Barney made a 'What can you do?' gesture to his giraffe-like companion, kissed her suavely on both cheeks and asked for her phone number, which she duly wrote on his hand in lip-liner.

'*How*?' Greg mouthed to Tanith, his face creased with bemused envy. 'How does he *do* it?'

'I'll phone you about the weekend, yeah?' said Barney

with a final, gorgeous smile, and he slid into the back seat next to Greg. 'God, where do they *make* those girls? Is there a Barbie factory in Fulham I don't know about? Hi, Greg, I see the IRA got you as well. Shift over, will you?'

Greg shunted over to the other side, keeping his wine bag between his feet and swallowing furiously at the pills which had got stuck in his suddenly dry throat.

Tanith turned round in her seat. 'Hello, Barney. I don't think I've ever seen you on your own. You're like an oxygen molecule.'

'Hello, gorgeous.' He leaned forward and managed to plant a kiss on each cheek. 'Mmm, you smell nice. Don't tell me Robert splashed out and bought you some perfume?'

'Shut it, you,' said Robert, steering forcefully around a bus. 'I'm not in the mood, all right?'

'Rob, why the *Sweeney* routine?'

'Don't push your luck. It's *that* far from turning into a *Reservoir Dogs* routine.'

Barney satisfied himself by directing his special sexy look at Tanith – a slow, deliberate double blink of cheeky conspiracy, sweeping his long lashes in a manner guaranteed to reduce most of Parson's Green to willing jelly.

To her chagrin, Tanith felt her own heart speed up, but she was too smart to let Barney see. Instead she winked coolly and cut her eyes at Robert, to indicate that she knew exactly what his next comment would be.

'And don't get that slapper's lipstick on my upholstery,' Robert added on cue, swinging the car into Rosetta's street. 'This car's just been valeted.'

'Do you have a pen I could borrow, Tanith?' asked Barney, with disarming politeness.

Tanith found a biro in her Filofax and extended her arm over her head to pass it back. Then without waiting to be asked she tore out a piece of paper and handed that back too.

Barney started to transcribe the phone number from his hand. 'Would you say that was a four or a six?' he asked Greg.

'I'd say she was a ten, no question.' Greg's headache picked up a gear. 'I think it's a kiss, actually.'

'Really? Yeah, think you're right. Ah, bless.' He drew a box around the mobile number, and the pen hesitated.

'Don't tell me you've already forgotten her name,' said Greg, sourly.

'Ehm, no, I haven't, her name's . . . oh, shit, she used to share a flat with Katie Bleswick . . . God, I'm so dreadful with . . .'

'Her name was Georgie.' The three men turned to look at Tanith in amazement.

'It was on her necklace.' She rolled her eyes. 'Honestly. The difference between men and women is a mere three inches focus range.'

Greg and Barney looked blank.

Tanith held her hands up in a balance. 'Jewellery, tits? Jewellery, tits? Tits, jewellery?'

'Jewellery,' said Barney.

'Tits,' said Greg.

'Get out of the car, children, we're here,' said Robert.

Supper passed under a typical cloud of barely repressed tension. It reminded Tanith of one of those Victorian party games, in which one person leaves the room and then has to guess which of the remaining guests is a murderer, while the remaining guests pass coded clues amongst themselves. Except, as usual, she had no idea what the dark allusions were about, and despite the lads' fervently expressed disbelief that none of them could possibly be related to each other, they all behaved exactly the same.

Rosetta, on the other hand, was in a very odd mood. Tanith noticed that her hair and eyes were shining as if a spotlight was following her round the room, and yet she would suddenly break off mid-sentence, pick things up and look at them distractedly as if she hadn't seen them before. More than once, she stared at Robert as if she hadn't seen him before either. Though Tanith conceded that that was understandable, given some of the deranged things he was coming out with.

But what really interested Tanith was that alternating with the dazzled spotlight look was a disturbing vacancy, which she hadn't imagined was part of Rosetta's range. Tonight, though, Rosetta even sat oblivious through Robert's half-hour tirade about parking restrictions in Kensington and Chelsea, despite Barney's sinking his head on to his hands and Greg's twenty-five-minute absence in the loo.

'Is there something wrong?' she asked Robert in an undertone, when Rosetta went through to the kitchen to get the coffee.

'Yes, there bloody is,' said Robert, making no effort to lower his voice. 'I've had a bloody awful day trying to get receipts out of a man whose idea of filing is something women do to their nails, I've had to run round town after these two helpless bimboys, no one in London understands how to drive a car, and my own mother has tried to feed me some kind of lead-encrusted deathtrap of a supper, despite the fact that I haven't ever eaten game in my life. She should at least remember things like that, even if she has forgotten my birthday for the last three years.'

'Oh, give it a rest, will you?' muttered Greg, leaning back on the spindly legs of his chair, trying to see down the hall into the kitchen. To his annoyance, despite filling in time by reading most of last month's *Vogue* in the loo, he had still returned to hear the closing part of Robert's tirade against A & R men who attempted to claim drugs on VAT returns. 'I've never seen her so weird. It's like someone's playing her in a film, but not very well.'

'I know what you mean,' said Barney, finishing off his wine. 'They've got the basics right, but the shameless egotism just isn't there. You could have cast it better, Tanith. Who *would* you cast in a film version of my mother's life, then? Drew Barrymore? Joan Plowright?'

'Is she all right?' Tanith asked Barney in an undertone. She didn't bother to direct the question at Robert or Greg. Barney, who still spent time at home, was the only one whom Rosetta actually talked to about anything.

He shrugged. 'We'll soon find out. She doesn't like to keep bad news to herself, on the whole.'

As he spoke, Rosetta shimmied through, carrying a large plate of cheese and a sort of Indian gourd canoe containing water biscuits, which she placed in front of Tanith. Then she ran her fingers through her thick pale gold hair and coiled it up into a knot at the nape of her neck, absently hunting through her pockets for pins.

Tanith hoped she had a neck like Rosetta's at fifty, all long and swan-like, without a wrinkle or crease. But then being able to afford all the latest designer neck creams must have helped. Being able to turn your nose up that high probably ironed out the creases too. She noticed that the boys were all fixedly watching the hairdressing performance with some concern.

'Take notes. First sign of nerves with her,' murmured Greg. 'She does her hair over and over again. Sometimes when it's still up. She'll put a fork through it in a minute.'

'That's a lovely comb,' said Tanith politely. 'Is it tortoise-shell?'

'Oh, for fuck's sake, Rosetta, why don't you just sit down and tell us what's happening?' said Robert. He helped himself to a large slice of runny Brie and smeared it on a cracker. 'We're not kids any more. You can't expect Dad to break all your bad news to us.'

'I thought it was usually the *Daily Express* that did that,' Barney interjected. 'Are they not interested any more? Pass the cheese, will you, sexy?'

'Do you mean me?' asked Tanith. 'Or your mother?'

Rosetta seemed to break out of her trance, and an unreadable look twinkled into her eyes.

Damn it, thought Tanith enviously, she really does twinkle. That's such an old-fashioned glamorous thing to be able to do.

'I don't know what you think is so funny.' Robert glared at his mother. 'See the poor paranoid children you've raised? What would Freud make of a unmarriageable wedding photographer, a compulsive flirt and a man with two ulcers in his late twenties?'

'Suspected ulcers,' Tanith added. 'And you're now early thirties.'

'And I prefer serial lady-killer, if you don't mind,' said Barney. 'But unmarriageable wedding photographer is a pretty lenient assessment.'

'Can you just leave me out of this?' demanded Greg. He fished in his pocket for the rest of the Nurofen. 'All right, Rosetta, now you've got our attention, why don't you spit it out, will you, whatever it is?'

Rosetta pushed a teaspoon into her hair to hold it up, and stood with her hands on her hips, ruching the velvet of her skirt between her fingers. In the candlelight of the dining-room, she looked exactly like a photograph of herself: vivid, but oddly two-dimensional. 'You three are so *negative*. Why do you assume it's bad news?'

'Because you haven't spilled the beans immediately, and there aren't about fifty other people here to share in your good fortune,' said Robert. He bit into his cracker and it splintered over his plate.

Greg met her eye and nodded sadly.

'Oh. OK.' Rosetta looked thoughtful and sat down. She poured herself some more wine. 'Well, it's not really bad news. Or at least, I don't think so. I've decided to take up a long-standing offer to write a book about my life,' she said. 'And I thought I might move somewhere abroad to do it. Ireland, probably. Have you finished with those biscuits, Robert?'

Robert's hand froze over the plate and his eyebrows knit-
ted together. 'You're going to *Ireland*? Why?' Tanith
thought he looked exactly like a Victorian paterfamilias,
recently informed of his wife's defection to a lesbian
brothel.

'Why not?' said Greg quickly. 'Ireland's a lovely place.
Lots of time to think about things. Nice pubs. Horses. And
it's not like you're too old to make a change, is it? Lots of
people your age just decide to up sticks and move.'

'Yeah, into bungalows with no sharp edges and lots of
handrails,' said Barney.

Tanith stared hard at the dripping mass of candles in front
of her, to stop herself laughing out loud – not at his joke, but
at his sheer rudeness. Only the truly gorgeous could get away
with that.

And – like mother, like son – only the truly gorgeous could
ignore it completely.

Rosetta lifted her chin and looked at Robert from over her
nose. 'I need to have somewhere peaceful and inspiring to
write my autobiography, and I'm going to find a very nice
little house by the sea, where I can be on my own and think
about what's happened in my life, and put it into some kind
of order, without any distractions.'

'Or shops,' added Barney.

'That's a very brave thing to do, Rosetta,' said Tanith,
feeling a gap had been left in the conversation for her to con-
tribute.

'Oh yes, right, brave,' Robert snorted. 'Very brave indeed.
That's why she's going to Ireland. You want to see what
Dad will do to her when he finds out what's she up to. And
all those other people. Are you going to include Coke King
Danny in your memoirs? Or that mad astrology guru bloke
you used to go to – the one who had a sex change to avoid
going to jail for bigamy?'

'It's *my* autobiography,' said Rosetta calmly. 'And it will
be like a tapestry of life in the sixties and seventies. Not

some . . . some groupie's phonebook account of Studs I Have Shagged.'

There was a challenging pause.

'Are you sure about that?' asked Robert.

Tanith choked on her wine.

Rosetta gave him a glare that started off outraged and moved to wounded. 'This is a book about *me*. And what *I* did. If it hadn't been for me, that band would never have *had* a contract. You have no idea how much work I did behind the scenes. *Nobody* knows. Just because no one ever wrote about it . . .'

'Yeah, yeah. Anyway, I thought you said you'd never write an autobiography,' said Greg. '"I'd rather invite the tabloid press into my house to rummage through my laundry, rather than stoop so low." Or am I misquoting you?'

Rosetta helped herself to some more cheese. 'I'm allowed to change my mind.'

'Has someone actually commissioned this great work of literary genius, or are you just doing it to piss Dad off?' asked Robert.

'Of course it's been commissioned.' She looked up with a frosty glitter in her eye. 'Not only has it been commissioned, but I have a signature cheque.'

'Oh, so *that's* why you want to go to Ireland!' exclaimed Robert, pointing his knife at her. 'The mists clear. For the *tax* breaks!'

'You're *very* like your *father*,' said Rosetta, the frost now manifest in her voice.

Robert gave her a very leading, very sarcastic look and opened his mouth to say something, at which point Greg met Tanith's querying eye and hurriedly spilled some water over the tablecloth to create a diversion.

'Jesus Christ almighty. It's like having supper with the Black Queen and the PG chimps,' said Robert, not quite *sotto voce* enough.

'Who's commissioned it?' Tanith asked to cover Greg's

embarrassment as he mopped at the spill with his napkin.

'An old friend of mine, Susie Morton-Thomas.' Rosetta helped herself to the towering block of Stilton, her equilibrium now restored.

'Sue, that dreadful friend of yours with the black fright wig?' Barney reared his head back in horror and his blond fringe swung into his eyes. 'Sue the one who used to hang around Anita's shop stretching the seams on everything and telling Anita she was making it all too small?'

'Sue used to be a journalist,' Rosetta explained, for Tanith's benefit. 'She was one of the first writers to move into television. Before that she was,' she stressed for Barney's benefit, 'one of the most *successful* Fleet Street columnists ever. She always used to claim that Polly Filler in *Private Eye* was based on her. Anyway, now she works in publishing. She's called Susie, these days, anyway.'

'Horse shit's called organic fertilizer these days but it doesn't make it less horse shit,' retorted Barney.

Robert buttered himself another biscuit, so hard that it cracked under the stress of his knife. 'Well, that's perfect, isn't it? Your own in-house ghost. And she'll know where all the skeletons are, ho ho. Just make sure she's not doing it for her own dubious reasons. That's all I'll say.'

'Robert . . .!' Tanith glared at him, but he was too busy wrestling the cheeseboard off Barney.

It made her feel really uncomfortable, the way the Mulligans spoke to each other. There was a complete lack of the usual family rules and niceties that made the whole experience very unsettling. She wasn't necessarily Rosetta's greatest fan, but something about this house seemed to propel Robert – and the others – to previously unexpected heights of sarcasm, which Rosetta seemed to accept, almost with resignation. Quite why she didn't put her foot down, Tanith had no idea. Particularly when she didn't hesitate to put her foot down about other, completely irrelevant stuff.

'So when do you plan to go?' she asked, aware that she

seemed to be the only one conducting the conversation
Rosetta wanted to have. How weird would that be? London
without Rosetta at the end of a phone, invisibly pulling all
Robert's strings? London without mild panic setting in each
time she had a casting near the King's Road? Who knew
what happy repercussions that might have for Robert and
his blood pressure? And as an even happier side-effect, for
their sex life?

'In the next few weeks. I need to get some things sorted
out here first. Decide which shoes to take with me, you
know what it's like.' Rosetta suddenly smiled privately at
Tanith in a confiding, girl-to-girl way. To Tanith's amazement, it made her chest swell up with automatic happiness
that Rosetta was directing that smile at her alone, and for an
intoxicating instant, Tanith could suddenly see why Rosetta
was so good at wrapping men round her little fingers in
interesting tessellating patterns.

Robert snorted from the other side of the table. 'Rosetta,
there *are* more important matters to worry about shoes. How
long do you intend to be there? Are you going to be resident?
Have you investigated your tax status? Have you actually
bought this pretty little cottage? Or is this going to be like
that forestry place you and Dad wanted to buy in Scotland to
save us from international rock pigs? The place that turned
out to be purely theoretical and yet highly tax-efficient?'

Rosetta carefully removed the rind from a melting piece of
Brie and applied it delicately to a water biscuit with a tiny
pearl-handled cheese knife. 'Well, that's really what I wanted
to talk to you about tonight, sweetheart. Not quite in those
terms though.'

Robert rolled his eyes. 'I bet not. What is it? You want me
to go through your accounts?'

'Well, it's either that or hand them over to someone else.'
She pulled a sad face. 'And I don't really want to do that.
Not when you're so good at it, anyway.'

Robert looked at his mother with what he hoped was a

stern expression. Brian, obviously, had been in charge of the family accounts until he made a break for Geneva, and frankly he wouldn't put it past Rosetta to have persuaded Brian to carry on poring over her books, in the interests of nurturing their labyrinthine divorce settlement. Money hadn't exactly changed hands as much as moved between off-shore umbrellas. There was a lot of it around, just none of it in their bank accounts: Brian and, annoyingly enough, Rosetta firmly believed in making their children work for their livings.

Robert's quick mind flicked up several good reasons to refuse outright. It would be a real pain to sift through the accounts, not to mention the faint shudder of distaste he had about knowing his parents' finances – it felt too much like knowing their old sexual habits. And yet he was enough of his father's son not to want someone else – someone like him – flicking through the books, finding all sorts of tax loopholes and then pocketing a sizeable percentage in return for not pointing them out to the tax man.

'All right,' he said. 'I'll have a look at them. God!' He helped himself to a couple of ripe apricots from the dish, crossly pulling off the leaves. 'I might have known this wouldn't be supper without strings attached. You're so predictable.'

'Oh darling, *will* you stop being so selfish?' said Rosetta, touching her hands on his shoulders, smiling over his head at Barney and Greg. 'I'm about to go away for a while! And it's not going to be a holiday, you know. Some people can only write their autobiographies after years of therapy. This is a very serious project for me, and I'm not doing it lightly.'

He gestured towards the other two with his glass. 'And what are they down for on your to-do list? Is Greg going to do the photos for the estate agent?'

Greg coughed on his cheese biscuit.

'You're selling the house?' Barney looked genuinely shocked.

The fire left Rosetta's eyes. 'No. No, I'm not going to sell the house.' She pressed her lips together, and exhaled slowly through her nose.

It was an unusually vulnerable gesture, and for the first time, the enormity of what Rosetta was proposing to do struck Greg. It was a *huge* step for her to make, at her age, to leave everything behind her, to go somewhere deliberately empty and clean of memories while she tried to put her whole life down in words. This house *was* Rosetta, for a start – from the little attic studio she and Dad had bought first, gradually spreading down from floor to floor as their lifestyle grew and money flooded in with each tour. Rosetta – or her divorce settlement – owned the whole tall, narrow house now.

'Oh, good,' said Tanith, then hastily offered the coffee round again.

'Well, Greg?' Rosetta turned to him. Some of the fight had returned to her face. 'Aren't you going to weigh in with some sarcastic yet naïve comment?'

He shook his head. 'No, why should I? Go ahead and write the damn thing. It's not as if I'm going to feature in it very much, is it? And who knows what we might actually learn from it.' He picked an apricot off the top of the fruit bowl and started peeling it with a knife.

Tanith topped up Robert's coffee with cream and handed it to him, but her eyes never left Rosetta. Doing what she did every day, Tanith wasn't easily rattled or impressed with histrionics, but there was something weird constantly rippling beneath Rosetta's beautiful placid exterior, as though she might erupt at any time, or persuade someone to do something dangerous for her. There was something about Rosetta that wasn't exactly real life. The fact that she had four adult sons, consorted with rock stars, and still only looked about thirty-five, for starters.

Before Tanith could wonder why she'd addressed that last question to Greg and not Barney or Robert, Rosetta was shaking her hair loose again and smiling like a perfectly normal mother in the flattering light of the massed candles dotting the table.

'That's exactly why *I'm* doing it,' she said. 'I might learn something too.'

Robert rolled his eyes, but no one saw him. They were all looking at Rosetta.

Chapter Six

London, 1969

"Why couldn't we have gone in the van?' demanded Glynn. 'I don't want to arrive looking ... *crumpled*.' He gave Red a shove, and smoothed out his shirt which was ruching up but not creasing due to its high level of man-made fibres. 'And don't put your arm around me, you Geordie bugger. No! Get off me! I can still feel you touching my neck.'

He shot Red a viperous look out of the corner of his eye. 'You haven't washed, have you?'

'Hey, Glynn,' said Red aimiably. 'You're wearing eyeliner, aren't ya, y' great jessie?'

Somehow Rosetta had shoehorned Red, Glynn, John and Simon into the back of a black taxi while she and Brian perched on the flip-down seats and scrutinized them with some concern. Since both Glynn and John were well over six feet tall and Red was built like the bricklayer he still was by day, it was amazing that they'd all got in, more amazing that the driver had agreed to take them.

'Now, now, lads,' said Brian. 'Let's not get personal. Red, you can move up a bit, can't you?'

'No,' said Red. 'I cannut.'

There simply wasn't room for four male shoulders to fit next to each other and Red had had to spread his arms out along the back of the seats, forcing Glynn into uncomfortable intimacy with Red's armpits. Rosetta noted too late that

Red's shirt wasn't as clean as it could be, with ghostly rings of sweat circling the armpits like tie dye. She made a mental note to talk to him about deodorant.

Fortunately, Simon's ability to slither into small spaces had come into its own. He was wedged under Red's other arm like a stoat in a poloneck. John was cramped up by the door, pretending to be unaffected by the tension in the taxi, but Rosetta could sense the excitement from the way his eyes moved from side to side, taking in all the busy streets and shop windows.

She too was buzzing with excitement, but naturally wasn't showing a glimmer of it. Instead she was retouching her lipstick and looking as bored as possible.

'Pack it in now, you two,' she said, without bothering to take her eyes off the powder compact. 'I told you before: it's a record company. They're looking for first impressions. And they're hardly going to take you seriously if you arrive in the van.'

'Why not?' Glynn had been truculent all morning. 'Makes us look like a proper working, *gigging* live band, arriving in the van.'

'It makes you look like a bunch of labourers,' Rosetta replied.

'But we *are* a bunch of labourers,' said John, innocently.

'Don't mention that!' Brian interrupted.

John shot Rosetta a conspiratorial grin which she caught over her mirror.

'We went over this last night, didn't we?' said Brian, hotly. 'I don't want you to mention that, about you working on building sites, John.'

'Why not, man?' demanded Red. 'You never told me I couldn't mention about my bricklaying.'

'Red, honey, you're obviously a bricklayer. Even *I'd* have a hard time passing you off as a fine art dealer,' said Rosetta. 'Anyway, it's good for your drumming. All about power and tightness, isn't it?'

'Well, Red *is* normally tight,' sniped Glynn. 'In all sorts of ways.'

Rosetta snapped her compact shut and looked at the band, squashed up in a row like compressed schoolboys on their way to the headmaster's office. That would make a great album cover shot, she thought, with a thrill of excitement. Now that they were actually in with a chance of *making* an album. God, it was so exciting!

'What's wrong with that van, anyway?' Simon whined. 'It's a good van, that. Fantastic load capacity. It'll do us another good few –'

'Simon.' Rosetta put her hand on his knee to interrupt him and fixed him with a friendly but hard stare. He wriggled slightly under her touch. 'You're going to talk to some men this morning who want to change your *life*, do you see what I mean? The whole *point* of this meeting is that when you walk out of it, you'll be going to your next gig in a new tourbus. On your own aeroplane!'

Simon tried hard to convey unconcern, and failed.

'Come on!' said Rosetta encouragingly. 'Your own Learjet! You've got to think big! Because if you won't, they won't!'

Brian nodded. 'She's absolutely right there, Simon. Not that it isn't a great van. It's done you proud, that van. But the day of the van will soon be over.'

Simon looked wounded. If Glynn had the trousers, and Red had the chicks and John had the solos, he'd had his van. It had been his only bargaining chip for years, that and the fact that he never got drunk and was always able to drive them home.

'Yeah, the things that van's seen,' said Red. 'You wouldn't want to know what some girls call that van. Eh, Glynn?'

'You what?' Simon leaned forward to see what was going on between Glynn and Red. 'What you on about? What've you been doin' in my van?'

Rosetta looked at Brian and let a flash of despair cross her face. He raised his eyebrows in quiet agreement.

This was what she was really worried about. The PR job she'd done on the band to get them this interview had practically resulted in contracts being brought out then and there. By the time she'd finished, coyly revealing details with a carefully judged lack of finesse, the A & R guy had been convinced he was about to get his hands on the last great undiscovered supergroup of the sixties. The only problem was that his boss at the record company actually wanted to *meet* them.

'Forget the bloody van!' said Brian, in a higher tone than he meant to, breaking through the familiar squabbling.

Four heads swivelled in unison to look at him.

He cleared his throat and straightened his tie. 'I mean, come on, Rosetta's right. We've got to look at the bigger picture.'

'You've got to give the impression that they're *lucky* to be seeing you right now,' urged Rosetta. 'You've got to make them think that you're seeing Atlantic this afternoon, that EMI are waiting for you to get back to them, that –'

'But don't actually say that,' said Brian, hastily. 'Don't say anything that isn't . . . true. We don't want to *lie* to these people.'

Glynn looked at Rosetta with narrowed eyes. He still hadn't forgiven her for her outburst in the dressing-room the night John had joined the band. The balance of power had definitely shifted since then, and not only did he have John and his flamboyant solos to compete with on-stage, he had the distinct impression that it wasn't just a case of keeping Brian on side any more off-stage.

'They just phoned you up, did they, Brian?' he said. 'What was it you said? Their A & R man came to a gig and liked what he heard?'

Brian didn't miss a beat. 'Yeah. He phoned me up and asked if you had a tape he could listen to.'

Mike Norman, the A & R man Rosetta had met and charmed at a cocktail party thrown at Anita's latest

boyfriend's art gallery, had indeed phoned him for a tape –
after Rosetta had spent the best part of the evening sitting on
his knee, asking questions about the music industry that she
already knew the answers to, and assuring him that if he
didn't sign The End, he'd never work again. Good back-up
work from Sue and Anita had convinced him; all Brian had
had to do was to fix the date for the meeting.

'And which tape did you send him?'

'The demo tapes,' Rosetta replied quickly.

Glynn's eyes narrowed further. Their last demo tape had
four tracks on it: 'I'm a King Bee', 'Little Red Rooster',
'Train Kept A-Rollin'', and a particularly excruciating version of 'Babe I'm Gonna Leave You' which Glynn had
delivered with far too much cod-blues screeching and impro-
vised lyrical emphasis on the burden of being the most
attractive man in central London.

'The last set of tapes?' he asked, deliberately directing the
question at Brian. 'Is that a good idea?'

'What do you mean, is that a good idea?' Brian said,
stalling.

'That's very shrewd, Glynn!' Rosetta interrupted with a
brightness in her voice that made John glance up at her curiously. 'That was my first thought too – why would an A & R
man these days sign any band who just did covers? It just
wouldn't be an accurate reflection of your potential as a
growing group. I mean, I know you've been working on
material yourself –'

Glynn had the grace to look guilty; 'this amazing new
song I'm working on' had been referred to frequently over
the past couple of years but had never actually seen the light
of day. 'Yeah, well . . .'

'So, rather than not give them any original material at
all,' Rosetta went on, 'I . . . *Brian* gave Mike Norman a tape
of John's own demoed material, as well.'

'Just a few songs, you know, just ideas, really,' said Brian.
She looked over at John, hoping her expression was

suitably casual, for Glynn's benefit, but also hoping that he wouldn't think that was *all* she thought of his songs – which had made chills run up and down her skin. The night she and Brian sat down and listened to them, even he had been so excited that he'd initiated unusually enthusiastic amorous advances; although whether he was aroused by the delicate, catchy songs, or the possibility of managing a signable act, Rosetta wasn't sure. She herself was horrified that she couldn't stop thinking about John throughout.

Rosetta crossed her fingers superstitiously in her lap and smiled broadly at the band; she *knew* the combination of John's instinct for a hook, the practised professionalism of their demo tape and – she hated to say it, but it was true – Glynn's Viking marauder looks would get them the deal they needed. John was a natural songwriter, just not enough of an exhibitionist to stand up and do his material justice, she could see that straight off. But Glynn certainly was.

The only trouble was the lads themselves.

Rosetta felt exactly like a mother taking a disruptive child to a smart party and being forced to leave him at the door, praying he wouldn't swear or pick his nose or maim the host's dog.

'I will *tell* them about my song-writing though,' said Glynn defensively. 'Even though I don't have the tapes with me.'

'That's great,' Brian soothed. 'The more song-writing talent in the band, the better.'

'That's not what you said when I wanted to do *my* song,' protested Simon, wriggling out from beneath Red's meaty armpit. 'You said it wasn't –'

'Life is unfair, Simon,' said Brian. 'But just as soon as surf songs come back into fashion, then you can give 'Little Bromley Surfer Girl' another run out, OK?'

Red sniggered.

'I don't hear you writing anything, Red,' whined Simon.

'I don't need to,' Red replied and stretched his arms out

along the back of the seat to annoy Glynn, who opened his mouth to complain again.

'Have you heard John's tapes, Glynn?' Rosetta asked. She tried to sound casual. 'They're really very, very good, you know.'

Glynn affected serious disinterest, but Rosetta could tell he was narked. Good. She didn't want him going in there and making out like he was the star and they were just his backing group.

'Ah, no, they're very rough,' said John, modestly. 'Just doodling around . . .'

'No,' Rosetta interrupted. 'No, they're really good.' She was conscious of how keen she sounded and flushed.

'Just a shame you haven't aired much of your stuff in rehearsal then,' pouted Glynn. 'If it's so good.'

'Well, I suppose he's a bit like you,' said Brian, with a conciliatory smile. 'He just wants it to be perfect before he shows it to anyone else. Given that you've all got such high musical standards and everything.'

The taxi slowed down and stopped outside an anonymous office block.

'Not exactly the Brill Building, then?' sniffed Simon.

'I think we're here,' said John, before Rosetta could unleash her tongue. He opened the door and slid gratefully out. Simon and Red unfolded themselves and followed him, while Glynn made a show of getting out of the other side.

John held the door for Rosetta while she carefully stepped on to the pavement. He extended a chivalrous hand, but she steeled herself not to take it, even though she wanted to.

'I know these heels are high,' she said, 'but I can manage.'

'Christ Almighty!' said Red. 'There are *chicks* here!'

As one, the band turned round and swore with delight at the nine or ten girls hanging round the entrance to the building, kicking their chunky heels against the steps and chatting in little groups.

'Are they here for us, do you think?' said Simon.

'I should think so,' said Glynn. He adjusted the opened buttons of his shirt, which Rosetta noted, now she could see it close up, was from Anita's shop. It was, in fact, a woman's blouse.

'Of course they're here for you,' she said witheringly. 'They're Anita's Saturday staff. And a couple of Sue's editorial assistants from the magazine.'

Simon and Glynn looked crestfallen, although Glynn recovered quickly.

'You organized this?' said John, impressed.

Rosetta smiled modestly. 'Well, you want to look in demand, don't you? Make sure the receptionists know they came for you, won't you?'

'Are you *sure* they're not real groupies?' said Glynn, deliberating over his last button. 'Might they not have turned up because they knew we were coming?'

Rosetta gave him a hard look. 'Have you told anyone?' she asked.

'Well . . . no,' Glynn conceded. 'But they might have –'

'OK, boys, good luck then,' she said, surveying them all for one last time. 'Red, come here.'

He ambled over and she squirted him with some cologne from her bag. 'Next time, you wash, you hear me? Or I'll come round and do it for you.'

Red submitted to her tweakings with a docile grace. 'Don't imagine for a second that I'd let any other girl do this, Rosie, will ya? Because I wouldn't.'

'I know,' she said, doing up one button on his shirt and standing back to check the effect. 'But then not many other girls would get this close to you, smelling like that.'

'I can't believe you don't use deodorant,' said Glynn disparagingly. He ran his hands through his hair, using the wing mirror of the cab to make sure he didn't have anything stuck between his small teeth.

'Nothin' wrong with a bit of carbolic,' said Red happily. 'Least I smell like a man. *I* don't reek o' hairspray.'

'Simon?' Rosetta beckoned him over while she pulled the heavy belt out of Red's belt loops, then slung it round Simon's skinny waist before he could stop her.

'Oi? What're you doin'?' He struggled, but she batted his hands away, and fastened the metal buckle on the tightest notch. It still hung low on his hips but made his horrible too-tight poloneck look a bit less like something you'd wear to a golf club party. She bit her lip thoughtfully, wondering if there was anything she else she could do short of giving him her own coat, then, steeling herself, she ran her hands through his carefully flattened hair, trying to tease it into a semblance of casual curls.

'What are you *doing*?' he whined, trying to stroke it down again. 'Brian!' he yelled. 'Tell her to stop it!'

'You don't want to go in there too formal,' she explained impatiently. They really had no idea at all. 'You've got to look a bit more . . . underground. You're not trying to sell yourselves as the Dave Clark Five, are you?'

'Or the Glynn Masterson Four,' said Red.

Glynn spun on his stacked heel and drew a deep breath prior to launching into a tirade.

'And Glynn,' said Rosetta, in a warning tone. 'Don't start. Don't even think those thoughts.' It was one thing making them look half-decent, but stopping them blowing it just by opening their mouths was another thing entirely. They weren't a group of lads that you could confidently say 'Just be yourselves' to in a situation like this.

At that point Brian rolled up, cracking his knuckles. In an attempt to put some managerial distance between himself and the band before this meeting, for the past week he had taken to wearing tweedy clothes and talking mysteriously about percentages and long-term touring strategies.

'Are we all set then?' he said. 'All set? Everyone happy?'

Rosetta could see he was bravely gearing himself to take on a completely unknown quantity, and she longed to tell him that Mike Norman was a total pussycat. But she knew that would make him feel even more out of his depth, so she gave him a big kiss and muttered, 'Don't sign anything yet, will you? Don't look too keen and *don't let Glynn bollocks it up*!'

'I won't,' said Brian through gritted teeth. She could feel his heart beating fast. 'Fingers crossed, eh?'

'Absolutely!' she said, stepping back and patting him on the shoulders. At least Brian looked convincing.

'Aren't you coming in with us, Rosetta?' asked John.

Glynn looked horrified. 'No! Of course she isn't!'

'No, I don't think so,' said Brian genially. 'Rosetta's got other things to do, haven't you, darling? Weren't you going to pop round to Anita's and pick up that new dress?'

Rosetta was gratified to see disappointment written all over John's face. 'I don't want to ... be in the way,' she explained. 'I'll meet you when you're finished and you can all tell me how it went.'

'OK, then, lads!' said Brian and began to shepherd them towards the door. 'Onwards and upwards!'

Rosetta could hear him talking confidently to Red about what he was going to say to Mike, what *they* should say, the number of assistants he would need, the new offices they'd have to have – all of it rubbish, as far as she could tell.

John was the last to turn round and he gave Rosetta a nervous smile. 'You haven't done that thing where you lick a tissue and wipe my face like you did for the others,' he said.

'I don't need to. You look just fine,' she said lightly.

Their eyes caught for an awkward second or two and Rosetta felt as if there were a ball of fire burning very obviously in her chest. It was like having very exciting indigestion when she was around him.

'Go on,' she said, touching him on the arm. 'Just be yourself, and don't let Glynn take over. *You're* the reason they'll sign the band.' She grimaced apologetically. 'But don't tell anyone I said that. Especially not Red.'

'Ah, no. Your secret's safe with me.' He paused and

blinked at her. Rosetta quivered at the sexy crinkle around his dark eyes, and hated herself for being so *predictable*. 'And thank you for saying that, it, er, means a lot.'

'My pleasure. Now, hurry up!' She ushered him into the building, and watched as the girls went convincingly mad as they arrived. The receptionist looked impressed, even when Glynn winked at her as they went past.

Through the long glass windows of the reception area she could see Brian patting John reassuringly in the small of the back, pushing him into the lift behind the others. Red and Glynn were still jostling for position and she could see Simon was fiddling with the belt. Then the lift doors closed, and the band disappeared as the little indicator arm swept them up to the tenth floor.

Rosetta took a deep breath and hailed another cab for the King's Road. She'd done all she could. For the time being.

Chapter Seven

Fulham, 2001

'She won't go,' said Maggie confidently. She handed Greg a pre-loaded back, on to which he screwed a 50mm lens and wound on the film by running off a couple of shots of the trampled grassy knoll they were standing on outside the church. From long practice, this handover was smoothly transacted without requiring either of them to take their eyes off the interesting situation developing between the usher and the best man, who were, in Maggie's words, 'putting the eye through each other' over by the car intended to transport the bride and groom to the reception.

So far, of the star turns, only the best man had arrived, and, rather ominously, he was on his own.

Over at the Rolls Royce, cravats were being loosened.

'I mean, it's like *King Lear*, isn't it?' Maggie went on, after a brief pause to fold another stick of sugar-free chewing-gum into her mouth. 'She's just doing it to see which of you, ungh ...' She loosened an old bit of gum from her back teeth '... loves her most.'

Greg lined both men up in his viewfinder and focused. 'Are you telling me that as a psychic, or as a literary critic?'

'Both. And also as an avid observer of your mother for the past five years.'

'Maggie, you must never *ever* say that to her face.' Greg took his eyes off the territorial barging now under way to impress her with a very serious look. 'She's not *like* other mothers. You do realize that Rosetta should have one of those "Do Not Feed This Ego" signs round her neck at all times? She gets even worse when she thinks people are watching her.'

Maggie shrugged. 'If you've got it, flaunt it.'

'I take it you saw her on the *Late Review* then.' Greg moved the Nikon back up to his eye and discreetly took a series of shots of the best man, now poking the usher in the shoulder, for the collection of arty black and whites he was 'collecting' for an ironic exhibition. He had more or less given up on the Wedding Photographer of the Year this time. Again. No weddings he attended in a professional capacity ever seemed to include moments of unsullied tenderness.

Or, indeed, any weddings he attended in a guest capacity.

'Anyway, she will go,' he went on. 'She's found the house. And she's got this book to write.'

'She's writing a book?' Maggie looked impressed.

'Yes. Well, she says she is. That's the whole reason for going, to write her autobiography. I did tell you that. Pay attention, will you?'

'Will you be in it?'

'I don't see why I would be. I haven't slept with her. Or with Dad.'

Maggie looked reproving. She liked Rosetta. She also had half a degree in linguistics. 'You know, you're very hard on your mother.'

'She's a very hard woman, in all senses of the word.'

'Greg,' Maggie snapped. 'This is your *mother* we're talking about.'

'And as I may have mentioned before, that's just a biological fact, not a sociological one. I had more maternal driving instructors.'

Maggie rolled her eyes. 'Have I talked about karma to you?'

'Yeah, yeah, it's a Volkswagen sports model. Jeez. What the hell is that?' he said, and adjusted the lens on his camera.

'Fancy,' said Maggie. 'She's dressed her bridesmaids as rainbow trout. That's a new one.'

One of the bridesmaids came shimmering up to Greg, a strangely frothy vision of lilac satin and superfluous netting overlays. Despite being a pretty girl, the light bouncing off the satin gave her the greenish pallor of a fish. The bride – still absent – had sensibly avoided all bridesmaid arguments by opting for a colour that didn't suit anyone.

'Hi-ya,' sing-songed Maggie, in a sudden and incongruously sweet tone.

'Hello. Oh . . . shit.' The bridesmaid looked as if she was struggling to overcome a crippling need for a swift fag with the awareness that bridesmaids smoking was the stuff of *You've Been Framed*. Her hands fluttered about her skirt, looking for pockets that weren't there.

'Can we help you?' asked Maggie.

Trout-girl chewed her lip nervously, leaving fish-scale traces of iridescent lip gloss on her teeth, and said, 'Carolyn says can you do some more of the reportage photos while we're waiting for the bride, please?'

Carolyn was the Wedding Organizer. At the mention of her name, both Greg and Maggie drew in a shuddering breath.

More and more weddings seemed to have wedding organizers, presumably because the bride's parents were too busy recovering from the stress of paying for it all to sort out place-name holders. Greg tried not to get involved with the inevitable power struggle between the bride, the bride's mother and the wedding organizer; he got Maggie to establish who was paying for the photos, and then took instructions exclusively from them.

Carolyn Mackenzie, a regular on this circuit, was one of the most annoying women Greg had ever met – which was saying something – and she was about as far from being an advert for holy matrimony as Greg could imagine. She and Greg had already established that he did not fall under any of her assumed jurisdictions, refusing to be part of the wedding, or the organization. Or rather, Maggie had. Greg had slunk off after the first round of fake smiles and pot shots about timings, and let Maggie get on with what she did best. Since then, Carolyn had taken to sending emissaries to do her bidding.

'I *am* doing reportage pics,' he said, defensively.

'Of the *wedding* guests?'

'I *am*.' Greg nodded towards the best man and usher, who were now shoving each other and yelling 'Yeah?' 'Yeah!' 'Yeah?' 'Yeah!' like a pair of aggressive delegates at a Beatles convention.

'He'll have the wing-mirror off that Roller if he's not careful,' observed Maggie.

'What? Oh, Christ! Ben! Ben! Stop it!' yelled the bridesmaid and minced towards them as fast as she could in her pencil skirt and backless kitten heels.

The usher, who had clearly seen too many Guy Ritchie films and not enough real fights, suddenly pulled back his fist to deck the best man, by which time the best man, who obviously got out more, had punched him in the waistcoat, just above the pocket watch. One slumped against the Rolls, winded, and the other stumbled back with an outraged howl of pain, trying to insert his entire fist into his mouth.

'Ah, I was right,' said Maggie, as the wing-mirror buckled under the best man's momentum and sheered off with a sickening crack. 'There it goes.'

Greg clicked away, the camera motor whirring in a very satisfactory manner. It was at times like these that he felt like a real snapper. He came to the end of the roll and started winding it back briskly. 'Film, please.'

The usher lunged for the best man while the other's back was turned and slipped on the wing-mirror. The sharp sound of tearing fabric rent the air. Or, indeed rented fabric tearing the air.

'Now *that's* what I call karma,' said Greg.

Maggie's hand hesitated in the film bag, as her better nature made a last-ditch stand. 'Oh, Greg, shouldn't you leave it now? When the bride said she wanted reportage pics so she could make up her own scrapbook, I don't think she meant scrapbook literally.'

'Give me the film. She'll thank me for it later.'

'You're not as nice as you look, are you?' Maggie handed him another film.

'No, I am not. Well, they'll want them for the insurance, won't they?' He snapped the moment when the bridesmaid finally reached the two men, which coincided – unfortunately – with the wedding car giving up the unequal struggle and beginning its slow roll down the hill outside the church. It looked as if it were trying to slope off surreptitiously. 'Or for when she throws him out because his friends are such a shocking influence on him.'

In his viewfinder, all three stood frozen in horror staring at the car, before springing into life like a silent movie.

'Why can't we do normal weddings, Greg?' asked Maggie, plaintively. 'And stop snapping! This is car crash stuff. Again, maybe literally.'

'These *are* normal weddings. This is what happens at weddings. Anyway, you can talk.' Greg reloaded as they disappeared from sight. 'If your psychic antennae were on form, you'd have spotted that little accident there.'

Maggie looked shifty. 'I didn't say I didn't foresee it happening,' she protested. 'I just chose not to mention it. I'm not the wedding organizer. I'm just some girl with a clipboard.'

Greg raised his eyebrows at her. 'Then maybe you should offer your services to Carolyn Mackenzie.'

Maggie raised hers until they disappeared into her shaggy fringe. 'Maybe I don't want to work for the organ-grinder. Maybe working for the monkey is more fun. Anyway, don't you think we should alert the relevant parties to the disappearance of the bridal transport?'

'I think they're more concerned about the disappearance of the bride, to be honest.'

Greg picked up his bags and started to walk round to the lychgate, using his zoom lens to home in on the gently trundling car. The best man and the usher were pushing against the boot as it rolled elegantly down the hill, as if in a very unequal rugby scrum. The lens was so sharp he could even see the sweat on the best man's face and – no shit, Sherlock – the hickey on the usher's neck.

'Did Carolyn give you an ETA for the bride?'

Maggie flipped through her notes. 'About fifteen minutes ago?' She pulled a face. 'She won't get that nice flattering shot of herself with All Women Over Fifty if she doesn't get here soon.'

'She could always use the Over Fifties from the next wedding. I don't suppose it would make much difference.'

'What I want to know is who she expects to look after the horse during the service.'

'The what?' Greg put his camera down.

'Er . . .' Maggie showed him Carolyn's neatly word-processed agenda, annotated with her own spiky handwriting, and shrugged. 'She's coming on a horse. At least, I thought that's what Carolyn said on the phone. That or a hearse.'

They looked at each other, unable to decide which would be less appropriate.

'Carolyn has a very direct phone manner,' said Maggie defensively. 'As you'd be aware, if you ever spoke to her.'

'Dearie me,' said Greg, rolling his eyes. 'These posh girls – so difficult to understand, don't you think?'

'I wouldn't know,' said Maggie darkly. 'I don't go out with them. But then neither do you.'

Greg was prevented from responding by the distant clatter of hooves round the back of the church.

'Well, let's just hope she hasn't gone for a Lady Godiva wedding,' he said, stuffing some films into his pocket. 'That would be a theme too far. Or, failing that, let's just hope the

Roller doesn't flatten the horse on the way in. I'd like to see them claim for that on the wedding insurance.'

At this, Maggie's eyes lit up and she clasped her clipboard to her chest. It crushed the silk corsage she attached to her T-shirts as a concession to the occasion. 'Just think, Greg! This could be your Wedding of the Year shot!'

Greg wished she were being sarcastic, but he knew she wasn't. Maggie was uncharacteristically blind to reality when it came to the Fuji Wedding Photographer of the Year competition. 'Don't even talk about that.'

'We're not doing it this year?' She scuttled round after him, picking up bags and boxes as he strode off towards the sound of the hooves.

'No, we are *not*.'

'Why?'

'Because I am sick of the humiliation, Maggie, OK? And you would be too if you had any pride. I'm not even going to think about it. It's just like a constant source of mockery. I didn't even *want* to be a wedding photographer in the first place! I don't even believe in marriages!'

'But you're a great wedding photographer! You wouldn't be so busy if you weren't!'

Greg said nothing, and lengthened his stride. Around the corner, the bride was yelling at the best man from the top of her horse and the bridesmaid was leaning into the car, her lilac arse in the air like a giant boiled sweet, trying to find a handbrake. The usher, now sweating through his waistcoat, was backed up against it, holding it back precariously as the soles of his new shoes slid on the road. The bride's father was staring into space, unable to meet anyone's eye, mouthing furiously to himself and clinging on to the decorative leading rein crafted entirely from silk flowers to match the bridesmaids' outfits. All of them were swearing violently, and in the bride's case, inventively.

The horse seemed pretty nonplussed about the whole thing.

Greg took some discreet shots of the mêlée. The framing was nice: horse versus car, man versus car, traditional dresses versus timeless rage and frustration. It would look good in black and white.

'The groom isn't coming,' muttered Maggie, who had materialized at his side with a bottle of Coke and a pre-loaded back.

Greg looked down at her, impressed. 'That just came to you? Wow. Was it a little voice in your head? Or did it all just appear on a gravestone, like at the wedding in Henley?'

She looked a bit sheepish. 'Um, no, I asked another brides-maid what was going on. And she, er . . . filled me in.'

At that point, a tall woman in a ridiculous cloche hat came steaming out of the church, high heels clicking on the Norman paving slabs like spent bullet-cases. Her head was swinging from left to right as she swept the area for victims.

Carolyn Mackenzie.

'Fine, time to do some reportage in the churchyard, I think,' said Greg.

'Why don't we try the church?' suggested Maggie. 'In about ten minutes everyone will be out here, getting their money's worth, and it'll be totally empty.'

They shouldered the equipment and made their way round the back of the churchyard. The vicar and a few close relatives had already slipped out of the pews to find out what the delay was. As the groom's mother (identifiable by the too-small hat pinned to the back of her head) and her best mate (identifiable by the gleam of prurient outrage coming off her) trotted out as fast as their best clothes would let them, he was murmuring in a vicarly manner that it couldn't be as bad as all that. To Greg's experienced eye, this vicar just wanted to get there before the video man did.

Maggie hitched herself up on a mossy family tombstone and arranged her skirt to expose her legs to the feeble rays of sun now struggling with cruel irony through the clouds. 'What I don't understand is why they do it,' she mused, doodling on her notes in case Carolyn stormed back without warning and caught her slacking.

'Do what? Get married?'

'No, have these big fights outside the church. Why don't they just get on with the wedding, save the fights till later, and not show themselves up in front of all these people they'll have to drink in the same pub with for ever? It'll all come out anyway. Why do it when everyone is armed with cameras?'

Greg bit the cap off a marker pen and started labelling his films. 'They do it because organizing a wedding takes months, and it just gives everyone too much time to *think about it.* I mean, *obviously* the bride's father doesn't really think the groom's good enough for her – he's had all the reasons lined up in his head ever since they got engaged. And he's been thinking about that nasty old car and the funny earring with every cheque he's had to sign, so it's all there in his mind, but when's he going to upset his daughter by telling her? You'd hope he'd get to save it all at least until the divorce, but suddenly, after a couple of drinks the night before, here's an opportunity and, before he knows it, out it all comes. It only takes a tiny little hitch to open the floodgates. Turns out she doesn't know what love means either, *now she really thinks about it*, and she's been shagging the best man out of panic, anyway.'

'I'd call it off,' said Maggie decisively.

'No, you wouldn't. Not when the wedding cake costs about the same as a month's rent. Not when you'd have to phone everyone you'd invited and explain *why* it was off.'

There was a pause, as a few more family members drifted over-casually past them and then scurried towards the gates.

'You know, I feel sorry for the brides,' said Greg. He sighed. 'God knows why they do it. I mean, the way I see it, marriage is like smoking – seemed like a good idea in 1650, but we now know it kills you. And do people stop smoking? No.'

'God, Greg, you depress me,' said Maggie.

'This is their Big Day,' Greg went on, regardless, 'maybe the only time in their lives that they're the centre of this much attention. And it's over so quickly, and so much can go wrong that they don't really enjoy it. I can see it on their faces sometimes, even when they've just walked down the aisle – will Auntie Barbara stay sober, will the food be all right, what are all his lot saying about me in the loos, will I slip over during the first dance while everyone's videoing me . . .'

Maggie looked at him, shading her eyes with her hand. 'Is that why you're so nice to them then?'

Greg blinked. 'Am I?'

'You are. You're really sweet with the brides. Total waste of time, if you ask me – it's the *bridesmaids* you should be hitting on.'

'I don't *hit on* people.'

'I know.'

He reloaded his camera thoughtfully. 'Families these days are just rubbish at . . .' Greg stared into the clouds, which had turned white and fluffy after being grey and sullen all morning. Evidently the next wedding had a better wedding organizer. 'I don't know . . . at *being together*. We're not used to being on display, normally. You think you should get on with people, just because you're related, but why should you? No wonder people get all freaked out by weddings.'

'Ah, no, I reckon it's the costumes,' Maggie interrupted. She began to pick the petals off a straggly daisy, which had grown into a crack between the stone angels. 'Put people in unfamiliar, expensive clothes and they're bound to start acting weird. Why is she wearing white, for God's sake? She's been living with him for five years and their eldest daughter's the youngest bridesmaid.'

'Are you listening to what I'm saying?' Greg looked at her. Sometimes he really wondered if she chatted through the voices in her head. No wonder she missed key details.

'I am listening,' Maggie protested. 'But I also think you've got too much time on your own to think about these things. And you talk shite.'

'All I want to do is make sure that these women have one really beautiful picture of themselves to keep for ever, even if the best man ends up in casualty or her mum gets pissed and snogs an usher because she wanted to look desirable in front of her ex and his new girlfriend, who used to be in the year above her at school. Is that so weird?'

'I don't think one picture is going to make up for all that.'

Greg sighed and rubbed his ear. 'I think one picture is all some of these marriages end up with, and I'd like to hope I made it a good one.'

'Why haven't you got a girlfriend, Greg?' asked Maggie, wonderingly. 'You're so sensitive.' She stopped and looked at her daisy, trying to estimate the outcome before she actually plucked out. 'Or maybe that's it. You understand women too well.'

'I don't understand women *at all*,' said Greg heavily. 'Or else I would be at these weddings, and not just photographing them. Come on, let's see if there isn't something we can salvage from this.' He picked up his cameras and walked into the back of the church.

Chapter Eight

Chelsea, 1969

'OK, so they had floor-length velvet curtains in the *main* room, but what about the skylight?'

Rosetta adjusted the phone underneath her chin and forced down another big mouthful of lukewarm peppermint tea. She didn't like peppermint tea, but Lucy, Brian's new press assistant sent by the record company, claimed that it was good for calming down red skin. Lucy used to work for *Vogue* and from the length of time she spent on the office phone, a casual observer would think she still did. Despite serious effort on her part (and substantial use of Mary Quant foundation), Rosetta's cheeks still flared up like raspberries when she was embarrassed, and embarrassment was not part of her new look. Fortunately, her blush threshold seemed to be dropping daily, possibly due to her own iron determination that it would, coupled with increased exposure to Red and his endless repertoire of socially challenging habits, both sexual and pharmaceutical. Now the band were officially signed to the label and were busy 'writing material for an album', the record company had bought the mews house behind the flat as the band's official management suite – and the band were constantly lounging around Rosetta's studio, littering the place with discarded clothes and beer bottles.

'The sky-what?' Sue sounded uncertain. Urgent sounds of the news desk clattered away behind her voice. 'There was some kind of *Jaguar* parked outside, but . . .'

'The *skylight*, darling. In the house.' Rosetta forced down the final mouthful of tea with a grimace and put the empty cup down on a stack of fashion magazines as high as her wicker chair. She was now claiming them as research. The record company paid for them. 'I read, in your own publication, I might add, that they've got a skylight and a minstrels' gallery with separate windows above the main room, and it's all decorated with Indian wall hangings and embroideries of the Kama Sutra.'

'The karma's *what*?' Someone about three feet behind Sue's desk started yelling about taxi receipts.

'The Kama *Sutra*, Sue.' Rosetta wiped off the smeary half-circle of pearly white lipstick from the black tea-cup. 'You know, the Indian book of love? Madly complicated. You need to be a black belt in yoga to get into half the positions. Haven't you read it?'

'That? No! It's disgust— I mean, I, yes, er . . .'

It never failed to amaze Rosetta how little attention Sue paid to the details of things, especially as a journalist. For a woman, she was even worse.

'Susannah! It *was Keith* Richards' flat you went to, wasn't it?' Rosetta demanded. 'And not *Cliff* Richard's?'

On the other end of the phone, Sue spluttered with outrage, but before she could get the full force of her affront going, Rosetta's doorbell rang.

Rosetta immediately looked up into the mirror by the phone to check that her hair was still flat. The landlords had installed a buzzer system so you could buzz people up without traipsing down to open the door – which was a blessing for Rosetta who no longer had to negotiate the stairs in high heels and/or short skirts to let visitors in. Naturally, on swinging open the door at the top of the stairs, she liked to make the most of her immediate advantage over panting visitors.

'Of course it was Keith's flat!' roared Sue. 'I had coffee there! And he offered me a joint!' There was some coughing, and she lowered her voice to a more discreet office level. 'But you seem to forget, darling, that I'm a proper journalist and I've got better things to do than take notes on interior design for –'

The bell rang again, more forcefully. Rosetta hoped it wasn't Lucy with another sheaf of badly-typed nonsense. She had already had to rewrite one gushing press release this morning.

'Sue, I'll have to call you later, darling,' said Rosetta, ignoring the fact that she had phoned Sue for information and had dragged her out of an editorial meeting to get it. Or not get it, as the case had been.

'Listen, Rosetta, do you want to meet up for dinner?' asked Sue quickly. 'There's a new restaurant opened over the road from the office. What about, um, maybe making it a foursome? I, er, seem to have some free nights this week.'

'How lovely.' Rosetta stared into the mirror and practised her mysterious photograph expression, the closed-mouth half-smile that hid her slightly overlapping incisors, which she fully intended to get fixed as soon as she had the money to go private. She didn't mean 'how lovely' at all; Sue was constantly inviting her and Brian out for dinner, on the understanding that Rosetta would magic a blind date out of thin air in return for another feature on Red's favourite drums or Glynn's haircare tips, and it was wearing very thin. Especially now *real* journalists wanted interviews with the band.

Really it had been like this since school. It wasn't as though Rosetta *begrudged* finding Sue a date – she genuinely wanted everyone to be as happy as genetics would allow – but she was running out of simple sacrificial lambs to sit opposite Sue and absorb her constant stream of self-deprecating savagery.

Rosetta increased the wattage on her smile, spotted the offending incisors emerging and switched it off. Thank God Brian never seemed to notice the flirting she had to do to secure Sue's dates. But then Rosetta had suspected for some time now that she could run naked down Wardour Street with the Rolling Stones and their entire road crew and Brian would merely smile and buy her a handbag for getting such fabuloso publicity for the band.

'Supper? Ye-ee-ee-ees . . . We could do,' she said, stalling. 'Who were you thinking of bringing along?'

Rosetta could almost see Sue doing her simpering lip-chewing on the other end. 'Well, I had rather thought that *you* might ask . . .'

As long as it wasn't John, thought Rosetta, crossing her fingers unconsciously. Sue couldn't have John. Like every other woman in London, Sue had been struck dumb by John, and for once, Rosetta had some sympathy with her, since her own efforts to stem the rising tide of desire were being thwarted by the long chats they seemed to find themselves in over band dinners and the like. And every time Rosetta drew a mental line of things not to tell him, his kind manner and sympathetic eyes would draw out secrets and private hopes she hadn't told anyone, not even Brian.

The doorbell rang again.

'Well, I was wondering . . .' Sue was being horrendously coy, which meant she really wanted something.

Rosetta fidgeted. It was too rude to answer the door while on the phone, but she had a sinking dread of Lucy sending off another terrible pun-laden press release.

'No, no, forget it, I'll find someone,' said Rosetta, rather more briskly than she intended to. 'Phone me later, OK? Bye, darling!'

She clunked the phone down, but it was too late. Whoever it was had evidently been let in by the old lady in the garden flat and was making their way upstairs, clumping up the steps.

Rosetta surmised from the clumping that it wasn't the twig-like Lucy.

Her own front doorbell chimed and she smoothed down

her smock, counted to fifteen in order to give the impression that she'd been engrossed in something complicated, like meditation or tapestry, then walked slowly over to the door and opened it.

On seeing who was standing there, peppermint tea notwithstanding, Rosetta felt a deep red flush spread over her face.

It was John, but, disconcertingly, he appeared to be standing there in her private fantasy version of himself. Instead of his habitual faded jeans and T-shirt, he was dressed head to toe in the new gear that she recognized from Anita's latest collection, apparently inspired by some acid trip she'd had while reading Tennyson. Brian *had* been muttering about image overhauls for a while. It was hard to picture John stripping wallpaper in his overalls now, as he leaned against her doorframe, six feet three inches of draped satin and ribbons and tight velvet bell-bottoms.

Very, *very* tight velvet bell-bottoms.

'John!' Rosetta held on to the door. She hoped it looked casual, but it was really for support. Her legs had suddenly gone very fluid, as if her kneecaps had been kicked out from under her.

'Rosetta!' said John, as if he were surprised to see her opening the door of her own flat.

Rosetta smiled as mysteriously as she could and swallowed hard. On anyone else so much costume would have looked ridiculous, but on John's rangy frame all the peacock velvets and ribbons just made him look like a Grimm prince who'd dropped in on his way down the King's Road in search of opium.

'Hello,' she said. 'Are you here to exorcise my flat?'

'Well, that depends,' he replied, making no attempt to move. One hand went up to his forehead where the heavy fringe had been until someone (Anita, probably) had parted his hair in the middle, so the dark curls fell over his face like Jimmy Page. He obviously wasn't used to it yet either, as finding no fringe to push back he tried to turn the gesture into something else, and, scratching his head unnecessarily, he smiled from under his hand in a self-deprecating way.

'Brian said something about your balcony windows needing looking at?' he explained. The practical joinery enquiry sounded hopelessly incongruous, accompanied as it was by the gentle rattle of tiny bells on his jacket as he scratched his head. Rosetta now realized that the cool leathery bag by his feet was in fact a joiner's bag of tools.

'Um, yes, one's sticking. Do you, er, want to come in?' she asked automatically, still clinging to the door. One of the balcony windows *wasn't* shutting properly and she'd been on at Brian to get it sorted out before a summer storm flooded the studio. Since things had started moving with the record company Brian hadn't been at home long enough to buy a saw, let alone sort it out, so it was only obvious that he'd send round the cheapest carpenter he knew. The four-album deal was theoretically done, but they were all still waiting on the money. It was some consolation to Rosetta that Brian would almost certainly see his share before the band did.

'If that's OK.' He drummed his fingers on the doorjamb (jingle, jingle) in an amiable carpenter manner, as if to prove he wasn't desperate to get inside, while his eyes tried to look around the flat, but kept returning to her face.

Rosetta cheered internally. And yet all this fitted in a bit too well with her favourite 'shelves fantasy': in which John effortlessly put up the shelves Brian had failed to start, while holding nails in his mouth and doing all that 'capable builder' stuff with planes, and then ravished her dramatically against the step-ladder.

As a fantasy, it had filled many a quiet evening, alone with the *Radio Times*. And yet here he was, offering to do some DIY she actually needed doing. It was too freaky.

She searched the hall for her mother, who normally popped up when Fantasy John was about to enfold her in his strong arms.

There was no sign of her mother.

John smiled shyly at her, and Rosetta couldn't help herself smiling back.

There was silence apart from the faint jingling of John's decorative bells and the hammering of blood inside Rosetta's ears.

'Right.' Rosetta bit her lip and tried to get some action going in her head. Nothing was happening. It was as though her brain had been switched off for the night. Her gaze flicked in a manic triangle from John's dark eyes, to his full lips, and back to his eyes. He wasn't quite real, all that vivid colour in the dirty ecru background of the communal hall.

'So?' His eyebrow lifted, making his eyes twinkle. 'It would help if you could let me near the window? Or are you after stalling so your lover can climb in the wardrobe?'

Oh my God, thought Rosetta with startling clarity. If I let John over this threshold, I *will* try to kiss him, even if he makes no attempt at building work.

'You're all right there!' He leaned forward and yelled past her ear. 'I'm not the husband! You can stop hanging off the balcony now!'

The air between them thrummed with tension and she didn't dare to meet his eyes. Rosetta was very aware of the sudden silence. Despite the ridiculous medieval lacings they were both wearing, she knew it could all come off in seconds, slashed sleeves and red stockings, the lot, if she let him in. She'd never felt more conscious of being dressed, of being naked beneath these arbitrary garments. Now sheer possibility had winkled open the door of her imagination, her mind was flooded with the narcotic temptation of abandoning all resistance – how could she help it, what was the point, when it was so obviously going to happen?

And consequently, since it was fated, how could it be her fault?

Desperate not to look up at John, Rosetta turned away and the first thing she saw was a photograph of Brian, trussed up in a suit at a smart drinks evening, with a gin and tonic in one hand, and her handbag in the other. Her forehead turned clammy and she struggled to get a grip on the situation. It was all very well for these groovy rock-stars to be all louche and casual about free love, but it wouldn't help anyone or anything if she and John did cross the line between flirting and well, *anything else*. If Brian found out, at the very least, it would mess up the tour he was planning with The End and an array of specially selected groups, inept enough to make them look like The Who by comparison. And that was without the shriekings of her conscience.

'Um . . .' Rosetta tried to compose herself. It was her duty to be responsible here. She was the Road Mother who washed all their stage shirts and had their fan-club questionnaires doctored so they looked more mysterious. She was Mrs Brian. Not some dizzy groupie.

'Um,' she said again. The smell of roses in the big vase by the door was like a reproach. Brian's roses, delivered to make up for a series of very late nights away. It wasn't as if he wasn't *thoughtful*, she told herself sternly. 'Um, listen, actually, do you want to go for a walk?'

'No, I want to come in and take the weight off my poor feet in these *ridiculous* shoes,' said John reasonably. His brown eyes glinted in a very unhelpful manner. 'Then I'll have a look at your window. In that order.'

Rosetta smiled drunkenly at him, then reminded herself that she was the cool one here, the one who was meant to be instructing The End in the ways of grooviness. The smile vanished and was replaced by an arched eyebrow.

'It feels like my feet are being sharpened,' he explained. 'You might tell Anita that. Please give me a cup of tea to take my mind off it.'

A cup of tea. What could go wrong with a cup of tea?

She opened the door and stepped backwards so he wouldn't have to press past her.

He inclined his head ironically and the heavy black curls bounced like a shampoo advert. 'Thank you.'

Rosetta followed at a safe distance as he loped fitfully into her sitting-room. The door to the balcony – the one that wasn't sticking – was open, and the room was light with spring air, lifting the muslin drapes and spreading the musky smell of roses and patchouli through the little studio. At the moment, everything in London smelt of patchouli. Going into Anita's shop virtually required breathing apparatus.

John settled himself on the chaise longue and patted the small area remaining. He looked more like Browning than ever. A sensible, well-nourished Browning. 'Now then. Will you not come and sit down with me?'

'No, thank you,' said Rosetta automatically. She had found – when dining out in a city full of fashionable emaciated-looking women – that it helped to refuse what you really wanted immediately, before you had time to think about it.

A smile nipped at the corner of John's mouth and he crossed one long leg over the other. 'You sure about that now? It's just that your shoes look awfully uncomfortable too,' he added by way of explanation.

'Cup of tea, was it?' she asked, nervously flicking her emerald ring with her thumbnail. If she sat down on that chaise longue, that would be it. Resistance: over. Relationship: over. Hard work: over. Band: over.

But it would be fun! And everyone else is doing it!

'Or would you prefer something else?' she added, so as not to look like an impolite hostess.

The sudden poshness of her voice betrayed her nerves and it pissed her off that while at the moment Marianne Faithfull would be shimmering across the carpet in a see-through scarf and authentic Arabian mules and a haze of exotic smoke, she had been possessed with the spirit of a Ladies' Golf Club Captain.

'Doesn't Brian keep champagne in the fridge?' asked John. The amusement was visible in his eyes now. 'Surely, *you* do, now. No, listen, I *know* you do! I read about it in the papers.

Rosetta Martin's fabulous Frigidaire, stuffed to bursting with pop-star goodies and nail varnish.'

Rosetta stared at him boldly, trying to assess whether he was winding her up. Did he really buy into all 'The Daily Rosetta' stuff, as Red called it? Maybe the clothes were making him behave like a real pop-star, instead of a trainee one. Whatever it was, there was a new slipperiness about him that was more than unsettling. He was *real*. Rosetta didn't like not knowing exactly what people were thinking, especially ones she had down as totally predictable.

'Er, yes, there is a bottle in there, chilling.' She smiled nervously. 'Now you mention it.'

'Great,' said John, levering himself to his feet. 'You get that and I'll take a look at your window.'

In the tiny kitchenette, Rosetta found the two champagne flutes and rinsed them quickly, took out the bottle of champagne Brian did indeed keep in the fridge, and wiped a smear of coleslaw off it. They only had a tiny fridge, and the champagne had been there for a long time. In fact, it had been there since the photoshoot in which Rosetta had proudly opened her fridge door to *Pop Miss!* in order to reveal the decadent things groovy pop-stars kept to hand.

There were no elegant little nibbles to go with it. Rosetta frowned at the bare shelves and picked a desiccated strawberry off the side of a half-empty milk bottle with her fingernail. She was forever torn between wanting to offer round little plates of things on one hand, and regarding that kind of cocktail-stick-hostessry as hopelessly Jackie Kennedy on the other. Consequently, there was usually more bacteria in the fridge than food. Brian wasn't aware that fridges got dirty and she didn't want to get into the habit of being his cleaning lady. Anyway, trailing round the supermarkets never seemed worth the effort to her, when they barely ate in, even for breakfast. And that was the way she liked it.

'Rosetta, you're no wife! A man could die of thirst out here!' John's voice floated back from the sitting-room.

She flicked the water off the glasses and carried them in, the champagne in the other hand, dangling as casually as she could make it, making her wrists slack so they'd look longer and more graceful, fixing her gaze on the far window, forcing herself to avoid the eyes she knew would be trained on her.

Rosetta put the glasses down on a side table as carelessly as possible, using Brian's unread *Record Mirror* as a coaster, and handed the chilled bottle to John. Looking less than casual now would be ruinous, she thought, gazing blankly out of the window at the white walls opposite.

John looked at the bottle, theatrically holding it a little way away to read the label, and Rosetta waited. Suddenly it felt very bad, drinking Brian's champagne in the middle of the day, but she didn't care. She was casual salon Rosetta. That was why Brian had got this flat, wasn't it? So she could promote their image?

John looked up at her, seemed surprised to catch her eye on him, blushed, and immediately started to wrestle with the champagne bottle.

Rosetta's eyes weren't seeing the houseboats bobbing on the Thames outside, though she carried on gazing out of the window. Her heart rate hadn't dropped since he'd come in, and she knew that with every moment that passed she was wading further and further out. Rosetta wasn't dumb and she knew when men were coming on to her, but suddenly, now, she wasn't sure. Had John *really* dropped in to sort out the window, or was that just an excuse to see her?

There still hadn't been a pop from the champagne bottle.

'Problem?' she asked more casually than she felt.

Small beads of sweat had broken out on John's forehead and his hands were slipping on the cold neck of the bottle.

'Sorry, um . . . I can't . . . I can't, er . . .'

Their eyes met and embarrassment rebounded over her in a hot flush, accentuated by the restrictive non-breathe lacings of her smock.

Christ! We've been saving that bottle so long there's something wrong with it! she thought, horrified. *The cork's solidified or something! It looks like a stunt bottle of champagne!*

Rosetta seethed, more like the Ladies' Golf Club Captain than she cared to note. Brian and his business ostentations! What was the *point* of looking like you could afford to live in Cheyne Walk if it was obvious you could only afford to drink instant coffee? It was all right for him – it was worth it for the address on his business cards. She was the one who had to cover up all the cracks and orange boxes when people actually came round to the place.

'Sure, I'm sorry, Rosetta,' John began apologetically, 'I, er . . .'

Then she realized that maybe John didn't know *how* he was meant to open it, and, nearly knocked over by a rush of affection, suddenly she didn't dare to sit and get drunk and let matters take their course. This wasn't some suave Hollywood seduction scene – John was as much of a dressed-up child as she was, playing with stupid shoes and champagne, and equally clueless.

'My fault entirely,' she said, getting up. She swiped the bottle from his damp hands and dumped it in her bag. 'Forget the damn window, it's too nice outside for home improvements. Let's go for a walk.'

They ambled down the Embankment for a while, enjoying the sensation of the river wind on their faces and the admiring glances from the passing cars on their backs. The champagne was stuffed in Rosetta's huge bucket bag, along with a couple of plastic glasses. Touchingly, John insisted on walking on the road side of the pavement, a courtesy that Rosetta hadn't even been aware of before, let alone been offered.

'Where's y'man?' asked John. Out of the flat he had returned to his normal amiable self, even if his green trousers still looked more like hose than was generally considered normal in Chelsea.

'I don't know. Sorting out roadies for your tour.' Rosetta irritably pushed her big round shades back up her nose and pulled her tortoiseshell hair out of its ponytail until it fanned around her shoulders. 'I've not seen Brian for more than three hours in the past week. The only reason I know he's at home at night is because he wakes me up, arguing in his sleep with promoters.'

John laughed, and Rosetta felt relieved to be saying this aloud to someone other than her mirror. Having The Perfect Relationship meant that she couldn't let slip to Sue or Anita that there was ever a single moment of discord between her and Brian, especially when Sue was so keen to find problems with the age gap and the hectic lifestyles and a million other potential problems that Rosetta denied had even crossed her mind.

She knew it was unfair to be irritated by Brian being busy, but something inside her couldn't stop it. For a start, he hadn't even told her he'd asked John to come over about the window. What else was he organizing about their lives without bothering to mention to her? And what was the point of her telling *Record Mirror* that they were blissfully happy in London if he was constantly planning trucks and buses and hotels for the band and had virtually no time to talk to her?

She reminded herself that it hadn't always been like this. And that Brian's efficiency and ambition had been hugely sexy when she first met him.

'When's he back?' asked John.

Rosetta snorted inwardly, but turned it into a wry smile for John's benefit. 'You tell me. Monday, I think?'

He looked at her, surprised. 'You *think*?' he said. 'I thought you two knew each other's every move?'

'Despite what Brian might imply to the contrary, I'm neither his mother nor his secretary.'

'Now, I thought that summed up the ultimate English male sexual fantasy.'

Rosetta laughed, although something inside her sank like a stone. 'Ah, well, that'll be where you're wrong. Brian doesn't get cheap thrills from secretaries unless she's got seriously good shorthand. *If* you know what I mean.'

'Sure now, I wouldn't know about that,' he said breezily. 'I am a simple West of Ireland boy with strong moral values and a rosary in every jacket pocket. There are people praying for me every day back home, being all alone as I am here in this terrible depraved city.' He pulled an ambiguous face at her. 'I have even been known to go to Mass now and again. But for the sake of my reputation, let's pretend it was a Black one.'

Rosetta blinked at him, unsure as to how much he was joking, how much he was flirting and how much he really meant. It sounded a little too much like that familiar voice at the back of her own head, the one that woke her every Sunday in time for Mass, though she never actually went.

'*Seriously*?' she asked.

'Seriously,' he said, suddenly looking serious too. Their walking pace slowed. 'I know it's very unfashionable, but, um . . .' He shrugged. 'I just think there's so much *madness* going on out there – you know, the drugs, and the booze and the pissing around – that if you don't have some kind of safety rope . . .' John frowned at himself, and grimaced, as if to apologize for being so heavy. 'Even if it is a load of Popish horseshit.'

'Ah,' said Rosetta, knowingly. 'Red?'

John nodded with a grin.

'He's very outspoken for a thick Geordie nonce.'

'Well, he spends so much time chucking beer down his neck, I suppose he has to talk out of his arse.'

There was a friendly pause, as they waited to cross the road, then Rosetta heard herself say, 'So you have the Voices of Catholic Doom in the back of your head too, do you?'

'Ah, whole celestial choirs of the beggars! Doesn't mean I have to listen to them the whole time, though.'

'But they're still there.'

'Well . . . Yes. And I'd miss them if they suddenly stopped. I don't want to be swept away, you know?'

Rosetta looked at John and knew he meant it. She liked that. He believed in what he believed in, even if it was unfashionable. That was good.

'Anyway,' he went on before she had time to formulate a reply, 'that's why Brian's such a good man to have in charge of a band like this. He's very straight, isn't he? Compared to a lot of these eejits I've heard about, fiddling the books and beating up promoters and the like. And he's been so good to me, since I've joined. Really . . . helpful.'

'Well, you're the one that'll make his fortune,' she said lightly. 'Which is why he spends *so much time* with you and none with me. But then I am just his girlfriend.'

'Fiancée,' said John sternly. He held up her left hand, with its sizeable rectangular emerald, and shook it in front of her face. 'Fi-an-cée,' he repeated slowly, shaking her hand on each syllable.

Rosetta grabbed her hand back. It was tingling as if John had an electric shocker in his palm. 'Well, whatever you want to call it, it's not like I'm a deb or something. The ring was just a present, not a . . .'

She suddenly found it painful to think of Brian.

'Anyway, don't be so square,' she said trying to drag back her faithful mental photograph to recompose herself into her cool persona. 'Girlfriend, fiancée, wife – what's the difference these days? I don't need a piece of paper.'

Funnily enough, that hadn't exactly been the way she'd seen it when Brian had given her the ring. Then it had seemed like the most exciting thing in the world.

'Come on, Rosetta. Red says this time last year you were practically marching Brian down the aisle.'

'Well, this time last year he wasn't quite so married to

you lot. Anyway, what the hell does Red know about anything?'

She strode on, feeling a little cheap for making that the reason for her apparent distress, distress that John was genuinely sympathizing with, even though, deep down, she didn't really care how much time Brian spent with the band. It was what he did best: it made them money, it made him happy, it made her contacts – why would she complain about it?

Because it's a good excuse, observed a small voice in her head, which she chose to ignore in favour of a cherry tree scattering sugared almond petals all over the pavement.

They sat down on a bench near the river, and Rosetta expertly opened the champagne. She was pleased to see that there was nothing at all wrong with the cork, the bottle or the champagne which fizzed out into her scratched Habitat plastic cups.

Rosetta deliberately didn't catch John's admiring glances at the way her iron wrist absorbed the force of the cork, or the way she lobbed the cork precisely into the litter bin with her strong rounders throw. Opening champagne bottles properly was one of the first things Brian had taught her – how to open them casually and with the minimum of fuss, as if it was something one did several times a day, though not in a professional capacity, of course.

She poured a glass for John, delicately touching the bubbles with the neck of the bottle to make the froth subside, then topping it up to the brim.

'You're very good at that,' he said.

She smiled self-deprecatingly. 'Thanks.'

He held the glass up to the light, to see the sun shine through the green plastic and amber champagne. 'I can't honestly say that three years ago, when I first came over here to London, I'd ever have imagined myself drinking champagne at eleven o'clock on a Tuesday morning, with a beautiful woman, by the banks of a river. In a pair of green velvet trousers that make my bollocks feel like sardines.'

Rosetta smiled and sipped at her champagne. That was
the trick of it, that cool thing the really cool people did: pretending, in the face of unimaginable glamour, that you never
expected it to be any other way.

There seemed to be a new feeling of intimacy between
them now; she wanted to know everything about him, and
felt that there wasn't much that she couldn't ask.

'Where *did* you imagine yourself?' she asked.

'On a building site. Maybe in London. Playing guitar in
the evenings . . .'

'Don't let Brian hear you say that.' Rosetta laughed and
nudged him. 'Haven't you seen your own press release?
You're a boy genius in the style of Gary Moore, and all
you've ever wanted to do is play guitar.'

John raised his eyebrow again and carried on,
'. . . *Wishing* I could be drinking champagne at eleven on the
banks of the Thames with a beautiful lady by my side who
knows how to open champagne bottles and waves away the
change from taxis.'

'Well, you're easy to please, then,' said Rosetta. 'Most
working girls can do that.'

It occurred to her how unfair it was that labouring on a
building site would probably only enhance John's mystique –
how those hands could ever have laid bricks was impossible
to imagine, whereas for her to be mysterious would require
distinct vagueness about her suburban parents, if not down-
right lies. And although Rosetta was prepared to do almost
anything to scale the celebrity heights, there was something
about lying about her parents that made her kind of uneasy,
karmically speaking.

As if he could read her thoughts, John said, 'Your parents
in the music business, are they?'

He looked at her as he spoke, and her heart skipped at
how young his eyes looked, all wide and questioning. Well,
she could tell him that her mother wrote songs with Carole
King and her father was a Viscount. He'd believe her. It

wasn't beyond the bounds of credibility, given her current ridiculous outfit and her carefully filed-down accent...

'No,' she blurted out. 'My mother's effectively a housewife and my dad runs a catering business in Richmond.'

'Oh, right?' he said, and there was no trace of disapproval or disappointment in his voice. It was just a piece of information.

She wasn't sure if it was the little champagne bubbles spreading looseness through her muscles, but suddenly she felt very light. Very happy. Rosetta relaxed in her velvet shift for the first time that day, tilted her head back on the park bench and shut her eyes while the sunlight turned the insides of her eyelids blue and yellow.

She smiled up into the sun. How had she been lucky enough to get this life?

'Ah, you've got such a gorgeous smile!' said John, hamming up his accent. 'Gorgeous, so y'are! You could charm the birds out of the trees when you smile like that.'

Rosetta shut her mouth defensively and opened one eye. He was looking at her with a very warm expression on his face. She suddenly felt conscious of her crooked teeth and rearranged her smile into the version she practised in the mirror.

His brow creased. 'No, no,' said John. 'I preferred the first one.'

'No, you *don't*,' she corrected him, swatting at his hand. 'I've got a crooked smile. I was told on very good authority that I have to smile like this –' she demonstrated '– or else spend a fortune having my mouth rearranged. Oh, damn. I don't know why I just told you that. It's not very demure of me.'

'Don't you smile any other way!' said John. 'When you smile, it's like . . . it's like the sun coming out. Now I don't know why I told you that, because it's not very demure of me either.'

Rosetta smiled at him, remembered her teeth and

rejigged her face jerkily until she burst out laughing and gave up.

She and John held each other's gaze for a little longer than was comfortable.

'You're so beautiful when you laugh,' said John without thinking and his eyes clouded with embarrassment. 'I mean . . . I didn't mean to . . .'

'*Thank* you . . . for the compliment,' said Rosetta gracefully, though her skin was prickling with excitement. She stretched out on the grass and put her arm over her eyes.

Her heart was hammering, and it wasn't just the champagne pounding through her veins like that. All she could see now in her mind's eye was John on stage, playing blues licks like an angel, long brown hair dangling in his eyes and his red guitar slung low over those narrow hips . . .

With an effort, she collected herself. This wasn't how mature women were meant to behave. Crushes were for schoolchildren, after all. Not adults with their own fridges. And serious, grown-up boyfriends.

Fiancés, even.

'Listen, I'm really sorry, John,' she said. 'You've got me on a bad day. I didn't mean to be so narky about Brian.'

'You must miss him.'

There was a pause.

'Yes,' said Rosetta, eventually. 'I suppose I do.'

'Do you want me to put up those shelves once I've done the window?' he asked in a conversational tone. 'Oh! Hang on! You've a ladybird on you.' And she felt him brush something off her forehead.

The cool fingers lingered on her cheek for a moment, feeling the peachiness of her skin, then suddenly, abruptly, they were whisked away.

Rosetta's skin suddenly felt cold and bereft and it was at that exact moment that she realized she really was in serious trouble.

Chapter Nine

Clerkenwell, 2001

'Good day at work, dear?'
'No.' Tanith threw her bag into the sagging easy chair on the other side of the kitchen and didn't even flinch when all the papers and head shot photos slid out of it, scattering in a flaky waterfall on to the Tuscan tiles. After a pointless meeting with the director over lunch, her search had moved sideways on to the twenty-something Amber and she was having even less success than with the teens. For every fifteen-year-old trying to look twenty-five, there were three twenty-five-year-olds trying to look fifteen.

Then, on returning to the office, Frances had grabbed her arm and shepherded her into her inner sanctum, where Warren was sitting on a beanbag, grinning like Marc Bolan on steroids, and she had revealed what all the subterfuge and accountants had been about.

She and Pixie Boy were moving to New York. And she wanted Tanith to run the London office of her casting agency, all on her own.

'No,' said Tanith, ruffling some life back into her hair, 'it was a very odd day.'

'Excellent.'

She looked over to the breakfast bar, where Robert was preparing supper. Which was to say, he was eating toast in his stripy Boden pull-ons and comparing a selection of takeaway leaflets with the sort of relish normally associated with perusing the menu at Le Gavroche.

Tanith shrugged off her jacket and hung it over the back of the chair. It slid off too. She shut her eyes and counted to ten, then added another five for good measure. When she opened them, everything was still on the floor and a particularly gruesome shot of a recently dyed redhead with eyebrows like Noel Gallagher leered back up at her.

There was a faint tsk from the direction of the breakfast bar.

'Is there any wine open?' she moaned, looking for sympathy. 'I need a drink. I might need two or three.'

He didn't even glance up from his leaflets. 'On the table. But don't drink it yet, it needs to breathe. It's a Barolo.'

Tanith stared mutinously at the bottle on the work surface. Robert liked wines that took a long time to get ready. He seemed to relish the inconvenience involved. And yet it was a typically Robert contradiction to want to drink a wine so stupidly complicated that it required two hours to sort itself out as an accompaniment to pizza or a Chinese takeaway. He had a thing about fast food deliveries, claiming that they reminded him of the happier bits of his childhood. By which she knew he meant weekends at school.

'I can't wait that long,' she moaned, dragging off her jacket. 'I had a meeting with the director today and he drank Bloody Marys all afternoon and I had to pretend I only drank still water.'

'Why?' Robert frowned, possibly at her, possibly over an unusual spelling of bhajia.

'Because one of us had to stay sober to remember what he was talking about! According to him, over the course of a *very* long afternoon, everyone from Goldie Hawn to Diana Rigg is 'perfect' for the lead role. *God*.' Tanith reached into the drinks cupboard, pulled out a bottle of vodka and made herself a very strong vodka and tonic. She shook the bottle crossly over the glass to get the last drops out. 'My only consolation is that this film will probably never get made, even if it does ever get cast.'

'No money?'

'No, just a director who seems to communicate entirely in hints and a writer who's still writing the damn script. I mean, if I'd told Frances I was going to start casting a film that hadn't even been finished, she'd think I was crazy. Crazy! But she wanted me to do it. And now she's off to New York, if I mess it up, well . . . I don't know what'll happen.' Tanith held up her glass to observe the level of vodka in it, decided it wasn't enough and looked in the cupboard for another bottle.

'Steady on!' said Robert, automatically.

Tanith met his eye steelily. She wasn't in the mood for being parented after an afternoon of being treated like a small child by a director old enough to be her slightly senior cousin.

Robert acknowledged the fight in her face. 'OK. OK. I'm only saying . . .' He raised his palms and gave her his lop-sided smile. 'Take it easy on the spirits. You haven't had any supper, you're stressed, I don't think it helps. You don't want an ulcer, do you?'

'Well, I'll be the judge of that, thank you.' Tanith could feel herself bridling and tried to shake the feeling off. Robert didn't mean to be smothery. He just cared about her in a very hands-on way.

She picked up her drink, then as an afterthought picked up the bottle and took it all over to the sofa before he could stop her, then kicked off her shoes and closed her eyes.

It all went pleasantly dark for the first time that day. Things were so much nicer when you could close your eyes.

'What did you mean about Frances going to New York?' he asked.

'I had a very weird meeting with Frances this afternoon,' she said. 'She's moving to New York with Warren and wants to move the agency there.'

'Oh, yes?'

Tanith knew he probably wasn't listening. He would be weighing up the pros and cons of ordering organic Gujarati food, but having to wait an hour for it to be delivered from Tooting. That was the thing about Robert; he was very one-thing-at-a-time. Once the food issue was completely settled, his searchlight attention would fall properly on her again.

'She thinks she'll have to have everything wound up by August. Warren has found a studio to do his jewellery in, and she's found an unfeasibly expensive flat to do her shopping from.'

'Jolly good. How do you feel about tofu? Could you live with meat substitute as long as it was cooked by South London's leading curry specialist?'

'Robert, she wants me to run the London side of things. Buy into a partnership, maybe.'

No response. Whether he was so stunned by this news, or merely weighing up tofu against marinated lamb, she couldn't tell.

Tanith didn't bother to press it, and instead followed her own train of thought about how easy it would be to transfer all Frances's contacts to her own patent pending filing system. Would she have to bribe them to take her seriously? How much would it cost to lunch 350 actors? Could you do it at Pret A Manger? And agents . . .? Could you do some kind of crate deal with Majestic Wine Merchants? Would she need a new haircut so they didn't recognize her as Frances's old assistant?

'You'll have spoken to her about a new pay structure, I take it?' said Robert. 'Oh . . . *no*! Damn!'

He sounded so distressed that Tanith opened one eye. 'What?'

Robert had four takeaway leaflets splayed out in one hand like a game-show host and the cordless phone in the other. 'I forgot about that marvellous North African place that just opened in Muswell Hill!'

'Oh, for crying out loud, just call Pizza Hut,' said Tanith and sank her head back down on the cushions.

The hardest part of it all, she thought, was going to be reinventing herself as the boss. Doing Frances's job wasn't exactly going to be hard, since she was already doing a substantial element of the actual *work* element of it, but *being* Frances was something altogether different. Being Tanith these days took more concentration than she liked. Though she tried hard to resist it, Tanith could feel some of her spikiness being rubbed down by Robert's constant gentle smoothing. It was like living with a pumice stone – only one of them could remain spiky. And she was becoming increasingly aware of not quite remembering how she would typically react at key moments. It was very unsettling.

'I need to get an office,' she said. 'Apparently she can't keep our current place on and pay the rent on the flashy one she wants in New York.'

Robert nodded slowly. Tanith could see the cogs moving in his brain, relishing the thought of a knot to untangle. 'OK,' he said. 'Whereabouts?'

'I don't know yet, somewhere cheap. But fashionable. And not so dodgy that people won't want to come.'

He walked over, stood behind her chair and put his arms around her. Tanith leaned her head into the crook of his strong arm. 'Why can't she keep both?' he asked. 'She's doing all right, isn't she?'

Tanith rolled her eyes. 'I mean, yes, she's busy, but she would have to be casting *Heaven's Gate* every day since 1981 to afford Duke Street *and* this new place. She showed me the brochures this afternoon. Even the doormen wear Armani. Anyway, I think Warren was using Duke Street as some kind of front for the import/export side of his covert business empire.'

'So why don't you ask if that's part of the deal? You could do import/export.'

Tanith huffed wryly and sipped at her drink. 'Unlike

Warren, the Man Who Ate All The Carrots, I will never achieve the necessary level of fake tan to make it look kosher. Anyway, back in the real world, I need to think about what this is going to mean for my freelance status, and all that kind of stuff . . .'

'Of *course* you need somewhere smart,' Robert said firmly. 'I'm not suggesting you work from some dive. OK, you want somewhere business-like but approachable and with decent off-road parking. Why don't we have a look at some places next week?'

For some reason, the word 'we' really jarred in Tanith's head. The last thing she wanted was Robert deciding where would be suitable. Not that many casting agencies were based in Canary Wharf, for very good reasons. 'Shouldn't I be speaking to that financial adviser bloke about my self-employment status?' she asked, as a delaying tactic. 'And I can't do that until Monday.'

'You mean you haven't already?'

She bit her lip. 'No.' It was galling to admit to sloppiness so soon, but in truth the whole idea was too pleasant to spoil just yet by spending an agonizing morning trying to explain to a very suspicious accountant why her business projections were about as fact-based as the films she was casting.

Robert rolled his eyes. 'Well, I *really* think you *should*. If you're running the whole London side of her business you need to know what you're responsible for. You need to speak to her accountant and speak to the person she deals with at her bank and then go and set up a meeting with –'

'Rob, stop!' Tanith put her hands over her face, then took them away, aware that she looked childish. 'I don't want to . . . I don't want to get into that tonight. I'm too tired.' If she started wading through impenetrable financial details when her mind was too weary to take them in then he would swoop down and tell her exactly how pointless the whole plan was and how she should really just get out of it, and she had a worrying feeling that she would end up agreeing with him.

He shrugged and Tanith knew without looking that he was wearing the same reproachful expression as her father used to adopt when she hadn't done any piano practice before her weekly lesson. The 'What's the point? It's your own loss' look.

'Look, we'll talk about this tomorrow, if you can just restrain yourself from saying whatever it is you're about to ...' she said weakly. She hated being weak, but it had been a long day and after her strength ran out at four thirty on the dot she'd been impersonating a strong woman for the last three hours, running only on caffeine, buoyed up by Lily-Jo's stroppiness. '*Please* can you just be blindly and uncritically supportive in the manner of a Hollywood husband for a while?' She softened her expression. 'At least until the bank tells me I'd be better off running an office sandwich operation.'

He grinned at her. 'A-ha, the sandwiches at last.' That was their little joke, that if Tanith couldn't cope with actors any more she would open a mobile sandwich operation, with Robert as executive adviser. It was a joke because there was absolutely no chance of it ever happening while there was breath in her body since Tanith could no more make a saleable sandwich than she could skin a seal. 'You can give one of my brothers a job riding the bike. Barney would love that.'

'No. No, no, no.' Tanith widened her eyes at the thought of Barney on a bike. 'I don't want him anywhere *near* butter or dairy products. Not with his reputation. Is that Barolo ready yet? Or would it like a massage and pedicure too?'

Robert stroked her ruffled hair with his big hand and went back into the kitchen to get the wine.

Tanith re-ruffled her hair crossly. It needed a wash. Annoyingly, that was the only time it achieved the look bestowed on it by her very trendy hairdresser, Luther. Luther had offered her various products which would effectively simulate two days of London grime, and she had refused in amazement. No wonder hairdressers all drove convertible Mercs.

'What would you prefer for supper?' Robert shouted through. 'Lebanese takeaway, or pizza? I found a proper place round the corner with a wood-fired oven.'

'Just whatever you want.' Tanith fingered a lank curl and debated whether she could be bothered to get in the bath or not. Horrible as it was to admit it, for the first time since they'd moved in weariness had started to take precedence over lust, and she knew that if she sat around in her dressing-gown Robert might want to fit in a quick roll on the sofa before supper. It made her feel bad to acknowledge that she didn't want to give him the opportunity, but she didn't have the strength or cunning to avert the situation if it arose. As it were. Her whole body ached and she felt defensively protective of it.

Her eye fell on a old school photo of poor Greg, who would willingly shave his own legs just for the chance of a snog – with anyone at all.

'Oh . . . listen to yourself, will you?' she said, under her breath.

In the kitchen she could hear Robert ordering lavishly from the organic Gujarati menu. He always ordered far too much, but never ordered rice. He made that himself while he was waiting for it to arrive and claimed that what he saved on the rice covered the delivery charge. Old habits died hard.

When the doorbell rang, Robert had reached a critical stage in his rice operation and Tanith had to lever herself reluctantly out of a semi-slumber to pick up the food. On her way back through to the kitchen, juggling Robert's change with three precariously splitting bags, she stubbed her toe on a stack of cardboard document boxes that she hadn't noticed when she came in.

'What's that stuff in the hall?' asked Tanith, dumping the bags and the instructions on the work surface. Several of the little boxes were leaking colours not normally found in natural food preparation.

'What stuff in the hall?' he said innocently, busying himself with spoons.

Tanith gave him a hard look. 'The pile of boxes, and that mangy-looking trunk. I nearly fell over it on the way in.'

'Oh, yeah . . .' Robert's face was open but he flushed around the ears, a sure sign that he was lying about something. 'That. It's, er . . . receipts and stuff.'

'Bringing your work home again?' Tanith stopped opening the bags. Robert's clients didn't tend to keep their accounts in files. One writer dropped his accumulated receipts into the office in Tupperware containers. 'Didn't we agree that you wouldn't do that any more? I don't want this house filled with the paper evidence of lives spent in strange pursuit of alternate truths. And I definitely don't want you thinking about their tax exemptions when I try to seduce you in the hall.'

Robert pulled a face. 'No, no, it's not work. It's, er . . . Oh God, look, it's Rosetta's. Weren't you listening at dinner? You know she asked me to go through her accounts and I couldn't say no, could I?'

'Oh, Robert!' Tanith steadied herself against the kitchen counter. She felt woozy as well as irritated, which irritated her even more. If she sounded drunk he'd accuse her of being irrational when she knew there were *very good reasons* for him to have refused point blank to have anything to do with Rosetta's accounts. But now she thought about it, he *had* promised to have a look at her books, when they went round for dinner. Not that she was going to back down though, just because she'd been too cowed by the occasion to say anything at the time. 'Now we really *did* have an agreement about that! You *promised* you'd never do accounts for anyone in the family again! You made me promise I'd stop you if you even volunteered! Not after Greg messed up that tax return and nearly got you professionally discredited!'

'That wasn't my fault,' said Robert, his lips tightening. 'He just didn't tell me about a load of stuff. He has a typical photographer's approach to what constitutes declarable income.'

'That's not the point. Did Rosetta blackmail you into doing this? Why can't she just employ a proper accountant! Don't tell me she doesn't have one! I don't *believe* Rosetta doesn't know what she's worth to the last pound coin.'

'She *doesn't* have one. Dad used to do all the accounts. Then his accountant did them. And the only reason *he's* stopped is because he's . . . decided to go and live in Spain. Anyway, that's not important. She needs to have all her financial records in order if she's going to move abroad and she asked me if I'd have a quick look.' Robert slumped in his chair. 'I assumed – stupid me! – that it would be a case of looking through some bank statements.' He let out a mirth-free laugh.

'And?' Tanith looked amazed. 'Come on. Don't tell me she doesn't have bank statements.'

'Oh, she does. In those boxes. All individually stuffed in by her own fair hand.' He took a big mouthful of wine and closed his eyes to appreciate it. Then he took another one, and didn't bother. 'Turns out she's got *no idea* what her complete financial situation is, because Dad and his accountant just made everything up between them. So not only have I got to unravel this ridiculous spider-web, some of which is pre-decimal, I have to recreate it in the rough shape of her previous tax declarations. God!' He massaged his forehead. 'And who says accountants aren't imaginative?'

'Isn't that illegal?'

Robert laughed again and refilled his glass. 'Oh, yes, of course it's illegal. But I've got to have a look through the whole thing before I can tell what to do.'

'Robert! You can't *do* anything!' Tanith's eyes flashed.

'You're not running the risk of discrediting yourself just because your mother's too much of a bimbo to open her own bank statements! I refuse to let you!'

Robert stopped with his fork half-way to his mouth.

Ooops. Had she gone too far? Tanith set her jaw and prepared for the torrent of wounded feelings. But someone had to say something, she thought defiantly. They couldn't all behave as though Rosetta was some kind of Marilyn Monroe lovable airhead when even they knew she was more of a Scarlett O'Hara lovable egomaniac underneath.

Robert put his fork down and his face underwent the instant transformation she'd seen many times before. He turned from irritable but fundamentally sweet Robert into Dad-Robert. His brow furrowed and Tanith could swear his hairline receded, like an electric sunroof going back on a car.

'Tanith, setting aside the issue of family loyalty, what do you *expect* me to do? If I advise her to go to another accountant, there could be very serious ramifications, not just for her, but for all of us. Rosetta's affairs are ridiculously complex – there are various trusts and investments for us where she's the nominal administrator ... God, I'm sure I don't even know the half of it. Anyway, this is my specialist field. If anyone can sort it out, I can.'

'Oh, right, I see.' Tanith wished she didn't sound so belligerent. It wasn't as if she was enjoying it. It wasn't as if she *wanted* to get locked into one of these 'we've been married for fifteen years and I hate your mother' rows. 'So it's a pride thing, then?'

'Let's not continue this conversation,' said Robert. He managed to inject a mild note into his voice, which only made Tanith feel more patronized. 'I'm simply going to have a look through Rosetta's finances, so I can advise her on the best course of action. I'll put everything in my study and you won't have to fall over a single box, or see a single dry-cleaning receipt.'

'She's got dry-cleaning receipts in there?'

'Tanith, there are taxi receipts for three shillings in there. My mother's entire life in cheque-stubs.'

'Oh, how appropriate. Why don't you suggest it to her as a title for her autobiography?'

He raised his hands and gave her a tight smile. Robert didn't like rows. 'I'm changing the subject now. When is it you're taking Greg out for more clothes? How is he for socks? Or have you moved on to accessories?'

Tanith ignored him and helped herself to more salad and then a bigger glass of wine. 'Did you phone your dad?'

Robert immediately looked shifty.

'Why? Why would I need to phone him?'

Tanith gave him a disbelieving stare. Brian frequently seemed like the sole voice of normality in the whole set-up. 'Well, apart from the obvious fact that you might want to ask him what the fuck he was playing at, keeping your mother in a delicate pre-war state of financial ignorance, because it's his birthday at the weekend and he's going to be away in Italy.'

'Is he? How do you know?'

'Because he always goes to Italy this week.'

Robert looked at her curiously. 'Actually, he does, yes. How did you know that?'

'You told me.' Tanith stuffed a forkful of rice and okra curry into her mouth and returned his curious look with sarcastically raised eyebrows. 'And *he* told me too. When he phoned the other night, and you didn't return his call. That's the trouble with you lot, you listen to all the irrelevant stuff and ignore the important details. The bits that might actually make you all think you care about each other.'

'Oooh, fresh!' said Robert, playfully.

Tanith levered a piece of aubergine skin off her back teeth with her tongue to distract herself from snapping back at him. At some point during the bottle of wine he had obviously switched from Dad-Robert to Fourth-Form-Robert.

'How come you don't mind my father and all his old-woman habits, but you've got a real problem with my mother?' demanded Robert. 'Is it a girl thing? Or do you subconsciously fancy my dad because he's a richer, more unavailable version of me?'

Tanith looked up, surprised. 'I don't *have* a problem with your mother.'

'Don't you?'

'I don't have a problem with your father either. And – honestly – I really don't fancy him.'

Robert looked oddly disappointed.

'I mean, come on. You lot have got more than enough problems to share around equally,' Tanith went on. 'I'm not committed to finding fault with just one person and letting everyone else off.'

'But you *do*. You're exactly the same with my brothers. You think Barney's a ridiculous waste of space, *even though* you go all gooey-eyed when he's around, and yet the sun shines out of Greg's scrawny arse. Why is that? They're both just as useless as each other.'

'They're not.' Tanith struggled to couch it in polite language and gave up. 'I mean, yes, they're both equally pathetic, it's just that ... Greg knows it, and wants to change – sort of – but for some reason I obviously can't put my finger on, Barney thinks he's God's gift to the Fulham Road.'

'I bet he *would* let you put your finger on it.'

'That's a very cheap gag. Especially coming from his own brother.'

'Ah well, ours is not as other ... families.' Robert trailed off and looked down at his plate.

There was an uncomfortable silence.

Tanith felt that it was her duty as the cause of this embarrassment to break it. 'Well, never let it be said I didn't give you all a fair road test. You bunch of freak-show, rock 'n' roll, psycho brats.'

She looked up, but Robert wasn't smiling.

'Come on,' she said. 'You're the fabulous normal one! You win!'

'Don't hate them just because they're different,' said Robert unexpectedly. 'That's a form of inverse snobbery.'

They stared at each other over the table and not for the first time recently Tanith wondered how the hell they'd managed to collapse twenty years of marriage into twelve months.

Chapter Ten

Knightsbridge, 1970

'So,' said Sue, discreetly touching up her pearly lipstick using one of the discs from her chain belt as a mirror, 'this is nice, isn't it?'

'Yes, very,' said Rosetta. Even though it *really* wasn't.

Sue and Rosetta were lurking politely in the far corner of a very dimly lit private members' club down a street in Knightsbridge. Someone had recommended it to Sue as being the place where everything was happening, more or less on the basis that it was the most unlikely place for *anything* to be happening other than the occasional brawl or raid. It wasn't looking particularly groovy from where they were sitting, on malodorous stools that appeared to have been stolen from the set of *Steptoe and Son*, but although it had been Sue who had insisted on coming, to report in her column, somehow Rosetta felt responsible for the place, and oddly defensive towards the sniffy glances Sue was sending round the room like fly-spray.

It wasn't helping the ambience that it was now only just gone five, that in order to get a drink they'd had to pick at the least impressive prawn cocktail Rosetta had ever seen, or that Sue was sitting there in full-on 'I'm a journalist, impress me' mode, her back ramrod straight, waiting to be amazed at the crowds of celebrities jostling for space at the bar.

'Is this a column feature?' asked Rosetta tentatively. 'Or were you expecting some sort of happening to break out?'

Sue smoothed down her glassy fringe, a new nervous tic she had developed since submitting her hair to a radical restyle at Vidal Sassoon, and snapped, 'Well, that *was* the point in coming here. Or rather, the point of *you* coming here.'

In a supremely masochistic piece of manoeuvring, Sue had got herself a Girl About Town column which relied heavily on Rosetta providing her with gossip about her daily round of shopping, chatting, having drinks and fascinating conversations with all sorts of famous people who routinely turned down Sue's interview requests. The pay-off for Rosetta was a stream of flattering mentions of The End and her and Brian. It was killing Sue, having to spend all her time listening to Rosetta's enviable life and embellishing it, but it was advancing her career at the same time.

It just gave their friendship yet another warped twist.

Rosetta restrained herself from reminding Sue that they were in fact there because someone had told Sue they'd seen George Best drinking Scotch with some bloke the previous week.

Even though Rosetta knew for a fact that he'd been *at* The Scotch all evening.

On the next table from her, Glynn and John.

She shifted on the uncomfortable seat and wished John was here. Or even, God help them, Glynn. But there wasn't any chance of any of them galloping to her rescue: John was in the studio doing some demos, Glynn was 'in Paris' (for which read: having a nose job in Surrey) and Brian and Red were both in New York with some people from the record company, checking out venues for the tour coming up in the summer, their first in America. Brian had insisted on going, wanting to keep an eye on the management, and Red had fancied a trip away, after another bust-up with Janette, his long-suffering girlfriend.

'So, tell me, what have you been up to of late?' Sue asked peevishly, and swilled back the rest of her vodka and tonic.

'Oh, this an' that,' said Rosetta cautiously. It was impossible to tell what Sue might take as quotes. Most casual comments were fair game, as Brian had discovered to his horror on opening the paper in bed one morning and reading all about his own problems with rich food on his delicate stomach. 'Brian's away, so I'm just the little woman at home. Housework, shopping, you know . . .'

This was about as far from the truth as it was possible to be: as well as keeping up her stream of social butterfly engagements, Rosetta had also been supervising installation of the new fan-club office in the mews house behind the Cheyne Walk flat, and arranging the publicity pictures for the album's press release. Not that she wanted any of this to be repeated in Sue's column – as far as the band went, she wanted her role to be serenely decorative. But mentally seeing 'housework and shopping' embedded as a quote in Sue's non-ironic prose, she qualified it immediately by adding, 'I've found this amazing chandelier in a junk shop – it sends little rays of sunlight right through the flat. Looks fabulous when you're tripping, just like being in a star.' She blinked enigmatically.

It wouldn't do anyone any favours to mention that John had wired it in for her, and redone her fuse-box while he was there. Or that he'd just fixed her clothes rail again, which had collapsed for a third time under the weight of all her clothes, which were now largely velvet and contained three times as much fabric as last year. In Brian's absence, John had finished off all the outstanding home improvements. It was getting hard to find more jobs for him to tackle – both to keep him coming over with a legitimate excuse and to keep him busy while he was there so they wouldn't fall into another long and interesting conversation.

Rosetta wiped the involuntary dopey smile off her face before Sue noticed. If she so much as *thought* about John, Sue would leech everything out of her before she knew it. It was tough to have something so exciting occupying your mind, and not be allowed to breathe a word. Not that anything had happened yet, despite the agonizingly obvious chemistry between them.

It was torture, but so far, their mutual moral stances were holding out.

So far.

She sipped at her drink. 'How about you? Been busy? Still dating that ex-choirboy from Fulham?'

Sue's face, already tense, darkened even more. 'I don't think it can get any worse. There's no Free Love in Islington, I can tell you. If I meet one more recently divorced public schoolboy called Falcon, or Drake, or something, who's discovered himself with primal scream therapy, I'll . . . scream. No matter what you might read in the paper.' She stared into her empty glass. 'Oh fuck it, you wouldn't think I was a journalist, would you?'

'What you need is a nice man,' said Rosetta, with the smugness of someone keeping one nice man on hand and one in reserve.

'Yes, I know *that*. But I don't *know* any nice men. I just know a lot of . . . screwed-up boys. It's all right for you, meeting interesting people all the time. And hanging out and with Glynn and Red and that lot.' There was a pause, in which Sue started playing coyly with the stem of her glass. 'And John.'

'Oh, John!' Rosetta felt her face smile at the mention of his name. She hoped it looked fond, rather than leading, and struggled to think of something nice to say about him that wouldn't end up in the column as an admission of adultery or domesticity.

'You wouldn't believe how good he is at . . . plastering,' she finished lamely.

Sue gave her a strange look.

'He refaced the balcony wall for us. He's very good with his hands,' Rosetta explained.

'No, wait.' Sue's brow creased and she put her fingertips to her temples in amazement. 'Sorry, have I got this right? John O'Hara, Baby John O'Hara and his magic fingers, came round to your house and . . . *plastered your balcony*? Rosie?'

'Er, yes.' Rosetta snapped back to reality. 'Don't put that in the column. Brian doesn't like him to talk about the labouring. You know, "We found him in a blues bar" and all that.'

'Don't worry, I won't,' said Sue. She chewed her stubby finger. Slimming pills were playing havoc with her already tattered nails. 'They think I make it all up as it is. Do you realize your life is like a series of badly described dreams?'

'Really?' Rosetta was pleased. After all, it was more or less the effect she'd been aiming for. Brian liked her to go out and do things, because it gave the rest of the band a veneer of avant-garde-ness that none of them really deserved, her included. But she and Anita, who genuinely was on another planet half the time, seemed to have acquired the knack of being invited everywhere. Being a quick student, Rosetta was now accomplished in the art of sitting in beautiful, mute amazement at the feet of seriously clever people. She made sure Sue sent a photographer to those parties.

'Can I get you another drink, Sue?' she smiled.

'Get me a date with John,' said Sue suddenly. She spread her little hands out on the sticky table like dried starfish, all ridgy and flecked with Liquid Paper. 'Please, Rosie. You're good friends with him, you could put in a good word for me.'

Rosetta froze, her hand gripping her plastic bag. Whatever she allowed to come out of her mouth now could potentially ruin everything. She had to be really careful. Really careful.

'John?' she said, playing for time.

'Yes.' Sue blushed beneath her mother-of-pearl pallor and her fringe fell in her face. 'He's . . . He's so right for me, and

I just know that if . . . If I . . . Please can you talk to him for me?'

Rosetta managed to force out, 'Oh. Wow.'

'Is he seeing someone?' Sue asked anxiously. 'I wouldn't want to mess up some scene with someone else or anything.'

Rosetta struggled to keep her expression neutral. 'I don't think he is,' she muttered. Did sending her cosmopolitan little bunches of anonymous flowers – so obviously the florist's choice, not his – and popping round to sort out her ill-fitting wardrobe doors count as *seeing someone*, or just looking after the boss's wife?

Sue's heavy black liner went shiny round the edges with swelling tears. She still couldn't bring herself to ditch it, even though everyone else was into iridescent eyes like peacock feathers. 'I just . . . Oh God, I know it sounds ridiculous, but ever since that night I met him at that party you and Brian had . . . I've just been thinking about him all the time, and I know they're going on tour soon, and . . .'

She looked up at Rosetta, eyes full of supplication, and Rosetta was overcome by a dizzying sense of power. Sue hated begging for favours – it wasn't her style. Even at school she'd traded prep for blind dates. For her to have abandoned her usual scheming approach suggested something more than just a passing fancy, and that spelled a crack in Sue's formidable girls' school armour. Sue was normally about as vulnerable as a crab in a condom.

Rosetta's mind spun away at a million miles an hour and she sipped her drink to play for time. It wasn't that she wanted to dangle John in front of Sue and then snatch him away for herself, just to teach her a lesson; she wasn't *mean*. And she felt bad enough about wanting John herself. But this would put Sue in her pocket, it would mean a big favour racked up for safe-keeping. An investment.

And what if John prefers Sue?

Rosetta choked on the lemon in her gin and tonic.

That couldn't happen, could it?

And what right had she to stop anything if he did?

She looked at Sue, now sucking her teeth in that irritating way she used to when she had her brace.

No, it couldn't.

'Well, I can't promise anything,' she said cautiously. 'But I think he'll be coming over this evening so I'll see if I can, you know . . .' She had no idea what she was going to say, but then she never did when John came round and they still ended up talking giddily until three. Well after Brian's transatlantic goodnight phone call.

'Oh, you're such a good friend,' gasped Sue, but Rosetta knew she didn't mean it.

'Let me get you another drink,' she said and ordered double measures as the trippy lightshow started. Rosetta could feel a migraine coming on.

After three more drinks each, the club hadn't got a lot better, but Sue hadn't made a move to leave, even though she'd obviously got what she came for. Something else was clearly on her mind. Sporadically, she would open her mouth and seem on the verge of saying something, then just as Rosetta was about to ask what it was, Sue would snap her mouth shut and smile anodynely. It was a habit that she'd had ever since Rosetta had known her.

'S'when's Brian back?' Sue asked eventually. She went to pick up her glass and missed it by a fraction of an inch.

'Um, I'm not exactly sure. He has to be back by the end of the month for the start of the British dates, then they fly off to the States again.'

'Oh.' Sue gave her a baleful look. 'You must be *awf'lly* lonely.' Rosetta noted that Sue now *sounded* just like her mother too. The more she drank, the more the cool outer shell slipped, along with her eye make-up.

'I manage.' She sipped her drink, wondering how she could force Sue to get to the point. Was there some gossip she could trade? 'It's all part of the deal, isn't it? It's his job.

I knew that when we got together.' It hadn't really occurred to Rosetta to get mad about Brian's absences. She'd heard about too many band wives grizzling, whining, then flying out to surprise their husband on tour with predictably farcical results.

Not that Brian was the type to have a wardrobe full of secrets, but it was always preferable to look cool.

'You know, you're a very understanding woman,' slurred Sue, and patted her hand. 'I don't think people realize just how understandin' you are.'

Sue might be writing with the big boys now, but she certainly hadn't learned how to drink like a journalist, thought Rosetta. She was still relatively sober herself, having redistributed the gin every time Sue stumbled off to the loo – not an easy journey in five-inch platforms through a terrain of over-stuffed chairs and occasional tables.

'Really? In what way, understanding?' Brian always said, if in doubt, answer a question with a question.

'You know.' Sue adopted her mother's expression of sympathetic Round Table concern. ''Bout Brian.'

'Brian?' Rosetta was caught off-balance. Brian? What was there to understand? So he was a bit middle-aged sometimes, he didn't look comfortable in loon pants much, but they got on well, he made her feel safe, and they still had a good laugh together. Just because John was now occupying most of her waking thoughts – well, that was just a crush, wasn't it? That would pass. 'Brian's fine. We're . . . perfectly happy.'

'You are?' Sue belatedly rearranged her features into a rough approximation of fashionable ennui. 'Still, s'pose that's what it's like, hanging out with rock-stars and people. You have to . . . go with the flow.'

'Sue, I don't think I know what you mean.'

'*Brian*,' Sue slurred again. 'And Red.'

'Brian and Red?' *Brian and Red?* Rosetta wondered if she was being very slow. Had they had a row? It wasn't like Sue to know anything she didn't.

'Well, that's what they're saying,' Sue hiccuped, her eyes widening. 'Brian Epstein, Kit Lambert, Andrew Looooooog Oldham.' She put her hand to her mouth, then took it away. 'Brian Mulligan.'

'That's what *who's* saying?' Rosetta stared blankly at Sue's jiggling eyebrows, unable to put the words in any order that made sense, and then it struck her like a punch in the chest. She could feel the breath leave her body. Brian and Red? Like . . . *that*? 'Oh, for heaven's sake!' She felt her face flush, hot and bright in the darkness. 'What a load of . . . I don't believe you. No one's said it to me!'

'Well, they wouldn't, would they?'

'Because it isn't *true*! What the hell does anyone else know about what's going on in the privacy of our own flat?'

'But it's not going on in your flat, is it? It's going on in . . .' Sue's imagination failed her. 'Public toilets and that kind of thing. Aeroplanes. In America.'

Rosetta put the back of her hand to her cheek. It was stinging hot. She felt strangely removed from the whole thing. It didn't even occur to her that she was talking to a journalist. 'What do you mean by *they*, anyway? Our friends?'

'It's all round the goss'p columns, darling,' said Sue. 'Everyone's talking about it. How you've been together for ages to cover it up, how he's always going off with them . . . on his *own*.' The vodka had obviously broken down any prurient caution and her eyes were glittery with something Rosetta couldn't identify and didn't like.

'But *you know* it's rubbish!' Rosetta's mind was trapped in a loop of disbelief: she's talking about someone else, she's talking about someone else. 'But why would gossip columns be talking about *Brian*?'

Sue stroked her hand patronizingly. 'Because he's the man with the plan, darling. He looks after one of the hottest bands in the country. Y'can't blame the press for being interested, can you? I mean, Red's one of the most elihg . . . *eligible* men in London. You can't expect them to write about Red's new Biba leopard-print bedroom, and not be interested in what he *does* in it! And you're public property too, these days. Come on, darling, you love those gossip columns as much as anyone. 'Specially when you're *in* them.' She ended on a sloppy giggle.

Rosetta narrowed her eyes. How drunk *was* Sue?

'But,' the hand patting intensified, 'it's so typical of you to be so *cool* about it,' Sue went on. 'I think it's very modern, you know, to be able to see both sides of your sexuality. Typical of Brian too, maximizing his p'tential.'

'Sue, Brian is *not* . . . like that,' Rosetta said through gritted teeth. 'Neither is Red. Red would deck you if he could even hear you say that. I can assure you, *here and now*, that both of them are very, *very* straight.' Rosetta's voice was trembling and she noticed that though the club was now – finally – filling up with people, it was suspiciously quiet.

Sue just raised an eyebrow. 'And how would you know that, then? 'S'that an exclooosive?'

Rosetta dimly saw 'My Three In A Bed With Hubby Brian and Red Kearon' headlines but was too upset to think about it.

'You can tell "them", from me, that it's not true, Sue.' Her mind spun in circles round an image of Brian as he left, flight bag on one shoulder, copy of Wodehouse in the other hand. He was so sad to leave her. Fresh roses appeared every other day, direct from Covent Garden. How could he possibly be interested in men? 'Listen, we've bought the flat next to ours and knocked through, come and do a feature about it.'

Sue's hand stopped its patting. 'Rosetta, swear you're unbelievable. I tell you your husband's havin' an affair with another bloke and you tell me about your *extension*.'

'That's because he *isn't* having an affair with another bloke,' hissed Rosetta. 'And I think I would know better than the idle busybodies at the *Evening Standard*.'

They sat glaring at each other in silence for a few charged

seconds, waiting for the other to lash out. It was a horribly fine balance of dependency on both sides, and both of them knew it.

Eventually, Rosetta realized that if she didn't get home she would be sick, or go to pieces in public and she didn't want to do that either.

'I'm going home now,' she hissed. 'Can I call you a cab?'

Rosetta stumbled out on to the street and felt the night air, at blood temperature against her face. She had the sensation of being slightly out of her own body, like bad reception on a television, but there was some small consolation in the fact that Sue, now attempting to reapply her lipstick, very slowly, bent double around the wing-mirror of a Mini, was conventionally pissed. If that made them both vulnerable, then at least she would be able to remember every single humiliating detail in the morning.

She really hoped Sue, the silly cow, wouldn't. But then if everyone was talking about Brian and Red, and had been for the past year, what did it matter anyway?

Rosetta leaned back against the nearest lamp-post. All she could see was John. For some reason she couldn't even drag Brian's face into her mind. She stared at the flimsy teenage models milling around an E-type badly parked outside a brand-new nightclub and it shocked her to realize that she was only a year or two older than they were. They looked like careless children, spindly long legs encased in white cobweb tights and torn vintage flapper skirts.

The most important thing was to get rid of Sue and to get home herself. The thought of doing something practical snapped Rosetta back to reality and a shudder ran through her, making her hair shake into her eyes.

'Now, Sue, let me call you a cab,' she said. It took an effort to keep the amused unconcern in her voice, but she managed. 'You need to get home.'

Sue glared at her. 'That's what've been *tryin'* to do f'the last five minutes. 'S'*impossible* to get a taxi round here at this time of night.' She had gone over her lip-line all the way round her mouth, and looked as if she'd been eating jam doughnuts.

'Oh, don't be ridiculous.' Rosetta pushed her fringe back behind her ears and strode into the middle of the road, where she stood hands on hips in her knee-high boots, illuminated by the light from the pub like a shop window mannequin. As if by magic, a black cab appeared from round the corner and pulled up. Rosetta yanked open the door, said, 'The Angel, please,' and ushered Sue inside, maybe a little more firmly than was strictly polite.

Sue, still not really at one with her shoes, caught her platform heel on the sill and lurched on to the back seat. The driver looked round and groaned when he saw the heap of dishevelled plastic and velvet sprawled across the back of his cab.

'She's fine, honestly.' Rosetta threw Sue's bag in after her and scrabbled in her purse for the fare.

As the driver began his three-point-turn, her head emerged from the window, topped off by the new hairdo, now all askew and looking deeply wig-like above the narrowed kohl eyes.

'John's phone number!' she bellowed. She leaned out to make sure Rosetta heard her. There wasn't a trace of drunkenness in her voice now. 'Yes? You'll get it for me?'

Some cord of control finally snapped in Rosetta's head. What was she, a pop pimp? 'Jesus! What do you *take* me for!' she yelled back.

Whatever Sue said in response was lost in a rattle from the diesel engine, but it sounded a lot like 'A complete fool.'

Rosetta turned on her heel before the taxi was out of sight and began walking back to where she thought she had left her car, feeling like Mr Jekyll turning back into Dr Hyde. There were precious few moments these days when she didn't have to remember to *be* something: cool chick, devoted girlfriend, hip fount of insider knowledge. She wasn't sure what she was now.

She didn't feel particularly fit to drive, but a weird numbness had crept over her brain, evaporating all sense of mortality. Traffic was starting to whizz past on the road, and Rosetta didn't care whether it hit her or not.

Her cream Lotus Elan was parked beneath a street light round the corner. For a moment she jangled her keys in her hand, and contemplated leaving it where it was and walking home in the still night air. Not because she was too pissed to drive – Rosetta knew she had reached the level of inebriation at which her subconscious took over all controls and made her take instinctive Fangio-style racing lines round Hyde Park Corner – but because getting in the car would mean driving somewhere and she didn't want to drive home.

She eyed up the Lotus, sitting there remarkably accusingly for an inanimate object. Brian had bought it for her when the band's advance finally came through, protesting hard right up to the moment he signed the cheque; he thought it was much too fast and wanted to get her a nice MG, or something with a roof, at least. But Rosetta had seen Diana Rigg in one and had insisted, taking him on one white-knuckle test drive after another until he'd given in. Just looking at it now, gleaming beneath the sodium light like a magazine advert, reminded Rosetta of Brian and his care and concern and fatherly pleated brow the first time she'd reversed it too fast into the garage behind the flats and narrowly missed his nice safe Bristol.

The truth was, it *was* too fast, it roared like a lion, and it scared the shit out of her going round corners, but once Rosetta saw the photographs of herself in *Harper's*, perched on the bonnet of her new car – a car so cool it even made her legs look thinner – she wasn't going to give it up for anything.

If Brian knew she was scared, he had the decency not to say anything when he paid her ridiculous insurance premiums.

Lovely, accommodating, Machiavellian Brian.

Rosetta pressed her lips together to stop herself wailing out loud and made herself stare at her own wavering reflection in a shop window. Looking at her face always made her get a grip.

The face that looked back was even paler than normal, but didn't show too much of the dizzy disorientation she was experiencing. The curious thing was that she didn't feel distressed that Brian was carrying on with another man because she couldn't really *believe* that. There was something else upsetting her, something that she couldn't put her finger on.

But Rosetta still didn't want to go home.

She made herself look at her mask-like expression while she thought these embarrassing spoilt brat thoughts and, to her credit, felt mildly embarrassed.

OK, so what if she didn't go home? What then?

Anita was in India on some kind of retreat. Or yoga therapy, or something. Patti Harrison was there, apparently – it was very cool. Rosetta gulped back a sob. In dire straits, she could break into the shop and sleep in the stockroom, but there was something ridiculously melodramatic about breaking into a boutique and sleeping on a pile of cloaks when she had a perfectly good flat of her own and her allegedly philandering husband wasn't back for another eight days.

Rosetta took a deep breath and unlocked the car. It smelled of leather and oil and Polo mints.

There was of course one other person she could go and see. Just to make things even more complicated.

'No,' she said sternly. 'No.'

She switched on the radio, checked her own unsmudged lipstick in the mirror, did a swift turn in the road and headed out towards the river.

Rosetta often made bargains with herself in times of crisis and now, as she absent-mindedly floored the accelerator down Sloane Street, she promised that she wouldn't set foot in the house until she knew what she was going to do about the whole horrible situation, and if she could get it worked out before midnight, she would buy herself a pair of new driving shoes on Brian's credit card.

It helped to rule options out. For a start, she *wasn't* going to go round to John's. No, no, no. She drummed her fingers on the wooden steering-wheel emphatically. If *he* came to *her*, magically appearing on the doorstep, that was fine, but she wasn't going to descend into tit-for-tat shagging. There were some things about Swinging London that Rosetta couldn't bring herself to understand.

For one thing, Brian *couldn't* be gay with Red and straight with her. He didn't have a single pair of brown shoes. He played cricket. He had a couple of dog-eared copies of *Playboy* in the bottom of his wardrobe that he didn't think she knew about, the pages creased to the readers' letters.

She changed gear thoughtfully to avoid hitting a couple weaving over the pedestrian crossing. But then there had been that friend of her mother's, Edie. Her husband had been a cross-dresser for years before Edie found out. And they had four children. Loads more weird stuff than this went on behind the lace curtains at home in Richmond.

Rosetta didn't slow down for the roundabout at Sloane Square but hauled the steering-wheel round fiercely and took the roundabout far too fast. The back end of the car spun out but she grappled it back under control automatically as she shot off towards the river, tyres squealing. A couple of lads loitering on the corner looked at the Elan with admiration as it flashed past, but she didn't even notice them in her mirrors.

Rosetta didn't use her mirrors much.

She drove on autopilot while her mind churned arguments round and round, searching out examples to put her own life into someone else's context. Hundreds of suburban marriages were based on moments like this, weren't they? When the wife found out something about her husband, something that everyone but her knew about, and yet she chose never to admit she knew it. You put the house and the children and the grocery account in one hand and the unknown in the other. What was so different about her? Or Brian? Neither of them were posh enough to have a genuine disregard for this kind of thing, unlike the floppy aristos who slummed it round Chelsea and took infidelity and deception in their languid stride.

How amused Sue would be— How amused Sue no doubt *is*, Rosetta corrected herself, to watch me squirm like this. It's the most miserable thing you could wish on a marriage, and yet I'm meant to embrace it as part of the new sexual revolution or else I lose my Brownie points. Because weren't they part of the fashionable élite that shifted sex and shape at will – and were celebrated for it!

But that's the point, thought Rosetta grimly. We're not, none of us. We're all just human beings with stupid petty little feelings. Especially those of us who don't take enough drugs to think it's normal. At least Brian's had the dignity to keep all this to himself.

But she still couldn't quite believe there *was* anything.

The flat was still full of soft light when she unlocked the door and let herself in. She'd left the lamps on, to make it look as though someone was at home while she was out, but really so that when she came back she wouldn't feel so alone. It wasn't the poky little studio they had moved into in 1967. As she'd told Sue, Brian had negotiated the purchase of the flat next to theirs and some unfashionable yet reliable builders he knew from home had knocked through while The End had been on the road in England.

It seemed huge now, and it occurred to Rosetta, for the first time, that it was decorated for people to look at, rather than for them to live in. There were two televisions in the sitting-room, one at each end, for no other reason than to have two, and the whole flat was covered with long mirrors, which made it look twice as big – and twice as empty.

Silently, Rosetta unzipped her boots and stood them carefully by the door, poured herself a huge Scotch, and curled up on the big leather sofa. At home, amongst the framed photos and debris from their old life, it all felt more real – though she still didn't believe it, the reality of what she had to lose began to weigh on her chest. She felt about ten and sixty, simultaneously.

Rosetta swallowed a mouthful of whisky. She didn't normally drink it, but in all the films – and Rosetta had watched a lot of films – it was what heroines slugged when things were bad and they needed to be bruised yet feminine. She clunked the ice around in the heavy glass, watching it melt while she thought what to do.

For a start, it showed how much Sue or anyone else really knew about these people they profiled to death. No doubt Sue was rubbing her fat little hands in the cab right now, hoping that she would be hysterical with grief and panic, and that John would be delivered up to her on a plate in return for a four-page demonstration of Brian's heterosexuality and home-conversion skills. Rosetta set her jaw in a manner that made Desperate Dan look fey. Well, that's where Sue was very, very wrong indeed.

The whisky was beginning to work, taking the edge off her emotional panic and setting her thoughts in order. It was a cunning trap, Rosetta was prepared to give her that: Sue knew how much Rosetta wanted to slide into that glamorous, shifting world of the Stones and the Beatles and the other bands and actors who shimmied around the London scene with casual carelessness of life and details. She also knew that Rosetta had the same curtain-twitching roots as she did herself, roots that were hard to ignore in unguarded moments of crisis. And throwing a bourgeois hissy fit about Brian's casual carelessness would undo everything.

Rosetta snorted into her glass. Really, Sue couldn't have *given* her better copy, if she wanted to make the Mulligans look like London's premier swinging couple. For God's sake, she could think of two models off the top of her head who were making *up* this kind of thing to give their tedious husbands some groovy cachet!

No, she couldn't appear to be outraged, on any level. But this pathetic attempt at bargaining . . . Rosetta huddled her knees up to her chest and forced herself to imagine Sue and John together, sitting in Trader Vic's, drinking rum and Cokes in a dark corner, Sue regaling John with her bystander tales of media life, John with his head on one side, murmuring encouragingly, asking all his thoughtful, unaffected questions.

To her relief, the image was about as realistic as Red and Brian in a *Gone with the Wind* screen clinch at the LA Riot House.

But the whisky soured in her mouth as the obvious next step occurred to her: *not* setting Sue up on a date would be the quickest way to an 'anonymous' story about Brian in the Who's Doing Who column.

And though Red was big enough to laugh it off, Brian would hit the roof, the band would split up and it would just look sleazy and wasteful.

Rosetta corrected herself: *she* would just look sleazy – it was always the woman who came out looking like a tart or a fool. Not the free-wheeling, buccaneering man.

She swallowed her drink and thought furiously. What to do, what to do? The best thing would be to maintain a serene silence about Red and Brian, at least until they came home, whereupon she'd have to send John on a date with Sue, during which he could make up his own mind about what a mad trollop she was. It wasn't as though it would be hard.

'Oh, damn,' said Rosetta aloud and banged her glass down on the coffee table. Sometimes she wished she had a more dramatic turn of thought. It would suit her so well to use Brian's 'infidelity' as a springboard into John's bed, and they could sort out the details afterwards.

It was such a tempting thought, appearing fully formed into her head like that, that Rosetta held her breath for a second or two and her heart raced as she fast-forwarded the scene in her head.

But no. She wrinkled her lips. Brian wouldn't buy it, and she couldn't live with herself if she started thinking like that. Someone would find out. That wasn't a relationship, not the way she knew it. Revenge was one thing, but going hell for leather for your own self-interest – under the convenient cover of hurt feelings – was just sick.

Rosetta sighed, closed her eyes and leaned her head against the leather cushions, wishing she had someone who could tell her what to do. After all, what did you get for being good? Even with her morals intact, she still had a phi-landering husband (maybe, proof pending) and a severe case of itchy pants. She and John had been making meaningful eyes at each other for ages now, clinging on to their stupid moral values, and it wasn't wearing off, as she'd hoped it would.

It was pretty depressing all round.

Rosetta let her limbs go heavy, and listened to the faint sound of thunder, far away at the moment, but certainly coming closer, across the river. The whisky was now meeting the gin and tonics, and she felt her mind dislocating and slowing drunkenly for the first time that evening. Doing the right thing wasn't quite as consoling as it should have been – even if it was a relief that London hadn't corrupted her entirely. She hadn't done what Sue expected her to do: either fly into hysterics, or run straight round to John's for revenge on Brian.

No, she had been mature, and sensible.

And just as manipulative as Sue.

But without degrading herself in the process.

Rosetta smiled, her eyes still closed.

And just to show that I'm not trying to play her stupid game, I can give her what she wants, a date with John. Not that she'll enjoy it.

She licked the corner of her lip and planned the warm and photogenic welcome she would show Red and Brian at the airport, just to demonstrate there were no hard feelings or even suspicions. Maybe Sue could send a photographer?

Her grin broadened, showing her beautiful white teeth.

So that's what I'll do, she thought. I'll just give John a ring. No harm in that. It's not for me, it's for my poor friend, who has terrible . . . terrible mood swings, and who's awfully lonely since her last boyfriend emigrated without a forwarding address . . . and it would be such a favour if you could take her out . . .

Rosetta dialled John's number without looking at the phone and leaned back, eyes shut, listening to it ring.

John wouldn't be in bed, not yet. She knew he often stayed up through the night, playing and practising and listening to records, trying to work out how it was all done so he could do it differently and not be sued.

It didn't even occur to Rosetta that he might not be alone.

The thunder was coming nearer now and a white blast of lightning flash-lit the room and she opened her eyes in shock. The river was silvery with raindrops bouncing on the water and the reflections of the lights across the bridges were broken up like mosaics. Yet the wind gusting in through the window was warm on her face.

'Hello?'

Rosetta revelled, not for the first time, in how gorgeous John's disembodied voice sounded on the phone. He always sounded sleepy, like he'd just woken up, and it made her shiver with guilt, even though she hadn't done anything.

'Hello, there,' she said, wriggling back into the sofa. 'It's Rosetta.'

'Rosetta! There's a surprise.' His voice was a little slurred, as if he'd been drinking, but wasn't drunk exactly. 'You know, I was just thinking about you.'

'Were you?' He was so charming. She bit her lip and focused her concentration on being sensible and mature. Of *course* he hadn't been thinking of her, not at this time of night.

'I was in the middle of a song,' he went on. 'All about you and your lovely smile. Do you want to hear it?'

'No.' That would be embarrassing. But – her heart squirmed with guilty excitement – had he really been writing a song about her?

'Listen,' she said, quickly, before she could weaken any more, 'I need to ask you a favour.'

'Oh, no. No, no, no. Not now. Let me play you my song instead. Sure, it's a lovely song.'

'John, no, listen, shut up about . . .'

She could hear the phone bump as he put it down on the table and the clunks and twangs of him picking up his guitar from the floor.

Rosetta hastily swilled some more whisky into her glass for moral support. Or to provide the basis for an excuse later.

Still, anything to put off the moment of discussing Brian, or Sue, and having to decide what her official reaction would be to it all.

She let her eyelids droop shut and wondered whether she should close the windows. John was playing a series of arpeggios on his twelve-string, clusters of notes that seemed to fall like icicles into her ear against the distant rumble of thunder outside. To Rosetta's relief, he didn't sing, he just played around and around the same chords; the cadences fitted like a maze of dovetail joints, and it sounded so familiar to her that she began to wonder if she'd heard it before.

This is all right, she thought with a gush of relief. What was I so worried about? We have one of those nice courtly love relationships. He's like Lancelot and I'm married to his king and we can admire each other from afar and burn chastely with terrible romantic love. He can write me songs and I can inspire him and we can be tormented exquisitely because nothing can happen, even though we really fancy each other.

Excellent!

Rosetta snuggled into her leather couch, half-asleep with drink, smug that she had the situation under control and more intoxicated by the dreadful romance of it all than by the quarter bottle of Scotch now inside her, swilling around and making evil compounds with cheap gin and quinine.

Then John started singing.

'You have the sweetest crooked smile,' sang John softly, 'but you only smile for me.'

There was a moment of numbness, like the millisecond between hammering your thumb and feeling the pain, before Rosetta's heart lifted and fell inside her and was finally swept away on a torrent of mixed-up emotions. She touched her hated, sharp, overlapping teeth with her tongue and the tears that had flooded her head earlier now flowed soundlessly down her face.

'You have another smile for them, the one that they all see, but your heart is in that crooked smile, in private, for me.'

How did he *do* this? she marvelled. Surely this was a connection on a much higher level. It was as though he could see right inside her, and knew what would move her. And what a tender thing, to write a song about how she made him feel – that he could sing to everyone – because he couldn't tell her in private . . .

A voice in Rosetta's head cut through the alcohol and gush and pointed out sharply that this must be fate. Not only had she based most of her early romantic encounters around song lyrics, but this was the perfect – the only! – opportunity to spend a relatively blameless night with John. If Sue knew the rumours about Red and Brian, then John would too – he could come over and comfort her. And who could really blame them if things got a bit out of hand . . . Just the once? And it could be just the once. This might be all she needed to get it all out of her system and go back to being a proper faithful companion to Brian.

It's my duty, she thought firmly. John writes these wonderful songs about me – the very least I can do is give in to the guiding hand of fate and sleep with him. I am a muse. It's OK.

'Rosetta, are you crying?' asked John suddenly.

Rosetta nodded and realized that he wouldn't be able to hear that over the phone. 'Um . . . yes.'

'Oh, man! Don't cry!' said John. 'What's happened?'

'It's . . .' Rosetta bit her lip. Whatever she said now was critical. Especially if she decided not to tell anyone about what Sue had said to her. 'Brian's . . .' She choked, surprised at the flood of emotion that welled up in her.

'I'm coming over!' said John, a little too quickly. 'You sound as if you've had a shock!'

Rosetta nodded again, feeling guilty but sick with exhilaration at the same time.

There was a clunk from the other end as he dropped his guitar and the phone, then muffled swearing as he tried to pick them up. 'I'll be a couple of minutes.'

'John, are you OK to drive?' Rosetta asked, unable to stop herself being responsible even as she was mentally donning her Guinevere pointy hat and veil number. 'You sound a bit drunk.'

'Oh, get out, I'm fine, woman. 'S'only a drop or two.'

'Get a taxi on the office account,' she said. Honestly, it was like brain-washing, the way she looked after the band: she did it even when she was pissed. 'Charge it to Brian.'

The image of Lancelot borrowing Arthur's horse did not escape her.

'I'll be there as soon as I can. You poor thing,' John added, in case there was any doubt about why he was coming.

'OK,' whispered Rosetta and set the phone back in its cradle. The flat suddenly felt very empty.

Rosetta finished her Scotch in the darkness of the sitting-room and watched the lightning flash illuminate her pale curtains.

John was coming round. John was coming round.

Before she was really aware of any time passing at all, there was a knock outside – obviously someone had let him in downstairs. Another hand of fate.

She opened the door cautiously.

'Hello,' said John. 'Are you OK? You look really . . . pale.' His long dark curls were dripping with rain from where he'd run in from the car, and the mental image of the first time he'd come round to sort out her balcony doors, the first time they'd really talked alone together, streaked across her mind. It seemed ages ago.

'I'm fine,' she said. 'I . . .' Her mouth closed as he shrugged off his leather jacket and a wave of desire shimmered through her.

'No, you're not fine,' he said softly.

Rosetta shook her head. 'No. No, I'm not.'

He took a step in to the flat, and gently lifted the empty glass out of her hands. 'Now, I've been arguing with myself all the way over here, thinking what things we need to say, and I came to the conclusion that it's for the best if we don't say anything at all,' he said. 'Don't you think?'

Rosetta was just about to blurt out, 'Brian's having an affair with Red and I don't know what to do!' but as John was speaking, she realized what a lame excuse it would sound. And she didn't want this . . . whatever was about to happen – to be sold on a cheap excuse.

Instead she shook her head and stared down at her bare feet like a schoolgirl, unable to meet John's eye.

She heard him put the glass down on one of her occasional tables with a soft clunk and felt the air move in the room as he came near her.

Rosetta realized she was holding her breath, and couldn't release it.

John stroked the long fringe off her forehead so he could see her face. His hands were incredibly gentle on her skin, cupping round her cheekbone and stroking her jaw until she felt all the tiny little downy hairs rise up, tingling.

The blood rushed out of Rosetta's head and into her lips and she squeezed her eyes tight shut, as John lifted her chin with his finger and bent his head nearer to kiss her. She felt the disorientating warmth of his breath on her face before his lips touched hers, soft and reverential, and she pressed herself into him as his hand went into the small of her back to draw her closer. Then he pulled back, making her eyes snap open with shock, and she saw the stricken look on his face.

No, she thought with a rush of determination, we can't stop now, this is right.

'Oh, Rosetta,' he muttered, 'we . . .'

'Don't talk!' she whispered and pressed her mouth against his, feeling his lips part beneath hers.

After a few seconds of hesitation, he groaned and started kissing her hungrily, wrapping his arms around her narrow back, and she felt her entire body shiver in response.

Rosetta tangled her fingers into John's hair and traced her fingertips over the rough stubble on his chin. Every part of her body was tingling with desire, and she couldn't touch enough of him at once. It hadn't ever felt like this with Brian, no matter how much she'd tried to persuade herself real-life sex couldn't possibly be like in Anais Nin.

But kissing John like this, without any need for directions or muttered suggestions, and feeling his strong hands slipping beneath her clothes, and sensing her body responding before her brain even had time to register what was going on – how couldn't this be right?

They fell on to the deep sofa, still wrapped around each other. John's shirt rode up, revealing the long muscles of his stomach, and Rosetta yanked it off, with little thought for the individual mother-of-pearl buttons Anita had hand-stitched with such care.

She sat back on her heels for a moment with the cotton shirt bundled up in her hands and marvelled at John's gorgeous chest; from the number of times she'd seen him on stage, soaked to the skin with sweat in paper-thin shirts and tight jeans, she knew he had a fantastic body, strong, not too muscly, not too skinny, but until now, despite her sticky, guilty middle-of-the-night dreams, she'd been no nearer to it than any of the other fans.

Until now.

'Take off your jeans,' she said breathlessly. The words were catching in her mouth. Her voice didn't sound like hers, all of a sudden. She threw the shirt on to the floor. 'Please,' she added automatically.

'No, *you* take them off.' John held her gaze; his brown eyes were amused, but now dilated with desire.

'Can't,' she said, holding up her trembling hands.

John grabbed her hands and put his long fingers over hers, making her undo the big American buckle on his jeans. His hands, she noticed, were also trembling. 'Can't not,' he mumbled, with a shaky laugh.

Rosetta swallowed as she felt the heavy leather belt slide through the buckle. Part of her couldn't wait to be *there*, beyond any point of turning back, naked and touching the bits of John she'd only glimpsed backstage, but first she had to get there, and pass any number of points at which she *could* stop things.

But she couldn't stop.

Not when he kicked away his jeans and awkwardly tugged off his pants.

Not when she let the straps of her dress fall off her shoulders and then slither off her altogether like a snakeskin.

Not when he buried his face in her soft stomach, smothering entirely untouched parts of her with butterfly kisses with a skill that was at odds with the shy smile that wreathed his face as she sighed and twisted, and certainly not when he finally lifted her up in his strong arms, carried her to the balcony and laid her down on the pile of cinnamon-brown Turkish cushions she'd arranged under the fall of wisteria.

Actually, to be fair, that was Rosetta's idea. But John didn't stop either.

Afterwards, with pleasure still flushing her skin like blusher, Rosetta lay with her head against John's chest on the surprisingly comfortable cushions and stroked the dark hair on his arms. A church clock somewhere in Chelsea chimed twice – she had no idea it was so late – and the air was fresh from the rain and still warm on her bare body. She wondered if it was the alcohol or the adrenalin or just happiness keeping her so warm.

Behind her, John's fingers traced a fine line down the curve of her hip as if he were trying to spell out his words instead of speaking them. Rosetta felt the tiny thrills run up and down beneath his fingertips like iron filings underneath a magnet.

'Until I met you, I just used to play songs,' he said very quietly into her ear. 'And they didn't mean anything to me.'

'And now?' Her stomach fluttered.

'And now I have to write them, because it's the only way I'm allowed to say what you do to me and my poor wrecked heart.'

Rosetta smiled beatifically. 'But isn't that a good thing?'

'No.' John put a hand on her waist and rolled her over on her back so she was looking straight up at him. 'No, it's not.'

The moonlight threw shadows along the strong lines of his jaw, and glittered in his dark eyes. Rosetta wanted to live in this tiny bubble of time for ever, because nothing could ever be more perfect.

'Why isn't it a good thing?' she breathed uncertainly. 'And careful how you answer that. Please don't spoil it.'

John dropped a soft kiss on her forehead. 'Because that half-wit Glynn gets to sing about how much I need you. And I just get the guitar solo.'

Rosetta curled up into his chest, her heart flooding with relief. 'But that's the only bit I listen to anyway,' she murmured into his left nipple.

'No talking,' he said and kissed her again.

Chapter Eleven

Duke Street W1, 2001

'But I thought I *had* the finished script,' said Tanith, look-ing aghast at the folder in front of her on the desk. 'I mean, if you could *call* it that. I *had* been hoping that half the pages had fallen out when Lily-Jo photocopied it, but apparently it really *was* seventy pages of "improv scene to go here".'

Frances shrugged and tapped her biro on her teeth. 'Well, it's very much a work in progress, sorry.' She looked up and smiled. 'It'll be worth it in the end, honey. I know it's a bit of a pain for you, but I don't think the new version alters much about the lead character. She's still an innocent young woman . . .'

'. . . who is swept along by the tide of fashion and music and turns into some kind of Jackie Collins reject super-woman in organic face pack and diamonds by the middle of the film. I know, I know. It's the casting challenge of the century,' said Tanith. 'I've seen the inside of more primary schools this week than Gary Glitter.' She rubbed her eyes, trying not to smear her eyeshadow down her face. Already her tired eyeballs felt like they were about to fall out and that was with all the Californian moisturizing oils Lily-Jo fed into the air-conditioning system to improve her dry skin.

Frances put her head on one side and pulled a sympa-thetic face. 'Tanith, sweetheart, you would tell me if I'm putting too much on your shoulders, wouldn't you? I don't want you collapsing with a breakdown before I go to America. Please don't make me leave Lily-Jo in charge of the office. I've checked and the insurance won't cover it.'

Tanith pulled herself together at the mention of America. 'No, no, it's fine, I'm just . . . you know, tired. And every time I think I've got someone, and send her on to these people, they come straight back with some new vague direction. And meeting the director didn't really help.' She raised her eyebrows. 'I think maybe they may have too specific an idea about who they want, you know?'

Frances nodded. 'You could be right. There was a lot of ridiculous nonsense about security and confidentiality agreements when we took this on.' She drummed her nails on the desk thoughtfully. Tanith noted that only a few scraps of lilac nail varnish clung to them. Stress. 'Sounds to me like the writer's a little bit too involved still. I might see if I can't get that knocked on the head . . .' She jotted a note on a Post-it and stuck it to her forearm. 'But, chin up and press on! The right person is out there . . .'

'. . . We just have to find them,' Tanith finished for her. 'I know. I will.'

She got up and gathered her various bits and pieces, her mind already scanning down the to-do list she'd made before her morning meeting with Frances. It was scary how fast the weeks were going in – she'd already been on this project for a month.

'Do you want me to give you the name of a masseur?' asked Frances. 'Because your shoulders are somewhere up around your neck, darling. You look like Herman Munster. Or an ironing board.'

Tanith immediately yanked her shoulders back and felt something pop under her neck. 'Ow!' she yelped and grabbed her spine. 'Do I?'

Frances flipped through her Rolodex happily. 'Tension at home, is it?' She took a soap-opera interest in Tanith and Lily-Jo's home lives, since Warren had made it very clear that his dynastic interests stretched as far as their matching Persian cats (pet passports pending).

'Sort of.' Tanith took the proffered card and tucked it in her diary. It looked expensive. 'It's just that . . .' A nagging thought had entered her mind shortly after dinner with Rosetta. A nagging thought that maybe what she'd read about Amber sounded rather familiar. Should she say something? Would it just land her deeper in it all round?

'No such word as just, dear,' said Frances, briskly. 'It either is or it isn't.'

'It's just that . . . OK, sorry, I mean, this film, well, *Amber* seems to be, um, not unlike a woman I know, and I've just . . . um, *only* been wondering . . . whether it's some kind of biopic thing?'

Frances looked thoughtful. 'I don't know. And if it were? Would you like me to enquire?'

Tanith bit her lip. This was her first solo project. If she couldn't handle this on her own, then Frances might rethink the whole issue of leaving her in charge. That would be a tough one to explain to Robert, who would probably try to sue Frances, before moving on to sue whoever was running the film.

And if it *was* some kind of biography project about Rosetta – then what? What kind of effect would that have on the boys, on top of the book thing?

And what if Rosetta herself was behind it?

Tanith had a hideously plausible mental image of Robert's monstrous Rosetta poring over her Polaroids in an office in Soho, deciding whether or not various girls were cute enough to portray her on the big screen.

'I'm sure it's not,' she said, decisively.

God. She's even got you thinking like a Mulligan now. Believing Rosetta's hype. Where will this end?

'Well, it's all useful for finding the right girl,' said Frances. She ignored the flashing of her desk phone where Lily-Jo was trying to transfer calls in. 'I know you're the right person for this project, Tanith, and I have great faith in you. I thought that from the minute I saw you in that funny little jumper. I thought, there's a girl who knows what she's doing.'

'Er, thank you,' said Tanith, although she didn't believe her for a minute.

With a sense that she was slamming the stable door shut long after the horse had bolted, bolted again, bolted for a final farewell bolt and then been turned into dog meat, Tanith spent the rest of the morning on the Internet in her office, feeding in 'The End' to as many search engines as she could find.

It hadn't particularly concerned her up until now that she didn't really know much about The End, beyond the fact that they were a fairly typical if not world-beating British rock group of the seventies: somewhere between Free and Dumpy's Rusty Nuts, as Patrick had put it. She wasn't sure whether that was a joke or not.

Tanith wasn't into music as much as some people, and certainly not anything before about 1990. The variety of blues metal country sludge that she understood The End specialized in was definitely not her thing; and if Robert said they were a seminal influence on eighty-nine per cent of all subsequent bands and suffered the fate of the truly influential (i.e., being totally ignored by their successors), well, she was prepared to take his word for it and leave it at that.

What was more interesting to her all of a sudden was where Rosetta fitted into the whole set-up.

Tanith hit 'search' and was astonished when more stuff than she could have believed possible rolled up on the screen in front of her. Admittedly, an Internet search for 'The End' did produce a lot of unrelated pages, mostly concerned with putting your parents to sleep, and far too many about *Apocalypse Now*, but a surprising number were actually related to the band, from listings on lyrics sites (including two entries on the Top 100 As Voted By Users Of the

Internet Rock Bollocks List), to obscure French fan sites, to numerous 'Where are they now?' features and lots of fleeting references on other, more famous groups' websites. According to the pictures, many of which featured Rosetta in a variety of outfits, Tanith noted, they had a lot of rather famous mates.

Not that Tanith recognized the famous mates specifically. But any men dressed that badly, or that sparsely, in the seventies had to be famous.

She waded through a gig-by-gig review of their first American tour on the Official American The End Site, compiled by some obsessive who relentlessly detailed all equipment used; quite monotonous, as it turned out, as they didn't have much at that stage. Tanith hoped for the fan's sake that they owned more than three amps between them by the later years. Though they started out with pitifully small gates, by the end of the tour The End were dragging in respectable numbers and even selling out venues in the smaller towns. John and Glynn were the only ones mentioned by name in most of the reviews, Tanith noticed; Red was only mentioned in connection with some explosives or when he fell off his drum-stool.

By the time she'd downloaded a section about their albums and their history and their collected interviews and their solo careers, Tanith was feeling a new respect for Rosetta. Even though she hadn't consciously heard a note these guys had played, they seemed to be pretty cool and they weren't bad-looking, if you liked a lot of hair on a man.

She could happily have surfed for the rest of the day, but Lily-Jo came in and tersely informed her that the laser printer was now jammed up with a grey-scale line drawing of Glynn Masterson by a Japanese fan, and Tanith took this as a sign to stop. She could have downloaded a whole lot more, but satisfied herself with signing up for an Internet mailing list about them instead. The Internet seemed to be The End's natural home, their memory nurtured by a lot of people who hadn't seemed to notice that no one was wearing denim any more and who liked to analyse lyrics using *The Hobbit* as some kind of translation crib.

What was really interesting to Tanith was that Rosetta was in nearly all the pictures but, for some reason best known to whoever was writing these things, rarely appeared in the text portions.

But then maybe fans were like that.

Tanith's hands hovered over the keyboard as she considered putting in Robert's name, just to see what came up, but something stopped her. She wasn't sure how much information she could usefully process.

Chapter Twelve

Rosetta spotted John coming through the Arrivals doors with his bags over one shoulder and felt her feet ease off the ground with excitement while her insides detached themselves and floated free. As her eyes made out his familiar profile, she could almost see her bright red pulsing heart floating out of her chest towards him, the way Red said he'd seen his liver talk to him when he was on acid.

It had been a long month since Rosetta had watched John walk through the departure gate with the rest of the band, shepherded by a nervous Brian who was promising to anyone who'd listen that next time they'd have their own plane. Since then there had been hurried, difficult phonecalls and cryptic postcards, and the lack of contact after three intense months of sneaking around had driven her mad. But they did confirm her instinct that John really was the one and true soulmate of her life.

The month had gone agonizingly slowly: The End had sold out every date of their last British tour, but America was much, much harder, and though Brian was bullish and Rosetta was encouraging, she prayed fervently and lavishly every night that it was working out for them, that they wouldn't have to slope back, tail between their legs, broken by apathy and half-empty venues.

With some 'happening' to attend every day, three photo shoots that she didn't even really remember, and her brain full of dilemmas thrown at her by the management people to sort out, Rosetta's nerves were strung tenser than they had ever been at any point in her life so far. And they'd been strung pretty tense before John left; they could only meet when Brian was busy, and he was usually busy with the band. Added to that, Brian knew her diary as well as his own, since they now shared a secretary – supplied by the record company. In the end Rosetta had gone down to Battersea Dogs' Home for a puppy, just so she'd have an excuse to pop out for a walk in the park without an appointment. Who she met there, of course, was her own business. The record company, naturally, had her photographed choosing the new pup. She called it Gibson.

With the band away, even Sue had commented on her lack of sparkle – although with Brian away at the same time, her moping around the usual haunts had been interpreted as wifely loyalty. And that made her feel as though she might as well be walking around with a big A on her chest, despite the fact that Anita was having a very open affair with some outrageously camp hairdresser called André, which Sue was peevishly ignoring in her column in return for twice-weekly blow-dries. Even Sue had started sleeping with the morbidly thin playwright husband of one of her work friends, though she made it plain to Anita and Rosetta that it was purely for the sake of her reputation, and she really wasn't enjoying it.

Rosetta 'hadn't got round' to arranging the blind date with John for Sue, despite being reminded weekly. Him being in America helped, and she hadn't thought further than that.

It had been a very difficult month all told. Rosetta vowed never to be alone with her conscience again.

But finally, here he was now, just as gorgeous as when he'd left and – amazingly – on his own.

'John!' She waved her hand above her head, a schoolgirl wave, not caring that she didn't look cool. She pushed her big black Jackie O sunglasses off her face in case she was a bit *too* incognito and he missed her in the crowd. Although with her tortoiseshell hair and long legs, Rosetta looked about as incognito as a horse on an ice-cap. 'John!'

A couple of people looked round at her, as if they almost recognized her, but on closer inspection she didn't look like the person they thought she was. She wasn't quite laid-back enough to be famous. The involuntary beam of delight spreading across her face made her look about fourteen, and instead of her usual King's Road psychedelic velvets and ribbons, Rosetta was dressed like any other nineteen-year-old, in jeans and peace beads and a loose cheesecloth smock which slipped off one soft white bra-less shoulder as she walked towards the gates.

John strode through the crowd in his tight bell-bottoms, looking like Gulliver in Lilliput amidst the drab, beige knot of weary and crumpled travellers. His beard had started to get quite thick while he was away and he was showing no signs of whatever it was that had made him miss the earlier plane that the others had caught, or indeed of having just endured a seven-hour flight. He had an old bag over one shoulder and his guitar case in his other hand and, without all the other lads, the roadies, the suitcases, Brian flapping about trying to create a buzz, he looked like a student hippie getting back from the kibbutz.

Rosetta stopped beside a pillar, leaned back, and smiled all around her, revelling in her cast-iron, fib-free alibi for seeing John alone. Brian, ironically, had handed it to her on a plate: he'd phoned her at seven the previous morning, spitting feathers that John had managed to go AWOL from the hotel, so they'd gone without him, 'to teach the bugger a lesson', and booked him in on a later flight. Rosetta rather suspected Glynn – now sporting a girlish Robert Plant-style blond lion mane in an attempt to divert attention from John's lengthening solos – behind the lesson teaching.

If she'd wanted a private, passionate reunion, she couldn't have planned it better herself. So there was no need for any of the white lies that still niggled her conscience: she had the

keys to the car, she was picking up this naughty, irresponsible musician and taking him to the secret rehearsal place
Brian had had her sourcing in his absence.

Rosetta's eyes shone under the hard strip lighting, and her
skin glowed as if she'd just sprinkled herself with Biba glitter.
Today she felt gorgeous and that was without anyone telling
her she was looking great through the lens. Today – she bit
her lip – *today* she had some news for John that might
change everything.

He was almost out of the thick of travellers now, and
Rosetta lifted her hand to wave again but, even as she felt
buoyed up with joy, she stopped herself with a shiver of shy-
ness that she hadn't felt since she was at school.

Let him see me.

She wanted to watch the expression change on his face
when he picked her out from the crowd. Her heart started to
skip as he carried on walking.

It's a test, she thought, panicking. *If he doesn't stop, he
doesn't care. If he stops, it will all be all right.*

But even as she was daring herself, Rosetta couldn't decide
how she thought it would turn out. Normally she knew these
little tests were just teases to send cheap thrills through her
spine, before it all turned out the way she planned. Yet the
way John was walking, apparently oblivious, sent a new,
real fear through her.

Maybe things really weren't going to go as planned.

'John!' she shouted suddenly, unable to stop herself. She
couldn't let him fail.

His head turned at the sound of her voice and Rosetta was
relieved to see a smile spread across his face like sunlight. He
lifted the arm that wasn't carrying the guitar case and began
to trot towards her, long legs covering the ground easily, his
denim flares swinging as he moved.

Rosetta longed to be swept up into a big-screen hug, but
at the same time her ever-alert photo-conscience was
scanning the hall – who might recognize them? Was there

anyone around who might read a little too much into an affectionate kiss? Seeing John in the flesh instead of his more controllable imaginary version, walking towards her in living Technicolor, slowed her thought process down in the most frustrating way. She just wanted to stare at him, like one of the sad-eyed little girls who hung around outside their house, hoping to catch a glimpse of Red hanging out his washing.

But suddenly he was there, wrapping his arms around her, and she felt herself being pressed against his strong chest. Rosetta drew in a deep breath and smelled him. Soap and lemon and patchouli. It almost made her sick with anticipation.

'John!' From within his bear-hug she dropped her bag and wrapped her own arms around him. Whereas she and Brian fitted together exactly, like stacking chairs, there was a sexy mismatch about her body and John's that reminded her that they weren't about cuddling, they were about something far more exciting.

'God almighty, Rosetta, I barely recognized you!' he said into her hair. His voice was catching with excitement as he ran his hands up and down her slim back.

'What do you mean by that?' she demanded.

'I just mean . . . that you look so gorgeous and normal,' he said simply. 'Like a real girlfriend.' Then a cloud passed across his open face and Rosetta pretended to fiddle with her hair so she didn't see.

Awkwardly and unwillingly, John and Rosetta pulled apart.

'Shall we start again?' she said, with a wry smile.

He nodded and blushed.

'John!' she said, and politely offered her cheek to kiss. 'What time do you call this! Did you have a good flight?'

'Mrs Mulligan,' he replied softly and placed a careful kiss on one cheek. 'Thank you so much for coming to meet me.'

Her heart hammered guiltily. 'I won't tell you again,' she said lightly. 'I'm not Mrs Mulligan yet.' With her eyes shut and a broad smile lighting up her face like a Botticelli angel, she turned her cheek for the second kiss.

'I can't tell you how good it is to see you again,' he murmured and kissed her on the little daisy she had painted under her left cheekbone.

As the rest of the passengers – who had not been ushered from the plane as promptly – began to swell around them, John and Rosetta stood about three inches away from each other, rooted on the spot, feeling the disconcerting energy that passed between them like radio waves.

'Oh, shit, Rosetta,' said John – something that she would regard later as less than romantic – and dropped his bags, grabbing her in the sort of uninhibitedly passionate embrace that she normally found really embarrassing and laughed at when she saw it in the street.

But she wasn't embarrassed now. Far from it. John's strong arms pulled her tightly into him, spreading tingles of pleasure all over her body, and it was impossible to resist the flooding need to touch him everywhere, as her hands slid around on his back and their lips jostled, bumping hungrily as she remembered how he tasted, all sweet and hot.

'John, John!' she said, pushing him away after a few head-wrecking seconds. 'People! Cameras! Hasn't being in America made you paranoid at all?'

Rosetta hoped it look like self-control, when in fact it was nothing more noble than fear.

John, his half-open mouth still smeared with her peachy lipstick, did a double take, and looked at her, then smiled.

'You are a very cool chick,' he said, and there was something in his voice that didn't sound straightforward. 'Come on, where are you taking me?' And he held out his hand. It was all calloused from a month of playing and sweating and doing all his own roadying. John didn't trust guitar techs.

She took his hand and there was no thunderbolt.

They walked from the airport to the car, Rosetta bouncing

six inches in the air with each step. A light seemed to surround her, and with John's arm slung round her shoulders, she glowed with the same kind of unchallengeable gorgeousness that she felt when she slipped her feet into a pair of beautiful shoes. Look at him! She wanted to yell at all the grannies wheeling their cases through the departure lounge. Look at this beautiful man! He plays the guitar like an angel and he wants me! Have you heard the songs he's written about me? You would just *die*!

She opened the door of the Lotus and he threw his bag in the back. It wasn't a car for more than two people. Another of the reasons she loved it.

It was what Brian called a sports-car day – bright skies, crisp air, lots of sun and enough breeze to lift her long hair off her neck as they drove along, well over the speed limit. For the first time in a long year of stress and pressure and constant concentration on being someone else, Rosetta felt exhilaratingly young. She sang along loudly to every song that came on the radio and John joined in, without telling her how flat she was singing. Her smile grew so wide it almost hurt her face.

On an impulse she pulled over into a lay-by with a squeal of tyres.

'Come here,' she said and ran her hand along John's strong jawbone to the point of his chin, pulling him near so her nose was filled with the smell of him.

'What?' he murmured, amused, into her hair. 'What can you possibly want now?'

Rosetta laughed into the warm crook of his neck as the hot engine ticked over in the background and ran her lips along the roughness of his scratchy beard. She felt as if her whole body was lined in red velvet, like a guitar case. No, *this* was right. *This* was where she should be. Everything else – Brian, the band, all those silly interviews – had just been a series of stepping-stones: good, strong ones, but just a path to being with John.

'You make me feel like I'm on acid,' she sighed. 'I can't describe you except in boring, stupid, weird colours.'

He bent his head and kissed her hungrily, then broke off abruptly.

Rosetta's eyes were still shut, watching the explosion of colours in her head. She felt exactly the way she had done at seven, when her mother had taken her to Westminster Cathedral and she thought she saw the Blessed Virgin in the mosaics. John O'Hara and his Near-Religious Experience.

'John,' she said. 'There's something that I need to talk to you about.'

At exactly the same moment, John said, 'Look, Rosetta, I have to talk to you.'

Rosetta's wide green eyes snapped open and she saw his face tight with misery.

There was a heavy pause. Rosetta understood what all those religious tracts meant about the air being full of angels. Only they were coming for her this time with their little sticks, not to spread any more happiness.

'So? You *are* talking to me, aren't you?' she replied, too quickly. She wasn't dumb. Somehow she knew what was coming next: this was the payback for being so happy. Sickness spread up her throat and she racked her brains for some gossipy nonsense to push the final words away. Something really light and hip, that gossip about Ginger Baker, gleaned from Anita, so he'd think the right moment had passed, so he'd have to wait a bit longer, leave things as they were . . .

'Ah, come on, Rosie, please don't make this harder for me,' said John. He pushed back his hair, until the curls stood up, all matted with old sweat and the wind rushing through it. He looked about twelve, despite the beard. 'You know I don't . . . It isn't that I don't love you, because you know I really do. But y*ou* know as well as I do that it's not right, so don't make me be the one to get all moralizing.'

'Well, if *by extrapolation* you know it's wrong too, stop

trying to make *me* feel worse than *you* do,' Rosetta said faintly. Something was churning around in her stomach and she knew it wasn't just stress that had made her periods erratic.

Not erratic, she corrected herself. Non-existent.

She stared off into the distance, not wanting to see the look on John's face. Where had this gone wrong? God, how she wished there was some way of stopping time and rewinding it! Re-recording it. Overdubbing all the bits that seemed to be going out of tune.

'Brian is my mate, as well as our manager,' John was saying. 'I just can't *do* this to him. I don't think you can either. God, he really missed you while we were away – he loves you so much, you know that. And I can't let you . . . I couldn't be the one to . . .'

Now she had made herself look at him, Rosetta could only stare at John's confused and distressed face, her eyes widening with shock and her heart pounding in her chest. She'd run through all the scenarios, and yet in all the rehearsed noble rejection of her traditional relationship and lovely home, she hadn't even imagined this as a possibility: that he would *force her to be good*. And that he was saying it with such seriousness in his eyes was . . . just terrifying. Hot tears suddenly swept up her throat and she had to fight to keep them back.

And the fact that he was trotting out all the oldest clichés in the book was almost insulting.

Fiercely, she tried to summon up the image of herself in the last lot of pictures she'd had taken – cool, chilly, in control.

It shimmered and shattered before her eyes.

'Don't think I don't want what we have,' he was pleading, holding her hand. 'God, it's been . . . more than I could have ever hoped for, but I've been goin' over and over it in my mind and it can't be right, when you're someone else's lady.'

'But it's not like I'm *married* to Brian!' she blurted out.

Even as she said it, she could hear how childish it was, and she despaired of herself.

'Oh, come on, Rosetta.' John looked reproachfully at her. 'What difference would that make?'

'A big difference.' She felt her lip jut, and at that point, some exterior force seemed to take over the controls. It was as if a thread running through her spine had just been yanked by an invisible hand. Then the invisible hand gave her a quick slap.

'You didn't say that when you came over the night before you left. The night that you skipped the band meeting Brian wanted to have in town.' The night she said she was having dinner with Anita, who was ever ready to supply an alibi she could call in herself one day.

'I know.' There was pain in John's voice and she knew he was too honest to be faking. 'And don't tell me that everyone else is doing it so it doesn't matter, because I've been running that past my head for the last four weeks and no matter how incredible it is when we're together, I just can't make it stick.' He looked up at her. 'Call me a fucking square but I *can't*. What I feel for you is too good for that. I don't want half-measures and I can't make you . . . I'm sorry.'

'You're sorry?' wailed Rosetta. 'You're *sorry*?'

She tried to find the words to put the plug back in the bath, to stop it all running out, but none came. Her hands felt paralysed in his and the breath stuck in her throat. This wasn't the way it was meant to happen.

'We have to stop this before something serious happens,' John went on. 'Someone will find out, or tell Brian, and –'

Rosetta held up her hands. She didn't want to hear whatever venal reason he had for not wanting Brian to find out. If he dared to say that he was petrified of being summarily ejected from the band, on account of his being seduced by the wicked lady of the house, she honestly thought she would punch him or drive them both into a brick wall.

That would give the papers something to write about.

But even as she tried to drum up some outrage, she knew that that wasn't his reason. His reason was that he was just a good lad, and in his eyes this was the first step on a slippery slope he didn't dare take.

'I don't want you to—' He began miserably.

The hands went up further.

'But, Rosetta, please don't—'

More hands. Rosetta's long fingers splayed so she didn't have to look at him. She was feeling sick again. More sick when she thought of the alternative: John breaking up the band to run away with her, taking away The End's real chance of making it, leaving Brian and the others in the lurch, never hearing those soaring, yearning solos again, never seeing *him* again . . .

'Janey Mary, I don't want us to part like this.' He sounded genuinely devastated. 'I didn't think it would be like this, I really didn't.'

So *he'd* had a plan in his head of the way this little meeting would go, thought Rosetta. And it had been royally screwed up too, by reality. Good.

She scrabbled in her bag until she found the tiny Smythson's diary Brian had given her. A casual little present, typical of his dual mission to please her and to organize her. And to think that Brian's own elegant Smythson's diary had been one of the first things she'd found attractive about him. She yanked the tiny silver pen from its neat hole and ripped out a page.

I'm trapped, she thought. *And I set the trap myself.*

'Rosetta?' said John. He sounded miserable. 'Rosetta, will you please say something?'

'Here.' She scribbled the name of the country house that she'd found for them in the middle of nowhere, perfect for thrashing out rehearsals. They had someone's mobile studio set up in the ballroom. Brilliant acoustics, apparently. 'That's where everyone is.'

'But I thought you were going to take me there?' said

John, bewildered, and, Rosetta was pleased to note, not a little pissed off. 'I thought we could talk, discuss this?'

'What's to discuss?' she said, making her voice airy with a supreme effort. Her stomach was light with misery. 'As the lady in the film says, I'm a very stylish girl. You want to call this scene off, then I'm not going to argue about it.'

She held her face steady, but around her it felt as though everything was crashing soundlessly down around her like a bad silent film. Mentally, she tried to project that gorgeous icy image of herself over the disintegrating reality but the tears burned at the back of her eyes.

'Oh, Rosetta, God, no, not like . . .' John groaned.

Rosetta looked in her bag again and pulled out her purse. Her hands were trembling like an old woman's as she riffled through for some notes. 'Here, here's some money for the cab fare. Give him an extra fifty not to tell the *Daily Mail* where he left you. Or just get him to drop you in the nearest village and Brian will drive out and pick you up.' She dropped her shades back on her nose so he wouldn't see the hot little trickle of tears escaping.

'Where are you going?'

'Where do you think I'm going? I'm going *home*, John. I'm going home to drink a bottle of whisky and cry until I'm sick, and then I'm going down the King's Road to spend a small fortune on clothes until I've forgotten what I was so upset about. Very Delta blues, don't you think? And when I see you again, no matter how you try and look at me . . .' Her voice cracked as she thought how many times she would have to do just that. 'You'll just be the guitarist in some band that my husband does tours for – that's what you want, isn't it?'

'No! No, I . . .'

Rosetta forced herself to be nasty, or else she knew she'd lose it completely. It was bad enough to be reduced to this. 'Don't say you love me, because you obviously don't. And you obviously have no idea what I feel for you, how much I feel for you, otherwise you wouldn't treat me like some groupie you've just got sick of!'

'You know that's not what I'm saying! I've never *had* a damn groupie! And I *love* you,' protested John, 'and that's why I don't . . . why I *can't* carry on like this.'

Rosetta tossed her eyes skywards, even though she felt like howling. 'No, if you loved me, you would at least make the *gesture* of wanting to run off with me, instead of dumping me to keep your job. Haven't you *heard* about Eric Clapton?'

John's head turned and he looked as if he were about to say something, then changed his mind. Instead, he ran his hand across his forehead. 'You're asking me to do something you don't even want, not really, Rosie.'

'No, I'm not asking anything *at all*. What am I asking you to do? Marry me? Challenge Brian to a duel? I'm not even asking you to . . . to . . .' She stalled, thinking of all the stupid things she had imagined him doing for her, none of which seemed to involve actually replacing Brian.

'But you don't *want* me to fight for you!' yelled John, exasperated. 'You want me to keep quiet so you can have your happy celebrity couple life with Brian, and your nice Chelsea flat, and have me waiting on the side, for whenever you want to run off and be irresponsible! I know you *love* me, but that's how it is, isn't it? Come on now, Rosetta. How can you want a man who'd settle for that?'

She flinched at the sudden shock of realizing that that was exactly what she was doing. Somehow it had never occurred to her in such bald terms.

'For Christ's sake!' he said, in a gentler voice. 'This isn't some teenage photo love-story. We're adults, with . . . responsibilities. And consequences. I know Sue's forever doing features about how fashionable it is to get stoned and sleep around and claim you never knew what was happening, *man*, but we know exactly what's going on and cheating isn't ever . . .' He looked miserable and yanked off the beads dangling from his neck. Rosetta knew some groupie had probably made them for him, and she felt sick with jealousy. 'I know this isn't what your groovy rock-star's meant to say, but cheating isn't *ever* right for people like us. And we both know that. Otherwise you wouldn't be protesting so much, would you?'

Why *doesn't* it feel like cheating? wondered Rosetta, through the white noise of misery that was now filling her head. *And why can't I have both?*

They sat in silence for some minutes. Rosetta didn't want to speak, because she didn't think she could find the right words under such pressure. She wasn't even sure what she wanted to say other than 'Don't leave me.' And that was so hackneyed.

'I want to be with you, of course I do,' said John, gently, blending in with her thoughts. 'You're the most amazing woman I've ever met. You do things to my head that I can't even describe. But, honey, come on – you're another man's wife, in all but name, and I can't be the one to break up you and Brian.' He smiled sorrowfully and laid a hand on her hair, with careful tenderness. 'I've had eighteen years of priests yelling at me about what's right and what's not and I can't just change me head like that. It's too late. I can't give you what you want. Brian needs you, you need him, he's right for you.'

Rosetta couldn't stop the tears running down her nose, and she shook her head. At least he hadn't brought up the band.

'Ah, come on now, he is, so,' said John. 'Just because he lets you get away with murder doesn't mean to say he doesn't notice and he's not upset by it.'

She shook her head again and strands of her hair stuck to her eyes. In her head, her voice was yelling all about true love and their future and what he was turning away, but it was all silenced by the horrible knowledge that he was right and she *was* nothing but a cheating, undeserving trollop.

'Rosie, this will make much better sense in the morning,'

he said gently. The affection in his voice almost made her tip over into tears again and she couldn't speak.

'Wipe your eyes and drive me to this stupid place,' he said. 'We can talk about it tomorrow. But I had to tell you now.'

'Tomorrow,' Rosetta managed, bleakly. There was always going to be a tomorrow, and a tomorrow and a tomorrow. She would have to give one thing up: either John and this sensation of being really alive, or Brian and the security of her charmed existence. And if she gave Brian up, she also gave up the perfectly balanced band that made it all possible. The band that she loved almost as much as Brian and John.

What a choice. For the first time ever, Rosetta felt like going to Red and demanding he give her half of whatever drugs he had and swallowing the lot.

But that wasn't her way. She wiped her eyes on the sheer silvery slip she'd hidden into the glove compartment, the one she was going to slide into in the country-house hotel she'd booked down the road for their big reunion. Then she blew her nose on it for good measure, screwed it up into a ball, and drove him in silence to the ramshackle mansion, where the band were already stoned and giggly, and where Brian interpreted her black looks as appropriate disapproval for John's absenteeism.

That night, Brian went down on his knee in the shadowy rose-gardens, and Rosetta, to his delight, accepted.

Chapter Thirteen

Chelsea, 2001

'OK, come and stand on the box,' said Greg. He fiddled with his light meter. It wasn't easy setting up lights in a room designed specifically to give off the atmospheric gloom of some drug-dive from *Confessions of an Opium Eater*. The red velvet draping the walls and the rococo furniture absorbed any light he was throwing at it like a great big sponge. Though he wouldn't ever have mentioned it to her, Rosetta's dressing-room had always reminded him of an internal organ.

Greg stood back and surveyed his efforts so far. Every piece of equipment he had – and a couple of extra reflectors he'd hired from the Flash Centre on Rosetta's exacting instructions – was set up around an antique Turkish stool in front of a French dressing-table cascading with jewellery boxes and dishes of jet eggs. Greg had always been rather suspicious of those jet eggs. It had taken him over an hour to get it this right, he was ravenous and they hadn't even started yet. Only Rosetta would have demanded the whole kit, reflectors, multiple lights and all. Only Rosetta would have required 'a proper photographer' to do something so bizarre.

Greg twisted the adjuster on a redhead light with unnecessary force. Presumably he was meant to be flattered that she was actually lumping him in the professional photographer category for once. And it wasn't as though he didn't have things to do. If she made him late for his shopping trip with Tanith, then . . .

'Rosetta, can we get moving, please?'

There was no response from the adjoining bedroom.

Greg sucked his teeth.

'Rosetta?'

He checked his mobile phone again, just in case Tanith had called while he was dragging the lights out of the Beetle. Nothing. His stomach lurched with nerves just thinking about that. Much as he secretly relished spending any time with Tanith, whenever they met it was normally based on some deficiency of his (bad shoes, inability to cook supper, girl-repellent wardrobe, etc.), and her attempts to set it right. Which didn't exactly put him in a strong position, self-esteem-wise.

Where was she going to take him? he wondered, distractedly. What was the limit on his credit card? How much would she tell Robert?

'Well?' Rosetta appeared at the connecting door, in a short black skirt that finished exactly on her knees, and a violet cashmere sweater with a deep plunge filled by three knotted ropes of coloured glass beads. Her hair was twisted carelessly on top of her head and held with what looked like a knitting-needle, but which Greg suspected was probably a fourth-century bull-skewer or some such other expensive relic. She looked, as she always did in Greg's mind, like the modern-dressed Queen of Swords from one of her numerous sets of Tarot cards.

'Are you ready yet?' she demanded. 'Come on, Greg, how long does it take to set up a few lights?'

Greg knew she was doing this to bait him, hoping he would rise like Robert or Barney would, and spark off a witty little exchange of words, but something inside him couldn't ever risk upsetting her properly. It took so long and so much effort to get Rosetta to be nice to him in the first place.

'It's all ready when you are,' he said evenly. 'Are you ready?'

'Of *course* I am,' said Rosetta. 'I have had my photograph taken before, you know, darling. I'll just get the stuff.' And she disappeared into her walk-in wardrobe, from which he could hear the sound of many doors being opened and shut repeatedly.

Greg sat down on one of the lighting boxes with a big sigh and rubbed his eyes. She made third-time-round-with-all-in-laws-invited weddings look like a doddle. But then – never let it be said that she hadn't given him life skills – it was shamelessly agreeing with everything Rosetta said that had given him a headstart with Carolyn Mackenzie and other people's mothers. That and observing how nice their shoes were. Another habit formed of self-preservation.

'OK. I thought we'd start with boots,' said Rosetta, finally returning with a small luggage trolley loaded with boxes.

'Fine,' said Greg. 'Great.' He dragged himself to his feet and picked up the nearest camera.

'Oh.' She stopped in the middle of lifting a lid and looked at his Nikon. 'Aren't we doing it on medium format?'

'No,' said Greg, as calmly as he could. 'We're not doing it on medium format. That would take for ever, and I've got a couple of appointments this afternoon.'

Rosetta raised her eyebrows in jokey enquiry – as if it was a matter of global importance that he might be meeting someone – but Greg refused to let himself be drawn. If it had been anyone other than Tanith, he might have told her what he was up to and taken some, if not great, pleasure in her surprise. Rosetta never stopped asking him when he was going to get a girlfriend, as if it was some fault of hers that he hadn't had one since he was fourteen.

Right on cue, Greg's heart sank at that reminder, as it always did. *Eleven years without a girlfriend.* But typical Rosetta, he rejoined to himself: she even has to take centre stage in my own sex-life.

As Greg thought of Tanith, some protective instinct closed

around her image and he pressed his lips together, not wanting to hear her subjected to Rosetta's habitually harsh assessments of potential daughters-in-law. (Flora had not, to date, reappeared.) To associate with two Mulligans was surely a sign that Tanith appreciated quality. To mess with three, though, indicated that she was either a social worker, a journalist, or a glutton for punishment.

He looked up and his mother was now gazing at a pair of silver snakeskin sandals with the kind of tenderness normally reserved for over-achieving children. 'Come on,' he said. 'On the stool, please.'

Rosetta abruptly shook herself like a dog, clattering her beads, and climbed up deftly on to the ottoman with the confidence of a woman born in high heels. She stood there, in a pair of gold platform boots, her feet neatly arranged in ballet third position.

'Can you see the detail on the ankle?' she demanded as Greg moved in with his camera.

'Er . . . right foot round a bit, no, back a— That's it!' Greg snapped a couple of frames. 'Now reverse the feet. OK, great.' Two more. 'Fine, next!'

Rosetta clambered down. 'Aren't those fabulous? Your father bought them for me in New York. On their first tour of the States.' She looked wistful. 'He always was very good at picking out clothes.'

'Yeah, they're amazing,' said Greg automatically. 'Next?' His gaze wandered around the room while she tugged the boots off and pulled on a new pair.

'Do you remember all those times we used to go to Pucci?' asked Rosetta. She was back on the ottoman, this time in a pair of knee-high red boots, with lacings up the back. She lifted her foot in one so he could get the detail on the toe and didn't even wobble.

'Pucci? Was that the one with the funny windows?' Greg tried to get all the lacings in shot without throwing his focus out. He knew fine well which one Pucci was. He just wished *Rosetta* could remember that he didn't want to remember it.

'No, darling.' Rosetta's brow furrowed, fortunately out of shot. 'Pucci – those beautiful swirly acid print dresses.' She sighed. 'You remember, the one where they used to run out to the café and bring you Coke floats.'

There was a loaded pause, in which Greg dared her to say what she was evidently struggling not to.

Rosetta was unable to resist. 'Well, until you spilled them on the—'

'Yeah, yeah,' said Greg, flinching with a flush of residual shame. He blinked rapidly. No wonder he couldn't reconcile the adult vision of himself with a sense of reality. He couldn't even take himself seriously, with the Coke float disaster still causing him serious internal cringing twenty years on, so why should any sentient woman? 'Next boot, please. We've got a lot of boots to get through.'

Rosetta put down the ankle boot she'd picked up and looked at him with something approaching concern. She marched the boots across the bed towards him. 'These boots were made for walking . . .' she mugged, trying to make him laugh.

'Rosetta, stop it.'

She marched the boots over his camera bag. 'One of these days these boots are gonna . . .' She tried a winning smile, but Greg didn't smile back.

'Don't bother. They already did walk all over me. Can't you see the stiletto holes in my forehead?'

Rosetta pouted sadly. 'Oh, come on, Gregory, give me a smile?'

Greg frowned back at her. 'I hate it when you do all that mumsy stuff,' he said, and dropped one of the reflectors down a notch. He concentrated on tightening the screw until his fingers went white. 'It's not a look that suits you.'

Rosetta sat on the bed next to him.

'What do you mean, being mumsy?' she demanded. 'I'm

just being me. I can't be anything else at this late stage of play, darling.'

Greg's brow remained creased. Rosetta sighed and when he didn't respond, she stuck her fingers into her thick hair as if she was trying to massage the right words out of her head. 'You didn't come with some kind of guidebook, you know. I swear, Greg, in thirty years, I've never known what a single one of you wants. I don't know, you lot are only happy when you're putting labels on things. You're a generation of emotional trainspotters. I don't know where you all get it from. I sometimes wonder if Robert was born in 1920 and just fell through a hole in space.'

Greg bit his lip and listened to the very faint sounds of traffic outside. He didn't want to get into Rosetta's clinical dismissal of His Generation. It was always so hard to resist pointing out that Her Generation had generously agreed to die before they got old, and then reneged on the deal, leaving them free to talk down to successive generations about how to be young.

'Why are you taking all this stuff anyway?' he asked. 'Are you chartering a plane?'

Rosetta picked up a gorgeously embroidered ankle boot and held it up to the light. The paisley swirls on the toes glistened like butterfly wings. Greg had always believed that they *were* made from butterflies – not unreasonably, since Rosetta was the kind of woman who would have shoes made of butterfly wings.

'I'm not *taking* everything necessarily,' she said. There was another pause, and Greg knew she was assessing how much to tell him.

'Oh, I get it,' he said crossly. 'You just don't think I have much to do on a Friday and you want to keep me busy.'

'Greg.' Her voice was reproachful, and he didn't even want to look at her eyes, which would be even worse. How she climbed on to her high horse was a mystery to him. Particularly in shoes like that.

'I'm trying to get a sense of what I *have* in my life,' she explained. 'For the book. I need to see what there is, and what I need and don't need. I need to strip everything back and see myself underneath it, without all the dressing-up.'

Greg wondered about suggesting that, in that case, a family portrait might in fact be more appropriate than photographing her shoes. He didn't say it though. Robert would have done. He satisfied himself with a baleful glare, though glares weren't proving that satisfying recently.

But Rosetta didn't notice, or if she did, she didn't let it put her off her stride. Her eyes were miles away, green eyelids drooping sleepily as she turned the boot round in the light, so the spiky heel gleamed purplish and sharp. 'You know, looking at these shoes – they each remind me of times . . . places I'd almost forgotten. It's so easy to forget things. Well, not so much things, more like the kind of *person* I was when I wore them. I mean, look at these.' She held up the boot with a half-laugh. 'Have you any idea how much these cost?'

She pulled a 'bad girl!' face and grinned – the mischievous smile that even Greg in his bad mood couldn't help reflecting back at her. No one could. That was her big trick in life, he knew; eventually you couldn't help mirroring a smile like that, no matter how mad you were at her.

'Your poor father, Jeez-us.' Rosetta giggled. 'I only got them because some silly groupie had bought a pair and was showing off with them backstage. I went straight out and got a higher pair. I didn't care that these didn't go with anything. I didn't even care that they were about half a size too small. I loved them because they made me feel so *powerful.*' She looked up at Greg, and the smile turned seductively inclusive on her lips. '*Do* you remember them?'

'Of course I do.' Greg picked up the other one. It was the first time he'd actually held them. They didn't feel as soft as he'd imagined they would. 'I remember you used to wear them all the time. The summer before I went to school.'

The summer before Dad left. For the first time.

He put the boot down on the velvet bedspread and picked up his camera. 'So, this book,' said Greg, swallowing hard. 'What's it going to be like? *I'm with the Band*? Or something more erudite?'

'I'm with the band? Darling,' drawled Rosetta arching her eyebrow, 'let's get it straight: the band were with *me*.'

It was flip and they both knew it. Long exposure to journalists had left Rosetta unable to suppress sound-bites when they occurred to her. Greg wondered if she could even tell the difference between a conversation and an interview. But then, he conceded charitably, maybe it was an encouraging sign that she was getting defensive about this book.

Rosetta stood with her arms folded across the beads, and looked at him, challenging Greg to challenge her, but he didn't. Lack of encouragement was his best tactic. Instead he gestured towards the next pair of boots – a Victorian lace-up pair with gold leather toe caps. They still had the price sticker on the unblemished sole.

'Ho, ho, ho. OK, forget it,' he said. 'We've got a lot to get through and I need to leave by three.'

'No, come on, Greg,' she said. 'We need to talk about this book. I don't want it to be something that you're going to go into a decline about. No, darling, put the camera down. This is the first time in ages that we've had a proper conversation about this.'

'No, it's the first time you've talked about writing a book since Robert walked out of that family therapy bullshit,' Greg reminded her.

Rosetta rolled her eyes. 'I should never have let him do that. Look at him now. Totally screwed up. Mind like one of those machines that sorts post. But don't you see that it's something I need to do?' she persisted. 'I mean, even you and Robert don't really understand where I fitted into everything. It's flattering, but kind of depressing really to find myself still listed in the Groupie Database on Groupie

Central dot com when I'm nearly . . .' She stopped and corrected herself. 'After everything I've done.'

'Isn't that how you see yourself?' Greg countered. 'A groupie?'

'Of course not! I was a . . . *muse*. There was a lot that I did for that group that made them the way they were. Only I didn't make a big thing about it, because I didn't want to come over as some interfering wife and now . . .' She looked very sad. 'Well you can't go back, can you? You can't demand your own footnote.'

'Rosetta,' said Greg, 'fabulous as they undoubtedly were, I don't think anyone is saying that The End were exactly the Rolling Stones.'

Rosetta recovered herself and arched an eyebrow. 'Darling, don't knock it. Their very second-division-ness was the secret of their continued success.'

'Meaning?'

'Meaning, you can't go out of fashion when you're never *in* fashion.'

Greg stared at Rosetta as she giggled to herself. She must have been a real pain on drugs, he thought. I bet she never shut up.

Was that the kind of thought you were meant to have about your mother? he wondered.

As if she could read his mind, Rosetta's expression softened and she said, 'I wish you weren't so judgemental. I was married to your father when I was *nineteen*, for God's sake, Greg! I had Patrick when I was *twenty*! And before that I'd been going on the road with the band for two years. Sewing stuff, fixing up dates, listening to their problems, buying them decent clothes . . .' She ran a hand through her hair. 'God, I was more of a mother to the lads on the road than my own mother was to me.'

Greg fiddled with his lens to stop himself rising to the bait.

'Actually, let's not talk about my mother,' Rosetta added.

She breathed through her nose to calm herself down. 'That's a whole other chapter in the book.'

Greg stared into his camera bag and said nothing. He hated to see her whine, especially about his grandmother, who he'd never really met and therefore had to take on Rosetta's probably warped terms. Rosetta rarely whined, not even about his dad, since she wasn't the self-pitying type, but it didn't fit in with his image of her as the woman who was too cool to care, and too cool to complain. That was the easiest way of dealing with her, and once he'd worked it out, he'd stuck with it.

Rosetta saw him turn away and stopped tugging on the red laces. 'Listen, I'm not saying I didn't *enjoy* it. I *loved* it! But, Greg, by the time I was twenty-one, I was sick of men who couldn't even run their own baths.' She shook her head. 'And I felt *cheated*. Women were meant to be doing it for themselves, and I wasn't supposed to mention all the things I did for them, just look pretty in the pictures. Anita had three boutiques in Chelsea, Sue had her own column and I ended up working myself into the ground, making that band what it was while everyone thought I was some kind of rock Barbie doll!'

'Rosetta!' said Greg, just to stop her.

She looked at him and sighed. 'I knew some of that was in the deal when I got married. But I was your father's secretary, his PR girl, his hostess, his covert business adviser – everything apart from his wife. He left so much up to me, and didn't even realize he was doing it. And I didn't want you all to grow up like that, waiting for a woman to come along and sort out your problems for you, so you could take your love somewhere different. That's why I wanted you to grow up . . . independent. And I think you have, haven't you?'

'You think we can run our own lives?' Greg nearly laughed. 'Which one of us is the great life success? Barney the trainee gigolo? Robert the prematurely aged accountant? Me the terminally single wedding photographer? Pat the—

'Don't bring Patrick into this.' In an instant the eager vulnerability vanished from Rosetta's face and it turned back to the mask Greg had learned to dread. It meant she was concentrating on Being Rosetta.

There was another pause, but Greg wasn't bothered much by silences in conversation, especially not with her.

'Why *are* you going to Ireland?' he asked, out of curiosity. Not that he had the faintest hope that he'd get the real answer. It would just be interesting to compare and contrast with what she'd told the others. 'Is London too much of a distraction? Or is it tax, like Robert said?'

Rosetta sat down on the bed and stuck her finger through the red laces of her boots to loosen them. 'I'm going because . . . I don't think I can write honestly about my life in this house, darling. I've lived here for years and years – everything that's happened to me and your father happened here. I mean, when I look round this room, for instance – my sitting-room, you know – I try to see the first little bedsit we bought, but I can't. I can't un-knock down all the walls. We've made it too much of a whole house. And I need to be able to see that crummy little bedsit, at least in my head, if I'm going to remember what it was like.'

'So is that why you want me to photograph your shoes?' he said, sarcastically. 'So you can remember where you bought them?'

Rosetta smiled to herself, with a delight that Greg didn't miss. All at once, surrounded by all her old shoes, she suddenly looked very different, much younger, as if she was laughing at a joke he didn't understand. It made him feel oddly excluded. 'Honey, *no*. So I can remember what *I* was *like* when I bought them. Before I had all this . . . stuff. When your father and I were just a normal young couple with lots of plans and no money.'

They both looked at the piles of shoe-boxes stacked up by the door of her dressing-room. Some had sketches or Polaroids taped to the ends. Some even had yellowing press cuttings, with photos of Rosetta leaving a première or a party with those shoes on. Most were covered in a thin film of grey dust. Greg tried again to imagine what his mother had been like before she had rooms full of clothes, shoes and mysterious trinkets and couldn't. She was a woman born with accoutrements.

'I don't think I've ever seen you looking normal,' he said. It came out more accusingly than he meant it to.

Rosetta's hands traced dreamy figures of eight on the velvet bed-throw. 'When we first moved in,' she said, 'this room was our entire flat. We didn't have anything at all. Our fridge was smaller than that television. I had to throw saris over everything because the furniture was all second-hand and falling to pieces, and I swear we honestly made tables out of old packing-cases from Brian's dad's removal vans.'

Greg pretended to load a film to hide his interest.

'Bet Grandma Martin loved that,' he said casually.

Rosetta snorted. 'She didn't come round to the flat until Brian and I had been married for three years, and by then we'd bought the flat next door and knocked through, so it looked slightly more affluent. And even then she went round looking for evidence of our dissolute lifestyle. She accused your father of smoking opium.'

'Dad? Smoking opium?' Greg's eyes widened in disbelief.

'Your father never smoked anything stronger than St Bruno ready rub,' said Rosetta. 'But in the interests of looking groovy he bought himself a very mysterious little jar to keep it in and as I might have said before, your grandmother was never one for bothering with details when there was some drama to be had.'

'Good job Red wasn't staying with you then, eh?'

Rosetta's wide mouth twitched. 'Well . . . I did leave some of Red's stuff out to wind her up since she was so determined to be scandalized – not that she found half of it. And for God's sake, that woman took so many Valium she practically rattled. But then she *wanted* to find something, so she could go back to the bridge club and boast about how her daughter was utterly out of control and in the grip of long-haired degenerates, but in the most *expensively* appointed Chelsea flat . . .' She shrugged. 'I don't know why there's all this fuss about men having double standards when mothers are the worst of all.'

'Why didn't you just tell her to get lost? Or why didn't you just tidy it all up so when she came round there was nothing to see?'

Rosetta put her hand on Greg's head. 'That's so you, darling.'

'What is?'

'"Why didn't you just sweep it under the carpet and pretend you were about to have the local prayer meeting group over for a cheese and wine?" Darling, your grandmother might have pretended she knew nothing about rock 'n' roll, but when we went through her stuff, she had scrapbooks and everything. She knew more about the drugs busts and the rumours than I did. Even though she maintained *to the last* that Brian would be better off going back to furniture removal.'

'You never told us that,' said Greg.

She shrugged again, and the beads around her neck rustled. 'You were just babies. And I didn't want her to pass on all that disapproval to you. It was hard enough being a mother myself without worrying that I was making all the same horrible mistakes she made with me.'

'Did she give you a hard time?' asked Greg. 'I had no idea. I thought we just didn't see her because . . .' He stopped. He'd never really wondered why they virtually never saw their grandmother. They just didn't, and the day before his fifth birthday she died and Rosetta had refused to cancel his party, for which he'd been very grateful at the time since he'd seen the huge train-shaped cake already.

'I was really young,' said Rosetta. 'I thought I knew

everything and I thought I loved everyone. Or rather, I thought I should love everyone and then feel bad about it later. Oh God. What a mess. I was a very clean Catholic hippy.'

She tugged the red boots off and threw them on the floor.

'I don't think you need to photograph those, Greg,' she said, contemplating them with a wry smile. 'I bought those when I was going through . . . going through a very bad patch. Let's just give those away and pretend I never had them.' She paused, thinking. 'Listen, darling, stay there a second.'

Rosetta slid off the bed like a cat and padded through to her dressing-room in her stockinged feet.

Greg took a couple of frames of the discarded over-the-knee boots, lying with their laces snaking out like entrails. There was something creepy about the shiny red patent against the dark floor.

She must have been going through a *very* bad patch.

Greg had a dim recollection of some terrible photoshoot involving them. Had it ended in a row of some kind? There were lots of incidents like that in the back of his childhood memories, long and shadowy and often involving going to sleep in the back of a car.

Rosetta reappeared with a large leather box in her arms and a nervous, almost pleading expression on her face.

'Greg, darling, I don't just want you to photograph my shoes,' she said. 'There's something else I need you to do.'

'What's that? Catalogue your lipsticks on to digital format?'

'I need you to go through these.' And Rosetta put the leather box, bound at the sides with brass protectors and monogrammed with her initials, on to his knee.

He looked up and saw three more identical leather boxes stacked by the door. Unlike the shoe boxes, there wasn't a trace of dust on them and the leather was bright and deep red.

'What's in here?' he asked, still clutching his camera.

'Open it and find out. God help us, Greg, you really are suspicious, aren't you? Were you dropped on the head as a child?'

Greg ignored her and flicked open the brass hinges, and lifted the lid cautiously. Inside the box was subdivided into parchment month by month folders, each stuffed with press cuttings and photographs, contact sheets and loose strip negatives.

His heart sank at the mess of it all, but his curiosity was immediately piqued by a picture of his mother that he'd never seen before. And he thought he'd seen the lot.

He stared at it. Rosetta, in a ridiculously large pair of fashion sunglasses, laboriously parking her Lotus Elan. The sleek cream car in the garage that she never drove any more. The one he was secretly hoping she'd give to him – eventually.

'I need pictures for the book,' she explained. 'And I don't want to use the usual ones, the picture library ones. Everyone's seen those, they're so dull. People don't really see *you* in old photos, they tend to see *themselves*, where they were when that paper came out, whether they liked that dress or not. It doesn't really . . . *reveal* a lot about you, and if I'm going to go through with this properly then the pictures have to be as new as the text.'

'But *I* haven't seen these before,' said Greg, picking out photos at random. 'Where have these been?'

As usual, when he saw pictures of his mother playing up to the camera, he was struck by a mixture of awe and detachment. It was her, and at the same time, not her.

Like everyone else at his boarding-school, Greg – and Patrick and Robert – had had a large framed picture of his mother in his study, but unlike everyone else's happy Christmas snaps, their portrait had been by David Bailey, and featured a black and white Rosetta sitting imperiously in the wicker throne from the hall, laced into an Ossie Clark evening dress with her bare feet poking out underneath. Compared to that image, imprinted on his mind from all the times he'd been miserable and had only her haughty camera stare to sustain him, these photographs were of a woman he wasn't sure he'd met.

Rosetta swinging too high on a rope swing in some country house garden somewhere, her white knickers showing through her transparent dress and a knotted scarf wound round her narrow ankle, trailing like ectoplasm behind her.

Teenage Rosetta close up, smiling as though the sun was shining out of her eyes, peering through a heart she was making with her hands, her front teeth overlapping slightly, giving her a cutely rabbit-like expression.

Greg looked up at his mother in surprise. 'When did you have your teeth done?'

She blushed. 'Um . . . After Robert was born. It was your father's treat to me. I never used to smile like that before. Look.' And she showed him the wedding photo on her dressing-table: in which her pale face was illuminated with a slight and enigmatic Victorian smile. Pearly lips pressed tight together. No teeth.

'It was your *treat*?' Greg repeated incredulously.

'Well, some women get eternity rings, some get cars . . . I got . . . cosmetic dentistry. That's your father for you. Ahead of his time.'

'Did you *want* your teeth done? Didn't it hurt?'

'Um . . .' Rosetta pulled a face that Greg didn't understand, then flashed him the dazzlingly even toothpaste smile he'd seen a million times.

Somehow, he thought, it wasn't quite as nice as the shy uneven one in front of him.

He tucked the photo to the back quickly and flipped through the rest of the pictures. It was easy to be objective about Rosetta's beauty, even though she was his mother, simply because he'd seen in her in so many different guises over the years. She was startlingly beautiful in some of these,

with none of the poses he recognized from photo shoots or
the big leather-bound albums they had downstairs in Brian's
old study.

'Why aren't these photos in the albums?' he asked.

'Oh, darling, there were *so many* photos,' she said evasively. 'I just didn't have time, after a while. And some I
wanted to . . . well, some I wanted to carry around with me.
I didn't want them in an album. After a while, you get sick of
seeing your photograph fixed there, it doesn't feel like you
any more. You start looking at yourself as others see you a
bit too much.'

She took the photographs gently out of his hands and
retrieved the one he'd put to the back. She held it carefully
by the edges, as she held her tarot cards when she read them,
as if she were searching for something within the picture.
'And some pictures are . . . private,' she said, half to herself.

Greg suddenly had a horror that there might be nude pictures in there somewhere and flushed.

'You know, for someone who can run through forty different expressions a minute, you almost sound as if you don't
like having your photograph taken,' he said ironically.

Rosetta looked at him closely, searching his brown eyes
for the sarcasm, but she didn't find any. Of all her sons, only
Greg seemed to have learned the art of letting things go –
perhaps to extremes, given the state of his life, but he'd
learned it all the same.

'Sometimes I didn't,' she said frankly. 'Your father never
stopped snapping away, and it drove me insane. But you
learn what's necessary and you just . . . do it.'

'Did Dad take these?' Greg lifted a strip of negatives up to
the light. Even in reversed black and white he could make
out Rosetta laughing and posing around with an electric
guitar. They weren't professional shots, because some were
blurred or out of focus, but she'd kept them.

Dad would never have hung on to second-rate material
like that. Not that he'd have thrown it away, Greg corrected

himself, but he'd have stored it somewhere no one else could find it. When he was learning photography, apparently he'd shot five hundred rolls of film in a few months and kept all of them in a trunk, just in case.

The trunk was now in Geneva. Just in case.

'This doesn't look like Dad's stuff,' he said. 'He was totally anal about composition, wasn't he?'

She dropped her eyes. 'Not all of it's Brian's. I, er . . . It's mainly things I kept for myself, private memories – you know, instead of the version in the newspapers.'

Greg looked down at the negs. Now he thought about it, she *was* smiling a bit too freely at the camera for it to be Dad on the other side of the lens.

She pulled out a page of newsprint. 'Look,' she said, 'this is a feature about Robert's christening.'

Greg skim-read the columns. 'Glamorous party . . . Red Fearon, rock's newest godfather . . . champagne celebration . . . radiant mother . . . delightful baby . . . American tour dates . . .'

'Nice piece,' he said drily. 'I like the bit about Dad taking time off the tour to change nappies. Like *that* happened.'

'It's Sue, of course,' Rosetta replied then handed him a photograph. Like most classic seventies prints it had one main picture with two tiny clones on the bottom, ready for snipping and tucking into a wallet. It showed Robert, bright red in the face but wearing an expression of complete infant triumph, clutched by Red in an ill-fitting safari suit, obviously borrowed for the day, around whom everyone else was arranged in various states of strain.

Greg could tell immediately that Robert had been crying all day.

He held it next to the official photograph illustrating the piece – a very tight headshot of Rosetta and Brian and Red, all luminous and beaming, with Robert, enchantingly open-mouthed, between them – then looked again at Rosetta's private snap.

Apart from the many bottles of champagne littering the picture and the fact that there seemed to be a couple of well-known actresses in the background, it could have been any other suburban get-together.

'Why haven't I ever seen this?' he demanded. There was a vague feeling of having been swizzed in the back of his head. How much other visual evidence had Rosetta suppressed? 'I could have had hours of fun out of Robert with this.'

'Oh, he prefers Sue's version. The one where everyone comments on how beautiful and quiet he is in his Anita Crowther Indian christening dungarees.' Rosetta shook her head and took it off him. 'Look, there's the radiant mother,' pointing to herself wedged into what remained of the sofa once Red had made himself comfy. She looked catatonic with fatigue in her floor-length silk kaftan.

'Were you on smack at the time?' Greg enquired. 'Only you look as though you died about three days earlier and they just refreshed your make-up.'

She grimaced. 'That's what it felt like. But then there was no one around to tell me that having two babies in the space of fifteen months would do that to me.'

'Serves you right for being so quick to get back in the sack,' said Greg without thinking, then said, 'Sorry.'

Amazingly Rosetta didn't seem to have taken offence. Greg wished she would, just for once.

But she looked sad and patted his hand. 'I was *dreading* having you after that. But then you were the quietest and most amenable of them all.'

'Cheers,' Greg replied awkwardly. In a million years he would never relax into a conversation with his mother. For some reason, possibly autobiography-related or maybe inspired by seeing all her shoes all at once, she was in the kind of mood he barely associated with her and he didn't have a clue how she wanted him to react.

'So what do you want me to do with these?' he asked, indicating the box on his knee.

'Just go through them and pick out things you think would be interesting for the book.'

'But I don't know what you're going to write,' he protested. 'How am I meant to pick out the right ones?'

Rosetta smiled mysteriously. 'I rather thought I'd do it the other way round for a change,' she said. 'Between you and me, I'm having a bit of trouble getting started.' She lifted her hands and indicated the room around her. 'I mean, where *do* I start? What's the most important thing about me? *I* don't know. So you start with the pictures, then see what they say. I'd do it myself, but I know them too well now. I want you to look at them, since you haven't seen them before and you tell me which you think are the most interesting. After all, you're the professional photographer, darling.' Her smile deepened and she touched his hand with what almost felt like maternal pride.

So much so that Greg nearly forgot that she wanted him to do something for her.

'And the shoes?' he enquired with a raised eyebrow. 'Or was that just a ruse to get me over here?'

Rosetta looked around the room at the half-opened boxes and stray pairs of sandals and platforms and mules, scattered around the floor. It looked liked a decadent shoe fetishist's den of vice. 'No, I really did want you to photograph the shoes. I need them for research. Anita thought I should give some of them to the V & A costume department while I'm away. There's some exhibition on the styles of The Rock Years –' she put in the capital letters ironically '– she's lending a lot of her old pieces to.'

Greg conceded that bequeathing your shoes to the nation wasn't much worse than bequeathing a hall full of Ancient Greek knick-knacks. He checked his watch. Half two already. Amazing how quickly time passed when Rosetta wasn't being a pain in the arse. Then his heart thudded when he realized he didn't have long to get to High Street Kensington, especially at this time of day.

'Look, Rosetta, I have to go,' he said reluctantly. 'Can we do the rest of the shoes another time? I'm meeting . . . someone in Kensington.'

She raised her eyebrow. 'A girl?'

Greg flushed, unwilling to go through the whole avoiding-the-topic thing again but after Rosetta's unexpected revelations, he felt oddly obliged to be honest with her. 'Ye-ee-es.'

'A bride?'

'No.'

'A girlfriend?'

He considered. 'Sort of.'

Hmm, that felt too nice, didn't it?

He thought about saying, 'Robert's girlfriend, actually', but changed his mind and clutched the box to his chest. 'Thank you for these,' he said. 'I'll, er, have a look through and we can talk about them?'

Rosetta nodded and smiled. Greg noticed that she smiled without showing her teeth, even though they were now perfect.

Chapter Fourteen

Chelsea, 1970

Rosetta sat in front of her bedroom mirror, putting on her bridal face with a steady hand. It was the *only* thing about her that felt steady. But then she could apply eyeliner standing on her head – she'd been doing it since she was twelve, after all. In a funny way, she was glad to be able to do something that made a big show of her apparent nervelessness while inside she shook like a jelly.

As usual, she had an audience. But at least the record company hadn't sent it.

'You could have had a make-up artist, you know,' said Sue, picking at her bouquet of wild flowers as she sat, white knees firmly together on Rosetta's chaise longue. She sounded put-out. She looked put-out. 'Anita could have recommended someone really good, someone professional.'

'You mean, *I* could have had a make-up artist who could have done *you* at the same time.' Rosetta opened her mouth as she lashed on the mascara. No minimal bridal make-up was complete without loads of mascara, to run in photogenic streaks of appropriate emotion.

'I mean, there'll be cameras there, won't there?' Sue persisted. 'You want to look your best.'

'Sue, I keep telling you, it's a very quiet wedding. We didn't want anything dramatic. It's just . . .' Rosetta examined the array of cosmetics in front of her and picked out her blusher. She frowned at the little silver circle already appearing where it was worn through to the base. She'd only bought it three weeks ago. She'd been getting through a lot of blusher recently. 'It's just me and Brian.'

Rosetta filled a brush with soft raspberry shadow and circled it generously around her cheeks, trying to dispel the greenish pallor her skin had taken on. The early gorgeous bloom of pregnancy had vanished at about the same time as Brian had slipped the huge ruby engagement rock on her finger and John had flown off to Morocco with his guitar and tape recorder 'in search of inspiration for the new album'. Since then, Rosetta reflected with a twinge of regret, her skin had gone almost colourless next to her flaming hair, and she'd thrown up constantly. So far she'd managed to hide it, but there were only so many times you could rush away from a table in a crowded restaurant, especially when she knew so many people on the way to the loos.

'It's just going to be me and Brian. And a few close friends. Like you, darling,' she added in an attempt to distract Sue from the make-up issue.

But Sue clearly had the bit between her teeth.

'*Rosetta*,' she laughed in her most patronizing tone, 'I realize you *want* it to be *just you and Brian*, but didn't Paul McCartney want it to be just him and Linda? Honey, there's no such thing as a quiet register office do these days. There'll be photographers there, and journalists, and . . . all sorts of people.' A cat-like smile spread across her face at the thought of the attention she'd be getting, albeit second-hand, not to mention the scoop on the wedding pictures.

'*Sue*,' Rosetta contradicted her, 'there would be stampedes – but only if I were marrying Glynn.'

'Or John.' Sue gave her a significant look – Rosetta *still* hadn't set up the date as promised – and sighed heavily. 'Tell me why couldn't he come again? It's a real shame. I thought there might be some kind of bridesmaid's prerogative there . . .'

Rosetta pressed her tongue against her front teeth so the

sharpness matched the sharp stab of pain in her heart. But she kept her voice light and didn't look away from her reflection in the dressing-table mirror. In it, she could see Sue watching her for a reaction.

Rosetta turned round to make sure Sue saw her face clearly. 'And thank heaven I'm *not* marrying one of them!' she said, widening her eyes in mock horror. 'I'm telling you, Sue, if those little groupies that hang around the studio had to see Red squeezing his spots first thing, or Glynn checking the developing time on his Clairol Champagne Blonde, they wouldn't fantasize about getting on the bus after the gig! I've been worse than married to that lot for three years now and I am glad, *more glad than I can tell you*, that I'm marrying the one man in the outfit who uses proper shaving cream.' She turned back to the mirror and picked up a special highlighter powder that some magazine had sent her to test. 'And you can use that as a quote.'

Sue, who had been clandestinely changing the tape in her tiny dictaphone, fumbled the cassette guiltily.

'Just let me know if there's a photographer in the wardrobe, won't you, darling?' said Rosetta, dusting her cheekbones with pearlescent powder. She studied her various bridal grimaces. 'Want to be sure I give him my best surprised expression.'

'You don't need me to tell you. I thought you could smell photographers by now,' said Sue. She got up and fiddled with the fake laces on her knee-high boots, which were cutting into her calves something rotten. 'God, Rosetta, couldn't you have got married in about six months? Anita says hemlines are definitely coming down next season.'

'Anita always says that, darling. It's to make sure everyone comes back to the shop in search of nice long skirts. Anyway, there's nothing wrong with your legs. You look lovely.'

Rosetta was wearing a white lace tunic that finished halfway up her long thighs, teamed with high-heeled boots, made out of silvery crushed velvet. She looked like an ethereal principal boy. Sue was wearing a similar tunic in mint green satin, teamed with shiny PVC boots and ivy twined into her dark curls. She looked like a peapod, pea bulges and all. Anita had made both outfits – and reflected her loyalties accordingly, in Sue's opinion.

'Well, I don't see Anita wearing it.' Sue tugged at her skirt. 'Why didn't you ask her to be a bridesmaid?'

Rosetta cautiously looked at her in the mirror. It was written all over Sue's round face: say you picked me over Anita!

She buried her nose in the powder brush, and concentrated on the soft hairs tickling her nostrils. She had, in fact, asked Anita straight away – on the night Brian had proposed, partly to ensure that, having told someone the wedding was on, she wouldn't be able to back out. Anita had refused, claiming that she didn't believe in the social handcuffs of wedlock. But then she had to say that, since she had dumped the hapless André and was sleeping with the irresistible and very married lead guitarist from another band, much bigger than The End. Being Anita, though, she was getting away with it.

Rosetta looked at Sue again, bulging in exactly the same places as she had done in the tunic they'd worn in primary school, and her heart softened. Sue could be a cow, but then she always had been, and deep down, really deep down, she had a good heart. And since Anita was about as dependable as a white Christmas, Sue really was the best friend she had.

'Oh, I only wanted one bridesmaid. I wanted it to be really quiet,' Rosetta said. 'And it is a bit ridiculous, having more than one bridesmaid at a register office do. You're more of a witness, aren't you?'

'Guess so.' Sue looked pleased. 'Well, you could still have waited,' she said. 'Then John could have come back from Morocco.'

Rosetta's heart, which had only just stopped hammering, began skipping again. That was only one of a whole list of reasons she couldn't have waited. God, the guilt! Of all the things she never thought she'd do! She hadn't told Sue about the impending baby, and had no intention of doing so until the last minute. There would be time enough for intrusive 'at home' photo-features – Brian had already observed that a round of 'flower-child' shots would coincide brilliantly with the release of the second album. She'd even overheard him and Red discussing the possibility of using the baby on the cover.

'Oh no, no,' she said, picking up her eyelash curlers. 'No, it's much better to do it without all that press kerfuffle.'

Sue's face stretched in bewilderment. 'Rosetta! I can't believe you, of all people, actually *said* that! If you'd asked me to predict one thing about you three weeks ago, it would have been that when you and Brian finally got married it would have been orchestrated better than the *1812 Overture*.' She went back to stretching her boots with her pudgy fingers. 'I have to hand it to you, Rosetta, you certainly know how to surprise people.'

'Well.' Rosetta took a deep breath and picked up her coronet of roses and lowered it on to her head, adjusting it to get the right angle. To her horror, what had looked so pretty when the florist delivered it first thing now looked more and more like a crown of thorns as the moment came nearer. 'Sometimes it's good to surprise yourself. Remind yourself what you're really doing, instead of going down the usual tracks.'

'I mean to say,' Sue went on, apparently oblivious to the quick rise and fall of Rosetta's chest, 'you always wanted the spectacular romantic wedding, didn't you? I remember you saying at school how the groom would arrive in his own Rolls Royce, and you would have a long white dress and a diamond tiara and there'd be geese with blue bows round their necks wandering around in the churchyard, and . . .'

'Oh come on, Sue, that was ages ago!' said Rosetta. She fidgeted uncomfortably with her hair. 'That's what all little girls want. Didn't *you* want a wedding just like Princess Margaret's? I grew out of that when I was eleven!'

'You always had very specific plans,' said Sue meaningfully. 'And actually it isn't all that long ago.'

It's half a lifetime back! thought Rosetta, and her heart stopped beating for a second as she tried to remember back that far. Before the first thrills of sneaking out to the Crawdaddy Club, before Brian, before John, before this baby . . .

She squeezed her eyes shut. This wedding was the first of her plans that hadn't turned out at all as she'd intended. She wondered what Sue knew, whether she was driving at something.

'I suppose you've got *some* of that though,' said Sue. Rosetta opened her eyes and saw the naked eagerness to please in Sue's face.

'Which bit?' she said.

'The groom with his own Rolls Royce.' Sue giggled. 'Though that's not very right-on, is it? We're meant to be marrying for passion and freedom these days, not for status symbols. Though I bet you every single girl at St Mary's would kill for Brian and his bank book, rather than Red. And his little *black* book.' Rosetta noted that Sue snorted with the violence of someone recently dumped. Obviously she was trying to work her way round to John via the traditional groupie route. 'I mean, Red's got looks and money now, but how long will that last, the way he's going?'

'Who knows indeed?' Rosetta began fixing the coronet to her head with sharp-ended bobby pins. It hurt, but it was the only way it would stay on her poker-straight hair, according to her hairdresser. 'But he is the best man, so you might try to keep your predictions until after the speeches?'

'He's the *best* man?'

'As in, the best of a bad lot.'

Sue's eyes rolled like marbles behind the thick lenses of her glasses.

'Are you . . . Er, did you . . . bring your contact lenses?' Rosetta asked gingerly.

Sue's hand went instinctively to the bridge of her nose and she pushed the heavy specs up defensively. 'I did. They're in my bag. Only I'll wait till the last minute until I put them in, if it's all right with you.'

'Fine with me,' said Rosetta lightly. 'Do you want me to do your make-up?'

Sue squinted at Rosetta's fresh and shining face. She had just taken about an hour to put on make-up that made her look as if she wasn't wearing any make-up at all.

'Yes, please,' she said grudgingly. 'As long as you don't forget that the purpose of the brides*maid* is not to look virginal, but to click with an usher.'

Rosetta began to reorder all the cosmetics on her dressing-table while her mind worked to calm itself down. Reconstructing Sue's face wasn't just an act of mercy – it would at least keep her quiet for twenty minutes while she prepared herself for the biggest performance of her life. She could imagine at this second what John must feel before going on stage – that weird nervous sensation of having to be the person that everyone else expects to see, knowing that that person is you and yet not you at the same time.

Don't think of John. Not today. That's part of your old life that you're leaving behind.

She drew in a breath and squirted some foundation on to her palm. Sue shut her eyes accommodatingly.

This is the right thing to do, Rosetta told herself. Without doubt, *this is the right thing to do*. Getting married will sort you out. It'll get you back on track. It'll put some order in your life and whatever stupid crushes explode in your head, you'll just have to work within the rules of marriage. Marriage is a partnership, not a fairy tale. And Brian and I are *lucky* because we knew that from the start.

John had disappeared the night after Brian announced the engagement in the ballroom of the echoing and damp mansion house. Somehow two crates of Krug had arrived just in time to celebrate the happy news. John had had one glass, then had gone to the loo and not come back. In the drunken high spirits that followed, no one but Rosetta noticed he'd gone, and it wasn't the time or place to draw attention to it. She didn't believe he'd really been planning to travel, as Brian claimed, and she felt underhand that she hadn't been able to tell him herself. But Brian hadn't given her the chance, dragging the band and the technicians out of the makeshift studios, and anyway, she wasn't sure she *could* have told him. The words might not have come out of her mouth if she'd been forced to look into those brown eyes and say it.

So, for want of a stronger will, here she was, about to marry Brian, who was, she reminded herself, a good, decent, handsome, hard-working and ambitious man who she really did care for a great deal.

And that was the hardest part – Rosetta truly didn't love Brian any less because of what she felt for John, but knowing how she felt about John made her realize that this was all she *could* feel for Brian, and it wasn't anything like the dizzying, euphoric rush she felt when she and John just sat and talked.

Let alone did anything else.

Rosetta smoothed foundation over Sue's shiny skin with a steady hand. There was still time to pull out, she knew that. If she was really the independent, glamorous girl-of-the-world she made out she was in the interviews, she would get in her stupidly fast sports-car, drive to Heathrow and demand to be put on the first plane to Morocco. And they would do it for her, no question about that. There she would find John, tell him that she couldn't throw away her life on a man she didn't love quite enough, and sod the band, their happiness was more important. He would write a song about it that would go to number one and they could live the rest of their lives in ecstasy in Tangier. That's what Marianne Faithfull would do, she knew that.

But Rosetta was sharp enough to know that if she ran away from the wedding and flew off to John, she would have all the press attention anyone could ever want, maybe even becoming more famous than the band. And Sue would love her for ever for the scoop. But she wasn't sure that she was brave enough to take it all on, and for that she hated herself. It was one thing to pretend she was trendy and with-it in photo-spreads, when she knew different, but somehow she couldn't expose herself to that kind of personal attack and all the guilt and shame she would have to live with, surrounded by the wreckage of the lives she'd trampled over to get what she wanted. John, of course, would emerge looking irresistible and romantic, Brian would look dumb but tragic and she would be branded a cheating, if glamorously awful, whore.

That was without the emotional carnage she would wreak all round. It would be like throwing a grenade into the tour-bus.

And of course there was the baby now, too.

The lead band tightened around her temples. I'm just a big phoney, she thought, miserably. So if I'm not brave enough to go for what I want, I should take the bourgeois route and bloody well be happy with it.

'Oi!' yelped Sue. 'Are you trying to make me look like Looby-Loo?'

Rosetta looked down and saw that she'd turned Sue's cheeks an angry red with blusher.

'God, sorry,' she said. 'Sorry, darling.' She hunted on the dressing-table for some cotton wool to blot it off.

'Were you thinking of your vows?' asked Sue disingenuously.

'Yes. Yes, I was, in a way.' Rosetta's hands hovered over the little boxes and jars on her dressing-table. Did she have any Rescue Remedy left? Or would a couple of Mandrax be better?

What was that drug they used to give soldiers in their tea

to stop them thinking about sex? Bromide? How much of that would it take to blot John out of her mind for ever?

'Good.' Unexpectedly Sue's voice turned diamond-hard and Rosetta froze like a burglar caught in the spotlight as their eyes met in the mirror. 'Because Brian is a *good man*, Rosemarie, and there are only about three of them in the whole of London. So don't even *think* about messing him around.'

Rosetta creased her forehead in amazement, hoping that it would look as if she was dumbfounded by the mere suggestion that she might not be grateful for a man like Brian, rather than dumbstruck by Sue's perceptiveness. Maybe that was why she was so good at winkling out killer interviews from people – she really didn't look like the type to be so observant. And yet . . . Rosetta shivered.

'The trouble with lucky people,' said Sue heavily, 'is that they don't know when they're lucky.'

'Until their luck runs out,' said Rosetta.

Sue arched an eyebrow.

'Don't,' said Rosetta. 'I know *exactly* how lucky I am, thank you.'

'I don't think you do,' replied Sue.

There was a short silence. Rosetta couldn't think what she should say, so she said nothing and looked wounded. Which coincided nicely with the way she now felt inside.

'How are we getting to the register office?' Sue asked eventually.

'Um, by cab.' Her mother was meeting them there. Rosetta had overruled Brian's suggestion that she spent her last night in Richmond; there was absolutely no point in starting her married life incandescent with suppressed rage.

'Must be at times like this that you miss your dad, I suppose?' asked Sue delicately.

'Not really,' Rosetta lied airily. She picked up a green eye shadow and began loading up a brush. 'Might miss him if I could remember what it was like to have him there in the first place.' He hadn't featured much in her earlier wedding plans either. 'I never wanted to be *given away* like some old car,' she said passionately. 'Ever. There's just no nice way of looking at that.'

There was a long ring at the external doorbell and Sue checked her watch. 'Jesus, Rosetta, the cab! We're late!' The double-strength American diet pills she'd been knocking back – to little effect – for the past three months had made her more twitchy than normal.

Rosetta frowned. 'No, we're not. The car isn't due until half twelve.'

Sue looked at her in the mirror. 'Then who is it?'

'I don't know.'

'Well, I can't go like this, can I?' said Sue, pointing to her one made-up eye. 'Go on. It must be for you. Flowers or something. Or a telegram?'

Rosetta's heart hammered so hard she thought she was about to die. Her brain could only think of one thing: John had come back! She might be too weak to go with her ideals, but maybe *John* had managed to find a way round his conscience. And now it was up to her to match that.

Her legs suddenly felt boneless, and she grabbed the back of Sue's chair for support as the weight of the moment hit her.

'Go on!' urged Sue. 'It might be someone from Jennifer's Diary!'

'OK.' Rosetta took a very deep yoga breath, and started to walk across the room, trying to draw some confidence from her high heels. At least she would look beautiful when he saw her, not the hopeless flake she might have been.

The doorbell pealed again, three rings.

'No, wait!' yelled Sue, as Rosetta started down the narrow stairs. 'Stop! It could be Brian, it could be such bad luck for him to . . .'

Rosetta ran down the final seven stairs and flung open the door with her heart beating in her mouth.

It was a delivery boy from the florist down the road. He held a tight bunch of red rosebuds wrapped in ivy.

'Rosetta Martin?' he asked, then blushed when he realized it really was her, answering her own bell.

Mute with disappointment, Rosetta nodded and took the flowers, shutting the door with her shoulder and leaning back on it to open the envelope. The one day out of her entire life when getting roses would be a *disappointment*.

There was no message on the card, but Rosetta didn't need to see one – she knew that Brian wouldn't have sent her *red* roses, not on their wedding day.

Maybe that was the point: there was nothing to say.

Her breath was coming in short, ragged gasps and she knew she was about to cry. Thank God it would look appropriate. With a supreme effort, she picked up the intercom at the bottom of the stairs and dialled her flat.

Sue picked up the phone after seven rings.

'I've finished my other eye,' she said crossly, 'but it doesn't match. I look like someone out of *A Clockwork Orange*.'

'I'll do it in the car. Can you bring my white bag down, please?' said Rosetta. She put a hand over the receiver and took a couple of deep breaths. 'I want to go in my own car, I think. I don't want to wait any more.'

Chapter Fifteen

High Street Kensington, 2001

Greg had agreed to meet Tanith at High Street Kensington tube for their Reclothe Greg Mission. At the time, feigning serious disinterest to disguise his real excitement, he had suggested High Street Ken on the grounds that, one, there were plenty of coffee bars and so on to leaven the shopping intensity and, two, he didn't know anyone who might see him trying on embarrassing clothes. Tanith had accepted this with good humour, but Greg had regretted it as soon as the words left his mouth: being spotted with Tanith by anyone who knew him (outside his immediate family) could only be a good thing.

There was something about shopping that brought out a violent non-cooperation in him.

Even with Rosetta's prying, Greg managed to be ten minutes early – a small, private compensation for his fake reluctance, since he knew Tanith would be on time and therefore wouldn't notice. He waited for her by the fountain outside the Tube station as arranged, shuffling from one foot to another and trying not to stare at the ridiculously erect nipples on the plastic models in the window of H & M. Greg felt a faint sense of paranoia rising in the back of his head: did girls' nipples *really* look like that? Were there some girls you could meet that had nipples that doubled as coat hooks? Was this yet another piece of vital information no one had thought to pass on to him?

He checked his watch. The Beetle was in the car-park round the corner – it had lights hidden in the boot, ready for a quick portrait job this evening, some fledgling 'R 'n' B covers and two slow dances' wedding band that Maggie knew. Greg hoped that Tanith's transformation process wasn't going to take longer than two hours, or else the parking was going to cost more than the clothes. Besides which, Maggie had insisted on him getting changed before he met her mates. That boded badly.

He saw Tanith coming before she spotted him: she was striding down through the crowd in a short camel coat, talking briskly into her mobile, her eyes flicking back and forth at the people in her way, as though she couldn't stop auditioning.

He waved tentatively at her.

It always surprised Greg to see how short Tanith was when he saw her in the context of other people – in his head and over the phone, she gave the impression of being about six feet tall, and yet when you set her up next to normal-sized people it was clear she couldn't be more than about five feet three. It also amazed him that she could look as though she had just materialized out of a magic bottle, yet when she opened her mouth, all you could hear was a tough-talking city trader – an effect she could apparently conjure up at will. It frequently looked and sounded as if she was being dubbed.

'Greg!' She waved when she saw him, and gave him a big smile, but carried on her acidic phone conversation as she steered him out towards Gap. Clearly, the conversation hadn't started in such needly tones, but Tanith was hanging on in there like a Doberman.

'Well, do you think there'll be anyone there who could *pass* for sixteen?' she was snapping. 'OK, seventeen?'

Greg tried to remember when he had last been able to pass for sixteen. Never, probably.

'What are you, a school or a cotton mill?' she demanded. 'How hard are you *working* these children?'

Tanith stopped and leaned against a wall to rub her eyes, and Greg, his head still crowded with visions of his own dark and droopy teen years, walked on a couple of paces alone before he realized. When he turned back, fighting his way through a sea of people with some difficulty, she was scrabbling around in her bag for something, snapping out questions all the while.

'It doesn't matter about the hair, we can work around that,' she was saying persuasively. 'But she has to look young enough.'

Pause.

'I know.'

Pause. Tanith forced her tongue over her upper lip and frowned.

'I *know* there are regulations, but ... But ...' Tanith's eyes squeezed shut and then opened wide. She crossed them, perhaps for Greg's benefit, but despite all these facial contortions, she only succeeded in looking about as deranged as the Take It Easy Caramel Rabbit, and she still sounded well on the pleasant side of brisk. 'No, please listen to what I'm saying to you ... Shut up! Shut up! Now, will you please *listen* to me? I don't *want* her to be able to sing the aria from *Madame Butterfly* and I don't *care* if she's the High Barnet Gymnastics Champion. All I *need* is a very pretty teenage-looking teenager who's done a few school plays. That's *it*. The rest is make-up, believe me.'

There was another pause in which Tanith pulled an apologetic face at Greg and handed him a list, scrawled on blue notepaper torn from her Filofax.

He studied it with some trepidation while she carried on barking her orders, sounding like a sergeant major stocking a brothel.

It seemed to be a list of clothes. Whether it was a list of clothes she expected him to have, or a list of clothes she intended him to buy today, he couldn't tell. Tanith had quick, cross handwriting, which sometimes slipped into capital letters mid-word, creating the subliminal effect of making the reader feel inexplicably shouted at. Greg preferred her e-mails, which she liberally splashed with asterisks and smiley faces.

Her list was pretty specific, as he'd expected. Did women really expect you to have *five* pairs of jeans? He blinked. Did they come round and count them, or something?

Greg flinched at the number – and specification – of boxer shorts he was meant to have. He didn't do boxers. He wasn't even sure if his underwear had a generic description name. Most of it didn't have the label in any more. Most of it, now he came to examine it in his mind, had been stolen from the laundry basket and wasn't even necessarily his.

Good quality jogging pants.

One cashmere pullover – black, or dove grey.

But he did have a dinner jacket, he thought, rallying. A really good one, a Savile Row one.

That didn't seem to be on Tanith's list.

Neither did rugby shirts, of which he had three, worn to the gym in rotation.

A sick feeling settled in the base of his stomach, as he read down to the list of clothes Tanith wanted him to chuck out to make room for the new stuff.

No rugby shirts (unless worn-in school one and/or cute-looking)!

No amusing ties!

No short-sleeved shirts (no exceptions)!

'God, you'd think I was some kind of white slave trader,' said Tanith, fiercely stuffing her mobile back in her bag. 'Either they want their girls to be in this film, or they don't?'

'Mmm,' said Greg. His eyes were still running up and down the list. The Nots were scarier than the Must-Haves.

Tanith took him by the arm and steered him down the street, talking into his shoulder the whole time. 'I didn't know what you had in your wardrobe already, so I made a sort of checklist. I mean, if you've got some of this stuff, then ignore it. Unless you think you need to replace it. I might have gone a bit overboard, sorry. I went through Robert's wardrobe and worked from that. Not that he's anything to model yourself on, unless you're planning on seducing someone in the style of a 1940s film, but he does have all the basics, you have to give him that.'

She leaned over and scanned the list. 'I mean, sorry, you don't really *need* a macintosh. But you can't have too many pairs of jeans, I find – just from a merely practical point of view – it means you'll always have a clean pair to put on if you have a date, and we are approaching this from the point of view of getting you more dates, aren't we?'

'Er, yes,' said Greg weakly, as Tanith placed a firm hand in the small of his back and shoved him into Gap.

'Hello!' said the greeter on the door, bathing them in a professional smile of welcome. He had a Janet Jackson headset and reminded Greg of the best man at last weekend's Fulham wedding, the one that Maggie had confidently assured him was unusually lucky in love and had in fact ended up with a mysterious and copious nosebleed somewhere between the ceremony and reception, causing untold complications for Greg's group shots.

'Hi!' said Tanith. She returned the beam unselfconsciously and breezed past, heading straight for the biggest display of rainbow-coloured shirts, none of which, Greg knew right now, would do anything for his naturally sallow complexion. Suddenly he felt wilfully miserable. He shuffled past in her wake, wishing he could do something about his moods. They seemed to take him over like aliens, even when he wanted to be light and witty with every atom in his body. Sometimes he felt as if he, like his mother, were trapped for ever in the body of a teenager.

'Don't you find it faintly sinister in here?' he demanded, tweaking at a jaunty display of baseball caps, all of which had a G for Greg on the front. 'I mean, why do they want to dress us all like the cast of *Friends*? Is it marking us out for when the revolution comes?'

'What *are* you talking about?' asked Tanith. 'They just want us all to have access to casual, easy-care clothing for when we're having coffee with our mates in Starbucks.'

'I don't have any mates. And those I do can't afford Starbucks.' Greg had no idea why he said this. Maggie spent at least half her disposable income in there, trying to eyeball men she thought looked like photography students.

'Are we going to get everything here?' he asked suddenly. 'If I let you, then can we go home?'

'Greg. Calm down, will you?' Tanith started to fill her arms with wool and cashmere mix sweaters. 'Why *are* you so anti-shopping?'

'My mother.'

'Is *everything* about your mother with you lot?'

'Mostly.' He picked up a shirt and looked for the label. Polyester. Urgh. 'But don't tell her, she'll just be pleased.'

'But shopping?' said Tanith. 'Didn't she leave you with a nanny while she did that?'

'We didn't really have nannies. She liked to take us with her, for company.' Greg fingered a polo shirt with some suspicion. 'I don't think many of her girlfriends liked going shopping with someone so thin and famous. So she took us, to dilute the "bad mother" effect. And of all four of us, I reckon I clocked up more shopping-with-Rosetta hours than the rest.'

'So you should be good at it, then.'

Greg shot her a baleful look. 'She dragged me round like a slightly bigger than normal carrier bag and left me in a pile with all the other bags while she tried stuff on. If I said anything at all, she set the assistants on me.'

'Well, then, that's quality time, isn't it?' said Tanith. She held a red jumper up to him to see if it went, then tactfully returned it to the pile when it didn't. 'Trying to involve you in her favourite things.'

'I only have to hear the distant ting of a cash register to want to go home. THIS MINUTE,' said Greg.

In fact, standing in the main foyer of the huge new Gap, he could feel his brain zoning itself out even now.

Am I really here? How can I tell this isn't a dream? What does it feel like breathing?

Greg slowed his breathing down and unfocused his eyes until he was distracted by the familiar sound of hangers being shoved rapidly back and forth on a rail by a practised female hand.

'Greg? I said what colours do *you* like?'

He muttered something about her choosing whatever suited him, and the rattling stopped abruptly.

'Greg, work with me here. This shopping is all about *you*,' she said. 'You big fool.'

There was something in Tanith's voice that poked Greg in the stomach – was it tenderness? Or pity? Or something like that? He looked up and she was staring at him, her forehead wrinkled with concern, wrinkles which vanished as soon as he met her eyes.

'Call it a casting director thing,' she said lightly. 'But I don't actually see you in the role you're playing at the moment. There are too many of you rocking this weird Greek tragedy vibe for my liking. Now. Have you ever thought about lilac?'

Tanith promised Greg that she would get everything sorted out by five o'clock, at which point he could leave, regardless of what stage they'd reached. Which was fair enough, Greg thought, since he was pretty sure he couldn't go much longer than that without embarrassing himself somehow in front of her.

Consequently, she was speed-shopping him with the brutal efficiency of someone on a sixty second trolley-dash.

'Do you want some help in there?' she yelled through the changing-room curtains, as she had done every three minutes since he'd gone in.

Greg allowed his mind to flicker briefly over the tempting image of Tanith 'helping' him do up the ninth pair of jeans – 'button-fly only, zips equals Paul Calf' – but pushed it away. It wouldn't do for her to see his pants. Thank God she'd just given his waist a cursory glance and thrown a pile of multi-coloured boxers in the basket.

'Greg, are you going to show me what those jeans look like on?' The curtains twitched and he hastily finished buttoning up the latest linen shirt.

Tanith's head appeared round the curtain. She smiled at him in the mirror. She looked proud. 'Well, look at you! You look amazing!'

'Yeah, they're, er . . . all right, I suppose.'

'Sorry you had to try on so many, but it takes a while to find exactly the right fit for jeans,' Tanith explained. 'You can't tell just by looking. You know, bit like finding the right woman.'

Greg didn't believe this, but kept his mouth shut. All jeans moulded to you if you kept them for long enough. Quicker if you minimized the washing aspect. Fabric softener could put you back years.

Women, on the other hand, he didn't have the first idea about.

'But you're lucky,' she was saying, scrutinizing him from a lower angle. 'You've actually got a really nice arse. Robert spends *hours* playing squash but his is just hopeless, really. No definition. Looks like a wide-screen telly in jeans. Don't tell him I told you so. But you've either got it or you haven't, and you have. Patrick's was great too, but a bit more . . .' She stuttered to a halt, seeing Greg's flush appear at her words. 'Oops. Sorry, was that too much information?' she added, a light blush appearing on her own face.

Tanith dropped her gaze and Greg wondered where he had picked up the habit of feeling embarrassed for other people and then making *them* embarrassed to have embarrassed *him*. No one had ever said not to mention Tanith and

Patrick – she certainly hadn't banned the topic – but it wasn't really done, he supposed, to look as if he was angling for information, because he didn't know how much she'd told Robert, or how much they ever discussed it. At the back of his mind, he was flattered that Tanith felt relaxed enough to slip up and mention Patrick. His stomach gave a twist of guilty desire at her vulnerable expression. It was unusual to see Tanith look so embarrassed with herself. She was normally so grown-up and responsible.

She was normally standing next to the most grown-up and responsible man in London, for a start.

'Well, it's good that you've got that professional detachment about people's arses,' he said, attempting to sound casual. 'I suppose you can just look at them and think, "Oh, that would be nice in a pair of Regency breeches, buns of steel like that." Or, "Nice packet – must remember him for the Nijinsky biopic." And just be totally pro about it.'

Tanith looked up with the cheeky grin back on her face. 'Oh yeah,' she retorted, 'in much the same way that you must look at bridesmaids and think, "Maybe I should do some individual shots of these ladies, give them a fair chance away from the bride."'

'I don't *do* bridesmaids.' He could feel the flush spreading down his neck, which he knew only made him look guilty.

Tanith patted the small of his back. 'Well, I don't *do* Regency breeches.'

There was a pause in which Greg's heart bounced painfully around his chest cavity and he wished she'd patted a bit lower. He wondered if she had this effect on Robert.

'Problem?' she asked.

Greg swallowed. 'Do you want me to try these other jeans on, then?'

'Oh, no, no, no, those ones look gorgeous,' she said. 'Really nice. I could use you in this new film – we need lots of young men in tight jeans.' Her bright eyes snapped back to meet his in the mirror with a suggestive smile and Greg felt himself smiling back at her without actively being aware of meaning to.

God, she's cute, thought Greg. His stomach finished its loop-the-loop guilt manoeuvre and plummeted into his groin.

'Are you interested in auditioning?' she added.

'In what sense of the word?'

'Well, in *all* senses of the word?'

Greg's mind raced around the potential metaphors and his smile vanished instantly: he saw it wiped off his face in the mirror. *Shit.* Did she know? Had she read his mind? He felt the sweat prickle in the armpits of the new shirt, which just made him panic even more.

For a second or two he struggled to decide which was worse: Tanith knowing he had a crush on her, or Tanith not knowing he had a crush on her and politely, if inadvertently, telling him to forget it.

The complications of it all made his head spin in the over-heated changing rooms, where the strip-lighting now seemed to be bringing out his spots, lilac shirts or not.

The alarm clock on Tanith's mobile phone bleeped the *Star Wars* theme from somewhere deep inside her bag. 'Five o'clock, time's up! Let's go and have a coffee,' said Tanith brightly. 'You can wear your new latte outfit!'

They sat in one of the little booths in Coffee Republic, surrounded by plastic bags full of cotton shirts, and fresh jeans, and soft new T-shirts. Not all of them were white. None of them had slogans.

'It's just the basics,' Tanith had said reassuringly as the assistant folded them all up into squares at the cash desk. 'You don't have to wear it all at once, you know, mix and match with your own pieces. You don't want girls to think that you work at Gap and you've just popped out for a sandwich.'

Greg wasn't sure whether any of his clothes could really be called pieces. Although he did have that dinner jacket.

He stirred the herbal tea bag, watching it spread green slicks through the hot water, and squeezed it against the side of his cup. 'Do you really think of me as a Gap boy?' He tried to keep the pleading out of his voice.

'Er . . . not really. But we needed a shop that did cheap jeans, T-shirts and shirts all in one place. Once you've got an idea of what suits you and what colours to go for, then you can go wherever you want.' Tanith dropped a tube of sugar into her coffee, stirred briskly, and pressed some buttons on her mobile phone.

Greg felt touched that she'd switched it off in the first place while they were shopping.

'Sorry, just switching my phone off,' she said, studying it for new scratches. 'Never works round here anyway. Someone told me Princess Diana had a signal jammer installed at Kensington Palace.'

'Really?'

'Maybe. Anyway, Rob's been leaving messages about . . .' She rolled her eyes, as if she couldn't be bothered to explain the details. 'I think I'm going to be "on the Underground" for half an hour, if you follow me. I do love him, but you know what he's like when he gets a bee in his bonnet.'

'Tanith, do you miss Patrick?' said Greg, before he knew what he was saying.

Surprisingly, Greg thought, for such a personal and much-thought-but-never-articulated family question, Tanith didn't go off on one. Maybe that was the unforeseen bonus of being the idiot savant brother.

Instead she replaced the phone in her bag and tapped the wooden coffee stirrer thoughtfully against her perfect front teeth and said, 'Yes. I do miss him, sort of. Sometimes. How funny you should ask. I thought you were all politely ignoring it.'

'How do you mean?' asked Greg evasively.

'Well . . .' She smiled. 'Come on. It's such a weird coincidence, me going out with two of you, and no one ever remarks on it! Like I deliberately came down to London to seek out Patrick's brother as part of some elaborate Jacobean revenge tragedy. It was just a mad coincidence, honestly, but you all seem to want to make it into something far more dramatic – isn't that why no one ever talks about it?'

Greg stared at her. 'Actually, you've got a point there. Sorry.'

Tanith shook her head with amusement. 'Just goes to show how much you're dragging me into this bizarre way of thinking you all have. But, no, to answer your question, I don't *miss him* miss him, because first of all, I'm with Robert, who is a much more relaxing man to be with, despite his bees, and secondly, the things I liked about him are sort of family traits you all have.'

'Yeah-right!' said Greg disbelievingly. He fidgeted in his seat. 'We're about as different as it's possible to be.'

'Ah, *no*. You are all *very much* the same, I'm telling you, and I've had more opportunity than most to reach that conclusion,' she replied. 'OK, so you have different hair and stuff. And you're not as much of a psycho as Patrick. And Robert's more sensible than the rest of you put together. But . . .' She shrugged and helped herself to the icing Greg had been saving until last on his carrot cake. 'It's not all about eye colour, is it?'

'Don't give me that girl bollocks,' retorted Greg, unhappily watching her eat his icing. He could remember having this conversation with Flora, and being happily glib about the others and how unlike they were, but with Tanith – it felt very different. Like he couldn't lie to her about what he really thought. 'If it isn't about eye colour, and all down to our fabulous family personality, then how come Barney is fighting them off with a shitty stick and I'm . . . not?'

'Because Barney has a cashmere pullover in black *and* dove grey.' Tanith sipped her coffee without leaving a trace of lipstick on the cup. 'I'm joking, of course.'

'Well? There has to be more to it than just that. Doesn't there?'

'No, not really. It's more to do with . . . knowing what you've got. If you wrote down all that you've got going for you, and all Barney's got going for him, he wouldn't get a look in. On paper.'

'Meaning?' Greg knew what she meant, but he wanted to hear it come out of her mouth.

'Meaning,' Tanith rolled her eyes as if she thought it was unnecessary to state such obviousness, 'you're a successful photographer in your twenties, with your own flat, own car and a degree in Fine Art. Barney is a full-time slacker who doesn't know what he wants to do with his life, who still lives at home, effectively, and who behaves like someone who's seen *Breakfast at Tiffany's* one time too many. He lives in his own sit-com, Greg.'

'Be fair, he did pick that up from Rosetta,' Greg pointed out. 'And at least while he's living at home, it's a co-production.'

'But you see what I mean? You just don't see any of what you've got going for you as an advantage. Character is *not* genetic. It's what you *do* with your life. For some reason, you see it all as evidence that you're old and past-it. And you're not, are you?'

Greg ignored this by fishing out his teabag and splashing the cuff of his new shirt. 'Do you have any idea what it's like growing up with three other brothers? It's like being in The Beatles. Everyone wants to label you so there's some way of telling you apart – Patrick's the mystical one, Barney's the cute one, Robert's the clever one, I'm . . .'

'The funny one?' Tanith raised her eyebrow.

'The *other* one.' He sighed. 'I love them, but please don't ever tell me I'm like them.'

'You should think yourself lucky to have such a great gene pool,' said Tanith. 'You bunch of dark-eyed, pale-skinned, creative lanky bastards. All I got from my family

was weak teeth, a bad temper and a susceptibility to varicose veins.'

Greg didn't meet her eyes. This was where his big suspicion came in. And he didn't believe she had varicose veins,
for one thing. 'Yeah, but think of it as genetic *Double or
Drop*,' he said. 'You want a Scalextric and the *Girls' World*?
Well, there you go but here's three cabbages too.'

Tanith looked puzzled.

'With us it's like, you want your mother's eyes and snake-
charming personality? OK, well, you have to have your dad's
hairy back and addictive tendencies.'

'You've got a hairy back?'

'Figuratively speaking.' Greg's face adopted its signature
raspberry flush around the neck. He was unused to talking
about his brothers to someone who actually knew them. It
meant he couldn't tell half the usual stories.

Tanith realized he'd said more than he meant to, and she
felt an older sister instinct to spare his embarrassment. Even
though there was nothing he could tell her about the myriad
problems and failings of the Mulligans as a family that she
hadn't already heard from Robert.

'What did Robert win?' she asked, to spare the knots Greg
was tying himself into on the chair. 'Apart from the hairy
back and the short legs, which I already know about.'

'Oh, he got Dad's business brain, and Rosetta's inability to
understand the word no. But he also kind of lost out on the
looks thing. Well, I don't mean he's . . . I just mean, he's . . .
well . . .'

'He's not Barney, no. And you?'

Greg gave a self-deprecating shrug. 'Don't know. Dad's
irresistibility to the opposite sex? Rosetta's business sense?
Not a lot. I tend to prove Robert's theory about Dad.' He
stopped, and looked very unsure.

'Robert has a lot of theories,' said Tanith evenly. She
started to massage her cuticles, and didn't meet his eye. It
was the best way to get shy men to talk, not look at them.

There was something of the nervous collie dog about Greg. 'Mostly about natural selection and the master race. He gets a lot of them off the Internet. Go on, you can't shock me, hit me with another.'

'He doesn't think Dad's – Brian's – really our father,' Greg blurted out.

Tanith looked at Greg with her unreadable audition face. 'You really believe that? After all you've just said to me?'

Why was it, Greg wondered, that it seemed really easy to tell someone like Flora that kind of thing, and yet when it came to talking to Tanith, it was . . . suddenly much harder? He pushed away the tight sensation which pressed across his chest and tried to look blasé about it. Like he imagined Rosetta would in the same circumstances.

Tanith mentally revised the collie dog image – Greg was more like one of those inside-out jellyfish, or a see-through telephone where you could see where all the wires went to.

'He doesn't think Brian's your *dad*?' she repeated. 'In what way?'

'The usual way?' Greg went shifty, an expression Tanith was very familiar with, though she didn't think it was the moment to point out the fraternal resemblance. He started to back-pedal. 'Oh, just the way you put two and two together in big families,' he said, a bit too airily. 'None of us . . . ever thought that Brian was our dad. I mean, none of us *look* particularly like him, we're nothing like each other, and Rosetta was always going out with . . . other people, and . . . oh God, you've read the papers from that time. It was all just free love and dope and tour buses. And she was in charge of it all. You know what it was like.'

'Not really,' said Tanith. 'I grew up near Chorley. *Was* it like that?'

Greg flushed. 'Well, from what I read in the papers.' He went quiet, then said, 'But how would we know? She packed us off to boarding-school for most of it.'

Tanith was silent for a second or two, watching his face.

They were truly incredible as a family, truly incredible. It was as if they had no normality sensors. It was as if they couldn't see that they were *all* the spitting image of Brian and Rosetta.

'Is that why Robert's so mad about her writing this book? He thinks it's all going to come out?'

He nodded. Then shook his head. 'Well, I don't know, but yeah . . . I'd guess so. I know I'm . . . kind of interested in what she'll say.'

'But Greg!' Tanith protested. 'He looks just *like* Brian! They even have the same *hairline*!'

Greg returned her gaze steadily until she said, very carefully, 'OK, so you had an odd childhood. But I used to believe I'd been adopted, because my parents were just nice, normal, boring people and I wanted to be the love child of an Olympic show jumper and a teenage princess. But you seemed to spend your childhood *doing* the kind of things we were all dreaming about. So why can't you accept that sometimes things *are* just as normal as they seem on the outside?'

Greg flicked a look from under his long eyelashes that she couldn't quite place. 'Did Patrick ever say much about what it was like growing up?'

Tanith shook her head. 'He didn't like talking about his family. Which is ironic, since it would seem he's the one topic of conversation guaranteed to kick things off round Rosetta's dining-table.'

'Well, there you go,' said Greg darkly.

'There you go what?'

'There you go, doesn't that tell you something? Like, it wasn't all getting backstage passes and free ice-cream. You're very lucky you're not embroiled in the whole sorry mess that is the Mulligan family. Run away, little girl, run away before it's too late. Before Robert gets that ring on your finger. Because his view of normal marriage won't be anything like what you have in mind, believe me!'

Instantly, an image of Robert swam up in the back of

Tanith's mind; Robert sitting in a very expensive restaurant in town last week, dropping huge hints into the soup about getting married, but – typically Robert – refusing to come right out and say it before he had definite assurances that she would say yes.

'I think you're very wrong there. Robert's view of marriage is about as traditional as you could imagine.' Tanith took a bigger sip of coffee than she meant to and scalded the back of her throat. She hadn't said yes at all. In fact she had played scandalously dumb all evening, until he'd suggested that she must be going down with flu or something, and she'd agreed with the embarrassing swiftness of someone spotting a dog to blame their flatulence on.

It was amazing, really, that someone with such a free-wheeling background could be so determined to impose traditional orders on his life.

Or maybe it wasn't.

'How long has Robert thought this?' she asked. 'That you don't have the same dad? Is that what he thinks – different dads for all of you? Does he have a list of possibilities?'

Greg raised a wintry smile. 'Oh, I think he has a shortlist. I know several rock-stars he's bagged for their genes, not that he can prove anything. No, he's thought this for ages, you know what it's like.'

'No, I *don't* know, actually. I've always been pretty sure about my mum and dad.' She always forgot that even though Robert and Greg were the relatively normal ones, they weren't exactly your run-of-the-mill latchkey kids. 'Greg,' she said carefully, 'have you ever thought what this says about your mother? And how she might feel about hearing you say this?'

'The woman who told us to call her Rosetta because she wanted to be defined by her own terms and not by her capacity to bear children?'

'Your mother—'

'Who woke us up in the morning to show us the early

edition pictures of her and most of Britain's top lead guitarists emerging from Tramp at all hours?'

'OK, OK, so she wasn't exactly the most conventional parent. But this was the sixties, wasn't it?'

'The seventies,' Greg corrected her. 'Her excuse was Feminism, though she does throw in The Drugs and The Way Things Were Then occasionally. Do you *know* what it's like to have virtually no happy snaps of you and your brothers at the zoo, but to have seventeen albums full of press cuttings about you learning French on a tour-bus?'

He snorted and looked out of the window. 'And that's not the only thing we learned on a tour-bus, I can tell you.'

Tanith stirred the dregs of her coffee and tried to assimilate the various spinning strands of information in her head without letting the disbelief show on her face too much. Why did this always happen when she tried to probe into the Mulligan family – everything appeared more or less as normal but when she touched stuff it all slid sideways. Could Robert *really* believe that about his mother? He'd said some fairly unbelievable things about her in the past, but this . . .

And more interestingly, wondered Tanith, sneaking a covert glance over the top of her mug, could Greg actually be more of a grown-up and less of a comedy younger brother than she'd previously thought? It had been a bit of a shock seeing him come out of that changing-room looking like he was related to Patrick, rather than Robert. Maybe she was falling into the trap of seeing them all as little Beatles too.

Greg was peeling strands of balsa wood off the coffee stirrer. His face had returned to its normal pensive anxiety. He did look as if his father might be a tormented singer-songwriter, rather than a tour manager/accountant.

Tanith watched him with a certain pained affection, and thought, *God, Rosetta's screwed them up like little balls of paper*. None of them know what they really want. But maybe if Greg had a *normal* woman in his life, someone to unscrew him, flatten him out again...

Determination swept through her, just like it did when someone put a new script her way.

Surely I must have a friend he could be perfect for, she thought. He deserves a good girlfriend. It's not his fault he doesn't have the skills.

'Greg,' she said. 'You've got the clothes, which is great. Now all you need is a dinner date.'

He rolled his eyes at her. 'Tanith, the last *date* I had was at prep school.'

'OK,' she said lightly. 'Then you need some practice. You can take me out for dinner next week.'

'For real?' said Greg, flushing again.

'Call it a dress rehearsal,' said Tanith. 'Text me in the middle of next week, and we'll take it from there, OK?'

'OK,' said Greg, and swallowed.

Chapter Sixteen

Chelsea, 1971

'He's a very quiet baby, isn't he?' said Sue, peering doubtfully into the cradle, which was festooned like an overgrown pond with floppy daisies crocheted from psychedelic wool – a gift from the groupies who hung out with Red and the road crew. Brian had insisted she made a note of that. Red's little band of 'friends' had been getting some bad press of late, and not for their handicrafts. Sue stretched out a long finger as if to poke the sleeping baby into participation, but withdrew it suddenly as he stirred a tiny fist in her direction.

'He's an angel,' said Brian proudly. There was a linen burping square over the shoulder of his pristine corduroy blazer, and flakes of dry sick in his sideburns.

Sue wished Rosetta would step in and make Brian dress the way he had when the band had first been signed: viz, a three-piece Serious Manager suit and short back and sides. The clothes Nature had intended for Brian and his squirish figure. He hadn't dropped his poshness – if anything, since they'd started doing well in America, he'd ratcheted his accent up a notch – but his broad chest and slightly stumpy legs were definitely more suited to tweeds and a shotgun than narrow-lapelled jackets and that ridiculous American cowboy belt. Typical manager, thought Sue; wants to run the band, then ends up wanting to *look* like them too. Brian, no matter what he'd like to think, was about as hip as a bassoon.

She straightened up with a rattle of bracelets and looked over to the window, where Rosetta was sitting patiently on the chaise longue, having her hair done for the photoshoot that was meant to follow the interview. Rosetta hadn't participated very much so far, which troubled Sue; such a quiet baby couldn't be exhausting her *that* much.

'Doesn't he ever cry, darling?' she asked.

Rosetta didn't answer immediately, but that might have been because she was having her hair smoothed into a shining wave by the hairdresser wielding an enormous paddle brush. She'd insisted on a hairdresser. Not that she needed cosmetic help, in Sue's vexed opinion, because motherhood just made her look even more translucent and elfin. No, there was something else behind it – more as though, for the first time ever, she didn't want the spotlight shining on her.

Rosetta, to Sue's sharp eye, had been uncharacteristically quiet all morning, when she wasn't being extremely attentive to Brian. Normally she allowed him to dance attendance on her, and yet today she was treating him with astonishing deference. And today she'd left most of the talking to Brian. In fact, it had been Brian who had phoned her up to arrange the interview. Most odd.

For a while Sue had worried whether Rosetta's pointed silence was something to do with the blind date she had had with John the previous week. It hadn't gone well – no, she corrected herself, it just hadn't gone as well as she'd hoped, for a date she'd planned and looked forward to so much. John had been charming, but more reserved than she'd expected. And she'd talked too much to fill in the silences. Still, he hadn't turned her down when she suggested he come with her for a restaurant review later in the month.

Sue pursed her lips. It was just something else she'd have to work at.

'No, he doesn't cry much,' replied Brian without waiting for Rosetta to speak. 'He's just like his mother. Fascinating, if a touch enigmatic.'

'So, this is just the first of many?' asked Sue, hoping it would provoke the famously 'no kids for me, thanks!' Rosetta into a reaction. 'A whole tribe of little Mulligans running around your ankles?'

'Oh, most certainly,' nodded Brian. 'A couple more sons, then maybe we can try for a girl. My brains, her looks, and all that. It would be a crime to waste genes like Rosetta's on boys, don't you think, Sue?'

'Rosetta?' said Sue, trying to keep the incredulity out of her voice. '*More* kids?'

Rosetta gave a mild smile in agreement, though her eyes were veiled beneath her long fringe. 'Oh, yes. Brian's very keen to have children. And I'm ... very keen on making them.' She laughed, to underline the little quote for Sue's ease of transcription. 'And I'm desperately keen on making Brian happy, of course. I've been reading *reams* on infant development and that sort of thing ...' Then she turned her head away and murmured something to the hairdresser, flipping a strand of hair with her fingers.

Sue bit her pen and scribbled down something anodyne about fatherhood agreeing with Brian's organizational capabilities. This wasn't going the way she had expected it to. At *all*.

'Brian, you've a reputation for being quite an old-fashioned businessman, despite working in the music industry, so it's rather forward-thinking that you've taken some time off work to look after Rosetta and ...' Sue glanced ostentatiously down at her notes for the baby's full name. She *hadn't* been asked to be godmother. She hadn't known there was even going to be a baby until three months after the wedding, when Rosetta threw up all over some appalling society photographer at a breakfast party. Rosetta, of course, had stayed skinny until the last moment.

'Patrick,' Brian supplied helpfully. 'Patrick Gawain Mulligan. Eight pounds ten ounces. Nice big baby. Well, the band are between tours at the moment, so it's all fitted in rather well.' He beamed again, and his broad smile turned his cheeks appley. Sue found the effect unsettling after the creased and stressed look that had been Brian's signature look, peace beads notwithstanding, for all the time she'd known him.

Really, she thought viperishly, I think I prefer it when he's being an arrogant control freak.

'Patrick . . . Gawain . . . Mulligan,' she said slowly, writing the names down. 'Not very rock-star names?'

'He's not a rock-star child, though, is he?' Rosetta said hotly from the other side of the room. It was the first time she'd really spoken unprompted for twenty minutes.

Sue raised an eyebrow.

'I mean,' Rosetta added, dropping her eyes to the hand mirror she was holding, 'he's going to have a perfectly normal upbringing.'

'So you'll be staying at home with him, will you?' said Sue swiftly, her mind running along a whole new direction for the feature – 'Rosetta Mulligan gives up her celebrity whirl for motherhood!' Recent new mothers flicked through her head like a picture library. She did this one about twice a year, and stored up pictures of glamorous women looking bloated and pissed-off specially.

Brian opened his mouth, but this time Rosetta was too quick. 'No, I'll be taking him with me when I tour with the band.'

Sue looked at Brian for the reaction, but there was only a momentary flicker of surprise before the broad smile and blissed-out expression returned.

'Well, we just can't spare her on the road,' agreed Brian. He offered Sue an almond tuile from the plate of patisserie-bought goodies Rosetta had put out for the photographer. She patted her stomach self-deprecatingly and he helped himself to two.

'The lads are just hopeless if Rosetta isn't there, kicking them into shape. And between you and me, Sue, the record company more or less insisted that she came out too, in an "overseeing capacity". Even with all the armies of secretaries and assistants and press people they send out to help us, they still need her "overseeing" them.' He chortled with amusement, although Sue noticed at the other end of the room Rosetta wasn't smiling. 'Isn't that what they called it, darling?'

He turned back to Sue before Rosetta could reply. 'Anyway, I can't be without her for ten minutes, not with a massive American tour and two big European tours planned for this year. Ticket demand, you know.' He raised his eyebrows, prompting her to write it down.

'Won't it be a lot of work, with the baby, though?' asked Sue, with some concern.

'Ah, she's had plenty of practice looking after the lads already. I mean, after Red, this little one will be a doddle for her.' He laughed his new fruity gentlemen's club chuckle and wagged another tuile in Sue's direction before biting into it.

'I'm very good at sweeping up sick,' said Rosetta, drily. 'But don't quote me on that.'

The hairdresser finished with her hair and added a last coat of powder to her nose. Rosetta shut her eyes and submitted passively to the attention.

'Besides which, I'm completely cool with the idea of Rosetta bringing the baby on tour,' added Brian, as if Sue didn't look convinced enough. 'We've all read Dr Spock in this house and I think it's very important for Patrick to have his father near him in these formative years.'

On a journalist's instinct, Sue looked over at Rosetta as Brian said that, but her face was implacable as she applied her own lip-liner in an enamelled hand mirror. She seemed to be staring hard at her own reflection.

'Shall we do the pictures now?' suggested Brian, getting up with a crack of his joints. 'Hello, you there?' he shouted up the stairs. The photographer had been despatched to capture the newly extended flat, the high point being a beautifully furnished nursery, full of toys and flowers and more strange hand-crafted gifts from the groupies, who liked to see any beautiful woman put out of action with a new child, particularly one who toured as much as Rosetta.

'Jolly good,' said Brian as the young photographer emerged clutching his camera. 'Did you get the skylight?' he asked earnestly, then turned to Sue and added in explanation, 'Rather proud of the old skylight – I put that in myself with John, you know, John from the band. Have you met . . .?'

Sue raised her eyebrows at Brian. 'Oh, darling, of *course*. Johnny and I . . . yes, we're *very* good friends.'

Brian looked pleased and surprised. 'Sorry, I always forget who knows who . . . Rosetta takes care of that side of things, you see . . .'

Rosetta appeared at her elbow from nowhere. Sue noted that while Brian smelled of baby sick, Rosetta smelled of violets as usual.

'Of course Sue knows John!' Rosetta's conspiratorial smile was seductively genuine, although her eyes were guarded. 'You had a date with him, didn't you? You never told me how it went . . .'

Sue slid a sideways glance at the photographer, who was testing the light against the side of his hand. 'We'll talk about that later,' she hissed. 'I need to, er, ask you a few things about, um...'

Rosetta smiled beatifically. 'My pleasure.'

'Oh, excellent!' said Brian, apparently catching up. 'Always nice to keep things in the family, eh? Lovely guy, John. Awfully good at architectural drawings, too. If you thought he was good when you saw them at the Marquee the other month, he'll blow you away after these last American dates. Honestly, I've never heard him play like this. The more time those boys spend in America, the better they get. I mean, if I didn't know how straight he was, I'd say he was on something pretty special. Er, don't print that, will

you, Sue, love? Total flake when it comes to punctuality, but
he's an awfully nice chap.'

Rosetta gave him a look.

'Awfully *cool*,' Brian corrected himself. 'Cool.'

'Do you want to do some pictures with Patrick?' she
asked, turning to Sue with a gracious incline of her head.

Sue was reminded of Princess Grace – shortly after she
stopped being plain Grace Kelly. 'That would be good,' she
said and cast her gaze round the room for the best spot to
put them in. She had to hand it to Rosetta – she certainly
knew how to furnish a flat. All the old Indian silver and
peacockery had been swept away and was now replaced
with lots of cream and coffee-coloured fabrics and soft paint-
ings lining the plain walls. Brian's contribution was a very
serious-looking record player and amplifier in one corner
and a bookshelf full of reference books. Big vases of lilies
made the room musky and Rosetta had even coaxed some
wisteria to grow around the balcony doors. The photographer had already set up one shot of Patrick in the cradle,
with wisteria fronds trailing around him. The place looked
twice as big as it had done when they'd first bought it, and
not just because of the new extension.

Sue twinged with a little jealousy, but then remembered
Anita's chaotic, remnant-strewn bedsit above her shop and
felt comparatively better.

'On the sofa, perhaps?' she suggested.

Brian adjusted his shirt cuffs and arranged the cushions
for Rosetta, as she lifted Patrick out of the cradle, trailing
long streams of lace behind him like sea spray.

As much an observer as the photographer, Sue watched
Brian gaze devotedly at the little scene, Rosetta lifting Patrick
high in the air to make him gurgle, exposing her long white
arms as the sleeves of her blouse fell back over her elbows.
Despite her pallor, she looked very strong. The photographer
snapped away, relieved to have been gifted a natural picture
at what was usually a hopelessly formal event, and later,

Sue couldn't see whether Brian's delirious smile was directed at Rosetta, or at Patrick, or at both.

'Can we do the pics at the same time as the interview, Sue?' asked Brian. 'Only we've got a date with the record company and I want Rosetta to have an hour's sleep before we go out.'

Brian's face might have been off-duty, thought Sue, but the voice wasn't. She nodded and looked over to Rosetta. 'Sure. I've got a date tonight myself.'

Patrick cooed and Rosetta buried her nose in his warm scalp, murmuring to him.

'So,' began Sue, 'it's been a very busy few months for you, hasn't it? First the wedding, and now the baby!' She looked up, throwing the question out to both of them, just to see who would answer.

Brian did, almost before the words were out of her mouth. Like Rosetta, he had the habit of slipping into journalese when he wanted something written down; Sue now knew to write it down verbatim, but to put invisible question marks around it in her own head for later. When she could check and examine it more carefully.

'Well,' he said, 'it's been the most exciting few months of my life, Sue. As you know, the band has really grown up in the last year, and we've doubled the size of our audiences in the States. And then when Rosetta told me that we were having a baby . . .' His smile broadened.

'You decided to get married. That's very, um, respectable of you, to make an honest woman of Rosetta,' Sue commented loudly. Again, there was no response from Rosetta, who sat tracing Patrick's nubby forehead with a fingertip. Sue wondered if she was drugged or something. Her hair was so bright and her face so pale that without the make-up she would look partially erased.

'Well, not exactly.' Brian patted Rosetta's hand. 'It's hardly a shotgun arrangement, is it? After all the time we've been together, we're a bit of an institution on the scene, aren't we?'

'You've been together for, how long now?'

'Four years,' said Rosetta.

'Is that all?' Brian looked surprised. 'Well! Guess it must be. Feels like for ever.'

Rosetta, Sue noted, said nothing.

'So, was it a formal proposal?' Sue persisted, hoping to catch Rosetta's eye and elicit some response.

'Absolutely!' said Brian.

'I was asking Rosetta!' said Sue, before she could stop herself.

Rosetta looked up from Patrick's head. 'No, let Brian tell it,' she said, sweetly. 'It's his story, after all. And I do so much talking normally.'

Brian patted her hand again. 'Well, I am rather proud of it, actually.' He coughed, ready to launch into his tale. 'I planned to propose to Rosetta after the band came back from the States for our first big tour – as you know, she couldn't come with us because she had the fashion show to do for Anita, didn't she?'

He smiled affectionately at his wife, and Sue wondered if he had any real idea how popular Rosetta was with the magazines in her own right, or indeed how much people knew she did for the band behind the scenes.

'I mean, we've been together for *years*, but I don't mind saying that it wasn't until I went away on tour with the boys to America that we realized how much we missed each other, and I knew I had to do things properly. Simply no sense otherwise.'

'No sense indeed,' murmured Sue, taking rough notes. She would no doubt get a call from Rosetta's press assistant later, telling her to throw some hipper vocabulary into Brian's interview quotes.

'*Anyway*, I'd found a very romantic old place for the band to record their new material in, with some fantastic little cottages in the grounds. The plan was—' he leaned forward, warming to his anecdote; Brian loved telling

anecdotes '– that I would come back from the tour, get
them all settled in the rehearsal venue, then take her off
somewhere for a weekend and get down on the old knee. I
checked in her diary before I went away and saw that she
had some ridiculous book launch that night, so I even had
her collect that reckless idiot John from the airport so she
would have to come out to see us. Chuh! John!' he added,
with a roll of his eyes. 'That great idiot! Did she tell you he
missed the plane because he was taping some local musicians or other?' Brian smiled indulgently. '*Anyway*, it
worked out fine in the end, an ill wind, et cetera. I'd never
have got her out of London, not with you organizing her
social life, Sue!'

Rosetta's head jerked up as if it were on a string. 'But you
could have waited for John, couldn't you? Did you leave
him behind *on purpose*?' she said sharply.

'Did you?' echoed Sue, latching on to the note of dismay
in Rosetta's voice.

'Um, well, not exactly on *purpose*,' Brian conceded. He
looked disconcerted at the unexpected interest from both
women. 'Well, look, I don't know. Sort of.' His gaze went
from one to the other, and he rallied. 'Well, *I don't know*, it
was what *you two* would call a karmic coincidence, and
what *I* would call an informed management decision,
because when Rosetta drove him out there, she told me that
she had some amazing news too, and . . .' He put an arm
round her and squeezed her shoulders.

'I told him I was having a baby,' said Rosetta tonelessly.

'Aaahh,' cooed Sue.

Brian's brow creased discreetly, as though he were concentrating on saying the right thing. 'I mean, it wasn't
exactly the way I would have planned it, no, but we certainly
didn't get married *just* because Patrick was on the way.
That's not the case at all. I would have been *totally* cool
about Patrick being born out of wedlock . . .'

'Some of our best friends are bastards,' explained Rosetta,

with a brittle laugh, and Patrick's sleepy head bobbed against her chest.

Sue laughed and wrote it down.

Brian twitched, casting an odd glance at her, then laughed and helped himself to another tuile from the plate. The thick gold wedding band glinted on his finger. Sue knew, from her experience of married men, that this was one ring which wouldn't ever come off in a hotel bar, or under a table at a restaurant. The flesh was practically growing around it already.

'So, how do the group feel about having a married man in their midst?' she probed. 'Will it spoil those mad bachelor nights out?'

'Oh, heavens, no, they were all really delighted when I told them!' said Brian. 'In fact, Glynn managed to find a really quite good bottle of brandy in this amazingly redneck town when I told them that . . .'

'*Glynn*?' murmured Rosetta. She stared at Brian. 'You told the band before . . .?'

'So you broke it to the band first!' crowed Sue. 'How fantastic! Ever the manager, Brian! I suppose you're really married to them first, aren't you?'

'*When* did you tell them you were going to propose, darling?' asked Rosetta, lightly. 'I mean, now you mention it, they didn't seem *very* surprised when we announced it at the studio.'

'We-ee-ee-ll, it wasn't really a shock to anyone, was it?' Brian looked a little self-conscious. 'Simon thought we already *were* married, actually. Mind you,' he added to Sue in a jovial tone, 'Simon never really notices much apart from the size of the tour-bus and whether it has on-board lavatory facilities. Oh, what the hell – you can quote me there if you want.'

Rosetta turned to Brian and he was disconcerted to see that her green eyes were glassy with tears, even though she was blinking rapidly so Sue wouldn't see.

'Rosetta?' he said, then added, 'Are you OK?' in a whisper.

Rosetta didn't say anything. Her lip, pale with peachy lipstick, was bitten between her sharp white teeth and it reddened dangerously as her eyelashes flickered up and down.

'And John?' she whispered. 'Was he there when you told them?'

'Of course!' Brian nodded emphatically. 'I told him before I . . . You don't think I would tell Simon and Glynn and not John, do you?'

'And what . . .?' Rosetta couldn't go on.

'He was thrilled, darling,' said Brian. 'He thought it was the best thing . . .'

There was a painful pause in which it dawned on Sue that this might be less of a funny feeling and more of a scoop, and she motioned for the photographer to move, while she herself edged round under the pretence of admiring a mirror.

The hand cradling Patrick's downy head trembled until he stirred and started to wake. Patrick began to grizzle and Rosetta appeared to snap back into life.

'Darling?' murmured Brian. '*Are* you OK?' He squeezed her and looked up at Sue. 'I don't know – you girls and your waterworks!'

'Rosetta?' Sue touched her hand.

'Oh, er . . . Fine,' she muttered back, 'it's just the baby, you know. Hormones. Sorry.' Then she wiped the corner of her eye with Patrick's trailing silvery robe, so her eyeliner wasn't completely ruined, and her eyes merely sparkled. 'Jesus, Sue!' she said, 'I don't know what came over me just then! The vision of Brian having a last night of freedom, stuck in a sleazy pool hall in Ohio, with only Glynn and Simon for company! Hardly Led Zeppelin, are they? My God, darling!' She dropped a kiss on to his hand. 'No wonder you couldn't wait to come home and get hitched!'

'I had to do it while Red was . . .' Brian looked mildly

embarrassed. 'While Red was out sampling the local . . . um, cuisine. He isn't exactly an ambassador for marital—' He spluttered to a halt, confusing himself. Sue made a mental note that if she wanted 'off-the-record' gossip in the future, Brian would be a much more fruitful source than Rosetta. 'He, um . . . Red, our drummer, is *very* happily engaged to his childhood sweetheart, Janette, you know?'

'It's OK, Brian,' said Sue, drily. 'I think we've got past the stage of pretending they're not distracted by other girls on the road.'

'Have you got enough there?' Brian asked, flicking concerned glances towards Rosetta, who was blowing gently on Patrick's head to make him gurgle up at her. He wasn't sure if there was a medical term for it, but she'd been acting a bit mad recently, and not entirely in character. 'I think . . . I think Patrick's getting a bit tired. And it's nearly time for his feed.'

'Um, it looks like I've got everything.' Sue looked back over her notes. Brian had been more than forthcoming, so why did she feel there was something missing here? Did she just know them too well?

'One more picture of the three of you,' she said, 'then we're done.'

'Rosetta?' said Brian. Damn, she was crying again. He frowned with concern so Sue couldn't see.

'What?' she demanded in a whisper. 'Is there something wrong?'

'No, no, I don't think so. You're just . . .' He rested his forehead on hers. 'So lovely. Both of you. I don't deserve you.'

She smiled through her tears and kissed his nose. The photographer inched in closer and took a tight head shot of Brian and Rosetta, their foreheads meeting over Patrick's sleeping face, noses touching, eyes closed. Patrick hadn't inherited Brian's manly forehead, but he certainly had Rosetta's long dark eyelashes. He was a gorgeous baby, even

Sue had to acknowledge that, and without any of the usual cajoling, he stared into the photographer's lens as if he could see something they couldn't.

They were a very handsome triangle, the Mulligans.

God, thought Sue, it was an effort not to hate Rosetta sometimes.

'So, will there be more?' she asked again, disingenuously. One last time, just to see if she could catch her out. Either Rosetta had been converted to motherhood in the most amazing way, or she was acting a little bit too well.

Brian tore his gaze away from Patrick and looked up. 'More . . .?' he asked, raising an eyebrow.

'More *children*.'

'Oh, most certainly,' replied Brian at the same time as Rosetta said, 'Who knows?'

'A difference of opinion there!' observed Sue, trying hard to disguise her glee – and the new direction the piece could take.

But Rosetta drew her lips into a broad smile and leaned her head against her husband's shoulder.

She looked as if she were readying herself for a parachute jump or something, thought Sue. Is this really what lactation does to you?

'Not at all,' said Rosetta in her 'quote me' voice. 'As I said before, Brian and I both love children, and I want to be the best mother and wife I can possibly be.'

'*Very* traditional,' said Sue.

'And what's wrong with that?' said Rosetta, arching an eyebrow.

'Nothing at all!' said Brian, and squeezed his new family tightly.

Chapter Seventeen

Clerkenwell, 2001

Tanith was woken from a fitful dream about being trapped on an out-of-control bus by the sound of an ambulance wailing close to the bedroom window and she sat up groggily, reaching for the alarm clock with a disorientated hand.

Oh shit, she thought, I've slept through. Her head was thick with too much drowsiness and her mouth tasted funny, but to her amazement, it was ten to two in the morning, and she was starving hungry.

She lay for a moment, unable to move her arms and legs. For one thing, she seemed to be on top of the covers, not underneath them, and there was something heavy on her stomach. She angled her eyes down as far as they would go and saw it was the script she'd been reading while her facepack worked. From the odd sensation of home plastic surgery on her face, Tanith deduced that she hadn't got round to removing it before she fell asleep. And that she was in her lounging-around pants and not even changed for bed.

'Oh, *bollocks*,' she moaned, and tried to move her arm to push the script off, but her limbs seemed to have turned into lead and she couldn't force her neurones to move them. Obviously her body was aware of what time it was, even if her brain wasn't.

Another painful angle of the eyes revealed that Robert was not in the bed either.

Her stomach rumbled and the tempting thought of a nice mug of warm milk finally forced her to lever herself up. It had gone chilly – not surprising, given that the window was still wide open – and she pulled her dressing-gown off the back of the door and pulled it tight round her waist. Part of her wilted with depression at the very idea of *owning* a dressing-gown, but it had been a gift from Robert and somehow after a year with the King of Sheepskin Slippers, it was impossible to imagine what else you would slip on in the middle of the night.

She crept down the stairs to the hall. Maybe he wasn't even back yet – all the lights were off and the place was silent.

Tanith flicked the lights on so she wouldn't fall over anything and the seven hidden lights glimmered on along the hall ceiling. The simplicity of the hall still impressed her now as it had on the first night he'd brought her back here. At the time she had seen it as elegant and sparse. Now she saw it more as a tribute to Robert's refusal to clutter anything – his home, his office, his life – with objects that didn't reflect well on himself. Even his drum-kit was hidden away in the soundproofed cellar.

Still creeping, for reasons she didn't understand, Tanith tiptoed into the kitchen, opened the fridge and poured herself a mug of milk, which she put in the microwave to heat up. The open door cast a triangle of yellow light on the kitchen tiles by her bare feet and made the frosted nail varnish on her toes gleam like tiny pearls. It was a huge fridge, which Robert had bought mainly for its powerful ice crusher and the fact that you could put five ribs of beef and a whole crate of beers in it. It hummed like a small car and used roughly the same amount of power.

While it hummed, comfortingly, Tanith peered into its strip-lit depths and pushed down the impulse to pick at the left-over bits of takeaway; instead she began to chuck out stale lumps of cheese and old cartons of hummus. Bizarrely, given his otherwise anal approach to sparse furnishing, Robert never threw anything away, maybe because he'd bought a fridge large enough to store a year's worth of shopping in, and at anything less than half-full it took on a forlorn and underfed bachelor flat look. Or maybe Rosetta had never maintained a welcoming fridge in his childhood. Whatever reason, with more elderly food in it than in the bin, Robert's fridge generally smelled as though some vegetable death cult had committed mass suicide somewhere towards the back.

Tanith wondered where he'd got to. There was no sign of him downstairs, and normally he left a trail of neatly folded socks, a paper, his briefcase, all in appointed places.

She stopped the microwave before the milk could boil over and took out the mug, cupping her hands around it, and kicked the fridge door shut. Hot milk usually put her straight to sleep. Reading through a couple of scripts would finish her off nicely.

She padded through to the sitting-room in her bare feet, thinking she might take it all through to Robert's study, where there was a comfy leather chair. But as she turned on the uplighter, she noticed there was already light shining underneath the door through to his study. There was also a smell of cigarette smoke and the faint sound of Chopin.

'Oh, God,' breathed Tanith and tried not to feel cross. But this was something his doctor had expressly told him not to do: working late at night wasn't good for his hypertension, and Robert knew it. He usually managed to get most of his stress worked out on his drums or on the squash court, but he was clinically unable to leave something unordered once he knew it was there and now he would be at those accounts day and night until they were done.

Tanith noticed that the basket of shirts she had placed by the washing-machine was still there. This single-mindedness was an affliction Tanith often wished he would apply to the laundry; generally, he refused to see housework and sailed past overflowing bins and unwashed socks in the manner of Marie Antoinette making her way delicately through the slums.

His excuse was a childhood of room service.

She put her milk and script down, went over to the door and gently pushed it open. She didn't want him to think she was criticizing. That was fatal.

'Robert, what are you doing?' she asked. 'Come to bed, honey, it's late.'

Her heart sank when she saw him sitting there, with his head propped wearily on one hand, surrounded by scraps of paper. They were all over his desk, round his chair, little piles on the bookshelf, heaps on the pulled-out drawers of the filing cabinet, on his briefcase, stacked up on the monitor, under the murky cafetière of cold coffee. He was trapped by thousands of pieces of paper and the *Creem* magazine screensaver was rotating on his computer.

Robert himself was partly hidden by a cloud of smoke.

He only smoked when he was stressed. Tanith could see from the ashtray that he was very stressed.

'I'm making a collage,' he said, an unlit cigarette clamped between his lips while he slapped his hands around the desk, looking for his matches. Papers lifted and fell gently in the draught. 'What does it look like I'm doing?'

Tanith saw his matches beneath a pile of taxi receipts, but wordlessly passed him a lighter in the shape of a Colt 45 that some client had given him shortly after Robert had hidden the price of their new home in Jersey for them in 'back-dated research expenses'.

Robert lit his cigarette and automatically blew the end of the gun as if it were a match. He looked at it stupidly for a fraction of a second and then handed it back to Tanith. His eyes had taken on the beady appearance of black ball-bearings, although whether that was to do with the piles of

papers, or having consumed the contents of their biggest six-
teen-cup cafetière, she couldn't tell.

'You're constituting a major fire hazard here,' she pointed
out. 'Isn't there some rule about not smoking while surrounded by millions of tissue paper Visa receipts?'

'This is insane,' he said. He didn't sound as if he was necessarily talking to her.

'I can see that,' said Tanith. She perched on his exercise
ball, which was free from papers only because he couldn't
make them balance.

'I started off trying to make proper piles,' he explained, as
if he'd already explained what the piles were. 'You know,
accommodation, food, clothes . . .' He sighed heavily and the
nearest five piles rose and fell in sympathy.

'But you've scaled that down to . . .?'

Robert swivelled in his chair and looked straight at her.
His hair was sticking up at right angles all over his head
where he'd been running his hands through it. Dark circles
had formed round his eyes and he had biro marks on his
cheek. He looked daunted, like a man who has approached
K2 in plimsolls, thinking it would be a pleasant way to pass
Sunday afternoon. 'Sixties, seventies, eighties and nineties.'

They both left a discreet pause.

'Come to bed,' said Tanith, putting a hand on his shoulder.

'What? And leave all this? It'll only look worse in the
morning. Oh, yeah, I'm going to have to be sick tomorrow,
so can you call the office for me? Tell them I'm going with
you to some kind of fertility clinic – tell them it's some
women's problem thing. Then they won't expect me in for
the rest of the day.'

Setting aside the jolt of shock generated by Robert bringing up *children*, Tanith was dumbstruck by the almost
unheard of sickie-pulling. Robert never blagged days off.
Ever. He would stagger into work with two broken legs
rather than take the day off. More than once he had refused

to phone in sick for a hungover Tanith, forced Berocca into her and driven her to the office himself, claiming things were only twice as bad when you went back in again. 'You're going to *skive work*?' she said.

'I'll have to.' He put his hands through his hair again and took off his glasses to clean them on his shirt. 'I said I'd get something ready for her by the end of the week, and Christ . . .'

Tanith picked up a small pile at random. A receipt from Gucci for three dresses from 1978, a restaurant bill from Joe Allen from 1982, an invoice from Rosetta herself for some article about living with a rock-star for *Cosmopolitan* from 1975 (no sign as to whether it was paid, or indeed sent), another invoice written on the back of a piece of headed notepaper from 1969 for 'the installation of three shelves, one wardrobe, papering and painting of two rooms and sundry handiwork'. Tanith looked at it curiously. It was doodled all over with pictures of a dolly bird trying to hang wallpaper and the words 'Paid in Full!!' were scrawled over the top in Rosetta's loopy handwriting.

'You don't have to do this, you know,' she said. 'She could get it into order, and then you could look at it. It's not fair. You've *got* a job.'

He spread his hands expansively. 'Tanith, you know what she's like.'

She gave him a hard look. 'Now, if *I'd* said that . . .'

Robert took off his glasses and rubbed his eyes. 'No, honestly. I *should* do it. Once I get going I can sort it all out quite quickly. Not everything is relevant. I mean, I can't quite work out whether she kept this box as financial records or just some kind of keepsake thing.'

As he spoke, a receipt from Habitat for a sofa slid off the printer and into his coffee mug. He fished it out and showed it to Tanith. 'Look at this, for instance. It's quite sweet, really – you can imagine how excited she must have been, getting a brand-new sofa, having it delivered. When's that from?' He peered at the date. 'Nineteen-sixty-eight. She was only seventeen or so. Still pretty young. It must have been exciting for her, you know, with Dad, fitting out a new flat in Chelsea, their first place together and all that.'

Tanith couldn't imagine Rosetta permitting herself to get excited over a sofa from Habitat, much less remembering to keep the receipt, but she took it from Robert and tried to imagine, as she held it, why on earth Rosetta was doing this. Surely there must be more painless ways of showing her youth to her children? Like photograph albums or home-video evenings? Unless this was part of her plan to break the autobiography to them gently, starting with the moving story of her home furnishings.

Carefully, she put the receipt down on the nearest pile.

Robert snatched it off and moved it to another pile, three piles away from the first.

'Rob, I have to go to bed,' she said. Suddenly she felt very tired, even without looking at the scripts. 'I have an early call in the morning. I didn't mean to fall asleep when I came in – I was just knackered.'

'Right,' muttered Robert, pushing the sleeves up on his jumper.

Tanith wondered if he'd even looked in on her, when she'd been nowhere to be found in the house. 'So, I'll . . . go to bed?'

'Fine, *fine*!' he exploded suddenly. 'So just fucking go . . .!'

'Hey! Robert!' Tanith's heart slammed against her chest, as it still did at his sudden and irrational outbreaks of temper.

He sighed and swivelled round. 'Sorry, sorry. Sorry. I didn't mean to snap at you.' He smiled at her through his tired eyes, and Tanith immediately felt bad for being so angry. 'It's the accounts. It's just so . . . typical of her. A whole lifetime's accounts in one fucking night. It's like trying to, I don't know, read the whole of the British Library all at once.'

'You can't do it that quickly. You're not meant to! And you wouldn't for any other client, would you? Come on, come to bed.' She tried a smile although her heart, still banging with shock against her ribs, felt very heavy at the brief glimpse of the darker side of Robert's insecurities, just as dark and driven as Patrick's. Was this what it would be for the rest of her life – patching up the holes of Robert's personality that Rosetta had damaged? Was that something she was up to? Or wanted?

To her surprise, Robert pushed back his chair from the desk. 'You're right, you know. It's too late.'

She held out her hand, determined to make the peace despite the warning bells ringing in the back of her head. 'You never told me I was infertile, by the way? I had no idea we were trying for a family. It's not even as if you've been trying very *hard*. Maybe you should make a last-ditch effort before you wheel me off to the egg-farm tomorrow, eh?'

He grinned and took off his wire-rimmed reading glasses. 'Sorry, I didn't mean to ... Um, I wasn't trying to make a ... It was a crap excuse. I just wanted something that the office wouldn't ask too hard about. I didn't mean ... Oh shit.' He gestured at the desk. 'It's not like she's a very good advert for it, is she? Motherhood?'

'No.'

Robert went thoughtful. 'You would let me know, if ... well, you know,' he said eventually.

'If what?' Tanith tried not to sound too evasive. The silence in the study suddenly felt oppressive. 'If I was pregnant?'

'Well, not so much that as ... you know, if you *wanted* to have children.'

Tanith's eyes slithered away from him, flicked round the room, round the piles of paper on the floor, but then she got a grip of herself and made herself look up, into Robert's open face. At least it was easy to be honest with Robert; he liked to have all the facts, however unpalatable. Making herself say it was the hard part. 'I don't,' she said, 'not yet. I'm not ready to be responsible for someone else.'

Tanith knew that this was the opportunity to push the rest of her unspoken fears into the open; that she wasn't ready to slide into marriage just because they lived together, or that his side of the relationship seemed to be working on a much quicker timeframe than hers, but she couldn't. She was too tired, and too reluctant to hurt him when he hadn't been processing receipts as much as sifting through his mother's life.

Robert shrugged but she sensed a slight hurt in him. 'Still,' he said, switching off the computer, 'it's as well to know your bits are in working order.'

Tanith held out her hand. 'Maybe we could give the old natural method one more try before tomorrow morning? Before the turkey baster?'

'We could.'

Robert slipped her cold fingers in his warm hand and Tanith led him through the dark house, up to their bedroom where he pulled off her lounging pants and vest tenderly and kissed her fingers and toes one by one. But all the time they were making love, and he was murmuring roughly in her ear how he couldn't be without her and she was the only one, Tanith's restless mind kept going back to the little receipts of Rosetta's materialistic life that were lying like snowflakes over Robert's study, and what exactly it was Rosetta had done to make her children so angry and resigned.

Chapter Eighteen

Los Angeles, 1973

LA was the half-way point through a tour that cats-cradled back and forth across America like corset laces, their seventh time in the US in three years, and the second one this year alone. Rosetta had heard Brian talking to Manny, the promoter, about squeezing another short trip in before Christmas. The record company were keen, and, as usual, Brian was in charge of making all the times and places and lorries add up. He was in charge of everything else, it seemed, albeit with a new troupe of 'assistants' and 'aides' from the American office, who didn't do much except fall into bed with Glynn.

Rosetta was exhausted, and she wasn't even playing. Plenty of times she'd felt like grabbing the babies and flying home to the peace and quiet of Cheyne Walk, away from stoned journalists and shrieking DJs and women who would just turn up at the hotel room with a couple of monkeys and a recommendation from the last band.

She leaned her forehead against the cold window of the limo and watched the snow piling up against the sill, trying to think what she could get the lads to say in their interviews in the morning that they hadn't said a million times before. She was almost asleep, but was trying valiantly to pass it off as boredom. Everyone said that she was crazy to go on tour with them. But there was a Guide Leader in her head yelling that it was her duty to be here, to keep a tiny room of normality for Brian in the midst of all the madness and to deal with the problems when there wasn't anyone sober enough to get rid of the evidence before the cops piled in. She did more and more of that; in fact, she was getting more and more interviews on her own, which she didn't mind, even if it did mean talking about the kids and spinning all the fairy tales they wanted to read about her 'rock 'n' roll gypsy lifestyle' (© Sue Morton-Thomas), rather than the more mundane organizational pressures she was under to keep the band sober and functional and interesting at the appropriate times.

Rosetta knew not everyone was keen about her doing interviews on her own. Brian, naturally, was suspicious of her talking about what she did backstage, not wanting her to be seen as some diabolical combination of Yoko Ono and Lady Macbeth, and Glynn disliked being displaced as the haircare spokesman for the band. She guessed that other people were bitching about her hanging around the tour for the sake of her own publicity – which made her laugh.

The real iron cord that kept her on the tour-bus – and she would never have admitted it to a soul – was sheer masochism: the reluctant desire to see exactly what slid into John's limo, rather than sit powerless at home imagining it and then having her worst fears confirmed in the newspapers.

Rosetta didn't believe for one second that she didn't love John. She knew she did, more now than ever, despite the arrival of Robert, whom Brian adored, despite his not being the hoped-for girl. Loving John while being Brian's wife was like being short-sighted, or colour-blind: a small personal flaw she'd learned to live with. The real torture was never quite knowing how *he* felt, now that they couldn't spend the comfortable time alone together that used to come so easily. Even though, trapped in dressing-rooms waiting for gigs, and hanging around at airports, they were together all the time, Rosetta never felt able to relax near him, in case she gave herself away, and he seemed on edge near her too.

Some nights when she lay awake, waiting with a maternal sixth sense for Robert to start crying for food and Patrick to start crying to keep him company, she marvelled at how it had all settled into a such a reasonable pattern.

Rosetta leaned her head back against the red leather headrest of the limo and watched the lights of the city stream past the sunroof like illuminated snowflakes. They were delicate and beautiful, against an LA sky that never quite got dark. She was pretty drunk, from the champagne the promoter had laid on in the obligatory stretch limo specified in Brian's increasingly demanding contracts. More annoyingly, she also felt passively stoned from the mountains of dope being smoked at the gig. Nothing was really connecting in her brain and that made her cross, despite the lovely lights being all the lovelier for the vague hippy significance they were taking on in her head.

In fact, beneath the outward expression of jaded amusement Rosetta displayed in public, her irritation was turning into something rather more potent. She knew, uneasily, that any minute now – if Brian and the groupies who'd stowed away in the limo as it sped out of the arena really didn't shut up – she would say something, if only to stop the relentless yatter that was filling the car, when something beautiful, and deserving of silent contemplation, was going on outside.

Added to that, John was in another car, and she didn't know what might be going on in it.

In short, things weren't cool.

'So, I think we need to talk to the people in Houston,' Brian was saying excitedly. 'We need to get something really special laid on – it's Glynn's birthday. I was thinking about covering the stage with rose petals and fake snow, you know, raining down from the ceiling in a bizarre seasonal juxtaposition.' He smiled and coughed shyly. In the sleazy glamour

of the car he looked more Jermyn Street than ever. 'Remind
him of home – England's rather like that in the summer.'

The two PR girls from the American record company (not
that Rosetta believed *that* introduction for one minute) giggled appreciatively, so much so that one of them spilled a few
beads of chilly champagne on to the tiny tight T-shirt she
was wearing; it had '69' stretched over her breasts, which
was obviously either her speciality or her price.

'Oh shit, I'm all wet!' she breathed, her blue eyes, with
their pinprick pupils, widening like a Disney deer. Manny,
the promoter, and Nev, who had made a smooth and total
transition from furniture remover to world class roadie-
pirate in a matter of five frenetic years, leaned forward with
hankies to help her out. Quite at which point The End had
started to attract first-division groupies, Rosetta didn't know.
But then she wasn't sure when they'd got this famous either,
though no doubt Brian could pinpoint it to an exact day
and pay cheque.

The girl widened her eyes still further as Nev patted her
cleavage ineffectually, and parted her lips in a sticky smile.
She looked as if she'd just fallen face first into a pot of honey.
'Thank you seeew much!' she giggled. 'I just love English
guys – you're seeew *chivalrous*!'

Rosetta amended her initial assessment of the two girls.
With acting skills like that she was obviously in films. Of a
certain type.

They look so young, she thought. The pair of them looked
about fourteen, if that. Just kids, like most of the girls hanging round the hotel lobby. Loads of them, new every day.
And they weren't really coming for the music any more – just
the after-party. Suddenly the skin around her eyes felt very
taut and dry from the air con, and the small Caesarean scar
Robert had left behind ten months ago ached beneath her
pull-you-in pants. Maybe it hadn't been such a good idea to
have another baby so soon; even if the constant adrenalin
was still keeping her going, in many ways she felt like she'd

been breastfeeding for ever. In fact, she felt like a twenty-four-hour petrol pump.

Still, she thought sternly, *you were the guilty one.* You were the one who thought another baby might make things better with you and Brian. A little girl was the least you could do.

She stared out of the window at the snow. No woman should be allowed to make a *shopping list* in the four months after childbirth, much less life decisions. But there wasn't anyone there to tell her not to be so stupid – and hadn't she vowed not to let her conscience run her life any more like some mental bulletin of the *Catholic Herald*?

But Robert was here, nevertheless, and she wouldn't wish him back for the world. *No. Not at all.* Not that it had really changed very much with Brian; he was still busy and a little distant, and now slept with her even less.

'Man, those guys there were just *grooving* this evening,' cooed the other girl, putting a glossy bougainvillea-coloured nail to her cheek in seductive admiration. 'I thought they would break down the doors outside the hall. Those boys are *seeew lucky* to have you running the show for them!'

'Honey, I think *we're* all the lucky ones,' oozed Manny, who had been about as genuine as plastic ham all evening. 'These boys are *on fire.* Can I refill your glasses, ladies?'

This was greeted with a cascade of tinkling fake laughter and some sub-farmyard mewing of pleasure as the champagne foamed over the glasses and on to their bare knees.

Nev shuffled himself further within the arm-reach of the better-endowed of the two groupies and made sure his 'Carol' tattoo was well covered by his tour T-shirt.

For God's sake! thought Rosetta, her temper spiked with alcohol and lack of sex and baby hormones. *If they haven't got any respect for themselves then they bloody ought to have some for me!*

She glared at Nev, who met her steely eyes with a look of fear. Then he dropped his gaze to the absurdly stacked glittery sandal inching its way seductively up his lower calf. It was attached to a long bare teenage leg that knew what it was doing, even if the face at the other end was maintaining an expression of serene innocence. Up and down, up and down, leaving little snail's tracks of glitter on his jeans and exposing the hairy white leg above his wrinkled socks.

Rosetta then glared at Brian, who affected not to know what she was glaring for. Then, under an intensified stare, he made apologetic grimaces and smiled his smallest, most conciliatory smile while trying to telegraph 'What can I do? He's the promoter?' using his beetly eyebrows.

Oh *please*, thought Rosetta wearily, it's like being married to your dad and your brother at the same time.

She knew she was behaving like a cow, but she couldn't stop herself. It had been a long, long day and all she wanted was to fall flat on her face on the vast hotel bed and sleep for a few precious minutes before going on to the after-show. Normally when it was just her and Brian and Nev in the car she could grab half an hour's kip but with these girls and Manny here, she couldn't relax – not with a public face to keep up. People expected her to be a certain way, as much as they expected the group to play the singles. Maybe that was what was making her ratty.

'Brian!' she murmured, glaring at the offending leg.

'Hey,' said Brian, nodding in Nev's direction, then at the smaller of the two girls. 'Pack it in. He's allergic to space dust.'

Reluctantly the spangly sandal returned to the shag pile. Nev looked disappointed.

'Are you OK, darling?' asked Brian. He lifted a hank of hair out of Rosetta's eyes. 'You look very pale.'

'I'm cool,' she said faintly and pressed his hand. She had to drag herself together somehow; there would be cameras and people as soon as they got out of the car. 'Pale' was fine. 'Pale' could be fashionable overdose on the wrong mix of drugs, it could be forgetting to eat again, it could be stylishly anaemic. 'Tired', on the other hand, wouldn't be good. At *all*.

'You just say if there's anything we can do, honey,' said Manny, anxious not to miss a trick. 'Anything we can get you at all, you just say now.'

He cast a concerned look at Brian. If Rosetta wasn't herself then the party after the show would be flat, flat, flat. Most of the time the journalists went straight to her table for a little gossip and a little glamour, skipping the other tables where drugs made the conversation too one-sided. The boys in the band were electric on stage, but once they stumbled off, they were amazingly gauche for such seasoned pros. Red could get violent when he was pissed and Glynn was a one-man campaign to get the age of consent lowered, not something Manny wanted the hacks to start writing about. Besides which, he was pushing this new freaky local band, and he'd promised to get them photographed with her tonight, in his brother's new bar. Like most of the other scenesters, they were dying to meet this smart English chick with the high-toned voice and the sexy eyes. She had a way of making everyone feel like the headline act, just by talking to them.

Manny added an ingratiating smile.

Rosetta waited a couple of beats, then returned it weakly, and relaxed into the seat with a brief swell of confidence, knowing she had control over the mood in the limo again. But before she could clear her throat and point out the stars and the snowflakes, Joe, who was, according to the record company payroll, the technical manager of The End but who had long since handed over all arrangements not concerning drugs to Brian, started talking about the logistics of getting the gear (or rather the electrical type of gear) to San Diego for the next day, and Brian got out his little notebook and began to make notes.

The two PR girls (Rosetta had by now concluded that PR stood for Penis Relief) were sitting opposite her in the limo, crushed between Nev and Manny, crossing and uncrossing their legs unnecessarily. They both wore hotpants. One of them had the leather stitching of the limo upholstery imprinted into the soft underside of her bare leg and the other, now Rosetta had a clear view, appeared to have been inhaling her face powder, which was coating each nostril like finely desiccated coconut.

Rosetta began to sigh but stopped herself, unwilling to show weakness in front of these kids. She massaged her temples with the tips of her long fingers. When had the groupie thing got under her skin like this? She used to find it amusing, but suddenly, in this last year, there had been a new swarm of real little girls outside the hotels, lured by the salacious teen-mag stories of the bands who loved tender, untried groupie flesh. They hung around the lorry entrance of the gigs, shivering in little lace skirts that barely covered their hairless legs, clamouring after every limo that went past. They didn't have any cards to play other than their youth – but the way they dressed, you couldn't imagine any of them were innocent. It made Rosetta feel like a million years old – as some of the lippier ones pointed out for her.

The real groupies, now she had more time for them. The original LA girls, the ones who'd wanted to be in the GTOs. At least they could tell you what the running order of the gig was likely to be. They were always there, the right place, the right time, the right hotel, holding their own little happenings in the long, long day before the gig and usually bearing gifts of shocking home-stitched shirts or embroidered guitar straps. Too bad most of them were leaving town now, marrying soap stars or 'going into acting', chased off by these little madams who just hung around not even bothering to fake their IDs.

Like these two, who didn't even have the nous to talk about the music. There were plenty of people to tell the band how *good* they looked. What they wanted to hear, especially now instead of being chilled out on pot, they were all snorting avalanches of coke, was how they were changing the world.

Rosetta thought of Patrick and Robert asleep at the hotel and wondered if the backstage pass bribe had been enough to get Sugar, Red's current two-night-stand, to read them their bedtime story all the way through.

This was only the first night of The End's three-day stay in LA; any longer and the fans would wreck the hotel and all the profits from the gigs. As they sped after the limo containing Red, Simon and their small troop of 'journalists' and 'astrologers', all kitted out in tight minis and Lurex halternecks, Manny had taken great delight in telling everyone that the police had already made three arrests and found five women naked in the dumb waiter.

Or *on* the dumb waiter. Rosetta hadn't been listening at the time, being more concerned by the girls who slipped a little envelope to one of the road crew and slid into the back of John's blacked-out limo while the band were still finishing their final number. Glynn now refused to share a car with John and had Nev chalk demarcation lines on to the stage at every gig.

Rosetta stared out of the window watching the storm intensify outside the nice warm limo, refusing to join in with the gossipy banter about the big English band that had trashed the hotel the previous week, feeling the champagne come-down begin to deflate what was left of her good mood. Like warm water running out of a bath, she thought. And to think that it was a really great night only thirty minutes ago.

At the gig, she'd been able to float away from all the external stress, sitting at the side of the stage listening to the band, really getting into the new material they were trying out for the album. The touring wasn't making them stale at all – they seemed to thrive on it. Red still did his stupid tambourine solo while everyone else had a quick drink, Glynn still pretended to come during 'Maybe I Will', John still

looked over at her during the solo in 'Your Smile' and Brian
still winked back at him over her head, oblivious.

No, the gigs were as good as ever, and the band got bigger
with every tour. Every night Rosetta felt proud that she was
there with them, a legitimate part of their scene. It was afterwards that was such a come-down, when there were poses to
be thrown and endless meet-and-greet parties, where she
met everyone in town and never made any real new friends.
Added to which, though she wouldn't admit it, it was getting
to be a real physical effort: she'd promised herself that there
would be no more coke and not too much champagne while
the boys were babies, so she had to listen to everyone else
being hysterically witty and flagrantly horny while she flirted
with journalists, and flattered promoters, and wondered
whether taking speed to keep herself awake would make her
a bad mother.

Of course, the boys stayed with her. Rosetta knew deep
down that the tour-bus wasn't really a place for children big
enough to know what was going on, but Brian and Manny
were really keen to have the kids on the road. Hippie kids
were the new tour accessory, running barefoot about the
place, smiling at the cameras at airports – most bands now
had at least a couple of blond toddlers in tow. There was
nothing like a cute kid to dispel the terrible rumours filtering
back to the other wives in London, for a start. Patrick and
Robert were gorgeous babies, who only seemed to smile
when there was a camera in the room. But then Brian and
Manny weren't truly aware how red Patrick's face went now
he was teething or the plainly evil looks that baby Robert
gave her some nights.

'Drop more champagne, Rosetta, honey?' asked Manny
in his most ingratiating tone.

She looked up. He'd opened a fresh bottle, obviously to
demonstrate the storage capacity of the in-car drinks bar. She
didn't like to think what the PR girls would have done with
the bottle if she wasn't there.

Rosetta's heart stung with the sudden image of what might be happening with the twins in John's car. It had been three days since they'd been able to spend any time together, and even then their conversation was more about what they weren't saying than what they were.

'Why not?' she said blankly and held out her glass. Then she remembered herself and flashed him a flirtatious smile.

Rosetta didn't really like drinking with people she didn't know; it was too hard to remember to keep your public face on and sometimes when the shiny-faced hangers-on offered her the little vials of coke and stuff she didn't even recognize, it just made her sad that there was no one here who had the first idea what she was really like. Sometimes she almost laughed.

Brian's big hand crept on to her leg and squeezed her knee through her metallic skirt. Stupid skirt, thought Rosetta, hating it. It made her feel about six inches older than the two teenagers sitting opposite. Not that Brian would have noticed – groupies passed him by altogether. His drug of choice was the power trip thing. But then everything he asked for these days, he got. He could have had any of the little groupies if he wanted, but he just wasn't interested. Maybe if he *had* a fling or two, that might make her feel less of a slapper. Less of a failed wife.

She looked at his big, reliable face, all gentle where John was angular and poetic.

'You OK, Rosie?' he whispered into her hair.

'Don't call me Rosie,' she hissed, more angry at herself than at him.

The broad hand merely increased its pressure, then added a couple of pats. 'That's my lady.'

But then how many failed wives went abroad with their men, ran households, brought up kids, assisted secretaries, massaged egos and generally did everything except sleep with their husbands? Didn't that cover most of Richmond?

'Don't call me your Lady, either,' she snapped without meaning to.

One of the girls smirked at the other and said something under her breath. Rosetta felt all the irritation in her body gather up like a cyclone and direct itself entirely on the vacuous little slut hoping to shove her out of the way.

'Oh, shit,' said Manny, catching the whispered aside out of the corner of his eye. He tapped the girl on the knee playfully, but his eyes were wary, flicking back and forth to Rosetta. 'Now, honey, I really wouldn't . . .'

'Well, now,' said Rosetta, feeling savage. She trained her eye on the sniggering kid, staring right through her. 'If you've had an amusing thought why don't you share it with the rest of us, sweetheart? God knows it probably hasn't had much company in that pretty little head of yours. Lead us down the echoing canyon of your mind, why don't you, so we can all admire the view?'

She was sitting so close to Manny that she could feel his thigh flinch, and Brian's thumb started to massage her hand. But it didn't make her stop. She was filled with a powerful kind of anger, and she knew it wasn't really directed at these little tramps.

The girl just stared back with a confident insolence Rosetta knew she used to throw at teachers herself at school. Only this hard-faced child used it confidently on real people. It was a look that said, 'Don't bother trying to put me down, because you're staying here, you're old, you're over, and your world's my oyster now.'

Rosetta felt angry and sick. She was twenty-three, for God's sake!

'Oh, I wasn't talking about you, if that's what you're so hung up about,' drawled the kid.

'C'mon, Dixie . . .' warned her friend.

But Dixie fixed Rosetta with a stare that came encrusted with sapphire blue glitter. She looked like a malevolent pixie. 'I was just sayin' to Storm here that it was a real shame we didn't get to ride in the limo with John, or with Red and the boys.'

'That's because little chicks like you don't get to ride with the band,' said Manny, trying to make it sound like a joke, and swiftly calculating that it was easier to piss off two pretend PR girls than have Rosetta going mad at all of them. She'd been kind of moody since Chicago, when those roadies had accidentally thrown firecrackers into her sons' hotel room, thinking it was Red's. He looked at Rosetta as if to say, 'Storm, eh? Where *do* they get these names?'

'Oh, we *ride* with the band,' Dixie corrected him, her eyes never leaving Rosetta's strained white face. She left a perfect pause. 'And sometime we travel in limos too.'

A silence fell, as chilly as the snowflakes now silting up around the windows. A few leaves of paper slid from Manny's lap, all city itineraries forgotten. In the background the radio, the DJ, well-bribed by Brian, was playing one of the tracks off The End's last album, one which Rosetta knew John had written about her – so aching with frustrated intimacy that she could barely stand to hear it on the radio – and it was that unsteadying, too familiar mixture of guilt and pride that sent her over the edge.

'What *do* you mean?' asked Rosetta, her consonants frostily English.

'I mean,' said Dixie, snapping her gum, 'that we're . . . good friends with the band. You dig?'

Rosetta released a scarily brittle laugh into the car and rested her hand on Brian's knee.

Brian hoped for a second that she was going to let it go. These days it was impossible to tell which way she would fall.

'Oh, how *cute*,' said Rosetta. 'I didn't think anyone *said* "You dig?" any more.'

Brian winced for the teenagers. She clearly wasn't going to let it go. And they were still five miles from the hotel.

'Well,' said Dixie, in a voice sticky with sarcasm and gum, '*I guess* it's gone out and come in again since the first time *you* used it.'

Storm sniggered beside her but stopped mid-yuck as Rosetta flashed her one of the most chilling glowers she had ever seen. Every sleepless night lying untouched by Brian, waiting for Patrick to start howling, every frustrating hour comforting whiny Robert, every yearning conversation with John about his tormented blues revelations, every slap administered to a comatose Red twenty minutes before a gig, every stupid interview wanting to know about which rock musicians fancied her – it was all distilled into a laser beam of absolute disdain directed at the embodiment of all that was wrong with her life.

'*What* a shame,' said Rosetta ominously. She didn't need to say any more. Her face supplied the rest.

Storm wanted to slide out of the window and run straight home. The coke was definitely wearing off now, her feet were aching, and she'd told Dixie it was stupid to get into a limo with Rosetta Mulligan in the first place. But Dixie had got this far and she wasn't going to be kicked out of the hotel at the last count by some elderly has-been who happened to be shacked up with the manager and thought she had a reserved sticker on the chief heartbreaker.

'Girls, we're all tired,' Manny began, making furious 'Shut up or fuck off' gestures with his eyebrows at the two teenagers.

'So I can see,' said Dixie. She fidgeted with her nose. 'Some more than others. Still, if you can't take the pace, I'm sure there's a nice comfy bed waiting for you back at the hotel. I know there's one there for me.'

'Really?' asked Rosetta. 'I trust you got cash up front.'

'Honey!' Brian laid a restraining hand on her thigh. She was steaming hot, as if she was running a fever. He wondered whether she was ill – it wasn't like her to be so aggressive.

Dixie pretended to ignore the barb, knowing she had a much better card to play. 'I have a date with a *Mr Tetley* tonight.' She smiled devastatingly. 'He's staying in the *Churchill Suite*, I understand.'

Rosetta flinched. The band never checked in under their real names, to stop fans getting into the rooms pretending to be journalists or personal yoga teachers, and, being more paranoid than most, John changed his every night. Last night he'd been Mr McEwan, and the night before, Mr Watney-Partypack. On Red's suggestion, he was working his way through the breweries of Britain on the grounds that it confused the American fans a bit.

'Fancy that,' she said, feigning disinterest while her heart hammered. 'Is he a friend of yours?'

'*Close* friend. You got a problem with that?' Dixie was on a lippy cocaine roll now. She'd never dreamed she'd get this far, or that it would be so easy to get past all the security that The End were so famous for. It wasn't that hard to read upside down and if roadies left hotel details lying around while she was persuading them to part with a backstage pass, then who could blame her for a bit of initiative? And even better, here was the celebratedly cool Rosetta Mulligan on the verge of a crying jag just because someone young and cute was in the back of her limo pretending to hit on John O'Hara!

It dawned belatedly on Dixie that with the info she now had, she probably could get in there for real and she squirmed in her seat with excitement. Beside her, Storm was silent and shivering.

'Why do you imagine I would have a problem with that?' snapped Rosetta. 'Other than the small matter of Mr *Tetley* going out with my best friend?'

Brian looked at her in surprise. This was the first he'd heard of it. First he'd heard of John having *any* girlfriend. 'Anita or Sue?'

'Sue,' said Rosetta, almost at once. Anita was in the States herself, selling her new clothing line to boutiques. Sue, on the other hand, was safely at home writing about how to order the best coffee in restaurants and which were the grooviest phone codes to have.

This news stopped Dixie in her tracks only momentarily,

as she weighed up where Rosetta's loyalties would lie – the band or the buddy. It was a toughie, and she had to decide quick to avoid being slung out. But since everyone on the scene knew there was something going on with John and Rosetta, she couldn't possibly be siding with the dumb friend, could she?

'Rilly? Too bad she couldn't come on tour with him,' drawled Dixie, shaking her head so her blonde curls danced on her bare shoulders. 'Should have taken a leaf out of your book, don'cha think?'

'Which book is that?'

'How does that song go?' Dixie put her finger on her lip-glossed mouth and made a moue of pretend thought. 'Stand by your man? Still, it ain't like he's *married* or anything, is it?' The glittery eyes widened innocently and then hardened. Oh, come on. Everyone knew. Surely?

'Stop the car, Manny,' said Rosetta, evenly.

Manny coughed nervously and pretended to look up from his tour notes. 'Sorry, did you—'

'I said, *stop the car.*'

Manny tapped on the smoked glass dividing the driver from the womb-like cabin and the car slid to a smooth, power-assisted halt.

Rosetta reached into her crocheted karma bag and pulled out a wad of notes.

'What are you . . .?' Storm's voice was wavering, and even Dixie's cool had turned panicky.

'I'm paying you off, darling.' Rosetta peeled some notes off the wad. 'Here you go. Hundred dollars should cover it. Buy yourself some clothes.'

'You can't just . . .' Dixie looked at Manny for support but suddenly all eyes were elsewhere.

Rosetta swung the limo door open. 'I'm sure you can hitch a ride.' She furrowed her eyebrows and the girls turned from glossy jailbait into sulky teenagers like fairy princesses turning back into frogs.

Dixie pulled on the long leather patchwork coat that had been balled up at her feet, so as not to hide her best assets, and seeing that resistance was useless, and no help would be forthcoming from the men, she wriggled out, pausing only to slip her business card into Manny's top pocket and chuck him under the chin.

'Hey, chill, grandma. And I'll see you at the hotel, honey,' she said with a nasty smile. In the distance there were three other limos carrying the rest of the tour party. And Dixie knew ways to make them stop.

Little Storm couldn't get out of the limo fast enough, but then stopped and gasped as the cold, snowy air hit her bare arms and legs. She turned back to the car with a scared expression on her face, misery written all over her shocked face.

'Go on, beat it,' said Manny, making to shut the door. 'And if I see either of you at the hotel, I'll make it my own personal business to phone your mother and your school principal.'

He slammed the door with a flourish and smiled at Rosetta and Brian with the satisfaction of a job well done. 'Now, drive on, driver, we've got a party to go to!'

Rosetta looked round at the men, none of whom wanted to meet her eye. Except Manny, who seemed to want a pat on the head.

'Stop!' said Rosetta, as the car purred into life again. She slapped the smoked glass screen with the flat of her hand. 'Stop!'

'Oh, what now?' demanded Brian.

Rosetta scrabbled with the silver door handle and staggered out into the snow, her high heels slipping on the wet tarmac. The coldness slapped at her tired face. Dixie was lying spreadeagled on the freeway, her leather coat discreetly protecting her from the puddles, pretending to clutch her leg, and Storm was standing on the grass verge, shivering and crying.

'Ah, quit it, Pammie,' Dixie was whining. 'I know Red's in the next car, he'll stop for me.'

Storm's big eyes turned to Rosetta with such fear in them that Rosetta felt truly horrible. She towered over the girl, despite the stacked heels which now had a pathetic dressing-up-box look. The mascara was running down Storm's face in long black lines and a couple of her stick-on silver stars had slipped. Rosetta was on the verge of taking them back home herself when she remembered that both these underage girls were trying to break into John's room and would doubtless have had no qualms about offering to screw Brian, Manny and Nev, in that order, to get there.

You had to keep standards.

'Here,' she said and pulled off her long fur coat. Immediately she could feel the spots of snow falling on the chiffon of her blouse like tiny stabs of cold on her skin. 'Take this.' She shivered and handed the coat to Storm, who didn't move.

'Come on,' Rosetta said more gently. 'Put it on, you'll catch your death out here.'

When Storm's eyes filled up with tears again, Rosetta put the coat round her shoulders. It reached the ground.

'If I see you back at the hotel, I will call the police and make sure you never *ever* get further than reception for the rest of your life,' she said sternly. 'And that goes even more for your trollopy little pal. Do we understand each other?'

Storm nodded.

Meanwhile Dixie continued to roll about on the road, unaware of what was going on behind her.

'Fine,' said Rosetta. 'And don't get in cars with strange men. Or take drugs from strangers.'

They looked at each other in silence. *What kind of a girl does this?* wondered Rosetta. *What does she expect from the men they're following round? Respect, or gratitude, or what? And does she think I'm just one of them?*

Suddenly her insides felt as cold as her skin and she turned and got back into the limo.

Inside, conversation ceased abruptly.

'Come on,' she said, 'let's get back to the hotel.' She sank into the corner of the back seat and refused Manny's offer of another glass of champagne. What Rosetta really wanted was a Mars bar or something, but American chocolate tasted like sick, and she didn't want to be seen eating, not when the Pucci wrap dress she'd brought over for the final night still wouldn't fasten at the waist. Brian put his strong arm around her and she felt about as small as Storm but much more of a fraud.

'You're such a doll, Rosetta,' said Manny, cheesily.

A blow-up one, or an untouchable china one, she wondered, but only gave him her best distant smile.

Back at the hotel, she went straight to the room, refusing all offers of food and drink and Swedish massages on the grounds that she had a terrible headache. Brian trailed after her, despatching messengers and worried concert officials with a sweep of his manicured hand, promising to sort various small problems just as soon as he had sorted out his wife.

Brian and Rosetta had a large suite in the Art Deco hotel, with adjoining dressing-rooms – for bed-hopping Hollywood starlets, she presumed wryly, when the dividing doors had been demonstrated by the porter. Robert and Patrick were tucked up and asleep in the corner of her dressing-room, where a bored-looking chambermaid was sitting reading the *National Enquirer* and stretching her gum between her teeth and forefinger.

So much for Sugar and her bedtime stories, thought Rosetta grimly, and slipped the girl twenty dollars to leave.

'Are you all right, sweetheart?' Brian called from the other room. Rosetta closed the door gently so they could talk without waking the children and walked back into the main bedroom. He was stripping off to have a quick shower and Rosetta felt a shudder of revulsion at the spots on his back. Brian came out in rashes when he was stressed, and his back was a lurid testimony to all the hassles he was currently under.

'I'm fine,' she lied. 'Just get sick of all those dumb girls littering the place. It's like Madame Jo-Jo's some nights.'

'I know what you mean.' Brian was peeling off his Y-fronts. Rosetta made a mental note to get him some better underwear. Maybe that might help. 'I keep telling the lads to encourage a better class of groupie, but you know what they're like. Quantity, not quality. I blame the road crew. You should have a word.'

Rosetta eased her aching feet out of her platforms and looked across to the dress hanging up ready for tonight's party. It was one of John's favourites: he claimed he was utterly unable to resist her in it – or so he said. His flirting was arch, like everyone around them. It was breaking her heart. Not that she really wanted to go out again tonight – she needed some peace to think. Things couldn't go on like this: on tour with her husband *and* the man she loved *and* their kids. It wasn't normal – it wasn't even avant-garde. It was a total head-wrecker. Much more of this and she'd totally forget what normal was; people accepted the most outrageous set-ups once they'd seen it twice.

Lately Rosetta felt she'd been peering down the rabbit-hole and was in danger of slipping over the edge herself. And in desperate times, you had to call on desperate measures. Kids hadn't worked, trying to be friends hadn't worked, being one of the lads definitely wasn't working. It was time for shock therapy.

Like most of the other women she met on the road, Rosetta had searched for something to occupy the hours and hours of sound-checking and hanging around at airports, and, not seeing much point in the painstaking macramé wardrobes many of them produced, she had thrown herself into learning tarot and astrology. Astrology she preferred, because there was something soothing about drawing out elaborate charts for people, but tarot was infinitely more useful to her in terms of keeping the highly superstitious roadies in line. And it meant she could use it herself, asking the same questions over and over again, letting her mind wander around the pictures and images until she got quite reliant on using the cards to explore things she couldn't talk about to a soul.

It was cheaper than therapy, and safer than confession, anyway.

For the past few weeks on the road a germ of an idea had been sprouting little shoots in her mind, about how she might manage to even out the terrible imbalances in her life, and now she just had to be careful how she planted it in Brian's organizational head. In a warped logic, it might even make everything make sense.

Elegantly, Rosetta undid her twisted knot of hair and laid back on the bed, slipping the complimentary satin eyemask over her red eyes.

The soft darkness rushed up at her and she sank into grateful relaxation, feeling the bed swallow her up.

'Darling, I've been thinking,' she projected into the bathroom, 'it's such a shame John's on his own. I mean, Red's got Janette, and Glynn's going out with that model – what's her name?'

Brian's voice was barely audible over the violently American power shower. 'Oh, er, the one with the legs . . . I know who you mean . . . God, what's her name?'

Rosetta's forehead creased into her eyemask, annoyed that she'd genuinely forgotten and wasn't just pretending not to know for once. Glynn had decided some time ago that he could only go out with girls famous enough not to require the additional definition of a surname. 'Oh, she was on the cover of *Vogue* last month. She's got one of those single word names, um . . .'

'He's going out with her?' Brian sounded impressed. 'That'll be great publicity for the new album, if she's hanging around.'

Why did everything have to boil down to publicity with

Brian, thought Rosetta, but she couldn't be bothered to argue, even for the sake of it, that Glynn and What's Her Name were less a love-match and more a mutual appreciation society.

'Can you come and scrub my back with that stuff the doctor gave me?' he wheedled.

She allowed herself one more divine moment of total oblivion then levered herself off the comfortable bed with a big sigh, and focused herself on the task in hand in the bathroom.

'I just think it's sad that John's on his own.' She smoothed some of the pink cream on to her hand and applied it gently to Brian's angry spots.

'Ahhhhhh.' The muscles in his back relaxed against her hands. 'Oooohhh. I wish you'd do that more often. You never give me massages any more. *Is* John on his own? I thought you told those girls he was with Sue.'

Rosetta bit her lip and tried to close her ears to the yells of protest coming from her conscience. She tried to imagine the words *The best thing for everyone* imprinted across her mind in jolly *Yellow Submarine* floating capitals. But they popped as soon as they appeared.

'Well, no . . . that was . . . no, he's not. But I know Sue's had a crush on him for years. And they've had a couple of dates. I think it might be going somewhere. Sort of.'

'Really?' Brian sounded surprised. 'Are you sure about that?'

'Honestly, Brian, I thought you read the press-cuttings file!' Rosetta tried to sound teasing although, mentally, she was throwing plates at his thick head. 'She's been taking him out all over the place. Restaurants, bars, dog-racing.'

'No, I had no idea. None at all. So you think they're serious?'

More screams of protest from the pit of her stomach as she rinsed her hands in the sink. 'Um, I don't know. I don't think John . . .' She searched in her mind for a good reason, apart from the most obvious one. 'Because John's been so busy with the band, he didn't have time to start a relationship. And Sue's not a part-time girlfriend. But maybe it's time to start . . . I don't know . . . encouraging them to take it on a bit.'

'And he does have time now? With this and another tour to do before the end of the year?'

Rosetta concentrated on folding the towels. 'It might be the stabilizing force he needs to get on and do some writing. Knowing she's back home, waiting for him.'

'Honey, he needs to have someone who can be *on the road* with him – like you and me. Unless you're there every day with someone, there's no *way* you can maintain any kind of honesty – look at Red and Janette! He makes one of the press assistants send Janette made-up tour itineraries, just so she doesn't know where he is!'

Rosetta flinched. *She* sent them. Janette had made Red promise that the band wouldn't ever stay in LA again. But then so had his girlfriends in New York and Chicago. 'John's different. He's very . . . loyal. He needs a good traditional set-up.'

So he can feel as guilty as you do.

'And he needs a nice woman,' she added.

That you've already vetted to be utterly unchallenging.

Brian turned off the shower and, out of habit, Rosetta immediately passed him the huge fluffy towel hanging next to the bath.

'Are you sure Sue's right for him?' he asked, towelling off his hair. 'I mean, is she really his type?'

'And what is his type?'

Thankfully Brian's answer was lost in the folds of the hotel towel and when his head re-emerged it was thoughtful, if oddly guarded.

'Well, do it then,' he said. 'Mind you, I never really thought he was . . .'

'Was what?' Rosetta's headache returned as the gentle thump of the pre-party drinks began to float through from Red's suite next door.

'Nothing.' Brian wrapped himself in the towel and gave her waist a paternal squeeze on his way past into the bedroom. 'And you call *me* a compulsive fixer. You just want everyone to be happy, don't you? Just like in your magazine spreads.'

Rosetta couldn't see his face. She wandered back to the minibar, which was stocked with yet more champagne and a selection of unfamiliar fruit. It was soothing to hear Brian's lukewarm response, because it reassured her that it was unthinkable to imagine Sue and John together. And yet in an odd way, that made the plan even more logical.

'But Sue's so keen on him,' she said, snipping off a bunch of grapes with the little scissors. 'Can we get some of these for home?' she asked, holding up the dinky scissors. 'She's known him for years, after all.'

She looked up in the mirror. Brian was obviously thinking hard. His spots were already flaring up again.

'You might be right,' he said slowly. He smiled and started towelling again, his floppy hair shaking with the effort. Brian didn't really suit the long hair thing. 'And goodness knows she's done you – done us – some big favours over the years, hasn't she?' he observed, clearly pleased to be writing off a debt so painlessly.

Rosetta paused with the last little grape half-way to her mouth as her brain temporarily froze, as always, at the hot and painful memory of driving drunk through London to the empty, tempting flat. The night she'd made her pact with the devil. That wasn't too melodramatic a turn of phrase, was it? Not when you compared it to what the tabloids regularly said about Glynn and Red and the legions of willing victims lining the lobby.

And Rosetta didn't like to think what they would be

saying about her – and Brian – if Sue didn't wield a certain amount of clout among Fleet Street gossip columnists on her behalf.

'Oh yes,' she said, 'I certainly do owe her one.'

Chapter Nineteen

London, 2001

Greg agonized about the text message he was meant to send Tanith to kick off arrangements for their dinner date. It was very odd altogether – he knew in advance that she would say yes, which made him feel a bit foolish from the start. But Tanith insisted he go through the process of asking her, so he would know for next time, when presumably the date wouldn't be quite so transparent. And since he wasn't even sure how much of a date it was meant to be, in terms of genuine enjoyment rather than simple coaching, it was hard to know what note to strike.

Nearly impossible in fact, when he was trying to disguise his very real enthusiasm while simulating dynamic, date-winning panache. All in 350 characters or less.

In the end he settled for '*Are you around on Friday night?*' Short, to the point and non-embarrassing.

Until he got a text back saying, '*Why?*'

Which rather threw him.

Greg was in the middle of a register office do run by Carolyn Mackenzie at the time, and had only texted Tanith because he had twenty-five minutes to spare – due to Carolyn's new policy of telling Maggie her weddings began half an hour before they actually did. Not that Greg was often late. Maggie was quite reliable at predicting traffic problems, even if her bridal psychic vibrations had been a bit off of late.

But by the time Tanith got round to replying to his text message, the guests had started to filter in and Maggie was starting to prompt him for crowd shots.

He stared at the phone in his hand as if the letters might form into something more revealing than '*Why?*' while, directly in front of him, the bride's mother adjusted her hat in an amusingly inadequate powder compact being patiently held up by her husband.

'What's that?' asked Maggie, flipping through her new computer-printed chart of poses from Carolyn. 'Footie scores?'

'Er, not exactly,' said Greg. His stomach churned with shock. Shit, had he read the whole situation totally wrong? Was Tanith just having a laugh with him? Was this whole 'reinvent Greg' just another of Robert's smug jokes? Or was this a particularly vindictive female method of flirting?

'Oh, *come* on.' Maggie nudged him sharply in the ribs as the bride's mother got a bridesmaid to hold up another compact so she could see the back of her head too. 'That is such a good picture,' nagged Maggie, 'the Fuji judges *love* shots like that! And you haven't even thought about what you're going to enter this year!'

'I think you're rather missing the point, Mags,' said Greg, crossly as he grabbed his camera and ran off a few frames to shut her up. 'The idea is to do pictures for the bride and groom.'

'And Carolyn.'

'And Carolyn.'

As Greg said this, the bride's mother spotted Carolyn arriving in the rear-view compact mirror, resplendent in a new oyster silk cloche that made her head look like a giant field mushroom, and she immediately engulfed her in a hearty Home Counties handshake.

'Oh, Carolyn, you have *made* this wedding,' she gushed. 'I don't know *what* we'd have done without you!'

'She's a lot more relaxed than most bride's mothers,'

observed Greg, getting a nice shot of Carolyn's poker face scanning the crowd over the maternal shoulderpad.

'She's been here before, I think. Secret sherry binger,' muttered Maggie. 'She's got that funny aura about her.'

'What? Polo mints?'

'No, third wedding syndrome. And why has Carolyn come as a penis? Is it fancy dress?'

Carolyn disentangled herself from the grip with a professional charm, thanked the woman without moving her shell-pink lips and made a beeline for Greg, who put his camera down hastily.

'Didn't I remind you that most of my clients expect the wedding photographer to turn up in something a little more formal than one of Les Patterson's cast-off velvet smoking jackets?' she hissed without preamble.

Greg, expecting some savage criticism of his last set of wedding pictures, was caught offguard. 'This is an original Ronnie Stirling,' he protested, picking at the frayed cuffs.

'Vintage,' added Maggie. 'So fashionable.'

'Not in Chelsea, it's not,' hissed Carolyn. 'Not in my book.'

'Well, that's why he's a photographer and you're planning the weddings,' said Maggie sweetly. 'You have a different sense of the creative.'

Greg stared at his phone. What did she mean, *Why?*

Carolyn glared at him, trying to get his attention. But Greg's eyes had taken on their familiar far-away glaze, and the wedding party was starting to swell around them.

'I'll just . . .' he said vaguely, gesturing in the direction of some guests.

Carolyn watched him drift off and chewed her thin lips. 'I don't *have* to use him, you know,' she said to Maggie, finally. 'There *are* other wedding photographers in London.'

Maggie drew herself up to her full height, which was a fairly average five feet five. If Tanith had been casting an actress to fit Maggie's personality she should have been small and petite, or buxom, tall and dark, both of which would have fitted the mystic look better, but she was neither. 'I know that. But they're not as good as Greg.'

Carolyn bit her pen. She couldn't disagree, much as she'd like to. Brides had started asking for him by name, on the strength of his flattering skills, and even with the savage pay split Greg's accountant had argued for him, Carolyn was making loads of money on the weddings he covered.

She turned her snarl into a sweeter smile with some effort. 'I don't suppose you could get the jacket dry-cleaned for him, then?'

'I could ask,' conceded Maggie.

'Good.' And Carolyn swivelled on her heel and marched off in the direction of the best man.

'Penis head,' Maggie added thoughtfully and drifted over to Greg, with her clipboard at the ready to cross off any shots he'd done.

Greg stared morosely around the wedding party and wondered if he was getting *déjà vu*, or all weddings were basically the same. The bridesmaids looked quite familiar, he thought. Was that Flora? He'd seen her all over London – or *thought* he had – for ages after that dinner. And she hadn't waved back, even when desperation had somehow made him bellow, 'Flora! Flora! It's Greg!' at her across Clapham High Road.

He needed a girlfriend. He *so* needed a girlfriend.

Greg looked down at his phone again in case Tanith's message had changed, and slapped his head. 'I mean, is she playing games with me? Is that it?'

Maggie looked at him. 'You know, you could be right there. I've often thought that – is Carolyn so horrible to you because she secretly fancies you?' She put a finger on her cheek. 'There's a terrible thought to go to a wedding with.'

Greg was furiously flicking at his phone with one hand while trying to keep control of a camera in the other.

Because I have a spare ticket for a film and a spare place setting for dinner.

He pressed send with a grin of triumph and put his phone in his jacket pocket. 'OK, then, my little psychic friend – who're the first victims?' he said and held his hand out for the list.

Greg generally preferred civil ceremonies since they didn't have quite so much inherent drama to spark off problems. Apart from the basic fact that there was generally less tulle and lace to get in the way, no confusing Chauceresque language to trip up the emotionally unstable, and no danger of grandparents dozing off during a sermon, there was a refreshing lack of opportunity for jokers to stand up and cough during the 'Does anyone know any just cause and impediment . . .' gag. Greg had photographed one wedding (Home Counties, Groom: rugby player, Bride: physio) where – for a 'joke' – the entire team, plus reserves, coaches and foreign professional, had stood up and coughed. It had made a great picture. Particularly the bride's father's face.

This wedding was one of Carolyn's finest moments – even Greg had to acknowledge that from his vantage point behind a large arrangement of snow-white roses. It would seem that the bride had had some revelatory moment with Walt Disney early on in her life, as the entire wedding could not have been more Walt Disney if the registrar had worn big black ears. A bride who could walk into her wedding, blush-free, to the strains of the Sleeping Beauty Waltz, while leading three Dalmatian puppies on white ribbons – at the age of thirty-two – must have put up a pretty strong fight to get her own way against Carolyn's normally impeccable taste.

Greg realized with a touch of disappointment that the only reason the bridesmaids had looked familiar was not because one was Flora, but because they were both dressed *in the style of* (Carolyn had evidently put her foot down about fancy dress) Tinkerbell or something. Presumably she would be faxing him later with instructions to Photoshop Donald Duck into the registrar's place and seven dwarves all down the aisles.

But mild taste issues aside, it was certainly going much better than the last three weddings he'd done, and Greg was almost starting to enjoy himself with the pleasingly photogenic bridesmaids, when Tanith texted back in the middle of the vows.

Greg was smart enough to turn the ring tone off on his phone during ceremonies, but hadn't planned for it to wiggle across the floor as it vibrated from its temporary resting place under his jacket, attracting the attention of the three puppies, who broke free of their ribbons and proceeded to chase it round the harp set up at the front.

Maggie was quick, much quicker than him, and scuttled in from the side of the hall, keeping very low to the ground like an SAS marksman. She had pried it out of their jaws before it had time to stop jerking around, even if she had to lift one puppy almost off the ground to do so.

'So sorry,' she said, in a much posher voice than normal, holding up her hands. 'My vibrator – *so* embarrassing!'

There was a shocked silence. A woman in the back row of the chairs reacted sympathetically and then blushed bright red.

Carolyn Mackenzie looked as if she was about to swallow her own tongue.

Greg took some reaction shots, since it was a waste not to.

The registrar carried on seamlessly while Maggie slipped behind the floral arrangement and thrust the phone at him.

'You didn't want to work with Carolyn any more, did you?' she whispered.

Tanith had texted: '*Which restaurant?*'

'Why is she doing this?' hissed Greg, shaking the slimy phone. 'Why is she making it so *hard*? She was the one who suggested it, after all.'

'Suggested what?'

Greg flushed. 'Tanith's taking me on a sort of . . . dress rehearsal date. She thinks I need coaching in taking girls out.'

'Tanith, your brother's girlfriend? The one you've got a crush on?'

'Yes, thank you, Mystic Meg,' snapped Greg under his breath.

Maggie rolled her eyes. '*Well*, coming from anyone else, I would be impressed by the cunning double-smooth manoeuvre. Women do it all the time . . .' She pulled an unconvincingly 'little me' expression and put a finger on her nose. 'You know, "Oooh! Just show me how to change that spare wheel again, will you?"'

The congregation shuffled to their feet to sing, 'Some day my prince will come'.

'It's not like that,' said Greg, able to speak normally over the powerful ghetto-blaster the best man had wired up to the hall speaker system. 'She knows I can't take a girl out, just like that. And she's not wrong. I *obviously* don't know the first thing about it. I mean, look at me. This is evidently some kind of ritualistic thing I've never even come across.'

Maggie studied the message. 'She's just trying to be as difficult as possible – presumably to show you how much hard work it can be with some girls? Look, *she* knows and *you* know that she's available – this is the *fun* part. Imagine if she really *didn't* want to go out with you? Then you'd be worried about the restaurant.'

Greg looked at his phone, then at her. 'I missed something really big somewhere, didn't I?'

'Forget it. Does Robert not mind?' asked Maggie.

He shook his head. 'No, he thinks I'm a total charity case too. Anyway, the only reason she's free to go out is because he's going through Rosetta's accounts and has cancelled all social activities and general fun stuff.'

Maggie gave him an odd look, and not just because the congregation had segued into 'The Bare Necessities'. 'I wouldn't say that. I mean, there are plenty of books she could give you. She doesn't *have* to go for the hands-on approach.'

'What?' Greg raised an eyebrow. 'She thinks I'm so dumb I need one-to-one coaching?'

'*Dur*! *No*, she thinks ... Oh, for God's sake! How can you be Rosetta Mulligan's son and understand so little about women?' demanded Maggie.

'That's the point,' said Greg. 'Now, tell me what to text back. Quick, before they bring the dwarves on.'

On Friday night, Greg sat in the bar of E & O and nursed a beer, waiting for Tanith to turn up. He was hoping the beer would make him feel less nervous, but so far it wasn't working. It was just making him feel more gaseous. It would have been helpful, from a learning point of view, if Tanith had given him a clue about what to wear, but when he phoned her, she had laughed and said that that bit was up to him.

For a pretend date, he certainly had very real grinding indigestion in his stomach, and twenty-four hours of Deflatine hadn't even made an impression on it.

In the end he'd gone through Barney's clean laundry and swiped a creamy-yellow shirt from the top of the pile. Turning up in the clothes Tanith had made him buy at Gap would have made him feel a little bit too much like a sad case. Besides, there had to be some advantages to having Barney still holed up at the flat, drinking his beer and hiding out from the Chelsea Girl Mafia. Sadly Barney himself hadn't been home for three days, and was unable to offer him any pointers, although Greg wasn't sure how, exactly, he would have explained the situation anyway.

He gazed round the restaurant beyond the bar and quailed at how busy it was; Tanith had booked the table for him, arguing kindly that it would be quicker all round. And it had been – he had listened in on her side of the conversation and was impressed by the easy and charming way she persuaded

them to give her a table where she wanted it, without resort-
ing to threats, or using the phrase 'Do you know who I am?':
a tactic he'd heard both his parents employ, much to his
embarrassment.

Tanith arrived dead on time. He could see her through the
long glass windows, sweeping towards the door, and then
she was there, heading towards him with a wide smile on her
face, weaving through the other diners elegantly.

As usual, his heart bumped in his chest as soon as he saw
her. Even if she did refine his pulling technique to a level at
which he could recruit his own girlfriends, would he ever
find one as perfect as the teacher?

Stop it!

'You look gorgeous,' she said, leaning over to kiss his
cheek. 'By the way, I'm on time, but don't expect other girls
to be.'

'OK,' said Greg, stunned. He'd never seen Tanith dressed
up for a date before and the effect was disorientating, particularly when a guilty but excited little voice pointed out
that the effort was all for him. She had done something to
her shaggy blonde bob so it bounced when she turned her
head, and she was wearing a black wrap dress that showed
off the pale smoothness of her clavicles.

Greg dragged his eyes away before she caught him looking.

'*You* look gorgeous,' he said. 'Have you had your hair
dyed?'

Tanith lifted an admonishing finger. 'Right, take out your
notebook. First off, if a woman *seems* to have had her hair
dyed, *don't* compliment her on the colour. Even though she's
just spent a hundred quid on it, she doesn't want to hear it.
It's not like men and cars. The more it costs, the more natural it's meant to be. Otherwise we'd do it ourselves in the
bathroom. Instead, say, wow! You look amazing! *Have you
been on holiday?*'

'Fi-ii-ne,' said Greg, looking confused. 'Why?'

'There *is* no why with women,' said Tanith, catching the waiter's eye. 'If you knew why, you'd be horrified half the time, so just go with it. That's the secret of successful woman management.' A barman appeared at her shoulder and she smiled charmingly. 'Hello, can I order some wine, please? And is our table ready?'

Tanith started with some kind of duck thing which she ate deftly while quizzing Greg about The End. He was too busy filling her in on the endless tours and the mind-numbingly dull hours of sitting around waiting for things ('. . . for baggage checks, for support bands to finish, for hairdressers, for aeroplanes, for Rosetta's interviews . . .') to be nervous about emitting the right vibes or dropping his squid.

'You're very good with chopsticks,' she said.

Greg smiled and picked up a tiny flake of ginger. 'It's no big deal. We ate out a lot as kids – Rosetta made us. It was hard enough to keep us all quiet as it was without having to worry about what we would and wouldn't eat, and whether we'd behave in restaurants.'

'You went everywhere with your mum and dad?'

'Had to.' He shrugged. 'We were living proof for the *Daily Mail* that Rosetta couldn't be running an opium brothel on board the tour-bus, not with small children around.'

'Do you know how often I've heard you lot say that? It's as if you've all learned it off by heart. Maybe she *wanted* you to be with her,' suggested Tanith evenly. 'Lots of women would like to be able to take their kids to work with them. That was the thing in the seventies, wasn't it? Trying to do it all?'

Greg nodded sarcastically. 'Well, *she* certainly did it all.'

'How do you know?' asked Tanith. 'You were far too young to know what she did.'

'Well . . .' He floundered. That was true, actually, if he was honest with himself. They just fell into the trap of trotting out the same glib one-liners as Rosetta often did herself.

He hadn't really thought of it from that angle. 'I just . . . know.'

'You don't know *at all*,' said Tanith, skewering some more duck. 'Robert's exactly the same. He says the most *appalling* things about Rosetta, and doesn't even *think* about what it means. Or how it sounds coming out of his mouth. Lucky you, having your mother looking after you as a child. You're just going on what you've read in the papers, aren't you? And what other people have said about her. Tell me something – what's your first memory of Rosetta? Your first proper memory.'

'I thought this was meant to be a date,' Greg scowled. 'Not family therapy.'

Tanith lifted an eyebrow. 'Most girls you're going to date are going to know who Rosetta is. And men who are scathing about their mothers normally have immense hang-ups elsewhere. Not sexy. So get used to it. Now, come on, what's your first memory?'

He poked at the remaining seaweed on his plate. 'Um, OK, then. I must have been about three and we were on tour somewhere in America. I was in a dressing-room with Patrick and Robert, and some groupies and I had an orange, a huge one, much bigger than you get here. Robert was singing a song and being quite nice for once when suddenly Rosetta burst in with her hair all over the place, looking exactly like a witch from a Roald Dahl book. I remember she was wearing a pair of very pale blue jeans and her butterfly boots. She grabs Patrick and starts shaking him up and down frantically.' Greg's brow crumpled. 'I remember thinking that he looked like a puppet – he went all limp in her arms. I was scared that she was going to come and do that to me next, so I ran under the table and got a huge splinter in my finger.' He went silent.

'And?' Tanith prompted him.

He looked confused. 'And what?'

'And why did she do that?'

He shook his head. 'You know, I really don't know. I can't remember ever being told. It all went weird after that. Apparently that was the night that Rosetta . . .' He stopped suddenly and fixed an apologetic grin on his face. 'Well, we can't all have happy puppies in the park memories, can we?'

Tanith was staring at him, full of curiosity. The shutters of politeness had gone down over his eyes, like a cat's third eyelid, hiding what he was really thinking. 'Come on, Greg, that was the night that Rosetta *what*?'

He shook his head at her. 'No, no, I've taken on board that point about not speaking ill of your mother at the table, so I won't. Anyway,' he smoothed out his napkin on his knee, 'I really don't have many memories after that, because we all came back to England, and she sent Rob and Pat off to boarding-school. And I stayed at home until I was old enough to be packed off, and there was just Barney at home with Rosetta and the au pairs. Learning how to wrap eighteen-year-old girls round his little finger. She always said it was because the constant travelling was unbalancing us, but, you know . . . it must have been a bit of a downer on her social life, always having kids to think of. Much better to get us out of the way, let her get on with her parties.'

Tanith let that pass. 'And your dad?'

'Dad?'

'Where does he figure in your childhood?' asked Tanith. 'He seems like a really nice normal guy. Wouldn't he have stepped in if Rosetta had been really off the rails?'

Greg screwed up his eyes as if he were trying to think. 'Er . . . No, you're going too far into therapy speak now. I'm closing up out of habit. Oh no! There! Did you hear that dull clunking sound? No, sorry, my mind has just shut.' He refilled her wineglass and then his own. 'Let's talk about something else. I don't want to talk about Rosetta all night. I would hate my date to think I was preoccupied with my mother. I mean, there's Interesting Parent and there's Classic Sexual Complex.'

'OK,' said Tanith. 'Good point.'

'Let's talk about you and Patrick instead,' he said.

Tanith recoiled visibly.

'Only fair,' said Greg. The wine seemed to be removing the time lapse between thinking something and saying it. It also seemed to be speeding up the time it took to think of things to say. Or that could have been Tanith. She *was* very easy to talk to.

'No, fine,' said Tanith quickly. 'That's not a problem.' She took a sip of her drink. 'Trouble with you lot is that you're so geared to producing urban myth where there really isn't any. I, um . . .' She cleared her throat and rapidly tried to shuffle her thoughts into some acceptable order in her head. How much did Greg know? Or need to know?

He smiled encouragingly, and said nothing.

Tanith decided to go for the bald truth while she was still just sober enough to cut it short. 'I met Patrick at college, we went out for a year or two, but he wanted to get more serious than I did, and . . . and I broke it off, so he could go and find someone who could give him what he wanted.' She looked up. 'And that's it.'

'Really? That's *it?*' Greg looked sceptical.

'That's about the size of it. Well . . . Give or take a few sonnets and cliffside declarations of love.'

'That's more like it!' crowed Greg. 'I bet he was a nightmare to go out with. Did he cry at you?'

Tanith widened her eyes, trying to convey disbelief rather than amazement. *How did he know?* 'Um . . . no, not that I can remember.' She paused, feeling a little bad for lying to Greg after he'd been so open to her. 'Did he do that a lot at home?' she asked cautiously.

'*Oh* yes.' Greg refilled his glass. 'We all had our own little tactics for getting our own way. Pat cried, Robert did his breath-holding thing, I went silent and naughty and Barney just sort of smiled and looked angelic.'

'Do you always think of things in terms of all four of

you?' She gave him a funny look. 'People only do that Beatles thing because you do.'

Greg acknowledged her point with a wry grin. 'OK, sorry. But I bet Robert seems almost normal after that, doesn't he?'

Tanith smiled diplomatically over the rim of her wine-glass. 'Let's just say that you're all mad in pleasingly individual ways. And he's the easiest to live with. Should we order some water?'

'No, I thought we were drinking wine?' He flashed her a confiding look. 'Don't want to look cheapskate.'

'Greg, *always* have water on the table for ladies,' Tanith reprimanded him. 'Even if they don't drink it, just having it there makes them feel more able to finish off the wine without looking like an alkie.' She gratefully seized the opportunity to break Greg's line of thought, grabbed a passing waiter and ordered some mineral water.

When she turned back, Greg was looking at her in a funny way. He had also two little red wine fangs on his upper lip. His glass was empty. She could tell, with a heavy heart, that he hadn't dropped the subject.

'If you had to choose between them, Patrick and Robert, who would you pick?' he said.

'*Pick*? God, what a choice!' she said, stalling. Then, when she saw that he really wanted her to answer, she sighed and said, 'It's not a question of *picking*, Greg. I love—*loved* them both very much, but different people are right for different times of your life. That's why I think marriage is such a headfuck. It's not like you can say, Oh, I'll live with Robert and get him to fix the plumbing, but have Patrick sending me sonnets and seducing me on sandy beaches at the weekends. That's relationships all over – it's why men find it impossible to settle down, because they're looking for the one woman who has everything. And they don't exist. You have to decide what you really need and then live with it. Or never make a decision, which is a bit immature, really. A bit Hugh Hefner.

Except I don't see any bunnies with cooking skills or cross-word-solving abilities.'

'But if you had to spend your life with one of them?' he persisted. 'Surely Rob would be the sensible option?'

'He would, I suppose,' Tanith agreed. 'But ...' She shrugged. 'Who knows? Where are those mains?'

'If Patrick wanted you back, would you go?'

'How much have you had to drink?' asked Tanith with a laugh. 'And who's meant to be giving the relationship advice here?'

'*Would* you?' Greg looked at her with direct brown eyes.

Maybe that's his gift, thought Tanith distractedly. You really do have to answer his questions, whether you want to or not, because he *sees* things.

'I don't know,' she said. 'And that's the honest truth. I'm a very different person now to the girl he went out with. Perhaps I would handle it better. Perhaps I'm not looking for that kind of drama in my life any more. But,' she spread her hands on the table for emphasis, 'I'm with Robert, who is a good, kind, interesting and attractive man, and, let's not forget, *your brother*.'

'If a little anal.'

'If a little anal, indeed.'

Greg held her gaze as if he were about to say something, then changed his mind. 'Can I order you some wine to go with that water?' he asked. 'I know I'd like some.'

After another quarter of an hour there was still no sign of the main courses, so Greg duly decanted the next bottle of wine into the huge glasses.

'God, you could get really drunk very easily here, couldn't you?' observed Tanith, looking at what was left in the bottle with surprise. She could feel the distinct beginnings of lightness in her head, and she knew how quickly that spread to her tongue.

'Isn't that the point?' Greg did a startlingly good

impression of Barney's sexy double eye blink, closing both eyes languorously, then opening them twice in succession, letting his long lashes flutter cheekily, and Tanith recoiled in shock.

'Wow! That could have been Barney Mulligan!' she said, a little too loud, on account of the wine. She covered her mouth with a giggle and dropped her voice. 'With the shirt and everything!'

'Like Lenny Kravitz *could have been* Jimi Hendrix,' scoffed Greg, and drank some wine to hide his flush of embarrassment and excitement.

Like Barney, eh?

'Now would be a good time to start asking me about my career and stuff,' said Tanith, remembering that she was there for educational reasons, rather than to enjoy herself.

'So, Tanith, tell me, what do you do?' asked Greg dutifully.

'I work in casting,' she said and patted her mouth with her napkin in case she too had a red wine moustache.

'Oh really?' said Greg, observing the careful way she didn't smudge her lipstick. This was so weird. But not unpleasant. Like watching a film you've already seen, but where you notice lots of new things. He hadn't ever really asked her about her job before. 'That must be interesting.'

She nodded. 'Oh, it is. It makes you realize how people are endlessly unique but ultimately replaceable.' She frowned at herself. 'Did I get that right? Anyway, at the moment I'm casting a film about a glamorous nobody who rises from nothing to become a famous . . . um, well, somebody. I think. Unless they change the script again.'

'Don't talk to Rosetta,' said Greg immediately. 'Don't listen to whatever Robert's told you to do. She'll think it's her.'

Tanith drained her glass. 'Well, I don't know. Robert hasn't said anything about it. But I'm beginning to wonder myself, I mean, there are a lot of similarities.' She frowned.

'I have to say, I don't really know much about the back-ground of this film, but . . . um.' She stopped.

She was learning quickly, though. Tanith had The End's greatest hits on her gym Walkman and for someone who hated squealing guitars with a passion, it was beginning to seep into her consciousness. It was getting very difficult to detach from the film, now she'd started to wonder if maybe the script and Rosetta's book were connected in some way. Very difficult indeed.

But now wasn't the time.

Tanith directed her attention back at Greg. Maybe it was the wine, or the nice shirt, or the easy conversation, but he was beginning to look very much like the optimum Mulligan blend. Not bad-looking, dry sense of humour, not self-obsessed, and – shock horror! – aware of the difference between conversation and monologue.

'Now, tell me something, Gregory,' she said, slipping into an appallingly overt flirtatious tone that she hoped he could tell was ironic. 'I don't really understand why you don't have a girlfriend already. Is there something you're not telling me? Do you have bizarre sexual preferences? Is this a cunning double-bluff ruse to seduce your brother's girlfriend? Hmm?'

Greg choked on his wine. 'No! I mean, no, of course not. That's what Maggie said. Of course I wouldn't . . . do a thing like that.'

He mopped at the wine droplets with his napkin and Tanith felt a frisson of wickedness run up her spine. It was a long time since she'd made a man choke on his wine.

'Only joking. Oooh, I'm really getting into this,' said Tanith happily. 'I can see why so many actresses go in for murderous bitch parts and tarts with a heart roles.' She slipped off her shoe and started to run her foot around Greg's ankle. He was wearing the nice silk socks Rosetta had given them all for Christmas, she could feel through her tights.

'What do you mean?' said Greg, faintly. All the little hairs around his ankle were standing up. He didn't even remember ever feeling them there before. He wanted to ask, 'What are you doing?' but was too afraid she'd stop.

'Oh, I mean, it's fun being someone you're not normally,' said Tanith. 'Isn't it? It's like having a night off from your normal life. You should be making the *most* of this!'

'Should I?' he replied faintly.

'Yes! I am! I never get to go out and be drunkenly glamorous any more! This is your chance to be as suave and cool as you like, and I can tell you how well it's coming over,' she said. The wine had added a huskier note to her voice. 'And I can be whatever type of date you think you need most practice with.'

'A live one?' suggested Greg. 'One that hasn't been generously recycled by Barney? One that has a basic command of English?'

Tanith smiled naughtily and sipped her wine. 'Don't be so defeatist. The only reason you don't have date-practice is that you never ask anyone out. Now, would you like me to be Sloaney, or stroppy, or pathologically shy?'

'I'd just like you to be you, to be honest,' said Greg, and then blushed as his cheeks caught up with his brain.

Tanith shrugged and smiled. She opened her mouth to say something, then stopped and pressed her lips together.

Greg noticed that her lipstick was wearing off now, leaving a sexy trace of scarlet pigment on her lips. He swallowed his mouthful of water too quickly. *Stop it!*

'Well, OK, that's not a problem,' she said, inclining her head. 'In fact, it's a lovely compliment. But this is my night off, so if it's all right with you, I might be someone else.'

'Who would you like to be?' asked Greg.

At that moment the main courses finally arrived and Tanith hesitated while the waiter arranged the plates and napkins around them. 'Thank you,' she murmured as he left.

Greg waited for her to speak, his heart hammering in his chest.

'I'd like to be the person I was when I was eighteen,' she said. 'She was much more fun and ... just more excited about things.'

'That's fine with me,' said Greg, and refilled her glass.

By the time Greg had finished pushing his sushi around the plate, and Tanith had given up toying with her noodles, they had started a third bottle.

Tanith knew she was drunk because although she had started off saying the most outrageous things under the handy guise of pretending to be Greg's nightmare date from Parson's Green, she was now flirting for real and somewhere along the line had gone beyond the point of feeling guilty because she could no longer make precise distinctions like that.

Greg knew he was drunk because he too had slipped off his shoe and was running his big toe around Tanith's ankle strap, while her other foot slipped further and further up his leg.

The waiter, who had been hovering for the past forty minutes waiting for them to stop playing with their uneaten food, eventually approached the table and said, 'Have you finished?' in a reproachful tone.

Tanith looked down at her plate and smiled back at the waiter. 'Oh dear. I just lose my appetite as soon as I've had a couple of glasses of wine.'

'Hey, lady. Maybe it's not just the wine making you lose your appetite,' said Greg, boldly. He was now using his Barney impression as a cover for his own unquestionable flirting.

Tanith giggled. 'Could be.'

He underlined it with one of Barney's trademark eyebrow flicks.

'No, actually, there's no need for that,' said Tanith. 'You've made your point.'

The plates were cleared silently and dessert menus arrived.

'I'll just have a double espresso,' said Tanith at once, not trusting herself to eat a pudding without making a show of herself.

'And for me,' said Greg, even though he hated coffee, just to get rid of the waiter before he went into some long spiel about specials.

Tanith circled her foot around Greg's calf. He had nice strong calves, she thought. 'So,' she said, pretending she had no idea what her foot was up to, 'are you going to drive me back to Parson's Green tonight?'

Greg looked confused. His calf tensed under her toes. 'But you live in Clerkenwell.'

'I'm not me tonight,' she reminded him. 'Concentrate.'

'No, you're certainly not! Oh, yeah, um, of course, yes.' Greg adopted a serious expression and tugged at his trousers under the table. They had gradually become uncomfortably tight in the crotch. 'I've had far too much to drink. I'll be taking a taxi home, naturally. Would you like to share it?'

'That would be nice,' she breathed, holding his gaze.

Greg stared at her in lustful fascination. Was she like this with Robert – all sexy and provocative? Talk about private faces and public faces. It was hard to associate this smoky-eyed, sexy woman now with the smart and creasefree businesslike Tanith he knew.

Not that he was objecting.

Greg realized that although Tanith was now sipping her coffee very demurely above the table, underneath it, her toes were slowly walking up his inner thigh.

'Do you feel tonight has been helpful?' she asked.

'Not really,' said Greg. 'I think you've raised my expectations of other women so high I'll never be able to find anyone else I want.'

Tanith's face was illuminated in smiles. 'That's so sweet of you to say so. I've had a great evening.'

Greg swallowed. How far exactly would this lesson go? Right up to the point where he made a move? Deep-set paranoia meant that he knew the wine was making him over-confident. 'I hope it hasn't been too much of a trial for you.'

Tanith shook her head so her hair fell into her eyes. She knew she should stop. In five minutes, she thought, I will ask for the bill and go back to being normal. I'll make it really clear that although I've enjoyed myself, that's the end of the evening.

But even as she thought that, she couldn't move her eyes from Greg's. He had all the things she fancied in Robert (*yes, and in Patrick*, yelled the voice in her head) but . . . new. And different. And easier. And more attentive.

She smiled over her coffee-cup, with a flutter of her eye-lashes, and was hugely gratified to see Greg blush.

It's just a bit of fun, she told herself. He doesn't get much attention. It's good for him to have an ego-boost once in a while – he deserves it. And it's not as though he thinks I'm trying to pull him, is it? He knows I live with his brother.

Oh, very good. You're trying to tell yourself you're play-ing a role here, said the voice in her head, *but it's just another side of you, isn't it? You can't disclaim responsibil-ity as easily as that.*

Tanith was dismayed to hear herself think, very distinctly, *I'm not* married *to Robert*.

She was so disconcerted by this that her foot slipped from its resting place on Greg's knee into his lap.

Greg misinterpreted this as an outrageous come-on and threw his remaining caution to the wind. 'No, Tanith,' he giggled, 'I think you should be aiming for here.' He grabbed her heel so she could feel the full embarrassment of his erec-tion against her sole.

At which point Tanith, who had been balanced on the edge of her seat to reach his ankle as it was, vanished beneath the table, along with her wineglass and a certain amount of tableware.

Greg froze and scanned around the room to see if anyone had noticed.

Everyone had noticed and pretended they hadn't.

When Tanith emerged from beneath the tablecloth, having given it a good three minutes to recompose herself and dissipate any remaining comedy value, Greg could tell immediately that she'd returned to her normal self. Her eyes were guarded and a hot blush had dusted across her cheekbones.

Disappointment spread through him, exactly like it used to at the end of school discos, where the final song was playing, everyone else was snogging and the unsnogged were getting their coats.

Still, he thought valiantly, through the drunken fug sitting on his brain, at least I didn't try to snog Robert's girlfriend. There's always that.

'Um, shall I get the bill?' asked Tanith, too brightly.

'No, I will.' Greg tried to smile. 'I couldn't possibly. Put your purse away, etcetera, etcetera.'

'It's OK, Greg,' Tanith replied. Greg detected a brittleness in her voice that only made his heart sink further. She looked through her wallet for her credit cards. 'You don't have to do the chivalrous thing. End of lesson.'

'Oh, and before the bit where I take you home,' he said, then looked around to see where the words had come from.

Tanith smiled sadly. ''Fraid so.'

'Why is it that you only realize you've drunk too much one glass after the event?' asked Greg.

'Why is it that you only realize a lot of things after the event?' Tanith replied, and caught the eye of the waiter. 'Can we have the bill, please?' She pushed the glass of water towards him. 'You might want to finish that. Damage limitation, you know.'

He flinched. 'I may not know a lot about taking girls out, but I do know that it's never a good sign when your date insists you drink lots of water.'

'Better that than throwing up on her in a taxi.'

He drained the glass and they waited for the bill in silence.

When it came, they split it (Greg doing furious mental arith-
metic and trying to remember when his camera insurance
direct debit went through) and left. Greg took the bill with
him, out of habit, thinking he might try to put it through his
accounts as staff training, or something.

At the door, the end-of-school-disco feeling intensified in
Greg's chest to an almost unbearable level. If it hadn't been
going so well, he thought as he scanned the road for taxis, it
wouldn't be so disappointing that he'd fucked up so badly.

'Greg,' said Tanith suddenly, taking his hand, 'please don't
let that last five minutes spoil this evening for you. I had a
great time. You're wonderful company, and any woman you
take out on a date should be charmed.'

'Really?' he asked. The heaviness in his heart lifted. 'What
grade did I get?'

She put her hand through his arm and squeezed her cheek
into his shoulder. 'You got a B plus on your practical and an
A plus on your listening test.'

He looked down at her clinging to his arm. She looked
very small. Tanith's eyes were tightly shut – she was pretty
drunk, it had to be said – and in the half-light of the street, her
lashes were gorgeously long and dark and her skin very pearly.

It was worth one last throw, just in case . . . 'And on my
oral?' he said tentatively.

Tanith opened one eye and gave him a cheeky look. 'Well,
we'll never know. But I would guess an A. Now,' she disentangled herself, 'there's a cab. Wow, look! There are *two*
cabs!'

Oh cheers, thought Greg sourly. Who would have predicted that in Notting Hill on a Friday night?

They both pulled up in response to Tanith's frantic waving
and gesturing.

'No sense in going so far out of your way, is there?' she
said. She went up on her toes and pressed her lips against his
cold cheek. 'Night, night. And thank you for a wonderful
evening.'

'No, thank you,' said Greg, weakly, and waved as she slipped into the back of the cab and drove off.

He leaned into the driver's window. 'Ellerby Street, mate,' he said and yanked open the door. He slumped down on the seat, trying to remember how much cash he had on him, and decided that if he didn't have enough, it was definitely Barney's turn to lend him some money.

In the other cab, Tanith was repairing her make-up and trying to make her face look the way it had done when she left the house that evening. But for some reason – and she hoped it was just the drink – she didn't look like herself. There were just too many traces of the eighteen-year-old Tanith still all over her face.

Chapter Twenty

'Uhm, Brian, listen, man, I think there might be a problem.' Simon grimaced and gestured towards Red, who was sitting on his bags looking as though someone had removed his brain and replaced it with water of a similar weight. Glynn was shaking him by the hair, but Red seemed unaware that the rest of the world wasn't actually swaying from side to side in real life.

'Ah, no. No, no, no, no.' Brian stopped jiggling Patrick around and put him down on a chair. Patrick looked bereft, so Brian gave him a huge bunch of keys to play with, and strode purposefully over to the rest of the tour party who were sitting in the VIP area, hopelessly out-of-place, scruffy and jet-lagged. It wasn't like he had the time to sort out Red again, but Rosetta, who was normally so good at these things, had disappeared with John to see if she could speed them through customs.

The sooner The End were big enough to get their own plane, the better, thought Brian. Now *there* was an incentive to make some money.

He bent over Red and tried to pry his eyelids back. It was all too easy. 'Red!' yelled Brian, about three inches from Red's nose. 'Red, can you hear me, you big fool?'

Red lifted his head to regard Brian quizzically, and he made a fish shape with his hands. 'Large onion,' he said, as if speaking from inside a well. 'Don't freak me with that *shit*, man.'

'Oh, Christ.' Brian stood up, and rubbed his eyes with his balled-up fists. 'That's not jet-lag, now, is it? Have the bags come through?'

'Some of them. Not Red's. Funny that.' Simon's weaselly face was wreathed in smiles.

'No, they're probably sending them to Hendon for testing. Oh, fuck. Oh, fuck.'

It had been a very long flight, with more turbulence than Brian was normally able to handle without a couple of brandies, and yet he'd restrained himself on the grounds that getting the band through the airport and back into the suspicious bosoms of their families would require all his concentration.

As usual, all his misgivings had proved depressingly accurate.

The sound of sharp clicking came nearer.

'You tell her about Red,' said Brian to Simon. 'She'll take it better from you.'

Simon looked thrilled to be handling some genuine bad news.

'What's the problem?' Rosetta pushed the heavy lock of amber hair out of her eyes and looked from one to the other. She was wearing a white trouser suit, cut as if to fit a fourteen-year-old boy, with a barely visible vest beneath. A turquoise necklace that Brian didn't remember seeing before hung down in her creamy freckled cleavage and her hair was streaked with blonde from the American sun. She didn't look like a woman who had given birth twice in the past eighteen months – and given birth most recently to the stroppiest baby Brian had ever encountered.

But then she knew there were cameras out front, and Brian had come to realize that Rosetta dressed up for the camera more than she ever would for him. Behind her, John was looking flushed and miserable. He guessed it had something to do with the end of the tour. John generally looked miserable at the end of tours. They all did, especially Red, but that had more to do with Janette standing at the arrivals gate, waving her fistful of press cuttings, than anything else.

He looked at Rosetta and tried to judge her mood. He couldn't. But, Brian reminded himself, never being able to tell exactly what she was thinking was part of her charm. She'd been in a very funny mood all tour, up one day and down the next, doing all the stuff she used to do before Patrick came along, and still finding time to be with the kids. She was amazing. According to Glynn, she'd even been helping John with some lyrics.

'What is it?' she demanded again. The good humour in her face faded as she made the connection between Red, who was singing gently to himself in tongues, and Simon, whose initial grin was fading as he recognized the steeliness in Rosetta's expression.

'Um, er, Brian wants to talk to you about Red,' Simon stuttered.

'Then I don't think he needs you as a translator, does he?' said Rosetta, and turned to her husband. 'What? What's the problem now?'

Brian sighed. 'God help us, Red's away with the fishes again. He wasn't drinking much on the plane, so I should have guessed,' he said. 'And I thought he was trying to get his head back together for seeing Janette.'

Rosetta gave him a look. 'That's probably why he's in this state. Anyway, it's not his *head* he should be worrying about. Did he tell you he got his test results back from that doctor in San Diego?'

The four of them stared at the drummer who was now moving his fishy hands round his head and staring at his fingers as if he didn't realize they were attached to his arms.

'He doesn't tell me, and I don't ask,' said Brian, woefully.

'I just don't know where he gets it, man,' said John. 'It's

like he's testing it for some laboratory. Glynn dropped some of the acid Red had in San Diego and he saw the inside of his brain for, like, five days. It got pretty boring in the end, apparently.'

'Well, I don't imagine it was exactly the British Museum,' said Rosetta. She tried a few experimental fingersnaps right in Red's face and got no reaction. 'Such a drummer cliché. I told you that Sue was going to send someone from the paper to cover your triumphal return, didn't I?'

'Jesus, you lot will be the death of me,' said Brian. He ran a hand over his brow, which was slick with sweat, and clammy from the cabin atmosphere. 'And I thought three months in the States would exhaust your ability to pull stupid stunts. Why'd you save this for coming home?'

'Oh, you know, it gets pretty dull without all the groupies around to . . . Joke, I'm joking!' Simon put up his hands.

'Yeah, right, those groupies, Simon,' said John sarcastically. 'What does that take your total up to now?'

'Eight three one,' Simon snapped back. 'I've got dates, names and places.'

Rosetta bit her lip and pretended to look in her bag for something. She was trying to get her composure back after the fifteen minutes she and John had managed to snatch alone in the Customs interview room. Most of the time she could disguise her permanent exhaustion, but occasionally when she was tired, like now, and knew she had to conjure up the glossy front-page Rosetta out of the frazzled, air-dried reality, it was hard to hide the dull ache in her heart, knowing that the situation with her and John was never really going to get any better, and if she went through with her plan for him and Sue it could potentially get much worse. But she still had to do it. It was her last hope of dragging the situation back under control. After all, he was the one with the big conscience.

'You realize that there will be more photographers than just Sue's out there?' Brian demanded. His artfully floppy scarf was looking less and less floppy by the minute. Back in the arrivals lounge of Heathrow airport, it had lost its casual West Coast grooviness and now looked limp and ridiculous round Brian's stout throat, like an Easter ribbon round the neck of a bull. 'You *realize* that since you've been away there's been a lot of press coverage about the drug busts? You *realize* that they're all just waiting for one of you to keel over and cark it, since Keith Richards seems to be refusing to play ball? You *realize* that wheeling him out in this state there is going to present serious problems with . . .'

'OK, Brian, we get the picture.' Rosetta bit her lip, and took off her pink-tinted shades. She ran her hands through her hair as she thought, her green eyes scanning back and forth across the hall. Though she didn't want to fan the flames of Brian's panic, he was right; it could be very embarrassing indeed, more so if they found anything in the bags.

In the background, Patrick began to murmur fractiously to himself, slamming Brian's keys experimentally against the formica of the table. Finding the sound interesting, he increased the volume.

'And I don't think Glynn's exactly sober,' said John, tentatively. 'I heard one of the stewardesses . . .'

'Don't . . .' moaned Brian. 'Jesus Christ, it's easier getting the kids through the airport than you lot.'

He rubbed his eyes, and for a moment, Rosetta saw how tired he was. He was looking old. Fed up with taking more responsibility as the band decided they wanted less. 'Please, Rosetta? Any ideas – apart from covering Red with a blanket and claiming he's got appendicitis? I'd do that,' he added, 'but I know . . . another drummer who we won't name, pulled that stunt last week.'

She frowned. She knew who he meant, and it hadn't stopped the papers running the story. It was such a short moment between wanting publicity of any kind at all, and suddenly being terrified of getting the wrong sort. The End were doing well, but were by no means the biggest band in the world, though that made them even more attractive scapegoats to the press, knowing that they wouldn't have the Stones' lawyers to fight.

Brian and John waited. 'Pass me that overnight bag,' she said eventually, and pointed to a powder-blue carry-on she kept Patrick and Robert's baby stuff in.

'Why? Has it got some kind of elephant tranquillizer in it?' John flinched at the weight as he hoisted it on to a chair. 'Or maybe an elephant?'

'Don't be ridiculous,' she said, rummaging around in the depths. Nappies, dummies, bottles appeared in heaps beside her. 'Red would have shot that up in about ten minutes. He dropped six of my contraceptive pills in Des Moines. Made him feel like a natural woman, apparently. Now, thank God for last-minute packing and worship at the altar of resourceful women.' She pulled out a long, shapeless maternity dress.

'He'll never get into that,' said Brian.

Rosetta gave him a brief, sarcastic look, then checked round the hall. The band had been let off the plane first, along with all the roadies – technically it was a favour, but probably so the customs people had a bit longer with their baggage. So far they were the only people off the plane, but once the other passengers started coming through, they would have to move on pretty quickly, leaving Brian trapped between the critical eyes of the public and the flash-gun assisted eyes of the press.

'Stand there,' she said, pushing Brian and John together as a human shield, and, in one swift movement, she pulled off her boots and whipped off her vest.

'Rosetta!' hissed Brian, his forehead getting visibly more clammy by the second. Nervously, he grabbed her vest and jacket up off the floor, folding them automatically and stuffing them in his own bag while his eyes raced round the room for lone photographers, ready to catch a glimpse of the long limbs wriggling into the dress.

'Needs must . . .' Rosetta's voice was muffled beneath the

layers of Liberty print cotton as she dragged the dress over
her head, and when she emerged, shaking her hair into a
demure centre parting, it was as though an entire personality transformation had taken place. The knowing rock chick
had vanished, and in her place – to Brian's bittersweet
shock – was the wide-eyed, clear-skinned schoolgirl he had
seen dancing madly in Richmond six years ago.

He felt a sharp pang of nostalgia and reached out a big
hand to touch the porcelain skin of her arm, exposed by the
slashed bell sleeves. Until that second, he'd had no idea how
much she'd changed. It was like watching the butterfly go
backwards into the cocoon.

But she was already cleaning off her iridescent mother-of-
pearl make-up with a baby wipe, sweeping it back and forth
across her face, and he drew back his fingers, knowing that
if he tried to touch her, it would turn into a grab, and give
the wrong sign. She'd got very prickly recently, where she
used to love his little caresses – the new baby, he supposed.
Still, this wasn't the time to have a row about misinterpreta-
tion.

Rosetta didn't notice his hesitation, or if she did, she didn't
show it.

'OK, go and get Robert,' she said to Brian, briskly. 'He's in
his bouncer-thing. And make sure that Patrick hasn't
dropped anything down his jumper.' She rummaged in her
own handbag and started to sweep blusher on to her pale
cheeks – cheeks that had for the past three months been
scrupulously hidden with hats and suncream to preserve the
glamorous, is-she/isn't-she? drug addict pallor.

'Right,' said Brian, suddenly glad to be doing something.
'Right, I will. Simon, come with me and help me get Red settled.'

Simon sloped off, casting backward glances at Rosetta,
trying to work out what she was up to.

Rosetta finished reapplying her make-up and knew without looking up that John was staring at her. She couldn't

bring herself to meet his eyes. She thought about her plans for him and Sue – cutting him off even further – and felt ill. There really were no limits any more.

'Don't even look at me,' she said, as her hands ran through her hair to smooth it down. 'I know what you're thinking. And it's not like that. It's an emergency. I wouldn't do this normally.'

John didn't reply and she glanced up, despite herself.

His brown eyes were weary and he looked exhausted. Still gorgeous, she thought guiltily, but exhausted. 'Do what?'

She bit her lip. 'Use the kids as decoy. I know it's wrong, but what else am I meant to do?'

'Rosetta, I can't tell you what to do with your kids. Especially if Brian's OK with it,' he said evenly.

Rosetta met his gaze and wondered if he was testing her.

Before she could say anything else, Brian returned, weaving slightly with the weight of Robert's bouncer. Inside, propped up on the cushions like a queen bee, Robert was fixing all of them with an ominous glower, his tiny forehead wrinkled with offence.

'Hello, darling!' said Rosetta and she bent down to lift Robert out of the straps, trailing yards of gossamer blanket from his fat larva body. 'How do you like being home, then?'

'Either that child weighs a ton, or Red's been stashing stuff in the lining of the cot,' panted Brian, rubbing his hands together where the straps had made red weals on his fingers.

Robert began to howl, with a kind of outrage as if he suddenly realized that he hadn't been crying before now.

'Ah, dear,' Rosetta joggled him up and down in her arms. It would usually take Birgit the au pair about two hours of joggling to get him mollified, but some kind of authority in Rosetta's joggling seemed to have a swifter effect. Robert's face turned sweet with smiles.

The two men watched with admiration. Brian had the horrible thought that despite the outward flower child, Rosetta was exactly the kind of mother who would have no qualms about rubbing opium on her baby's gums if it would stop it crying.

'OK,' she said, biting her lips to redden them, 'I think we're about ready.'

'Ready for what?' demanded Brian, still sucking his hands and casting nervous glances at Red. His drum roadie, Smith, was slapping him, to no apparent effect, although Red was fully conscious and watching with some interest. Simon and Glynn were standing behind, clearly itching to join in.

'Ready to *go*,' said Rosetta. She pulled her hands through her hair one more time and pulled it into two flowing bunches around her ears. 'Better get moving, before everyone else comes through and starts confusing Red. Look, get him over here.' She slung a now-compliant Robert on to her hip and hooked a scarf around her neck. 'John, be a love and bring Patrick over? You're so good with him.'

John picked Patrick up from his chair, and Patrick sank heavily into his chest, nestling his head into the crook of John's strong arm. When he passed the sleepy toddler over to Rosetta, their arms formed a loop around Patrick and for a moment she had a surge of longing to grab them both and run away, get back on another plane and take off together. Then Brian broke out into dry coughing, and she brought herself back to reality. Such as it was.

John awkwardly patted Brian on the back. He was much taller than Brian and he had to bend his arm so as not to smack him in the head. 'I'll see you outside,' he said.

'Great, OK,' Brian replied, suddenly protective. 'Now, listen. Make sure you don't carry anything. And don't talk to any of them. Don't . . .'

'Yeah, yeah,' said John, and sloped off to get his guitars.

Rosetta took a deep breath, and squeezed her children into her warm body. She felt unbelievably maternal, not just towards them, but to the stupid helpless fuckers in the band, who couldn't even get themselves to an airport and out the other side without feminine assistance. It almost made up for those quivers of insecurity she'd felt on this tour, catching glimpses of those knowing-eyed teenagers, all glitter and skinny legs, who melted away just as she arrived at the stage door, or let herself into a dressing-room unannounced. All her 'indispensibility' to the record company couldn't make up for that.

She looked at herself in one of the wall-to-ceiling mirrors. Just the glittery golden platforms emerging from beneath the flowing maternity dress could have hinted that she wasn't a beautiful young flower-child mother, returning from a holiday abroad with her round-eyed, fluffy-haired children.

Swiftly and instinctively, Rosetta slipped off the boots and kicked them towards Brian, who pulled a tense, long-suffering face and stuffed them in one of the many bags loading their trolley. Her bare feet still had the little henna stars painted on them from the leaving party the record company had thrown in New York, and the cold floor stung her soles. That was good. That would remind her not to hang around. Go in there, distract them, make sure Brian got the others out, then leave.

'Mummy *come*,' commanded Patrick.

She kissed the top of his head. 'Mummy's coming.' He had learned to speak very early – even if 'Mummy come' was a phrase that covered a hundred different situations – and it freaked her out, feeling the first tingle of proper communication with him. He knew everything. As if those searching little eyes weren't enough to break your heart.

Not to be left out, Robert started grizzling.

'Come on, Rosetta,' said Brian. He checked his watch. 'The cars will be here now.'

'OK. OK, let's all go. And make sure you get Red out while I'm talking.' Before she could see Brian's face, sensing that next to his gratitude he didn't really, truly approve of what she was doing, Rosetta strode out into the arrivals hall, smiling into the cameras that were waiting there behind the barriers.

Behind her, like a long train gradually lurching into
motion, Brian and John pushed a couple of trolleys, loaded
with luggage and the bits of special gear they hadn't allowed
to go in the hold – John's guitar, Brian's suitcase full of
papers. Red was firmly positioned between them, holding on
to the trolley for support, and in all the coos and cries
directed at Robert and Patrick and barefoot Rosetta, they
managed to slip him out of a side door, where two black
Mercedes were, as Brian had arranged, waiting.

'Oh man,' Red said, as Brian pushed him by the head into
the back of the car, 'where'd you get this amazing fish? It's
like . . . big enough to sit in!'

Rosetta held her children up to the cameras, and hoped that
Robert wouldn't start crying again. Patrick, having reminded
her of his presence, was silent again, looking from one
strange face to another as though he knew them.

She could see them doing the sums in their heads – how
old are they, how old is she, how long has she been married?
Rosetta merely smiled and searched the crowd of people for
Sue's round face, using it as an opportunity to make all the
journalists think she was looking out for them. It didn't
matter which conclusion they reached; it was more of a novelty for them to write that she was a traditional hippie
mother, stuck like a madonna in this circus of loose living
and bad behaviour. All she had to do was to persuade them
that it was her serene influence which calmed down the lads,
and not that their wild ways had depraved another ingénue
with a convent education and a centre-parting. They'd been
writing those articles for years now, and still they referred to
her as 'fresh-faced' like she was some kind of chorister.

'You must be very proud of two such beautiful children,'
said a male journalist.

'Oh, yes.' Rosetta nodded fervently, smiling until her
cheeks went appley. 'My children are my pride and joy.'

'Do you hope that they'll grow up to be musical?' cooed a

girl reporter from one of the teen papers, judging by her T-shirt.

'Well, they heard the Rolling Stones and Led Zeppelin in the womb,' said Rosetta. 'And Robert came out kicking, so he's going to be a drummer or a footballer!'

They all laughed, and she hoisted Patrick further up on her slender hip. He took his thumb out of his mouth and curled a long strand of apricot-coloured hair tightly around his fist, gazing about him like a small owl. It hurt like hell, but Rosetta carried on smiling.

'But do you think a rock and roll tour is really the place to take small children?' asked one crabby-looking woman, from over the top of her pointy tortoise-shell glasses. They matched her buttoned-up tweed suit.

'Oh, it's not so bad, really. You shouldn't believe all you read in the papers.' Rosetta flashed a naughty look up at the nearest photographer, who temporarily forgot the photo-op and grinned back, shyly. 'Besides, the boys need to be with their father,' she said firmly. 'And so do I.' She smiled to herself at the ambiguity, with a small thrill at telling the truth, but through the viewfinders she only radiated a Mona Lisa-like pleasure at her life.

The reporters laughed, and those at the back began to move out of the way of the trickle of passengers now emerging from the gates, all of whom stared and shuffled past the knot of reporters, wondering who it could be at the centre of such rapt attention. Rosetta discreetly shuffled from one foot to another, to get some feeling back in her toes, and seized the respite as an opportunity to rejig the boys, slip on her shades and start moving towards the doors. Brian would be sitting in the car, looking at his watch, and God knew what aquatic stage Red would have reached.

She could feel Robert wasn't going to maintain this unusual silence for much longer, and much as she loved him, she didn't want to have to demonstrate her tentative child-rearing skills in front of an audience. Patrick often tried to speak when he heard adults talk around him, and Rosetta suspected that some of the roadies had been trying to teach him swear words like a little parrot, coaxing him with sickly American sweeties while she was out finding places to get their stage clothes washed.

Now would not be a good time to demonstrate his advanced learning to the press.

Rosetta hitched Robert's sling higher up her shoulder and squeezed Patrick into her hip. He cuddled into her and she felt a sudden urge to be at home, alone with them. 'Would you excuse me?' she asked, as sweetly as she could. 'If you've got all the photos you need, I should be getting back to Brian and the boys.'

'But, really!' Valerie Jones from the *Evening Gazette* shoved her way to the front, looking as if she were about to explode with polo-necked self-righteousness. 'We read *all the time* about the drug problems this . . . *group* has, and I know for a *fact* that there were some very serious incidents with the police in America, and I think it's practically *irresponsible* to introduce children to that kind of atmosphere! And you're not much more than a child yourself! What can you possibly know about responsible motherhood?'

Rosetta stopped as if someone had frozen her on film, and even as the truth of what the woman had said hit her like cold water she drew herself up to her full height and glared in the direction of the question.

'Forgive me,' she said, her iciest, politest Richmond vowels coming up from somewhere she'd forgotten about. 'But I *hardly* think you're qualified to comment on a situation of which you can *know* nothing at all, except what's been reported in the press by journalists as prurient and judgemental as yourself.'

The tweedy woman merely pushed her glasses further up her nose. 'But is it not true that Red Fearon was arrested by the Los Angeles Police Department for possession of an illegal firearm and intent to supply a Class A drug?'

'I was under the impression you were asking me about my children, not about the band,' Rosetta snapped back as sweetly as she could. 'I can't possibly comment about anything like that. And the charges were dropped, anyway.'

'When are the two ever separate on a tour like this?'

Rosetta cast a sweeping look at the photographers ranged around her. 'I couldn't wish for more considerate help or inspirational role models for my children than the band. I know for a fact that they wouldn't *dream* of doing anything to harm them in any way.'

'So the rumours of all-night orgies and drinking binges are all just fabrications of the press, then?' This was delivered in such a way as to suggest that Valerie Jones had it on big tablets direct from God.

Rosetta's stomach flickered with nerves. What had they heard? She didn't ask most of the time, because she didn't want to know, and they usually had the decency not to embarrass her, but you couldn't trust some of these girls not to stagger straight out of the hotel room and into the nearest phone booth. And Glynn for one seemed to take pride in shagging journalists, mistakenly thinking they were a cut above. But while her mind raced, she forced out a light-hearted giggle. 'Of *course* it's all made-up. I make them all go to bed half an hour after the concert!'

The rest of the journalists laughed nervously and Rosetta relaxed fractionally, but she knew she had to get to the safety of the car somehow, before she stumbled out of her depth.

'Four young men in Los Angeles, all volunteering for *baby*-sitting. How nice,' the woman went on, her eyes glinting behind the glasses. 'I'm sure their wives are very proud.'

Rosetta saw the other writers begin to scribble things down on their pads and felt a leap of panic in her stomach. She knew exactly what the woman was getting at. 'You would be surprised. It amazes me how people can't tell the

difference between the act on-stage and the real life off it.'
Rosetta gave the journalist her best steely but cute look.

The look she got in return could have frozen petrol.

Adrenalin was surging round her system, mixing fear with
panic with triumph, forcing it through her heart. Was this
how John felt on-stage, when he had to improvise and solo
in front of ten thousand people, waiting for him to fly or
fall?

Cold sweat stung the inside of her arms, and Rosetta
knew she couldn't hold this control for much longer.
Timing – timing was everything, and she had to use every
little advantage she had, however petty.

'Now, please excuse me, but I really have to go,' she
announced into the simmering silence. 'I need to get my children home.'

The children were silent on her hip, for which she was
grateful. Her arms were aching and her back felt about to
snap. Those trousers might have been tight, but at least they
were supportive.

The photographers hurried to get shots of her leaving and
Rosetta's heart sank; she couldn't possibly beat them to the
door, with two children and no high heels. And how bad
would it look that Brian wasn't here to help her? In despair,
she caught the eye of a passing airline captain, who crossed
the foyer immediately like a knight in shining armour, swept
Robert out of her arms, and shepherded her towards the
door.

'Mummy come!' said Patrick into her neck. He sounded
distressed but not scared.

'Mummy is, lamb,' murmured Rosetta and cradled his
hot little head with her hand.

Before she could register much more, apart from the
agony on her calves of walking without heels, they were at
the car, and Brian was grabbing the children from her,
bundling them into the child seats, and making room for her
in the back.

'God,' said Rosetta. 'I could murder a drink. At the very least.'

'You did a brilliant job, darling!' he said, packing shawls and bags around her like ballast. 'I sent Red and John ahead with the others – get them well out the way, fantastic. Hello, my lovely!' He took Robert from the apologetic pilot and kissed his scrunched-up pug face.

Well done, Robert, thought Rosetta, and felt an instinctive reproach from his little coal-black eyes.

Chapter Twenty-one

Clerkenwell, 2001

'Explain to me what it was Rosetta actually did,' said Tanith. She leafed idly through the phone bills Robert had clipped together in date order. This particular batch started in 1990 and featured calls to locations Tanith had never even heard of. She wondered whether Rosetta might not be better off ditching the great writing process and just publishing the contents of her accounts box for the real insight it gave into her life.

'What do you mean, *actually did*?' asked Robert, guardedly.

'I mean, what did she do when she wasn't shimmering round the world having her picture taken with five trolleys of luggage and two or three angelic children.'

At the keyboard, where he was still hacking away at the rockface of Rosetta's accounts, Robert's broad shoulders lifted and fell dismissively but he didn't turn round. 'You're asking the wrong man.'

'Come on, you should know,' Tanith persisted. 'You were there, according to some of these photos.'

He grunted and bashed out a sum on his calculator, scribbled a figure down on his rough workings, then stretched back in his swivel chair until the joints in his shoulders cracked.

Tanith thought he looked very tired. For four nights now he'd come straight home from work and shut himself up in his windowless study, refusing all offers of help or back-rubs. It was as if he were punishing himself, Tanith thought. Too much coffee, too many cigarettes and far too much frenzied muttering were darkening the bags under his eyes, and traces of his eczema had reappeared behind his ears. Rosetta's books were taking far longer than he'd initially thought, mainly because he was very obviously seething at his mother the whole time, which ruined his concentration.

Still, she thought, he wanted to do it.

Robert spun round in his chair to face her. 'What did she do?' He pulled a 'search me' face. 'She . . . wrote a column for Sue's paper for a while, all about who was in and who was out, and what the band were wearing this week and how much a peppermint tea cost in Marrakech. Then she got bored of that and wanted to write the horoscopes.'

'And did she?'

Robert allowed himself a tight smile and decanted another heap of papers from the pile in his in-tray. 'Yes, she did. She was very good at it too. Pisceans nearly always had a fabulous month of parties and romance in the offing and Arians inevitably had to watch out for family traumas.'

'Well, I can kind of see her doing that, now you mention it.' Tanith looked impressed. 'No one could ever accuse your mother of being a bimbo.'

He snorted. 'Oh, that was just her idea of creative writing.' There was a pause while he put some papers in order, then he added, unexpectedly, 'What she was *really* good at was tarot cards.'

Tanith modulated her interest carefully; Robert got annoyed if she expressed too much interest – he said it just played into Rosetta's hands. 'Tarot? Really?'

'Oh, yeah. Gypsy Rosetta. God knows she had the silk headscarves for it. They all came to have their cards read – Sue, Anita, whatever groupies were hanging around, various deeply gullible journalists.'

Tanith had a sudden, very clear image of Rosetta earnestly

warning attractive young groupies off the bus with dire predictions of flood and venereal disease.

'Of course it helps if you know all the gossip, like she
did,' Robert went on. 'And if you have a vivid imagination,
like she did. And if you know when to combine the two,
then you are quite clearly a seer and a mystic of the highest
order. Oh, it's a great excuse is astrology. You can't help
anything once you've read it in the stars.'

Tanith peered into another box. It was odd seeing all the
glitzy ephemera of Rosetta's life filed in Robert's prosaic
document boxes. Another of his stoic attempts to bring her
down to orderly level. 'I think Rosetta is probably a very
good judge of character,' she said evenly. 'From the little
I've seen of her, she certainly seems to reduce people to their
component parts pretty quickly.'

'Meaning?'

'Meaning the way she seems to look straight through you
at first glance, like she's reading the back of your mind.
She'd be a good casting director. It doesn't encourage you to
pretend to be anyone you're not. I imagine she didn't suffer
fools gladly round the band.'

'You'd be surprised,' said Robert. 'There's a lot to be said
for being the smartest of the bunch, and keeping it that way.
Anyway, it's not piercing insight, it's myopia – silly bitch is
very short-sighted, but too vain to wear glasses. More coffee,
please.'

Tanith thoughtfully drained the cafetière into his mug.
Robert had made it very strong and gloopy.

'Aren't you supposed to tell me I'm drinking too much of
this?' he demanded.

She shrugged. 'Why should I? You already know you are.
Besides, I'm not your mother.'

'No,' said Robert ruefully, and turned back to the stack of
investment statements. 'Sometimes you're just a bit too
maternal for that.'

She put the phone bills back in the file Robert had marked

'Rosetta – yapping', and took the lid off the box on her knee. Most of the boxes Tanith had peeked into – the ones that Robert had sorted and sifted into 'bank details' or 'house documents' or 'investments' – just contained files of yellowing paper. This one, though, seemed to contain all the little bits of discarded junk he'd skimmed from the top: stray photographs, notes, postcards, a couple of solitary earrings. Tanith's heart thudded with prurient interest at this glimpse into Rosetta's – and by the same token, Robert's – past. It even smelled different: as she opened the lid, a faint trace of roses (or was it faded lipstick?) floated up.

'So she wrote horoscopes and frightened everyone into behaving well with promises of tarot doom if they didn't?' asked Tanith. She picked a couple of old concert laminates from the late seventies showing the band logo picked out against a Manhattan skyline in silver stars. Very kitsch.

'Well, to be fair, she pretty much ran the band. And she did look after the four of us full-time,' said Robert with a grudging air of admiration. 'Christ knows that can't have been much fun. She refused point blank to get a full-time nanny in. But we did have the highest au pair turnover in Westminster and Chelsea.'

'So, she made bringing you lot up her full-time job then,' said Tanith. 'Good for her.'

'Ah. No, don't get me wrong, it's not like Rosetta was the original Domestic Goddess out of the goodness of her heart.'

'What?' Tanith paused at a trippy hand-coloured photograph of an unsmiling Rosetta in a studio, with a baby on her lap – Patrick, going by the huge brown eyes – and John O'Hara sprawled at her bare feet, playing a purple guitar. At least, it probably wasn't purple originally.

'It was her *job*,' stressed Robert. 'Our nappies were probably tax-deductible.'

'Oh, don't be ridiculous,' said Tanith. 'You're all so self-dramatizing. God! I'd have *loved* to have seen more of my mother!'

'No, no, no, no. No,' said Robert, 'she invented the whole rock-chick mum thing long before Paula Yates and that lot. I tell you, she ran everyone's lives like some kind of black spider at the centre of a web. She was the head of the corporation. If she could have sold shares in our family she would have done. No one did a photocall at the baggage reclaim quite like Rosetta. And I speak as one who was put through the baggage reclaim so she could collect me for the cameras at the other end!'

'Really?' gasped Tanith, shocked.

'Oh yes,' said Robert, lighting another cigarette. 'And I was four at the time.'

Tanith stared at the photo in renewed amazement. Rosetta glowered back. And she'd thought there was nothing else he could tell her about his mother that would shock her.

'No, be fair, actually I *was* only a baby,' Robert admitted, exhaling a professional plume of smoke. 'I was in a Moses basket. It went through the plastic slat things better. But she would have done it. She once told me and Patrick that Santa had put our Christmas presents through baggage reclaim with the luggage so we would run through arrivals and look all happy, instead of jet-lagged and whiny. For years, we thought the *Generation Game* conveyor belt was some kind of airport thing.'

'Don't tell me any more,' said Tanith.

'OK.' Robert turned back to his desk. He sounded much cheered up. 'Just ask Greg about the time we did a trolley dash in Duty Free and he tried to trade Barney for a three-foot Toblerone because Rosetta . . .'

She held up her hand, pleased she hadn't flinched at the mention of Greg's name, despite the faint sense of unease pricking at her conscience after their night out. He hadn't phoned her, and she couldn't decide whether she was pleased or not. In the interests of his Dating Studies, of course.

You did nothing wrong though!

'OK, OK,' said Robert. 'But you asked.'

'That's not the same as wanting to know.'

Tanith sorted through more laminates and photos while he tapped away on his calculator and they passed the most companionable half-hour they'd had together since Rosetta's accounts arrived.

'Aaaah,' said Tanith at last, 'the little pageboy!' She held up a photograph of Patrick and Robert in violet velvet suits and matching caps. Despite the obviously cold day, their feet were bare and blue – an artful Victorian urchin touch that wasn't impressing a mutinous-looking Robert. Patrick, on the other hand, had a gorgeous expression of precocious misery all over his little face, which only served to complete the outfit.

'What?' Robert spun round and his face visibly darkened. He spun back. 'Christ, put that away. No, better still, *throw* it away.'

'Noo-oo-oo!' cooed Tanith. 'You look so *sweet*!'

Robert turned in his chair and snatched it off her. He looked at it with narrowed eyes and stubbed out his cigarette, suddenly really angry. 'You want an example of what a cow Rosetta could be, while she was pretending to be everyone's best friend? Well, this is a perfect one.'

Tanith straightened her back. 'What? Making you go in bare feet to a wedding? At least you didn't have to wear scaled-down morning suits and –'

He shook his head impatiently. 'No, have a look in the box, there'll be more of these.'

Tanith looked back in the box, startled by his reaction. 'Um . . .' She pulled out a group shot – fifteen or so people racked up on the steps outside Chelsea Town Hall: as usual, it was Rosetta who leaped out of the picture, resplendent in a long sea-green dress and fur hat, one hand on Patrick's head, the other splayed on her stomach like a white star.

'Whose wedding's this?' she asked, looking closer. There was Brian – it had to be, he looked exactly like Robert did now – and some other gangly lads, uneasy in their suits,

with beards that joined in with their hair in a sweep of
hippie-ish curls, that she recognized as The End. A burly
man in a tight velvet jacket was carrying Robert under one
arm as if he was a small log. Robert looked uncharacteristically happy.

'*That* is Sue's wedding,' said Robert.

'Sue who's commissioning Rosetta to write this book?'

'The very same.' There wasn't a trace of humour in
Robert's voice and he drained his remaining coffee as if it
were medicine. 'Her second best friend after that mad junkie
hippy Anita.'

'And who did Sue marry?' It was hard to tell, given the
informality of the clothes and the way Rosetta naturally
dominated the photograph.

Robert picked up a pencil, and was facing his computer
screen again, but made no effort to work.

'Sue married John O'Hara.'

Tanith peered at the photograph. So it was – John
O'Hara, resembling a crab out of his shell without his guitar,
trapped in a blue velvet suit that looked as if it had been
designed for someone else. It was evidently a scaled-up version of the ones the boys were wearing. Despite the
informality of the shot, he looked nervous and taut, as if
someone were operating him on invisible strings from above.
Tanith wouldn't have recognized him from the electrifying
shots of the band on stage, in which John was nearly always
twisting and arching centre-stage with Glynn, vying for the
white strip of spotlight. Next to John, curling a strong arm
around his slight frame, was Sue, Rosetta's friend, whom
Tanith now recognized from her old by-line shots in the
other cuttings, albeit without the distinctive owlish glasses.

'When did this happen?'

'Well, you can work it out from Rosetta's stomach,' said
Robert disdainfully. 'It seems to be a fairly reliable calendar
for the great stand-up rows and dramas of our happy family
life.'

'Just tell me what's going on,' said Tanith, impatiently. She picked up another handful of photographs and flipped through them for close-ups.

'Oh, *for some reason*, Rosetta, who is, you might notice, about seven months gone with your little friend Gregory at this point, consulted her cards and decided that it would be a good idea for Sue to marry John. Jesus!' Robert ran his hands through his hair in despair. 'See what I mean? You can behave in the most *appallingly* stupid fashion, just as long as you can claim there's some divine backing for it.'

Tanith flicked through the pictures until her fingers stopped at a close-up of Sue and Rosetta. Sue looked dazed but triumphant, not quite focusing on the camera, the red marks where her glasses had been still vivid against the pallor of her face. Rosetta looked sick. But then that might have been Greg's fault.

Then there was a band photo, and Tanith now picked out all the people familiar from her Internet research: John in the middle, flanked by Simon Parr the whiny bass player, his face as long as his lapels, and Brian, wreathed in genial smiles and lavish sideburns. Red loomed over them from behind, gurning for the camera and showing all the signs of a successful stag night the previous evening. Glynn stood a little apart, one foot up on a step to display his crotch better. He seemed slightly more at home in his smart suit than the rest of them, and his eyes were fixed on something, or more likely, someone, just to the left of the photographer.

'Why isn't this in with the photographs Greg's going through for the book?' asked Tanith suddenly.

'Greg's going through photographs?' Robert looked as though she'd confirmed his worst misgivings. 'Oh, fantastic, so she's saving on an accountant *and* a picture researcher. Is there no end to that woman's nerve?'

Tanith picked up the group photograph again and looked at the group. Though they were all standing close together, in the deceptively casual way that people regularly photographed in a group develop, there was an odd fragmentation to it.

'Why does John look like one of those Christians being led to the lions?' asked Tanith. 'Shotgun wedding, was it? Or was it just a very heavy night before?'

Robert rolled his eyes. 'Well, it *might* have something to do with the fact that John had been sleeping with the matron of honour for the past five years.'

Tanith's brow creased.

'Sorry? I don't follow.'

'You're not the only one.' He turned back to his accounts, then, sick of the sight of them, threw his pencil at the screen and got up. '*I don't know* why Rosetta got Sue and John together – maybe she even convinced herself that she was doing them a favour. Maybe Dad got sick of everyone whispering about why it was that Rosetta travelled in the tour-bus and he flew on ahead the whole time. But she organized that wedding and – Christ! she even had the gall to have me and Pat there as pageboys!' He let out a contemptuous breath through his nose and began striding up and down the small room.

'John, the guitarist?' asked Tanith. 'Rosetta had an affair with John O'Hara?' She hadn't known that but it didn't surprise her; Brian seemed an odd choice for Rosetta. Maybe not to begin with, when she'd been young and impressionable and needed his connections, but the marriage had lasted fifteen years or so. There must have been something else there. Brian must have had something she needed.

'No, John the dentist! *Of course* John the guitarist! It went on for years, apparently – before *and* after Sue and John were married.'

Tanith said nothing, but her mind was flipping backwards and forwards, trying to piece together all the rags of information she'd picked up from the Internet. The more she found out, the harder it was to match up the Rosetta she'd met, the Rosetta the boys talked about, and the strange, glamorous Rosetta that appeared at the side of these men in the photographs. She was reminded uncomfortably of how exciting it had been to pretend to be someone else while she was with Greg the other night. How easy it would have been to have slipped out of her depth and into dangerous waters.

'Really, sometimes I honestly wonder if Rosetta's got some kind of delusional illness,' raged Robert. 'She goes on and on about how tradition formed her entire life, blah, blah, blah, rebelling against parents, blah, blah, blah, don't want to tie you down with repressive religious fear, blah, blah, blah, and then she just uses serious, spiritual institutions like marriage and children like . . . like, set pieces in her little games.'

He stopped in front of the big photograph that hung above the sealed-off fireplace. It was an enlargement of a shadowy picture taken at a party: Patrick and Robert asleep like babes in the wood under a chaise longue at a party, surrounded by glasses and ashtrays and discarded high heels in the foreground, wrapped in a fur coat.

Tanith pondered why the boys always thought Rosetta was in charge of everything, as if her personality had deprived everyone around her of independent thought, when, from the pictures she'd seen, she was more decorative than decisive.

She looked at him, raking his hands through his hair as if he were trying to smooth his thoughts back into shape.

'People don't always get married for the same reason, Rob,' said Tanith evenly. 'There are some very good, very pragmatic reasons why—'

'Oh, don't even bother to trot out such total bollocks.' He stormed over to the desk and spun back in his chair. 'You don't believe that. People don't normally get married to please their best mate, do they?'

'So what would be your criteria for getting married?' she asked, casually.

Robert shuffled some papers, but kept his back to her. 'To make a statement of commitment. To say publicly that you love someone and you've drawn a line under your life before that point, so that everything from then on is for both of you. That old-fashioned but strangely sexy Catholic idea of fidelity and continence.'

The 'fidelity and continence' bit stung Tanith's conscience, and she wasn't totally sure you could ever draw lines under your life, but she persisted with the attack. 'But you were only, what, three? Or four when this happened? Who told you? How do you *know* Rosetta set it up? Couldn't it just have been one of those coincidences? It sometimes happens in those . . . tight-knit circles of friends. In those odd circumstances.'

He shook his head. 'No. It all came out, Tanith. I don't think it was even a secret at the time. Rosetta was always being photographed with different people – she used to bring the papers to show us. But I think John was different. Just because it was never mentioned at home didn't mean other people didn't know. That whole music business was a very small world, especially in those days.' He sighed and ran his hands through his hair.

'Then there was a big exposé in the newspapers when Patrick and I were at school. One of those horrible kiss and tell things, where you can't tell how much is planted and how much is made up. It was . . . it was pretty revolting. Lots of details. Champagne bottles, cocaine, groupies, the lot. Most of it was utter bollocks, even I knew that, but Patrick was really upset. He did a runner, as usual. Rosetta was meant to . . . Well,' he corrected himself grimly, 'Patrick often did runners. Can you imagine what it's like to have your mother's private life displayed in the newsagents? When you're trapped at school? It was one of the most miserable years of my life. And she wouldn't even move us. Said we had to learn to face it out.'

'What did Brian say?'

Robert's face darkened. 'We didn't really talk about that, funnily enough.'

'But you *must* have done!'

'Why?' asked Robert, with a humourless smile on his lips. 'He wasn't there, anyway. If your mother was having a long-standing affair, would *your* parents have sat you down and run through the details with you? I mean, I realize we're not exactly the most *normal* family in London, but we're not on Ricki Lake. It isn't like, "So, kids, I have something to tell you . . ." *Ding dong!* Hey, who's the mystery guest behind the door? Oh, it's the lead guitarist of your band! Your *real* dad!'

'But didn't it come up in the family therapy? I thought Rosetta made you all go to family therapy. Didn't you show me the bills she kept in her accounts?'

Robert laughed, and his laugh was chilling. 'The bills she kept for me to find? No. No, it didn't come up in therapy, actually. Rosetta hauled us all off to some quack in Harley Street to find out why none of us talked to her, then refused to discuss her own maternal shortcomings. Can you believe that? We all just sat there like lemons, so I walked out, which Rosetta *loved* because it gave her someone to blame other than herself for the fuck-up she made of her family.'

Tanith stared at Robert in shock. As the words tumbled out of his mouth he was trembling with anger. It seemed to shimmer from every pore. It struck her that maybe all the striving to get his life in neat lines was really an attempt to keep this anger under control, while it drove him on and on, underneath the surface, making him more successful and less dependent on anyone else.

For a second or two, she was really scared of him.

'Did Brian never ever mention it to you?' she asked bravely. 'Was it why he left?'

Robert's shoulders sagged and he rocked heavily on his chair, which creaked under the impact. 'When the band broke up, Rosetta wanted to stay at home more with Greg and Barney, so they wouldn't end up like me and Patrick, I guess, and Dad carried on organizing tours, so he was abroad most of the time. She flew out to see him and had weeks on, weeks off. We sometimes went out with him on school holidays, but it wasn't the same. I mean, for the first ten years or so, we'd been with Rosetta and Dad *all* day *every* day, and suddenly we barely saw them. We weren't that old and we just felt abandoned, like it was all our fault. And it was tough. You have to start every conversation at the beginning again – you know, what are you up to? How's school? Who's got the biggest lighting rig these days?'

He pressed his lips together, trying to be fair, and conceded, 'I suppose it must have got to be the same for him and Rosetta too, starting their relationship from cold all the time. And, you know, after a while, he came home less and less, and she was doing her own thing and eventually, they'd been living apart long enough to be legally separated and so they did. I expect there was some kind of tax break in it for Dad.'

'That's really hard,' said Tanith. She knelt by his chair and put her hand on his knee.

'No, I didn't really mind that, to be honest. The hardest part was learning all about your own life from the papers,' said Robert bitterly. 'Reading about people who had the same name as people you knew, but who acted totally differently. Having to read about parts of your life all over again, but with whole new explanations offered for things you didn't really understand at the time, explanations that changed *everything*. And now she thinks she can sit down and write a book, explaining it once more for the benefit of the general public, when she hasn't ever, *ever*, had the guts to sit down with her own children and tell us what went on herself. As if the Rosetta she was in public is somehow more important than being our mother. I mean, for God's sake! It's not even as if she's Cher or someone!'

'But why do you think she *hasn't* done that before?' asked Tanith gently.

'Because she's too fucking ashamed of being such a slut!' spat Robert.

Tanith shut her eyes. 'Sweetheart, have you ever thought that she's scared of you?'

There was a pause. 'And so she should be,' said Robert. 'Because we're exactly the way she made us. Now if you'll excuse me, I need to work out some accounts. I'm not going to be very good company. I've just seen a set of school fees bills clipped to some reports.'

Tanith awkwardly got up from her kneeling position. Another attractive family trait – the ability to touch on something very personal and then push it away with a slick line.

'Give me a shout if you want more coffee,' she said, trying not to let the frustration show in her voice. Now she really had to know who was behind that script. If it *was* Rosetta, then Robert was heading for some kind of breakdown. 'I'm going to make some calls.'

Robert didn't reply, but his computer chimed as he shut down his spreadsheets. 'I'm going into the cellar to play my drums,' he said, and five minutes later, she could hear him thrashing away as if they were on fire and he was trying to beat out the flames.

Chapter Twenty-two

Los Angeles, 1975

'And *so* the two shouty women take the little baby to King Solomon and they say, "OK, wise guy, if you're so smart, *you* tell us whose baby it is." And *King Solomon* says, "Verily, that's no problem, madam." And the mouthy woman looks at the first woman and says . . .' Rosetta jerked her thumb and dropped into gloopy stage-Brooklynese, '"Get ya bag, sister, here's where ya get awff!"'

Robert gurgled appreciatively.

Patrick stared at her, spellbound.

'And so King Solomon took out his big sword. And do you know what he did with the big sword?'

Rosetta looked between Patrick and Robert who were tucked up in a huge American emperor-size hotel bed. They stared back at her with round brown eyes.

'Did he chop off the women's heads?' breathed Patrick.

Robert's grin broadened, as if he'd been thinking that too, but didn't have the necessary communication skills to express it.

'No,' said Rosetta. 'But that's a good guess, darling.' She didn't dilute her Bible stories for the boys, just as her mother hadn't for her, and casual beheadings weren't that unusual in the Old Testament. 'No, he took his big sword and asked them to put the little baby on a table in front of him. Just like he was a teriyaki steak. And they did. And do you know what King Solomon said then?'

'Did he say, "I'm going to chop up the baby!"?' asked Patrick. His voice was full of trepidation.

Rosetta was pleasantly surprised by Patrick's precocious grasp of retribution and bloodlust. He was a very, very smart little boy.

'Yes, he did!' she said. 'He said exactly that.'

Robert's face shone with excitement.

Patrick looked horror-struck.

'He gave both the women a long, hard stare,' Rosetta went on, demonstrating, 'and said, "If you can't decide whose baby this is, then I'm going to cut him in half and you can share him. Now, madam, which half do you want? Top or bottom?"'

Patrick's lip wobbled.

Robert giggled. 'Bottom! The bottom!'

'And the first lady, the one who really loved the baby, well, she burst into tears as soon as King Solomon said that.' Rosetta mimed hair-rending and general Biblical tragedy. 'And she said, "No! Stop! Stop! Let her have him! But please don't hurt my baby!"'

She paused, recently plucked eyebrows aloft, to milk the drama. 'And King Solomon put his sword back in his bag, and said, "Guards, give the baby to that woman, because she is his real momma." And everyone gasped and said, "Gee, that Solomon sure is wise!"'

For some historically inaccurate reason her mother would doubtless disapprove of, all Rosetta's Ishmaelites and Philistines tended to be of the Technicolor Kirk Douglas Hollywood variety.

'They all came up to him and said, "How did you know whose baby it was? Did you use magic?" And he said, "I didn't need magic to tell whose baby that was. I knew that because only one of the two women didn't want to see him hurt." And that's how you can always tell the truth of a situation, because people will always give themselves away by the way they love.'

She finished up triumphantly and started to tuck in the blankets around them.

'But what if the other woman was his momma too?' asked Patrick.

'She wasn't, honey. She was just pretending.'

'Why?'

'Because you can only have one momma and dad. Maybe she wanted a baby too. And he was a very pretty baby. Not as pretty as you two, though.' She dropped a kiss on to his head.

Patrick's dark eyes followed her round the room. 'But why? Why would she want to steal a baby?'

'Because . . . because not all ladies can have babies.'

Rosetta turned piles of magazines and half-empty suitcases upside down, looking for her evening bag. She was meant to be at a record company party with Brian and John and she was late already. Not just late, as in 'not on time', either – late as in, 'Has there been an accident?'

It wasn't easy sharing herself out on the road between the band, and Brian, and the boys, with all the accompanying shifts in personality that required, especially now Patrick and Robert were older and couldn't be put in a cot under a table. But Rosetta didn't think that boarding-school was a substantially more 'normal' environment than a tour-bus and she had a job to do as much as Brian did, after all. And if the best place for the boys was with her, then they just had to get used to a rather different routine. Bedtime stories were a big part of her plan – if she could be there when they went to bed and when they woke up, that was pretty normal, wasn't it? She also hoped that a good dose of religion would act as a sort of moral penicillin against hanging out with a bunch of professional degenerates and constant exposure to the American cop shows playing on hotel TV channels.

The only trouble was, Patrick took them really seriously.

'Why can't all ladies have babies?' he persisted. 'Why doesn't Sue have a baby? Doesn't God love her enough?'

Rosetta unearthed her little velvet bag underneath a heap of newly laundered T-shirts and started filling it with make-up. Thank God for hotel laundries, maid service and baby-sitting facilities, she thought. How were you meant to bring up children in *Esher*?

'Of course God loves her, honey,' she said. Sue made a point of giving Rosetta blow-by-blow accounts of her fertility treatments, but Rosetta suspected a more basic reason for her inability to get pregnant. 'It's just that . . . she and John aren't ready to have a baby just now.'

And to think I was always going to be totally upfront about where babies come from, she thought crossly. At least 'Sue and John don't have sex' would be a fairly simple explanation. It even *sounded* like the title of a children's sex education book.

'But why doesn't she come on the bus with us?' he asked, sitting up in his little mini-Brian candy-stripe pyjamas. 'Doesn't she like coming on the bus?'

'Honey, Sue is very busy at home in London,' said Rosetta absently, as she coaxed her hair back into flicks with a round brush. 'She's got a very important job, writing newspapers and talking to famous people. Not everyone can just get on the bus and come with us, you know. We're all very lucky.'

And Sue is smart enough to let John get on with it here, and have her own life there meanwhile.

'Why? Why can't she come? Doesn't she love John?' Patrick's smooth brow creased. Ever since he'd learned to talk, he'd discovered questions only led to other questions.

'Honey, we can't talk about that right now,' she said soothingly. 'It's a very big thing to talk about and I don't have time to explain it to you properly.'

'But why?'

'If I had a pound for every time you've asked me why, I would be a very rich woman,' she said.

'So when?' Patrick replied immediately.

Rosetta bent down and switched on the hotel radio,

conveniently located in the headboard of the bed. It was
playing some kind of country music. Patrick and Robert
both liked to fall asleep listening to the radio, since they'd
spent most of their baby years in the back of the bus or in
dressing-rooms while the band were on, and she knew it
was connected to the listening service in case anything serious happened. They both also liked the vibrating beds in
certain hotels, much to Brian's embarrassment and her
amusement.

'Where are you going?' asked Patrick, changing tack.

'I'm going out to a party with Dad now, but I'll be back
soon.' Rosetta blinked a couple of times and checked her
appearance in the mirror, then threw a long-fringed shawl
around her bare shoulders, which she had dusted with
sparkly talcum powder.

Patrick stared back at her with the same kind of mistrust-
ful wonderment he reserved for Disney film heroines and
fairies in books.

'When are you coming back?'

'I won't be long.' Rosetta bent over and kissed his soft
forehead. Robert was already dozing off next to him. 'We'll
talk about everything you want to then, OK? You can ask
me five questions and I'll answer all of them. Now, darling,
please be good for me and go to sleep and I'll bring you
something back in my magic bag.'

'Promise?' said Patrick suspiciously.

'Promise.'

Rosetta descended the sweeping hotel staircase majestically,
on account of her floor-length skirt, and went straight to the
front desk to see if there were any notes for her. There were
some drooping flowers from a journalist she'd had lunch
with that afternoon, and a note from Brian, saying that the
limo had come and he'd gone ahead with Red and Glynn.

Rosetta wasn't irritated that they'd gone without her: Red
never liked to miss valuable drinking time at any party, and

Glynn wanted to be sure he got there before all the prettiest girls were creamed off by the hosts of the next event that night. Brian, ever aware of the delicate balance between his charges appearing mad, bad, and dangerous to know and being plain offensive, clearly didn't want to risk them rocking up unchaperoned at this critical stage of the tour, with journalists everywhere, a new deal in the balance and three senior executives from the record company hosting the party.

Brian's note reminded her, in his usual precise way, exactly who was giving the party and where and why, then asked her to pick up John, who had gone to the venue for the next night's gig.

'Yes, sir, no, sir,' said Rosetta ironically to the note. The way Brian constantly sent her into John's way you'd think he *wanted* them to have an affair.

'Evenin', Rosetta.'

She looked up and saw Simon sitting on the velveteen banquette of the hotel lobby, resplendent in a tie that looked exactly like a side of smoked salmon.

'Oh, hi, Slimon . . . *Simon*,' she said. It was a real effort not to call him Slimon to his face. Red had started it about a year ago, and now everyone referred to him as Slimon. It suited him. The more famous Glynn and Red got, the more they seemed to metamorphose into rock-stars – it was an attitude more than the actual clothes, or flowing hairstyle. And yet the more fashionably Simon dressed, or the longer he tried to grow his hair, the more he looked like an office supplies salesman in satin loon pants. There was absolutely nothing Rosetta could do, and God knew she and Anita had tried.

Maybe it was a bass player thing.

'Are you . . . waiting for someone?' she asked out of politeness.

'I'm waiting for . . . *someone*.' His weasely face was secretive and his little eyes flicked back and forth around the busy lobby.

Rosetta didn't want to know who he was waiting for. Mrs Slimon was at home in Blackheath with Slimon Jnr and Slimonetta, and if there was one thing Rosetta didn't do, it was keep secrets for people like him.

'OK!' She waved her hands in the air in front of her face. 'Don't tell me, don't tell me. I'm going to pick up John and go to the Rainbow,' she said. 'You want to come with us?'

Immediately his beady little eyes darkened. 'Er, no, love. Nah, I'll make my own way there. In a minute.'

Rosetta left a pause, short enough to convey fake disapproval. He was definitely up to something. If it was a woman, he might at least bring her along to the party so the poor cow got a decent night of it. Simon had to work hard for his groupies – they didn't just turn up in formation lines like they did for the other three.

'Well, be sure you get there before eleven,' she said sharply. 'You want this US deal to work, we've got to make these people happy. And take that tie off, yeah?'

Simon's hand flew to his collar then slowly returned to his belt-loop. 'I'm cool,' he said defensively.

'You absolutely are not,' said Rosetta and her car arrived to take her away.

Rosetta sat in the dark womb of the limo and reapplied her lip gloss, studying her face thoughtfully while her mind probed lateral avenues, trying to uncover what Simon was up to, lurking around like that, a tiny piece of the Dog and Fox snug bar in LA.

She hoped it wasn't a drug connection he was waiting for. The scene rattled with every kind of opiate, hallucinogenic, sedative and stimulant you could imagine but so far the band had largely stuck to their beer, grass and a social bit of cocaine, and steered clear of anything harder. Red had told her that the one time Simon had dropped acid with them, he'd claimed to be able to read the *Radio Times* without opening the cover.

None of them were really cool enough to develop a serious hard drug habit. Glynn was too vain about his voice and Red had a constitution like an ox but as he got older, he liked to keep with what he knew (preferably in tablet form).

It was John, though, who really worried Rosetta, since he was the only one with a real artistic personality and the only one with problems he wanted to get away from. It froze the blood in Rosetta's veins that every single guitar hero she had ever dreamed about seemed to have escaped into the oblivion of heroin at some point, and she'd made John promise that he'd never, *never* let things get so bad that smack would be an option. That was a place she knew she couldn't bring him back from.

But at least those stern moral values that kept him permanently tortured about their relationship would be good for something: he wouldn't risk his self-control, she knew, not while he hung on to his good Catholic fear of anything he didn't know. He even refused Red's generous offer of speed, even when they were all completely knackered. Whereas she had The Fear but could override that with her ambition, John *still* stuck his heels in.

Of course, none of this was to say that the group didn't pretend they were cool about drugs – Brian even employed one of the roadies to pretend to be the designated runner for the benefit of their reputations – but only Simon was insecure enough to think he needed drugs to join some kind of exclusive club.

Rosetta filed the thought away in the back of her mind to deal with later and rapped on the glass window to indicate to the driver to stop outside the venue.

Inside the concert hall the roadies were setting up the lighting rig for the three nights the band were booked to play. The sound and lighting rig was gradually getting more and more elaborate, and took up increasing amounts of Brian's time to coordinate. One of the sound techs had come back from the crew dinner so John could test his acoustic balances; Rosetta knew this was basically rubbish, since the whole place would sound totally different with sixty thousand screaming fans packed in, but John liked to play for an hour or so before a gig in a big venue, if time allowed. He admitted to her that it helped to calm the nerves that still attacked him before one of these ever-expanding American tours. Not that he would have told anyone else.

Not that Brian would have *let* him tell anyone else. He was still keeping a good tight rein on all the quotes and as far as the press were concerned, John was a Celtic visionary genius.

The hall smelled of old lager and stale teenage excitement, and echoed with the sound of roadies, yelling orders and crashing boxes and cables around. Rosetta walked down the aisle unseen, enjoying the feeling of being invisible for once.

From the back of the stalls, Rosetta could see John sitting cross-legged on the stage picking out the opening arpeggios to a song he'd written a few nights back – the melody was all there, but the words were taking longer to come to him. The lighting tech was practising the spotlights, but John played on, oblivious to the pools of yellow light that moved around him. He was murmuring lyrics to himself just out of reach of the microphone and jotting things down in a little notebook.

She stopped walking and slipped on to one of the seats at the back. It wasn't often she got to see him like this, natural and unobserved.

All the motes of dust stirred up by the crew shimmered in the spotlight, showering micro-confetti down the tube of light around John. She closed her eyes and listened to him strumming through mutating chords, and a shiver of sensation tingled down the front of her body. Listening to John play was still as exciting as the first time she'd seen him, auditioning at the Kingston gig, tearing up that student crowd. Virtually nothing else in her new life had kept its initial sparkle the way John O'Hara had.

He was singing under his breath, trying to make the words mingle with the tune, and Rosetta thrilled to think he was writing songs about her. She knew he was. That was the madness of the whole set-up: Brian might pretend he knew nothing was going on when she rode in the tour-bus and he flew on ahead to the next town with his briefcase, but every song John wrote was about being passionately in love, about being tormented by his heart and his woman, about finding a weirdly constrained salvation in loving something impossible.

Even if it was Glynn singing it for him to a crowd of hysterical teenagers.

She opened her eyes triumphantly, saw that John still hadn't caught sight of her, and for an exhilarating moment Rosetta felt as if her soul was filling with helium and she was being lifted high, high into the gods, looking down on the whole thing from the balcony. Somehow, by some weird mix of luck and fate and hard work, she'd swept the whole lot into her basket like a jackpot winner at the roulette table: she had the devoted, successful, perfectly pleasant husband, two beautiful children, the kind of career that wasn't as much a career as ten million people's real-life fantasy and, more than any of that, a lover who wrote songs about her and turned her into an immortal goddess muse woman.

It was so good, so thrilling that she forgot to feel guilty for a moment.

When he stopped playing, she stood up almost shyly and walked towards him. He peered through the lights, shading his eyes with his hand, and she could see his face light up when he realized it was her.

'Hi!' she said. 'Sounds fantastic.'

He jumped down from the stage and put his arms round her in a bear hug. They had to be careful not to make too much of a show in front of the roadies, who saw everything and then told everyone.

'You look just like Lizzie Siddall,' he muttered in her ear.

She pulled away. 'I might need to have a quick word with you in your dressing-room about tonight's party,' she said.

He nodded quickly. 'Let me put my guitars away and I'll be right there.'

'OK.' Rosetta smiled briefly and walked backstage, her skin already prickling with anticipation of his light and confident touch. Frenzied sex in dressing-rooms and rehearsal venues was the kind of thing *Cosmopolitan* recommended to couples trying to spice up their flagging sex lives, but it would never have the same adrenalin shot of fear, shame, excitement as when you were doing it for real.

That was the unspoken deal she and John had reached; yes, it was wrong; no, they couldn't stop. Hotel rooms and houses – anywhere that bore evidence of their other relationships – were out of bounds, as though they didn't deserve anywhere comfortable or convenient. It was, in many ways, an affair with the punishment already built in.

And yet whenever she was alone with John, it all seemed to make sense. As the band slipped further away from any normal existence, John heard the tremors in her soul that she couldn't articulate to Brian: the fear of being unmasked as a suburban fraud, the throbbing headache of constant contrition, the pressure of meeting everyone else's wild expectations. He understood all the contradictions that made her despair of herself in private, and didn't judge her, because he had his own to deal with.

Every little oddity of their itinerant lives, and the warped normality of doing what they did, fell away when it was just them together. It was, Rosetta sometimes thought, like being in a song, the way she had tried to make the lyrics fit her life when she was younger. But it wasn't just some 'bit on the side' thing, she knew that. No matter what she was doing with John, she was a good mother and the best wife Brian could have wished for. Everything good came with a price. She just hoped that this was the whole price, and not some down-payment for a much bigger punishment to come.

There was a single knock on the dressing-room door and John slipped inside, his black jeans dusty from the stage.

'Don't make a sound,' he said, holding a finger up to his lips with a grin. 'It's Nev's birthday and the lighting crew are all over the place, booby-trapping the loos.'

He crossed the room in a couple of loping strides. As the familiar lemony smell of his body reached her nose, Rosetta's breath caught in her throat and she lifted her face as he covered her neck with quick kisses.

With the same lean strength that he used to lift amps, he gathered her up in his arms and carried her to the chaise longue which was now specified in Brian's extensive rider, along with two crates of champagne and vases and vases of roses.

'We've only got twenty minutes,' she gasped as she came up for air.

'Do we have to go to the party?' asked John, leaning his head against the back seat of the limo. His eyes were dark and drowsy after the quick post-sex catnap they'd grabbed, still tangled up in each other's limbs. He shook a couple of vitamins and a couple of pep pills into his palm and swallowed them with a mouthful of Dr Pepper from the little chiller in the back of the car. 'Can we not just go back to the hotel and crash out together for a few hours, so? I know all those eejits from the bar last night will be in.'

'Honey, those eejits were from your record company and four of them were in a very big band indeed.' Rosetta concentrated on getting her high-shine gloss just right. Not *too* done. She didn't want to look *Sue*. 'Come on, darling, just do the meeting and greeting then go home to bed.' She gave him an exhilarated high-shine smile. Rosetta never got lipstick on her teeth. 'You don't have to stay long – just long enough for them to see you're not drug-addicted or getting fat. I'll come by and see you later. It'll look better if we don't leave together. Anyway, lucky you – I'll be there till all hours, flattering the suits and making sure none of the road crew try to crash it.'

John looked at her with a smile playing on the corner of his lips.

'Oh, but I know you, Rosie! Sure you'll leave before the end, but on the arm of some terrible pussy hound! You know you will!' he protested, only half-joking. 'It's page five in the Sunday papers every week these days, you know – Rosetta Mulligan goes off partying while hubbie Brian gets an early night.'

Rosetta pretended to sigh. 'The things I have to do for work, eh? I know. The nuns would be ashamed of me. And to think that I tell Sue to make half of it up.'

'*Half* of it?' Sue had recently been promoted to deputy editor of her paper; one word to her could get a diary piece printed or binned.

Rosetta flipped her compact shut and winked at his startled face. 'Yes, half. Because I make the other half of it up myself. Oh come on,' she protested, 'think about it! It's the only way to blow a smokescreen over you and me! If I'm going out every night with people other than my husband then who's going to count up the nights *we're* together? They're not saying, "Rosetta Mulligan swans off for a long night's chit-chat with Mick Jagger then goes home to the warm bed of her shady boyfriend, John O'Hara," are they?'

John's face darkened as it normally did on being flippantly reminded of their joint infidelities. They both knew Sue was implicitly included in that 'they'.

He would have made a heartbreaker priest, thought Rosetta, as a warm thrill ran through her stomach. He certainly had the conscience for it. And how many hearts would he have broken in confession?

'I know, I know,' he said. 'And I know you're not really . . . you know. But it makes you look . . .'

Rosetta set her chin. 'I don't care if people thing I'm a . . . party girl. All right, so I know a lot of people and I go to a lot of parties. It's my *job*, when I'm on duty. They don't know anything about the *real* me. Let them think what they want, you know? Brian's cool about it. He knows that I *might* go on to another party if there's a big band in town at the same time, but he knows it's business. He knows I don't go off with other *men*.'

John hoisted his dark eyebrows.

'Because I *don't*. And he does believe me,' Rosetta protested, trying to maintain a sheen of chic urbanity while she fought down a terrible desire to pull John's arms above her head and wrestle herself underneath his famous, lithe body again. Back seats of limos were so horny. There was a terrible groupie strand in her soul.

She concentrated. 'Listen, we talked about it. I keep telling you, we're very . . . business-like, me and Brian. On the road is *on the road*. It's all about the band, isn't it? He knows that column inches about me are column inches about you lot and . . . oh, come on, it's just *advertising*. I mean, *Glynn's trousers* are advertising.'

'Then Glynn's trousers want checking out by the advertising standards people,' said John.

'Maybe,' Rosetta replied. They were almost at the bar. She buried her nose in the crook of John's neck and breathed in the faint traces of the cologne he wore.

'Besides,' she went on happily, right into his ear, '*you* get the real me. Just you.'

John turned round to enclose her in his arm for a final kiss before they got out. 'And you know that I love the real you,' he murmured, 'but I'm surprised you can remember who that is these days.'

The party was, as John had predicted, full of eejits, with an equally lavish proportion of drunken heifers in Halston dresses.

Rosetta fixed her professional smile to her face and began to circulate in earnest. She had to communicate mainly through 'Hi-ii-ii-ii-!' smiles and intimate touches on the arm, since there wasn't any point trying to be heard over the deafening mix of loud chat and background rock music. Every corner of the club was full of record company people, journalists, some would-be stars and their would-be groupies, dealers and hangers-on, and some old friends she actually wanted to see. Not every party was a trial but there was always a certain amount to do before she could really enjoy herself. Parties in LA were not unlike the country dancing they'd done at school, as she wove her way from one clique to another in a smooth and constant movement, mixing up couples and redistributing pretty women to areas of heavy male grouping. And sometimes swinging undesirables out of the circle so they could be picked up and removed by sharp-eyed organizers on the outside.

'Hello, *Randy*!' she cried, seeing one of the A & R men from the record label. Randy Simons was a rising star and he'd been very helpful on the gossip front last time they'd been in town, very helpful indeed. But then, he'd explained, he was a big, *big* fan.

Of course he was.

'Hi, *sweetie*!' he cried and kissed her on both cheeks. He smelt strongly of Eau Sauvage and was wearing a rather ill-advised blouse-type top. 'So glad you could *make* it! The party can finally get going now.'

'Oh, no. You're too kind. But, honey, you look *sensational*!' she said confidingly. 'You must tell me where you got that blouse. I can get one for Brian!'

Randy giggled. 'Your Brian . . .?'

'Who else's?' Rosetta mugged. 'And I know Glynn's on the look-out for something new to break down the resistance of your teenage girls. Hey, listen, have you met Dominica? Dominica Dilieto, the music writer? Because I can see her over by the fruit punch. You'd *love* her. Look, can you see? She's talking to Cindy Barber? Come on, come with me,' she said, taking Randy's arm. 'Let's go and meet her . . .'

They wove their way through the chatting, swaying crowd of beautiful people, avoiding cigarettes extended casually over shoulders, and drinks dangled in animated waving hands.

Rosetta spotted Brian in earnest conversation with a suit from the record company over by the fire exit. He was looking a lot better since he'd given in to her gentle persuasion and had his hair cut short, the way it was when they first met. Amidst all the fakeos with their Grateful Dead split-end manes and bad highlights, Brian looked very English and debonair. Very trustworthy. Rosetta flashed him a smile as she shimmied past and Brian smiled back, obviously pleased to see that she was dragging Randy with her, and heading in the direction of two journalists.

With impeccable timing, Rosetta appeared at Dominica Dilieto's side at the very moment she and Cindy Barber paused in conversation to take a sip of their cocktails.

'Hi, darling!' she cried, feigning surprise and delight to see Dominica. 'Might have known you'd be here by the drinks!'

They exchanged enthusiastic kisses.

'Now, listen, Dommie,' said Rosetta confidentially, 'I really want you to meet Randy Simons. He's Armando's right-hand man in the A & R department, and he's so good. I mean, he's *so good*! And he's the most charming A & R man I know *in the whole of LA*.'

'And that's saying something!' said Dominica. She swopped her cigarette over to her left hand and extended her long fingers to Randy, jangling her love beads back down her arm. 'Pleased to meet you. Love your blouse.'

'And you *must* know *Cindy*. Cindy Barber?' Rosetta went on.

They didn't, but fell upon each other anyway and exchanged kisses.

'So, Randy, you'll be able to tell Cindy which drummer she should go for next,' said Dominica, taking a long slurp of punch and sizing him up with a blatantly shiny eye. 'She likes them unsigned. So much more grateful.'

Randy, like Rosetta, only went on-duty at these off-duty events, and was more than happy to fill Dominica in on his latest finds on the club scene. As soon as Rosetta could see the two women making a subtle wall of interest around Randy, she touched him lightly on the shoulder and murmured, 'Darling, must go and see what Brian's making faces at me for,' and she slipped off, eyes darting around the room to see where she was needed next.

It was tiring but somehow the very sensation of being tired kept Rosetta going. Tonight was a good night, she thought. For once, it all seems to be under control, and it's OK for me to enjoy myself.

She really loved all the flitting about from one group to the next, knowing everyone, making sure the right people met and mingled, then leaving exactly one minute before the party reached its peak. Little did they know that for every time she went on to another bar with a select handful from the previous event, there was another time when she'd get the first cab home and crash out listening to Robert snoring and Patrick sleep-talking and Brian making transatlantic phone calls to the record company back in London.

She shimmied across the room, smiling her way past acquaintances and friends, getting nearer and nearer Brian. He was her best mingling excuse – 'Darling, will you excuse me, but I must just go and have a word with Brian?' – but she did actually want a word with him now. By some amazing sequence of crises involving the band (him) and the kids (her), they hadn't actually spoken for nearly twenty-four hours, despite being on the same bus.

He seemed very engrossed in conversation with this same man, making his little hand gestures and nodding a lot. The man, for his part, seemed pretty engrossed too, and was mirroring Brian exactly. Rosetta narrowed her eyes and tried to think where she'd seen him before. A PR guy? Another manager? She ground to a halt behind a tight wall of women, and pretended that she was reaching for a glass of champagne from the table. Shoving through the crowd didn't look dignified, and she wasn't sure that her precariously attached top would stand up to a good shouldering.

The women were having a good gossip, and Rosetta could pick out a couple of British accents. She wondered if she knew them, or if they knew Sue. There was an annoying new fashion going round for wigs, which meant you could never quite be sure who it was you were talking to, especially from behind.

Glynn, in particular, had had some narrow escapes.

'No, it is a terrible shame,' one woman was saying, in agreement with the blonde next to her.

Rosetta loved a terrible shame as much as anyone else and began eavesdropping, running through all the possible victims.

'I'm not saying she isn't a very smart cookie,' the woman went on, 'and she does have the most *fabulous* clothes, but . . .' And she dropped her voice to a confidential level which meant that Rosetta couldn't hear any more.

With a shiver she knew that they were talking about her, and from the sniggers of delight that followed, it probably wasn't her fashion tips they were exchanging.

She took a deep breath. OK, so they were bitching about her. So what? She was the nominal hostess this evening. She wasn't so dumb as to think you could have a life like this and not be bitched about. That was the deal.

Anyway, they weren't bitching about her *personally*, they were bitching about that shameless party girl, Rosetta Mulligan, and probably discussing the very same fake gossip she'd fed them herself.

Rosetta took a deep breath and a sip of her drink and prepared to walk away discreetly before they saw her.

'But then *Brian*!'

There was a round of nodding, and Rosetta felt her stomach tighten protectively. Now this was *different*. They could say what they liked about her, because she made stuff up *specifically* so that no gossip would hurt her, but they couldn't say anything about *Brian*. Sweet, undefended Brian!

'I mean, he's really clever about arranging those tours and so on,' one of them bitched in a smug, whiny mid-Atlantic drawl, 'but I can't believe he can let them get away with it. He must be *so dumb*.'

'Oh, but, honey, he might not *want* to make a fuss,' intimated another. '*If* you know what I mean?'

Rosetta felt a surge of protective pride rise up in her throat, but she bit her tongue and held her breath, not wanting to be seen to lose her cool over a criticism of herself.

Luckily, the women were on a roll, and happy to oblige with some detail.

'Well, she's not the only one sleeping around – I've heard some pretty juicy rumours about *him*,' chipped in another. 'Him and the drummer, Red?'

Old news, old news, sweetheart, thought Rosetta grimly. But, no, wait – leave it, leave it . . .

'Oh, I've heard that's been going on for a long time,' drawled her friend competitively.

'No!' the women chorused.

No indeed. Rosetta's grip tightened on the stem of her glass. She really wanted to go, but she was trapped now by sheer mass of bodies.

'Talk about Beauty and the Beast!' said one.

Rosetta wasn't sure exactly who was meant to be who. God, women were the worst.

'And *did you know* that he's deliberately trying to get John O'Hara hooked on heroin so he can make him more . . . manageable? I mean, I know Brian looks like such a gentleman, but I've heard he can be real, real mean. Real . . . calculating, you know? Like he needs to be, because honestly, I don't think he's that bright when it comes to business, I've heard? I mean, maybe in England you can get away with being kind of . . . *amateur*, but he's playing with the big boys now and no one really takes him very seriously . . .'

The blood raced to Rosetta's cheeks and she felt light-headed and sick with anger.

Before she could speak there was an anonymous round of agreement, which encouraged another woman to add, 'And if you ask me, there's something very odd going on with him and John. A girlfriend of mine was with Simon and Glynn in a bungalow at the Marmont and they were having a private party, if you know what I mean, and Lord Brian came in wearing that ridiculous velvet smoking jacket he has and said –'

Rosetta couldn't hold herself back any more. She tapped the woman on her shoulder, forcing her hand to be light when every nerve in her body screamed to slap the gossiping, emaciated old witch.

The woman turned round with a raised eyebrow, expecting to see an industry friend. It was clear from the horrified look that developed over her starved face like a Polaroid photo that she wasn't expecting to see Rosetta.

Rosetta recognized her as one of the press officers for another band, one that The End had opened for a few years back, and who were now struggling to get another deal amidst rumours that their lead singer was up on charges of interfering with his pre-teen cousin.

Which made the lack-of-deal situation seem comparatively cool.

The PR reactions kicked in long before the shock faded from her eyes. 'Rosetta, honey! How lovely to see you!' she cried, extending her hand. 'Fabulous party!'

The other three around her shrank back into the crowd.

Rosetta ignored the skinny hand. 'How dare you speak about Brian like that?' she demanded hotly.

The woman flipped through her limited options and settled on attack. She looked, from the empty uncollected glasses around her, to have reached a pugnacious stage of drunkenness even quicker than Red did.

'I'm only saying what everyone else is saying,' she slurred.

'No, you're not,' snapped Rosetta. 'Every single thing you said was total garbage, and you know it.'

Ever since Sue's little bombshell in the pub, she'd made a point of knowing *all* the gossip about the band – good, bad and clearly fictitious – and somehow the more she heard, the less it bothered her. Yes, that little rumour was still doing the rounds, and she still didn't believe it, putting it down to jealousy and lack of imagination. But as far as she knew, virtually everyone in the business liked and respected Brian.

And God knew she would die before she let someone bad-mouth him at his own party.

The woman opened and shut her mouth and Rosetta slammed back in before she had time to gather herself. The blood was pounding through her temples, driven by absolute fury. How *dare* this woman be so rude to Brian? What the fuck did she know about *anything*?

'When you launch a band as successful and popular as The End, off your own back, as opposed to *on* your own back, *then* you can make moronic and ill-informed comments like that,' said Rosetta. 'And since I don't expect that to happen any time soon, I think an apology would be quicker.'

'To who?' the woman snapped.

'To *whom*,' Rosetta corrected her. 'To Brian, you cretinous slut. Via me.'

'Honey, forgive me for joining with the voice of common consent, but much as I admire your dress sense, I really think it's *you* that should be apologizing to Brian.'

There was now a circle of space around them. For once, Rosetta was so angry on Brian's behalf that she didn't notice the fascinated eyes of those guests lacking sufficiently in ennui to turn to watch the catfight unfolding by the bar.

A quarter of the party guests were still engaged in conversations about grosses and reliable security firms. The straight, male quarter.

'I can't imagine what you're talking about,' said Rosetta.

By some marital sixth sense, she knew that Brian wasn't particularly near her. She hoped that John had already left. This was the last thing he needed to hear, given that they'd only just got over his most recent bout of moral agonizing brought on by Sue's latest brat attack.

'Oh, you know,' the woman went on, giving her a nasty/friendly look that Rosetta found chilling. She put a finger on her chin. 'Who will I leave the party with tonight? Hmm? Ronnie Wood? Robert Plant? Rod Stewart? My husband? Oh, no, no ... not him,' she corrected herself. 'Far too dull and not nearly famous enough.'

Rosetta could have laughed, the woman was so far off the mark.

'You think you're so clever, don't you?' she said, and could tell immediately that her amusement pissed the PR girl off. 'Amazing what illusions drink can sustain.'

'Starfucker!' spat the woman and tossed her glass of wine over Rosetta's dress.

Rosetta blinked as the cold wine hit her, then raised her eyebrows and took a step forward. The thin silk of her top clung to her breasts and made her nipples stand out in a not-unattractive way, while the wine glistened on her porcelain-white skin.

Fortunately, it hadn't splashed her make-up.

Out of the corner of her eye, she registered the flash of a camera.

Rosetta grabbed the bowl of dry-roasted peanuts next to the tray of glasses and carefully tipped them down the woman's cleavage.

'I'm afraid that's the closest you'll get to spicy nuts tonight, darling,' she said. 'Now, if you'll excuse me, my *husband* and I are leaving to get some supper.'

'I'm peanut-allergic!' screeched the woman, as she desperately tried to brush peanut skins off her feather boa. 'You bitch! I flush really badly!'

'Yet another thing you have in common with a toilet,'

said Rosetta. She turned on her heel, and marched through the crowd which parted like the Red Sea in front of her.

Brian was standing on a chair at the other end of the room with Red, and they were both rocking with laughter. John was nowhere to be seen and she hoped he'd left.

There was a reporter with a radio mike standing quite near Brian and Rosetta made a beeline for her.

'Hi, have we met?' she asked, extending a hand. With the other, she beckoned Brian and Red over.

'Hi, Sonia Silver, Radio QTHX entertainment news,' the reporter replied excitedly. 'What was that all about?'

Rosetta slid an arm round Brian's waist. 'Oh, some girls are just jealous of the fact that not only do I spend time with the four most talented men in the States, I'm married to a real charmer too.' And she gave Brian a maternal hug. There was something undeniably comforting about Brian's solidity. Very grounding, as Anita often told her.

'Can we do an interview?' Sonia Silver asked, unable to believe her luck. 'Do you want to talk about it?'

'Of course! We were just leaving to get some dinner, weren't we?' Rosetta looked between Red and Brian.

Brian kissed the top of her head and said, 'Sorry, darling, you go for dinner with Red. I need to have a few more little chats here, OK?' He handed her his blue handkerchief to mop herself up. 'But thanks for defending my honour. Let me do the same for you some time.'

'You do every day, darling,' said Rosetta, trying to keep the trace of disappointment out of her voice, 'I'll catch up with you later? There are some things I needed to discuss with you. Look in on the boys, won't you?'

'Of course, later.' He clapped Red on the arm. 'Now then, don't let her leave with that Rod Stewart, will you, big lad?'

'Nah, man, she's leaving with me, isn't she? Are you writing all this down, pet?' he enquired of the reporter. '"Rosetta Mulligan leaves the party with famous rock skinsman, Red Fearon."'

Rosetta tucked her hand under Red's hefty drummer's arm and left the party for yet another unofficial press appointment. Within ten minutes of their oysters arriving, Brian had had another clean dress sent round to the restaurant, and was on the phone ensuring the PR girl was promoted sideways into the mid-West sales division.

After a glamorous and gossipy supper, at which Rosetta had been at her most charming and Red had been almost endearing, Sonia Silver left to file her report. Red and Rosetta stayed out drinking and talking until two, when the quiet underground hang-out threw them onto the street, celebrities or no celebrities.

It was good to go for a drink with Red now and again, she thought, making her way down the hotel corridors, which were still teeming with half-dressed teenagers and confused room-service boys, even in the middle of the night. Red hadn't really changed, deep down, from the lairy teenager she used to know. He just had marginally better clothes and drank champagne instead of Thunderbird. It was good, too, just to be herself for once.

She pushed open the door into the boys' adjoining room to check that they were both sleeping all right. The radio was burbling away in the background, and the little phosphorescent night light she'd left on against Patrick's nightmares was glowing in the corner like a comforting magic mushroom. Rosetta's ears rang with the peaceful silence, after the shrillness of the bar. Warm baby smells of talcum powder and hot breath filled the room, and Rosetta had a deep longing to kick off her shoes and get into bed with them, letting Patrick's warm body curl into hers.

But she couldn't. Her evening wasn't over until she'd had her night's chat with Brian, sorted everything out with him, paid him some attention, massaged his bad back, made love to him (he was trying to kick sleeping tablets) and then massaged his back again so he could get his six hours' sleep.

Then she was allowed to go to bed.

Her eyelids were sticking to her eyeballs with exhaustion.

Rosetta tried to remember if there was any Valium left in her bag, then mentally slapped her hand. No! *Bad* mother!

She crept through the room, avoiding the heaps of clothes and discarded room-service trays. Robert was sleeping, she could tell. He had a way of breathing that challenged you to disturb him. Brian did the same kind of thing. Patrick slept more fitfully, but even *he* had to be flat out at three in the morning, *surely*.

While her eyes adjusted to the faint light, Rosetta slipped off her heels and moved carefully between the beds to switch off the radio. She was about level with the pillows when she was stopped in her tracks by a clear, accusing little voice saying, 'You were on the radio, Rosetta.'

Patrick's round eyes gleamed at her from his pillow.

Christ! she thought, clutching her bumping heart. He's just like an M.R. James ghost story!

'Darling? Are you awake?' she murmured under her breath in case he was sleep-talking. Patrick wasn't a good sleeper and sometimes walked all over the house, arguing with himself. He came out with horribly complex sentences in his sleep, way beyond his four years.

'You were on the radio,' Patrick repeated, reproachfully. He sounded as if he'd been keeping himself awake for her return. 'The lady said you had a fight with someone.'

'No, I didn't, darling!' she whispered. 'That's just . . .' She faltered. How did you explain press hype to a little boy? 'That was just the reporter trying to make up a story for the people listening.'

Damn! she thought crossly. You couldn't trust anyone in this shitty town! Not even when you fed them oysters and Krug!

'Why?'

'Um . . .' Rosetta thought hard. 'Because Dad and I are . . . because you know how people come to see the band play?

Well, those people are interested in what Dad and I do, too. So they come to the party to see what I'm wearing and what Dad says to people and . . .'

Patrick blinked at her, as if he didn't believe she was telling him the whole story.

'OK, so it sounds pretty lame when you put it like that,' she said with a wry smile. 'But they really do.'

'They said someone threw a drink over you.'

'Yes, well, it was only white wine, so it didn't spoil my dress, darling.' She tucked the duvet round him tighter and scratched his head gently. That usually got him off to sleep.

'Didn't Dad stop her?'

'Dad got very cross. And I threw a whole bowl of peanuts down her front,' said Rosetta. 'And I know nuts make her face swell up, so it'll hurt her a lot more than a little splash of white wine'll hurt me.'

'Are you upset?' asked Patrick.

'No, no! Not at all, darling,' laughed Rosetta. Her hand stopped scratching and smoothed down his soft dark hair. 'Not at all. There's no need to worry about me.'

'But they said you were crying.'

'They say lots of things about me and Dad, darling,' murmured Rosetta. 'But not all of them are true. When we go out like that, sometimes we have to . . . we have to pretend to be different people, like actors and actresses on the television. It's not . . . real, not really. So you mustn't worry at all because when I come home, it's just us, isn't it?'

Patrick didn't reply and Rosetta put her lips to his hot head. 'Isn't it, darling? It's just us.'

When he didn't answer again, Rosetta kicked off her shoes, and slipped her cold feet under the blankets. The warmth of the bed hit her like a Valium and when Patrick nuzzled into her, they fell asleep together.

Chapter Twenty-three

Clerkenwell, 2001

Tanith had spent another strained morning with a school drama group from Wandsworth, listening to eight more impassioned renditions of 'Genie in a Bottle', and had begun to feel as though she were trapped in some kind of paedophile *Stars in Their Eyes* groundhog day. So when a couple of appointments fell through (due to exam resits), and Frances phoned to announce that she'd gone to New York on a cheap last-minute weekend flight to finalize arrangements for the new office, it only seemed fair to Tanith, especially given her impending managerial status, that she should bale out early, go home and lie on the floor, and try to lure her sense of reality back.

The street outside Robert's house was half-deserted, post-lunch and pre-school run, and Tanith parked easily. She sat in the car listening to the radio – by a weird coincidence it was playing one of Glynn's morbid solo efforts from the eighties, a dirge about being a divorced father of three, as far as Tanith could tell. She didn't particularly want to listen to it, but now felt a superstitious obligation to sit through every *The End* song *to* the end. While Glynn groaned on about tender lovin' and missin' the baby that he knew, Tanith tapped her nails on the steering-wheel and looked at the front door. Robert had recently replaced the brass number so it gleamed in the sun against the shiny black paint. It was a very nice house. She was very lucky to be living there. Nice house, adult boyfriend, prospective partnership in business . . .

'You trapped me with your love and threw away the kee-ee-ee-y,' howled Glynn in conclusion. 'And now the broken-hearted prisoner of love is me-ee-ee-ee.'

Maybe it *was* Rosetta writing lyrics for them until they split, she thought, and scrambled out of the car towards the espresso bar on the corner for a consolation coffee.

While she waited at the end of the counter for her full-fat cappuccino, Tanith automatically scanned the tables for the undiscovered face that might slot into the Amber-shaped hole in the back of her mind. More material had arrived since the last update, with new segments involving even more teenage groupies and an unfilmable incident on a private jet. She had asked for another meeting with the producer, and angled to find out who was actually writing this; he'd been even more patronizing than previously, as well as very evasive, which had only made her more determined to find out what he had to be evasive about. When Tanith steamed back into the office, she discovered he'd beaten her to it on the phone and had had a terse conversation with Frances about confidentiality agreements, and Frances had just shrugged and promised to get to the bottom of it for her.

She stuck her hands in the loose demonstration coffee beans and frowned as they trickled through, wondering what the directors had to be so confidential about. From what she was gleaning from Robert's analysis of the accounts, and from Greg's halting confidences about the photos he was apparently going through for the book, the rough story of the film would seem to be bizarrely similar to Rosetta's own – or at least based on it. How many other women were there who'd had that kind of life? Even if it wasn't anything directly to do with Rosetta, maybe she should know in case there were libel issues, or something. Tanith knew she *had* to talk to her about it at some point, and she hated herself for being such a wimp, but how the hell were you meant to bring it up? Was it her place to tell Rosetta what a film about her life might do to her sons, if it wasn't immediately apparent to her? And if it *wasn't* her behind the film, even on their brief acquaintance Tanith suspected Rosetta wasn't the kind of woman who would take kindly to the idea of her heyday now being viewed as historical drama.

Maybe she could hint at it when Robert took the accounts round.

She blanched and corrected herself. No, *that* was a strictly mother–son evening.

She picked up her cappuccino and walked back to the house, sipping it thoughtfully and enjoying the fresh afternoon sunshine. The combined stress of this casting project and Frances's imminent move seemed to lift from her shoulders as the sun warmed the top of her head. In the car was a folder of photocopied documents from Frances's business folder and the number of her and Warren's psychic, who would apparently advise her better than 'that accountant idiot' on the possibilities ahead for the business. It was hard to believe that someone as tough as Frances made most of her decisions on the basis of a gut instinct or a spook, but then the Medicis and half the emperors of Rome had operated on the same principles and hadn't done too badly.

Tanith unlocked the front door and let herself in. The house smelled funny, empty, and she was struck by an odd feeling of bunking off school. There was a stack of post piled up in the special letter-catcher that Robert had bought from the Innovations catalogue; the industrial size metal net was stuffed with the end-of-the-month glut of subscription magazines and bills. Tanith dumped her bag in the old wicker chair in the hall since there was no one there to tell her not to and wandered into the kitchen, going through the mail.

Which Hi-Fi, Evo, Mojo, three phone bills, some circulars and four brown envelopes for Robert.

Private Eye, Company, a couple of letters, fliers, plus coffee and a muffin and no interruptions for her.

Bliss.

Tanith decanted her coffee into a large mug, took her mobile out of her back pocket and gleefully switched it off, and left Robert's stack of magazines and Jermyn Street sale reminders by his bread-maker. Then she padded through to the sitting-room and settled herself on the large sofa, at the end with the suspended bag of remotes. Also from Innovations.

Sometimes, thought Tanith, systematically destroying three applications for fabulously cheap credit cards, it would be nice to disappear off the face of the world and away from all these computers that know where you live.

She ditched a flier for a new restaurant and came to a white envelope, with her mother's efficient forwarding sticker over her home address. That was the answer, maybe; have two identities, two homes, two lives.

She slit it open with her coffee stirrer, wondering who still had her old address – a school reunion? It was a long time since she'd had anything forwarded from home.

Inside was a hand-written letter, and as soon as Tanith saw the handsome handwriting looping across the page, it was as if time stopped in the room, and the blood stopped solid in her veins like a video freeze frame.

No wonder her mother had put the sticker over the address – it was from Patrick.

The last contact Tanith had had from Patrick was a seven-page letter in which he had delineated the three different ways he intended to kill himself and dispose of the body if she didn't write back to him. That was when her father had had to step in and write him a stern note, to which he'd received a perfectly polite, if pathetically Coleridgean, response. Patrick's manners towards her father, even when threatening his daughter with eternal misery, were impeccable.

After that, all communication had gone in a folder by the door marked Potential Legal Evidence. Tanith could only suppose her sister had been doing the post redirection chores

and slipped this one through without knowing. But she took
a deep breath and opened it. Patrick wasn't the sort to do a
'Stan' now Eminem had made a popular hit record out of
suicide notes.

Dear Tanith, *he had written.* It's a very long time since
I've put those words down on paper and sent them,
although I've got as far as Dear Tanith many times in
the last few years. And of course, you've never stopped
being Dear Tanith when I think of you, because everything I do I write in a letter to you in my head.

Immediately the old familiar creeping sensation tingled
up Tanith's back; the creeping fear that she didn't really
understand the workings of this mind, and that she couldn't
even *see* the pedestal he put her on, let alone be worthy of it.
There were a couple of photographs folded into the letter,
but she made herself read on and see the worst before she
looked at them.

It's been a very long time because I've been straighten-
ing out *all sorts of demons* since we last spoke. Some of
them I've come to terms with and some I realize I *never*
will, if only because it's not in my power to go back and
change my own past. You can talk for hours about *why*
you are the *way* you are, but you can't then decide to
have a different childhood and a different set of expectations. I know now that you just have to work with the
material you have, and realize that it's in mending your
defects that you make yourself a stronger person.

Tanith wasn't sure she followed that, but assumed it was
a veiled reference to Rosetta and her dubious gene pool.

Anyway (underlined twice), I am in Ireland, as you can
see from the address, and have stopped wandering

around. I've met someone who has changed my way of
thinking –

Tanith's heart plummeted as she heard Patrick's voice say
it in her head, and she was horrified to feel a stab of jealousy.

Not another woman, I should add, but a good friend
who puts things in perspective. You know how
unhappy I was, but I hope that pain's resolved now I've
accepted my past for what it was, and my future for
what it is. For the last couple of years I've been working
on these stone sculptures (pictures enclosed). They're
good for thinking and have helped me work through a
lot of bad things in my head.

With trembling hands, Tanith looked at the photographs:
round, fairy loops of rocks, set in barren fields of stone and
rusty bracken like magical rings breaking through the earth.
It was a series of overhead shots, and she could see the stones
move slightly with the seasons and animal interference, and
begin to take on moss and shifting colour. Every one was different and yet the same. They *were* perfect meditation pieces,
more complicated than they looked, and yet beautifully
simple. They were very Patrick: fat with metaphor and inter-
pretation, but perfectly set in nature.
She turned back to the letter, feeling calmer, if somewhat
cowed by a familiar feeling of not being quite on Patrick's
artistic level. The writing changed towards the end of the
page, becoming smaller as if he wanted to fit more in before
he ran out of space.

Will you let me know how you are? It's been so long
since we've been in touch, but when I'm working I don't
lay a single stone without thinking of you and where
you've got to, what you're doing. I haven't spoken to
my family in years and *frankly* I suspect that has helped

me get back to some semblance of normality, but I think
of you so much, *I sometimes forget to miss you.* I don't
expect you to phone – in fact, the house I'm living in
doesn't have a phone – but I would love you to write to
me, if you could bear to. It would really help me to
settle down the remaining ghosts, and, you must believe
me, Tanith, although I'm nearer to the proper version of
me these days, I'm not quite as good as I was when I
was with you. But I still could be.

    With love from Patrick.

Tanith realized that she'd been holding her breath since
she opened the envelope and as she let it out it shuddered in
her throat. She closed her eyes and they filled up with unexpected, embarrassingly childish tears.

When she thought of Patrick she always saw strong
colours in her head – blues and greens and reds – and
swirling around behind her eyelids now, they felt weirdly
vivid in Robert's tastefully sparse sitting room, intruding like
a bad trip over the fixtures and fittings.

A picture of Patrick sweeping across the beach towards
her in his black coat appeared in her head, and Tanith
opened her eyes quickly to dispel it. Just reading the letter in
that familiar handwriting had sparked off a flush of cheating
guilt, and she realized her cheeks were red hot.

She didn't want to read it twice, and stuffed the letter
back in the envelope, while trying not to let her gaze fall on
anything that reinforced Robert's ownership of the house
too much. But she propped the photos against her coffee
cup and stared at them, trying to work out exactly how she
felt and what she was going to do.

She couldn't tell Robert, for a kick-off. Patrick hadn't
mentioned keeping his whereabouts secret from his family,
but then why would he dream in a million years that she'd
be shacked up with his younger brother?

And if she did tell Robert, the first thing he would do

would be to track Patrick down, shout at him for five hours without drawing breath, and then drag him back on the first Aer Lingus flight out of Knock and into this ensuing debate about Rosetta's book.

Rosetta's book.

Didn't Patrick have a right to know she was about to open a whole can of worms?

Tanith bit her lip and picked up the envelope again, turning it over in her fingers.

It was so typical of Patrick to *write,* for a start. You wouldn't think this was the twenty-first century, she thought crossly, feeling the grain of the thick paper. So typical of Patrick to be in a house with no telephone, no mobile reception and no e-mail, but with laid notepaper. So typical of Patrick to want to hole himself up somewhere so remote that the entire address was in Gaelic. Robert went hysterical with nerves if reception dropped below two bars on his phone and didn't go anywhere that didn't have at least one place to eat that featured in the AA guide.

And now, of course, if she wanted to communicate with him – which, despite the warning bellow of her better nature, of course she did – she had to do it on *his* terms, and Patrick always *was* better at the written word than he was at face-to-face talking, whereas she couldn't write an e-mail without redrafting it four times, let alone the kind of dramatic prose he used as a first language.

God, they were a family of prime manipulators.

This was almost as bad as Rosetta leaving those exorbitant receipts from that family therapist in the accounts file for Robert to find.

Tanith sank back into the sofa with her coffee and tried to pretend that she wasn't excited to hear Patrick's voice again in her head. She hugged a cushion to her chest with her free hand.

It felt like a lifetime ago since she'd seen him and if he felt he'd come a long way since they were last in touch, then she'd come much, much further, she thought, with a faint touch of unconscious pride. There was something about working with actors that made you far more cynical about what people were really like under the surface; suspicious of the too-nice people and suspicious of the ones who claimed not to care.

And living with Robert had indirectly shown her a whole other side of Patrick; Robert had reacted very differently to a childhood of being dragged around, photographed, dumped on other people and generally treated like a teenager from the age of two. Ever since that, Robert wanted to organize the rest of the world his way, and Patrick just wanted to . . .

Run away from it.

Still, thought Tanith, I can cope with that now. I'm settled and mature and able to deal with life. Come on, I'm even thinking of running my own casting agency! I can deal with Patrick. I don't even have to bring Robert into it; Patrick doesn't know where I am, or what I'm up to – maybe it would just be easier not to mention all that until we've established some kind of communication.

And I don't want to set him back by complicating things, she thought. Not if he feels he's made some progress with all those family issues.

You don't want to tell him about Robert.

It was unusual to have someone from your past be so oblivious to your present, she thought, ducking away from her conscience. A bit like being able to be two people at once, but with all the benefits of experience. And it would be a real shame to waste this chance to resettle that part of her past and put it back in order, especially if she could help Patrick by doing it.

You don't want to tell him about Robert.

Tanith gripped her coffee cup and gripped her conscience at the same time. Now, *why* don't I want to tell him about Robert? she demanded of herself.

She squirmed internally.

'Come on,' she said out loud. Tanith sometimes had out-loud dialogues when she needed to force herself into a reaction one way or another. It was impossible to sit in sulky silence with yourself. She used the same tone she used with Robert when he got moody. The jolly, 'It'll all be fine as long as you don't start annoying me', tone that usually jerked an argument out of him at the very least. 'It's only a letter, isn't it?' she said reasonably. 'And you only have to tell him what you want to.'

She bit her lip. What exactly *was* she going to tell him? That her life was all sewn up here, thanks, that she had a good job with interesting prospects, Robert on the verge of proposing, and the potential mother-in-law from hell about to leave the country?

Heading his way, in fact.

Tanith was gripped with an intense desire to rush off to Ireland and stand with her arms blocking the entrance to Patrick's vowel-free Gaeltacht cottage.

Tanith remembered the dark looks that used to creep into Patrick's eyes on the rare occasions that he mentioned his mother. A mixture of total adoration and complete fear. Patrick might think he had the initial bit of his life under control, but it was going to take more than a heap of stones to get past this, and Rosetta wasn't even going to involve him in the process.

She sighed heavily, thinking of his lovely, brooding face. No, it would be easier to deal with this on her own first. Then see if he needed protecting from the rest of the Mulligans, and if so, what she could usefully do.

And a small voice in the back of her head pointed out that this way, she would have him to herself for a little bit longer.

Chapter Twenty-four

Dallas, 1979

'No, no, no. Stop a minute there,' said Rosetta. 'Don't put, "We'll go walking in the park every day." I can't let you.'

John put his plectrum down and looked at her. 'Why not?' he said with some difficulty. He had a pencil clamped between his teeth and his lyrics book open on the bunk in front of him. They were in the small sitting area at the back of the enormous tour-bus, which was, for once, deserted. There was an hour before the gig, and nineteen days before John had to give the rough demos of the new album to the record company.

'Because ... because it doesn't mean anything, does it? When was the last time we went walking in a park?'

He looked doubtful. 'Doesn't it? I thought it was one of those old blues things. I thought it meant ... something else. Like, *park* was one of your euphemisms for, I don't know ... *muff* or something. You know, like jelly roll. We'll go ... strolling through your muff every day.'

'I think most blues singers would just sing muff,' said Rosetta and tactfully went back to the chart she was putting together for one of the photojournalists covering the tour; a chart that would predict an impending romantic liaison with a tall, very rhythmic dark-haired man. Candice was giving her a couple of dollars for it, but Red was promising three nights of baby-sitting and the speedboat called *Zildjian* that he'd won in a bet. It was worth it, he claimed, since Candice wasn't the sort to be overly impressed with his usual chatting-up techniques.

'Oh God,' moaned John. He slapped his hand down on the open strings of his guitar, making it jangle discordantly. He'd been playing the same three chords over and over again continuously for the past hour, and only had half a melody and one line of lyrics that had met with Rosetta's approval. 'Why can't I have "We'll go walking in the park"? Half of Led Zeppelin's songs have it. That or *rambling*. Which is hardly rock 'n' roll.'

'Yeah, well, the way Robert Plant wrote songs you wouldn't think there was a single cinema in Wolverhampton. Come on, John. Don't write shite just because it's Glynn singing it.'

John laughed mirthlessly and grabbed the half-empty bottle of bourbon balanced within easy reach on top of a tape recorder. Rosetta noted uneasily that he looked completely exhausted. His pale Irish skin had gone from a healthy creamy white to a disturbing blueish cast towards the end of this tour and he was drinking far too much. More than once she'd found him dead to the world an hour before the gig – and she wasn't sure how much was sheer weariness and how much was . . . well, something else. None of them had been home all year for tax reasons and it was hard to remember what was a normal time to get up in the morning.

John poured himself a large glassful and offered the bottle to her.

Rosetta shook her head. 'No, I won't. I've got to sort out the kids when Brian gets back from that meeting,' she added, in case it sounded like a reprimand.

She watched with concern as he drained his glass too fast and shut his eyes while the alcohol burned into his system. When you hurt yourself you hurt me, she wanted to say, but couldn't.

'So what am I meant to write about?' he demanded, gesturing around the squalid tour-bus. 'What inspiration, no, what *life* do I have to write about? Maybe I *want* Glynn to sing shite,' John went on said recklessly. 'Maybe then he'll stop talking about breaking the band up to go solo and actually get on and do it. Claims he was going to announce it last night, after the gig – only Brian rushed us all out.'

Even though her heart bumped against her chest, Rosetta forced herself to stay outwardly calm, like she did when Robert threw hissy fits. This wasn't the first time Glynn's 'plans' had been aired. He'd started talking about his solo career roughly five years ago. Of late, though, he'd started talking about them to the press, and that made a big difference. Particularly to Red, who threatened to deck him most nights now, and frequently drummed right through Glynn's sensitive a capella blues moments. Even Simon was muttering darkly about Glynn now.

'Oh, darling,' she smiled, forcing amusement into her face, 'Glynn's an *arse*. I mean, isn't that what he's based his whole career on – his arse? He doesn't do much else, let's face it.' She pulled a face. 'He's only talking about going solo because you're coming up with all the new material and he knows all he does is stand up at the front in a pair of tight pants singing it.'

There was no response from John. His expression was bleak. 'Come on,' Rosetta persisted. 'He's just pissed that he's not getting any publishing and thinks that if he goes solo he'll get more money.'

'Ah, fuck the money,' said John, swiping at his eyes. There were tears in his voice. 'Who gives a flying fuck about the *money* now? It never used to be about that. I didn't join up for some kind of *accountancy* programme.'

Rosetta put down her notepad, took the guitar off him, and held his hands in hers. John's fingers felt dry and fragile and she remembered with a stab of shock how strong he'd been beneath the leanness the first time she saw him on stage. Tonight he looked like a husk.

Why haven't you noticed this before, wailed the voice in

her head, the stern, good girl voice that hung around despite everything. *Where've you been?*

'What is it?' she soothed, rubbing his hands between her own. 'Is it Sue? Is she giving you a hard time?'

Despite Brian's punishing touring schedule keeping him on the road most of the year, John wasn't away from Sue enough to pretend that the marriage was working out, even if she did diligently set up enough stories and diary pieces to make it look as if they were the happiest couple in the world – a media couple who thrived on their constant separation. But Rosetta knew that wasn't what Sue had hung around for years and compromised herself for. She also knew that while Sue was bull-headed enough to imagine she could *make* John love her by sheer persistence, just as she'd clawed her way up the career ladder by simply being around, there would come a point when Sue would put her foot down. The mutters about starting a family had risen to shrieking pitch in the last year.

So now, in a last-ditch attempt to save a marriage that had never even really existed, Sue had come on the road with them.

Finally, nothing, in Rosetta's opinion, could make this tour any more hellish.

What if she does get pregnant? the little voice whispered. *How would you deal with that?*

'Is it that fertility treatment Sue's having?' Rosetta asked nervously. 'Are they making you have tests too?'

'Sue?' said John, blinking as if it hadn't occurred to him. 'Oh, she's . . . fine. No worse than usual. You know.'

'Are you not getting enough sleep?' she suggested quickly, wanting to give him more reasons. 'Do you want me to get Brian to postpone some dates? He can do, you know, if you don't feel up to it.' And piss off the security, promoters, fans, police, road crew, accountants, support act, groupies . . .

Just tell me it's not me! she wanted to yell.

'It's not me, is it?' she heard a small voice say, and realized it was her own.

That in itself shocked her into silence.

'Jesus Christ, of *course* it's not . . .' John sighed, lifted his hands up and dropped them in despair. 'It's the whole fucking *thing*, Rosie. The whole fucking *thing*. It's Glynn pissing me off, it's Red drinking too much, it's Brian nagging me about the album deadline, that stupid little press girl in LA phoning me about photo-fucking-shoots, that eejit Nev not bringing the right guitars to the gig because he's strung out on something . . .' John buried his fingers in his thick brown hair, which was straggling over his ears. He'd refused to have a haircut in six months. 'Then when I'm *not* here, it's my accountant bugging me about tax years and . . . Oh *God*.' He groaned. 'And now Sue's on about having fertility treatment, because she wants a baby. A *baby*, Rosetta. Christ knows our marriage is wrong enough as it is! But bringing a little baby into it . . .'

Rosetta felt sick. He hadn't even noticed her mentioning it seconds ago. No wonder he couldn't write lyrics.

John noticed her head droop and put a hand out to her chin. 'Sorry. I didn't mean to go on.'

'No, no,' she said pulling herself together. 'If you can't talk to me . . .'

He smiled sadly and looked as though he wanted to say more than he could.

'But there're only a few more dates to go now,' she said consolingly, 'then you've got a month off.'

He shook his head at her and let out a tired breath through his nose. 'Oh yeah, great. Then I can't see you for a month because you'll be doing all your little At Homes with Brian and Rosetta and taking the kids to the park, won't you? And I'll be at home with Sue. Christ! On the road, I'm going insane but at least I have you. At home . . . it's like I cease to exist! Rosie, it's *not* an answer. You can switch on and off, I can't. And to be perfectly honest with you, much as she drives me mad, I feel a complete *shit*, treating Sue like this. It's not right. She wants kids, and she's running out of time.'

He sank back into the stacked pillows while Rosetta stared at him and twisted her rings in shock. Her heart was arrhythmic with lack of sleep and passively absorbed twenty-four-hour tension, and she was horrified to realize that things had got much much worse than she could have imagined and she had *no idea* when or how.

'But *John* . . .' she began. 'I . . . We . . .'

He looked at her with weary, dark-rimmed eyes and she couldn't go on. He didn't even look like someone she knew when he was like this.

'Rosie, when you're with me, on our own, with no one else around, you are still the sweetest, funniest, sexiest woman I know,' he said. 'I've gone through it a million times in my head, wanting to see a way out, but I *cannot* be with any other woman in the world. I mean, Jesus Christ Almighty, it's ridiculous when you think about it! Why else would I be messing around like this for all this time, just to be near you? It's crazy! It's like a *very bad* song!'

He tried to smile, but it twisted into a grimace. Rosetta pushed his tangled hair back out of his face, curling it round one ear. It was lank in her fingers.

John caught her hand and held it to his lips. 'It used to be all right. There used to be . . . more in my life! But now I only get you for an hour at a time before you have to put on your Social Barbie face and go off to some yoke of a party and I have to go on stage and go through all the motions and it's just . . . not enough any more.'

'John, you *know* I have to do all this for the band,' she pleaded. 'Don't you think I wouldn't rather just stay here with you and . . .'

'Sweetheart,' he interrupted her wearily, 'I played the demos of my new songs to Brian when we stopped in Denver, and do you know what he said?'

Rosetta shook her head bitterly. The bottle of bourbon was starting to look more attractive.

'He said,' and John adopted Brian's faux-public-school

snipped vowels, '"It's all fantastic, John, but does every song have to be about broken hearts? The record company are freaking out that there's no single on the album."'

'Oh *man*!' said Rosetta. It wasn't surprising that she was able to get away with living separate lives in her head. Brian never said a word, even when she came out of John's trailer at three in the morning. He only ever gave John an occasional baleful, reproachful stare like a kicked puppy. She had no idea why he didn't say something, especially when he was so full-on angry with everything else that was going wrong on the tour. 'Why doesn't he ever—'

'And you know what *Glynn* said?' John went on. 'He said, "I'm going to have to rewrite half of these lyrics, *mate*, because my audience don't mind me having a broken heart, but who would believe I'd be cheated on?"'

'That man is a cretin,' said Rosetta hotly. 'He ought to—'

'Rosetta!' shouted John. 'I'm telling you. I just can't *do* this any more.' He paused, and stared at the guitar propped up against his bunk. It was brand new, one that his contact at Gibson had sent him the previous week. 'When I look back at the last couple of years, honest to God, I don't even know how I've managed to do it for so long already. You might be able to let all these people take little pieces of you, but I can't.' There was total silence, apart from their breathing and the distant crashing of the road crew unloading equipment.

'I just can't play those songs any more,' he said at last. 'I don't *want* to do it any more. I've got everything in the world I ever wanted, and I'm just *miserable*.'

They lay together on the bunk, curled round each other like tree roots, and didn't speak for a while.

Rosetta tried to clear her mind of negative thoughts, but they wouldn't go. The more she thought about it, the more it was all her fault. She seemed to be holding the band together – keeping Brian happy and organized, and keeping John sane and clean – but it was completely wrong. How much longer could she keep *herself* together? And now it felt like the end of everything – end of the decade, end of the tour, end of the band, end of her strength – and she didn't think she had the energy to start all over again.

'How come I can be strong with everyone but you?' said Rosetta, not expecting a reply. It made the weight on her mind feel fractionally lighter just to hear herself say it.

'I don't know,' said John behind her. 'Maybe because you're not pretending to be anyone else when you're with me. You don't confuse yourself.'

She laughed under her breath but said nothing.

John put an arm under her shoulder and pulled her round so she was facing him.

'Rosetta,' he said. 'Who are you going to be when all this falls apart? Hmm?'

Rosetta blinked as she always did when confronted with John's eyes up close. Something about the precise dimensions, the exact measurement of beauty, made her heart quicken and melt. They were so deep and brown and perfect. But now they were very tired and sad, with tiny broken red veins around the dark, chocolate-brown iris. His pupils were huge.

'I'm ... I'll ...' she stuttered. That wasn't exactly how she'd have put it – falling apart.

'I love you,' he said. 'Please don't forget that.'

Rosetta blinked again. 'How can I forget it? I hear it on the radio three times a day.'

'After all this time,' John went on as if he hadn't heard her, 'all these tours and all these songs and hard slog and everything, I've got practically *nothing* to show for any of it.'

Rosetta knew what he meant, and he wasn't talking about the houses or cars or the gold discs that filtered back from the record company almost casually these days.

No, but you have! She wanted to shout. *You have! You've got Patrick!*

But the words were so heavy and final that they stuck in her throat and wouldn't come out.

It's too big, warned the good girl Richmond voice. *Once*

you've said something like that you can't take it back. You've
got to think hard, got to decide how to play it. It's your
biggest risk, Rosetta, don't throw it away.

I'll tell him after the show, she thought. The time's come
and he's got to know. But there's no point in making him distracted now, he's enough to deal with.

The weight on her shoulders shifted again just thinking
about it, and thinking about how happy she could make
him too.

There's no point holding it back any more, she thought,
kissing the pointed end of his nose, with complete tenderness. This could be the final piece of ballast that we can
chuck overboard and set us floating free. Sod the tour –
Glynn was on the verge of sabotaging it anyway. And with a
few whispers in the right ears, it could even look as if he
drove John to it . . .

Yes, thought Rosetta, wriggling further into John's arms,
it's time for *us* now. We've propped up this organization for
long enough. Let Glynn go his own way, let Sue sort herself
out, let Brian . . .

She stopped, her lips still on John's nose.

Brian.

No, she steeled herself, the time had come. Brian had had
the best years of her organizing and her caring and her company. He didn't pretend that his was a grand passion, he
never had done. It had been fun to start with and was now
more or less a business partnership, and he could survive
without her.

John couldn't.

She tipped his chin towards her and kissed his mouth,
tasting the bourbon on his warm lips. John kissed her back,
running his hands down her back and pressing his long body
urgently against her as if they could merge into one.

Then the alarm clock shrilled in the bunk above, the one
Rosetta had set earlier, to remind John to stop playing and
start getting ready for the gig.

They separated reluctantly, peeling their bodies away from one another, lips last. It was hard to leave the dark shelter of the bus.

'I need a couple of minutes to myself,' said John, without breaking their gaze.

'OK,' said Rosetta, Already – *already!* – she could feel her mind start to run back on its to-do list: speak to the promoter about the after-show, get the kids out of the makeshift groupie crèche, check Brian had done all the interviews he said he was doing this afternoon.

Rosetta got up and stretched, making all the vertebrae in her back crack. She hadn't been feeling too good recently either; all sickly and weak. But then mothers of three weren't generally meant to go on ninety-date tours.

'Have a shower,' she said, leaning in to kiss him goodbye. 'And don't have any more to drink, you hear me?'

John smiled his enigmatic Irish smile and his eyes twinkled manically in the half-darkness. 'You're far too sexy to be such a full-time mum. I don't envy your sons, having to find girls to match up to you.'

Rosetta had to press her lips together not to tell him everything, but her sense of timing stopped her. Instead, bubbling with the knowledge of how happy he would be when she did tell him later, she adjusted her hair in the mirror by the bunks and picked up the chart she'd been doing, to give to Red to give to Candice.

'I'll see you backstage,' she said. 'I'll be watching you in the usual place.'

John blew her a slow kiss goodbye, and she let herself out.

There were the usual dribs and drabs of lowlife hanging around the loading bay where all the transporters were parked – dealers, local paper reporters without press passes, ticket touts, the less well-informed groupies. A couple of them watched as she came out of the bus, and she made a note to have security check they didn't try to get in. Rosetta recognized a couple of scary obsessive fans who liked to send Glynn spirit drawings of them all together in the next life. Brian tried to them keep well away from the band.

It's all getting too *big*, thought Rosetta with a twitch of foreboding, as she passed a couple of drug-skinny girls eagerly handing over wads of dollars to a sleazy Hispanic guy. How did they go from Nev slinging three amps in the back of Simon's van to this? It was like having a little puppy that seemed really cute when you got it, then you turn round one morning, it's a Great Dane and your house is covered in mountainous dog shit.

She nodded as she passed the security men and went up to the dressing-rooms, trying to remember how much clean underwear she had left for the boys and whether there was time to get some laundry sent out. At least she didn't have to think about clothes for herself: Glynn had employed a new American stylist to source clothes for him now, and she had taken it upon herself to leave things for Rosetta as well. Rosetta surprised herself by not minding – putting on someone else's clothes was just like putting on a suit of armour: it was all just dressing up. She hadn't had time to see Anita in ages, especially now she was covertly designing for M & S in return for a huge fee and doing two detoxes a year.

If tonight's clothes weren't that great she would wear that old green dress of Anita's, she decided. It had sort of come back into fashion, if it was worn with the right stuff. There wasn't an official aftershow party but there were a couple of journalists hanging around, covering the tour for one of the English music weeklies, and she'd suggested that she and Brian take them out for dinner, on the usual charm offensive. Rosetta had a cynical feeling that it was a 'Last of the Rock Dinosaurs' piece, but she was doing all she could to be interesting for them.

In the lobby another security officer was bawling out some little cleaning guy about letting kids in to the back of the hall, punctuating each curse with a sharp jab to the shoulder, making the cleaner stumble backwards. The language made her flinch.

'Hey, you!' she yelled. 'Enough!'

They both turned and stared at her, giving her the 'And you are?' look down their noses.

Rosetta made another mental note to tell Brian and marched on.

I'm not bringing the boys on any more tours after this, she promised herself. They're getting old enough to know what's going on and they see too much already.

Robert, Patrick and Greg were in a dressing-room, plaiting leather strips with the small band of regular groupies who still turned up to run errands for the band, bring Red his stash and sometimes, if they were really favoured, do Glynn's hair. As well as the usual crowd of adolescent thrill-seekers, The End attracted a charmingly old-fashioned hardcore of followers, and despite the tantrums they pulled with her, the boys could be remarkably easy for other people. There were usherettes all over the Mid-West prepared to swear that Robert Mulligan should be used on the fresh milk ads. And in an odd reciprocal arrangement, these girls could be models of decorum and respectability with the children before leaving to offer blow-jobs and foursomes with dogs to the band, as soon as the gig finished.

Life on the road never failed to disturb Rosetta.

'Are you all OK in here?' she asked. It looked like a Women's Institute knitting circle. In a way, it was touching that there were still some groupies prepared to embroider guitar-straps instead of sending their thongs in with the roadies like calling cards. Greg was even laboriously eating an orange with his pudgy fingers, something he would never do for her.

Robert didn't bother to take his eyes off the plait. 'We're fine. Can you bring us some more KFC?'

'OK,' said Rosetta. 'Patrick? Do you want anything?'

Patrick had a heap of beads in his lap, but he was staring off into space, miles away inside his head.

'Don't mind Patrick, he's just tripping,' said Robert, tying off a plait. 'Misty gave him some pills.'

Rosetta clutched at the door for support as the room went supernaturally bright in front of her sleep-deprived eyes. This was the worst nightmare she barely dared contemplate. 'She did what? Oh Christ! Christ! Patrick!' She lunged across the room and grabbed for him, shaking him awake. 'Patrick! Are you OK?'

Patrick shuddered back into the real world as he flailed in Rosetta's grip. 'Fuck off!' he said very clearly, his brow creasing in outrage at the manhandling.

Rosetta dropped him as if he were on fire.

'God, Rosetta, only joking,' said Robert. 'He's just tired. He's been meditating with Sweet Charity.'

'Don't you *ever* joke about things like that!' screeched Rosetta, with what she hoped was a hell-fire stare. 'Ever!' She stopped running her hands madly through her hair and put her hands on her hips, wishing she could scare Robert, just once, or at least show him how scared she was. 'That is the one thing we never, *ever* joke about!'

She glared round the room at the groupies, wondering which one to vent her spleen on. But they all looked tranquil and mildly reproachful.

'It's nothing to do with *us*,' piped up one girl who had been following the band with cookies and hash cakes for so long she was virtually the catering manager. 'He doesn't get it from—'

Someone nudged her and she fell silent.

She reminded Rosetta of Sue when they were at school, unable to resist sneaking, just for the thrill of being in the right, until a swift kick to the shins from her or Anita shut her up.

'Don't tell me any more. I don't have time for this,' she snapped and spun on her heel.

'More's the pity,' floated back from one corner of the room, but Rosetta didn't have the energy to go back and knock it on the head. She wasn't even confident that she could speak without crying and that was her one rule on the road: never let anyone see you cry, particularly the groupies.

Even John didn't see the nights she sobbed angrily into her pillow, crushed by the restrictions and frustrations she'd set up for herself. And yet it seemed on the road anyone could get away with anything; the real restrictions, *still*, were in her head.

I'm right, she repeated over and over like a mantra as she walked back through the echoing corridors to the band's dressing-room. *I will tell him tonight. We can't go on like this for ever.*

The doormen had let the audience in and Rosetta could hear them running and yelling through the auditorium. She was surprised not to feel the usual chill of excitement that always tingled through her half an hour before the gig, and the numbness that filled her chest instead shocked her so much that she stopped walking and put a hand on the bare skin exposed by the deep V of her T-shirt.

She felt bony.

'Y'all reet there, lass?' A large hand clapped her between the shoulder-blades and she staggered slightly in her spindly boots. Red. She could smell him before she needed to turn round. And the longer they spent on the road, the more Geordie his accent got in compensation. He made all the roadies play football, just so he could be captain of Newcastle United.

'Shouldn't you be getting ready?'

He gave her an affectionate hug from behind. Rosetta felt engulfed in familiarity and for a brief moment, wanted to shut her eyes and fall asleep in Red's beery, sweaty shirt.

'Red?' she muttered into his chest. 'Let me pass on a little nugget of information that a very well-known drummer once gave me. "Just because you're a rock-star doesn't mean you don't have to wash."'

'Them punk lads don't.'

He wasn't dead drunk – Red was never *drunk* – but it was pretty clear from the brandy fumes coming off him in a mist of geniality that the gig wasn't the main focus of his evening.

'Just get in your dressing-room and have a shower, will you?'

'Can't. Sue's in there with Brian. They're having *words*.'

Oh Holy Mother of God.

'And,' he went on before she could give that a decent reaction, '*dinnut* tell me to go in the other one 'cos Glynn and Slimon are plottin' something in there with three or four black chicks, Slimon's dealer and a crate of champagne.'

Rosetta turned and buried herself in Red's chest and felt his beefy arms enfold her effortlessly. For a moment she wondered what life would have been like if that was what she'd settled for: a big bricklayer to look after her and make her feel safe as houses.

You couldn't swop.

It was nice and dark buried in Red's chest.

God, I'm tired, she thought.

No wonder you're hearing voices.

Red bent down so he could whisper confidentially in her ear. 'Promise me you'll get Sue sent home, will ya, Rosetta? I *cannut* stand lasses on tour, it's not reet. She's making us all eat baked potatoes.'

With a supreme force of will she pulled away and said heavily, 'Tell me what Brian and Sue are arguing about?'

'Fuck knows. John, probably.' Red's normally open face was perturbed and unhappy at the mention of John's name.

'John?' said Rosetta carefully. 'Why?'

'Ah, y' kna.' Red shrugged. 'He's been . . . knackered recently, behavin' odd, like.' He stopped abruptly, then said, 'Sue's on his case the whole time to do all them celebrity rackets, the ones you do, like, and . . . Well, y' kna.'

He gave her a searching look.

Red knew. He might look stupid, but he'd known her since she was fourteen, thought Rosetta. They all knew something was going on, that was the trouble. They *all knew* about the incestuous, destructive little knot of relationships, and in eight years not one person had stood up and told them to grow up.

But it was rock 'n' roll, wasn't it? It was Fleetwood Mac and Abba and the Bowies and all those other wife-swapping cool scenes. It made the band look decadent and modern when the critics said they were lame. Fuck what it did to her and Brian and John and Sue.

And the boys.

'Go and have a shower,' Rosetta repeated, her eyes glazing with weariness. 'I'll go and see if I can sort it out.'

Sue was very bad news at the moment, thought Rosetta, as she picked her way through the gaffer tape and boxes. A combination of dieting, tour sleeplessness, excessive jealousy and perpetual stomach acid were making her even more spiky than normal, even by her own exacting standards. Deciding to come on tour with John 'to save the marriage' showed a whole new level of kamikaze behaviour, eclipsed only by her determination to *stay* on the tour in the face of extreme discomfort and hostility from the entire road crew.

The previous Christmas Sue had decided that she wanted to move into television and had gone, very publicly, on the F-Plan diet, then charted her every fart and irregular bowel movement in her Sunday paper column. She had lost a fair amount of weight and got a spot on breakfast TV, but still smelt as though a couple of small animals had died in her trousers. Worse than that, Sue had taken to wearing leather trousers, which meant that Rosetta had had to ditch hers.

However, shrinking her ample arse hadn't made John fall madly in love with her, but the new Sue wasn't inclined to wait for things to fall into her lap any more.

It wouldn't have been much consolation, Rosetta realized, but she and John barely had time to be together, grabbing rare moments when he wasn't dozing off with exhaustion and she wasn't wired to screaming pitch with some new tour crisis to smooth over. She knew she should spend some serious time sorting him out, but there was Robert to worry about now, and Greg, and moody Patrick. It felt more like mutual consolation than ever, just holding each other up until the tour was over and they could have some time to work out where to go. And that very nearly was enough for John's conscience these days. In fact, all things considered, John's conscience seemed to be on its last legs, and although Rosetta never thought she'd live to think it, that in itself worried her.

She could hear the sound of raised voices in the dressing-room from twelve feet down the corridor, but didn't wait to find out what they were rowing about. Always better just to dive in while you were still brave. Rosetta knocked twice, then pushed the door open.

Brian and Sue spun round. They were both bright red in the face, and Sue, as usual, had smudged her lipstick yelling.

Brian took out a blue spotted handkerchief from his pocket and mopped his brow.

'It's showtime!' said Rosetta brightly, just to see what they'd say.

Automatically, Brian looked at his watch, although he didn't really need to – by now he had a precise instinct for where the band were in his schedule. It looked to Rosetta more as if he were looking to see how much time he'd wasted arguing with Sue.

'Rosetta,' snarled Sue, in a tone that suggested it was merely the opening salvo in a much longer stream of fire.

'I think Red needs this dressing-room to get changed in,' said Rosetta before Sue could launch into whatever she was about to say. 'So do you think you two could have your chat somewhere else?'

'Where's John?' demanded Sue.

Rosetta looked surprised. 'He's on the bus, working on a song.'

'I see,' said Sue.

'Well, that's great, so I can tell Red to come in and have a shower then?' she said briskly. There was a distinct aroma of baked potato in the room, although that might just have been one of Sue's residual smells. Rosetta felt nauseous.

'I might just go over there myself and tell John to get a wiggle on,' said Brian, casually, making a move to the door.

'I'll tell him!' said Sue immediately.

Rosetta barred the door to them both, amused. 'No, no,' she said, 'no need to interrupt your discussion. *I'll* go and tell him. I have to get some stuff out of the bus for the boys anyway.'

She stepped backwards slowly and saw both Sue and Brian take a subconscious step nearer to her and the door.

What was going on?

I really am losing my touch, thought Rosetta, as she skipped backwards and shut the door behind her. The argument started up again immediately.

She bumped into Red, who was listening a discreet distance away.

'Here,' she said, digging in her bag. 'That chart you wanted me to do for Candice. It's all there – the strong attraction to men with a Taurus moon, the need to find compatibility with your matching Venus signs . . .' She offered him the chart and he took it doubtfully.

Like all the charts Rosetta drew up, it was beautifully coloured and neatly written out. Half the trick was in the presentation, as she told Brian when he laughed at her pagan mind. Show someone something nice and of course they'll make it happen.

'This all true, like?' asked Red.

'Are you doubting my ability to see into the future?' she teased him.

For once, Red didn't smile.

*

With only twenty minutes until the band were due to go on (give or take quarter of an hour to whip the crowd into a frenzy), Rosetta came across Glynn taking delivery of three crates of champagne into his dressing-room. This was on top of the unbelievably lavish rider, which could have safely floored the entire New York division of Alcoholics Anonymous, and Glynn was giving out to the delivery boy that none of it was sufficiently cold.

The look he gave Rosetta as she walked past, however, could have chilled them all in a minute.

'Where is he?' said Glynn nastily. His eyes had a cocaine glitter.

'Where's who?'

'Where's John? Still in the bus writing turgid love songs? While the rest of us carry this band?'

If that was the line Glynn was going to take, Rosetta didn't mind encouraging him in it, not if it meant putting a quicker end to all this. There had always been a self-destructive tension in the band – it was what made them so watchable, albeit in a car-crash way. Now, though . . .

Simon hovered at the door behind Glynn. He was wearing his own tour T-shirt, which emphasized the splendid concavity of his chest, and kept shooting furtive glances backwards in case the giggling girls in the dressing-room escaped through a window while his back was turned.

Really, thought Rosetta, he gives bass players a bad name.

'No,' she said. 'He's in the bus doing an interview with *Rolling Stone*.' That always wound Glynn up, John being interviewed instead of him. 'But I know what time it is. I'll go and get him.' She turned to go, then added, 'He's such a fascinating interviewee, I'm not surprised it's running late. And get those tarts out of there before those people from *Melody Maker* arrive, will you? I'm trying to persuade them that you're not a complete cliché.'

Glynn just laughed as she strode off.

*

The door of the tour-bus was shut, which wasn't unusual, but when Rosetta tried to open it, she found it was locked as well.

That was really weird. She went round to one of the windows and peered in. Maybe John had left and gone for a walk round the building to get his head together before he faced Glynn?

But John wouldn't have the key to lock the bus and there were no roadies around.

'John?' She rapped on the glass. 'John!' Rosetta banged with the flat of her hands on the door, and noticed that one of the upper windows was open, the catch still swinging from her banging.

She watched the catch swing back and forth in slow motion, then sudden panic gripped her insides and she frantically looked round the loading bay for something to climb up on.

With a strength she didn't know she had, she dragged a packing case over to the tour-bus and crawled in through the window, not feeling the frame digging into her stomach or the skin scouring off her shoulders on the sharp metal. The window was above one of the deep window seats stacked with cushions and she fell awkwardly on to it, half-slipping on to the floor, half-crawling towards the back of the bus.

The air smelled stale, of sweaty bodies and smoke and empty beer bottles.

'John!' she yelled, trying hard to visualize his startled face when she found him listening to Fairport Convention on his headphones, unable to hear her banging.

But she couldn't make the picture stick, and all she could see in front of her eyes were her tarot cards – all the wrong ones that she showed the bad roadies, flipping over, one after the other.

John was lying along his bunk, very much, Rosetta thought distractedly, like *The Death of Chatterton*. One thin arm dangled down, the veins visible through the transparent skin like little rivers running up it. His eyes were softly shut, as if he were asleep, and his lips were a surreally beautiful pale blue.

Rosetta wanted to be sick. She fell to her knees and started to rub his hand, then dropped it, and frantically tried to find a pulse.

What did they tell you to do in case of overdose? What are you meant to do?

Her mind spun hysterically, like an engine roaring out of gear, and she couldn't focus on a single thought.

'John!' She slapped his face, but there wasn't a flicker of response. His eyelids were smooth and unfluttering – he looked as if he were having the most amazing dream.

'John!' she yelled. 'John! Can you hear me! John!'

No response. The pit of Rosetta's stomach burned white hot.

She grabbed him by the shoulders. Come on, come on, she panicked. What were you meant to do in case of overdose? Everything she'd ever read in preparation for Red doing this, or Nev, or one of the little girl-groupies, hid in some dark, unreachable corner of her head and she stared at John powerlessly, lying limp in her arms and wished that she was dead too, so she wouldn't have to be responsible. That she wouldn't have to wake up without him.

A black wave of misery swept over her, breaking down the last fragile fences of resilience and she dropped her head on his chest and sobbed with defeat.

There was a banging at the door.

'John!' yelled Brian's voice. 'That's it! I've had enough, open this door! I need to talk to you!'

Rosetta scrambled to her feet, still gasping with tears, stumbled to the door and fumbled with the lock. Her fingers slipped and slid but somehow she threw it open.

Brian took a step back in surprise at the sight of Rosetta with her hair dishevelled and her jumper ripped where she'd caught it on the window climbing in.

'What's going on?' he said. His face was dark with anger.

Next to Brian, Glynn stood with his arms crossed, now dressed for the gig in his cropped T-shirt and spray-on jeans, his hair a lion's mane mass of teased blonde curls.

'It's *John*,' panted Rosetta.

'We know that, darling,' said Glynn nastily.

Rosetta shot him a dirty look, struggling for breath. 'You little shit. Get an ambulance. He's had an overdose.' And she burst into fresh wracking tears.

'He's what?' Brian and Glynn were shoved aside by Sue, who'd appeared from nowhere like a steamroller. 'Let me in.'

Rosetta blocked the door. 'No, don't crowd him, just get a doctor, please.' Tears streamed down her face, smearing her mascara.

'You *will* let me in. I'm his wife,' Sue hissed.

Rosetta had never seen her like this and was so stunned that she let Sue shoulder her way past her before she could think of something sufficiently cutting to say. Nothing was registering through the white noise of panic filling up her nose and mouth and ears.

As she stood wavering on the threshold of the bus, Brian swiftly dispatched Glynn to find a doctor ('a proper doctor, Glynn, not that hippie space-shifter who's been dishing homeopathic trips to the roadies') and to tell Nev to delay the gig.

Brian didn't speak to Rosetta, but gave her a look that cut right through to her heart, making her feel fifteen again. Then he marched through the tour-bus, and gently moved Sue aside from the bunk where John was lying.

Sue was clutching a Pucci print headscarf tightly in her fist. When Rosetta appeared behind Brian she waved it at her accusingly.

'This is yours, isn't it?' she spat.

Rosetta nodded dumbly.

'It was round his arm! He was using it as a tourniquet!'

Oh God, thought Rosetta, stuffing her hand into her

mouth to stop the wail coming out, not heroin, please not heroin. She'd assumed it was sleeping tablets or Quaaludes or something. Somehow pills didn't seem that bad – there were always shedloads of them floating around.

It was shameful how quickly horror wore off with familiarity.

But smack was something else. Smack was big-league. Smack wasn't recreational – it was a statement about where your mind was.

It was, Rosetta realized with a stab of guilt, the classic, textbook cry for help cliché.

'When did you leave him?' asked Brian. He was trying to be efficient but something else was breaking through – a bitterness that Rosetta found chillingly unfamiliar. 'I assume you were the last person with him?'

'I . . .'

'Of course you were, weren't you?' Sue seethed. 'Very cosy, was it? And did you shoot him up? Did that keep him nice and placid for you? Hmm? How long have you been doing this then? All those hours when we thought you were just helping him write songs, you were –'

'Shut *up*, Sue,' said Brian. 'This isn't the time. Get me some water and see where Glynn's got to with the doctor. And make sure there are no press anywhere near the backstage.'

He began to rub John's arms and legs, trying to get some warmth into the cold limbs.

'Just go!' he yelled.

'No wonder we couldn't have a baby!' yelled Sue. The words tumbled from her mouth as if she couldn't spit them out far enough. 'You were ruining his sperm count with that . . . that shit!'

'Sue! Go!' bellowed Brian.

Sue gave Rosetta one last harsh glare and stomped out of the bus, making the floor shake under her feet.

'Brian, help me,' pleaded Rosetta. 'When I left he was fine, he was talking about –'

'Right now, I don't give a toss what he was like *when you were with him*,' hissed Brian. 'I don't even want to think about that yet. I just want to keep him alive.'

Rosetta crouched down beside him and saw that Brian's eyes were also full of tears as he rubbed John's hands between his own.

'Come on, John,' he murmured, as though Rosetta wasn't there. He sounded unbearably gentle, like he did when the boys were sick, a million miles away from his normal crispness. 'Come on, now, don't give up. Come on, you've got to stay with us, come on, John, can you hear me?'

Rosetta couldn't tell if there was a response. Brian felt around for a pulse in his neck.

'There's a pulse, but it's really faint,' he said, and the relief was obvious in his voice.

'Thank God!' Rosetta whispered.

'He could still die if we don't get him to a hospital. We've got to keep him moving around,' he said. 'He mustn't go to sleep.' He began loosening John's clothes with quick deft fingers, taking off his shoes and rubbing his skinny feet.

'You've done this before, haven't you?' said Rosetta slowly. Her voice rose hysterically. 'He's done this—'

Brian shook his head. 'Don't. Don't. Don't . . . Help me get him up.'

Between them they lifted John's arms on to their shoulders and began to move him up and down the corridor. He was pathetically light.

Each time they passed a window Rosetta scanned the loading area for signs of help, but it was eerily deserted.

Please God, don't let the press come. Don't let there be a photographer hidden in one of the packing-cases.

High above all the panic, Rosetta had an odd picture of the three of them, staggering up and down the tour-bus: her and Brian, with John in between. Despite John's fragility now, it was impossible to say who was more dependent on who.

All the time Brian kept talking to John in a low, urgent tone, so full of absolute tenderness that Rosetta had to bite her lips to stop herself crying. She hadn't heard Brian sound like that for years, not since she went into labour with Patrick.

Patrick. Rosetta put her hand over her mouth against the rush of bile.

'Come on, John, you can't leave us now, come on,' soothed Brian as they hobbled up and down the corridor of the bus. 'Come on. We need you here, we all need you here. You can't leave us just yet, there are too many people here who love you, John. I know you can hear me, wherever you are. Can you hear me?'

He looked across John's inert body to Rosetta. 'Come on, Rosetta!' he barked. 'Talk to him! We've got to keep a connection with him! If he's in some kind of limbo he's got to keep hearing our voices so he'll come back.'

She met his eye with disbelief. Now this really wasn't happening; this was how far her life had detached itself from normality. How could she talk to her lover – her lover of nine years – in front of her husband, also of nine years, who appeared to be acknowledging that he knew what was going on? She swallowed hard and looked at the swirling psychedelia of the bus carpet.

'Rosetta!' moaned Brian. 'Please! I don't think I can bear it if he dies!'

She looked at Brian and saw a pain in his face that she knew mirrored her own. And suddenly she understood why he hadn't said anything, why he'd tacitly encouraged her to carry on her affair with John, and stay on the road with them to keep the band together. Brian loved John as much as she did. Maybe not sexually. But it was all there in his eyes, and a heap of instincts suddenly fell together in her head with a ring of certainty: Brian loved John, and loved the way John could be everything he couldn't.

And if John went – then what was there left for anyone?

It wasn't her that had been holding things together, it was him.

How the hell did I get here? thought Rosetta bleakly, as they resumed the grim pacing. And why was I ever so arrogant as to think I *knew* any of these people at all?

The medics were quick, Rosetta had to give them that. They arrived in a very discreet Range Rover with blacked-out windows – their rock-star emergency vehicle? she wondered – and immediately began to work on John's inert body, asking questions in low confident voices, which Brian answered quickly.

Rosetta leaned back against the wall and tried to make herself believe all this was happening. If parts of her life had felt like a film, then this scene took the biscuit.

Sue arrived back five minutes after the medics pulled up, panting with the effort of not telling anyone what was going on. Whereas Rosetta was white with shock, so much so that she'd already been offered oxygen twice, Sue was bright red with anger and twitching with the physical stress of her rage.

She didn't waste any time in laying into Rosetta, even with her husband several feet away receiving medical assistance.

Perhaps it's her way of coping, Rosetta thought abstractedly, as the words rained down around her ears. She couldn't take her eyes off John, lying there like a waxwork.

Then suddenly it was just too painful and she closed her eyes and let the tears course down her cheeks. But the image of his inert body was imprinted on the backs of her eyelids and to her horror, she couldn't summon up any other picture of him.

I should have told him about Patrick! I should have told him then!

'Oh, that's so typical of you!' spat Sue. 'You close your eyes to everything you don't want to see, don't you? If it doesn't affect *you* directly *you* don't want to know!'

Rosetta waited for Brian to tell Sue to shut up, but he was crouched over the stretcher they were preparing for John, muttering arrangements, getting details and directions to the hospital. Ever the tour manager.

Odd phrases floated back to her: ' ... mixed with alcohol ... low resistance ... very pure local batch going round ... respiratory problems ...'

John – on heroin. How? How could *Brian* have known and not her?

Sue was flailing around like a Catherine wheel with her accusations, oblivious for once to the outsiders in the tour-bus. Rosetta hoped these medics were discreet. But then John wouldn't be the first tormented guitarist to drag a comfort blanket of heroin up over his head, to escape all the demons that made him play like a genius, but then wouldn't go away at the end of the gig. Not the first, and not the last. They weren't so special, after all.

Her attention was drawn back almost abstractedly to Sue, who was ranting hysterically and pointing her finger in her shoulder. Her breath, hitting Rosetta's face in great gusts, was foul.

She wasn't making any sense. Fragments floated back to Rosetta's slow motion brain: '... total fraud ... made you what you are ... not even your real name ...'

'What?' she said. Anything to make Sue stop. Her voice was bouncing off the metal walls.

'You know what you are, Rosetta? You're like a vampire,' roared Sue. 'You just go around taking what you want to feed your pathetic addiction to fame and celebrity and you leave the rest behind, all sucked out and empty. And we let you, because we're stupid enough to love you! Well, you're not going to skip on from this like you normally do. Go on, look – look what you've done.'

Rosetta stared at Sue, creasing her brow at the unfairness of what she'd said. She knew Sue was wrong, really wrong, but her mind was numb like she'd taken Quaaludes, and she couldn't find the right place to start. Her mouth opened and shut as the tears welled up in her mouth. Of all the times she'd needed a stream of smart replies, nothing would come.

She was John's muse, wasn't she? Wasn't that her reward for spending nine miserable years in love with a man she couldn't have?

Sue grabbed her by the hair and pushed her head round to face John on the stretcher. 'Go on, look! Look at him!' she screamed. 'Because this is all your fault, as much as if you'd tied the scarf round his arm yourself.'

'No, it's *not*!' Rosetta howled, suddenly finding an outlet for her pain. She had to stop herself from belting Sue, punching her until she was silent. 'How can you *say* that? How can you say that I do it all for myself? *Everything I've ever done* has been for other people – to help Brian, to help the band, to help your grubby little career! How can you stand there and say that *I* drain *you* of life when you're the one following us around, writing about the kids, using my name to get discounts in shops? You're a fucking *hypocrite*!'

'This isn't about me – look at him!' yelled Sue, yanking at her hair. 'You've killed the one thing that we all love, you selfish whore!'

And with a scream of frustration, she drew back her whole arm and slapped Rosetta hard across the face.

Rosetta wavered, not feeling any pain anywhere else except in her heart, and fell to her knees next to John. The ambulance man discreetly stepped to one side. She put her lips next to his ear and breathed gently on to his clammy skin, breathing in the familiar musky scent of him.

He *couldn't* be dying.

She couldn't feel this much love and him be dying.

'John,' she pleaded in a whisper, 'come back. Come back.'

'And you know what makes me sick?' said Sue from somewhere above Rosetta's head, her voice breaking in an effort to sound dignified. 'What makes me sick is that I *let* you carry on like this because I loved you both too much to see the shabby, pathetic truth. I *loved* John. Is that so hard for you to imagine? And I loved you. All I've wanted is to be your friend, ever since we were kids! God knows I've put up with a lot, Rosetta. But I can't ever, ever forgive you for this.' And she dissolved into painful, jerking sobs.

Brian steered her away into the other end of the bus. Rosetta could hear her sobbing diminish as she got further away.

'John, you have to come back,' she whispered into the pink fold of his ear. It was still warm. 'Please, you have to come back. There are things I have to tell you.'

And then the medics helped her up with firm but gentle hands, and carried him on the stretcher into the back of the Range Rover.

How could people imagine that rock 'n' roll was glamorous, Rosetta wondered bleakly as the ambulance pulled away. It was just as grim as the back streets of east London, just dressed up in someone else's free clothes.

The gig was cancelled.

And at 10.15 the next morning, so was the rest of the tour.

Chapter Twenty-five

Clerkenwell, 2001

If she hadn't had a headache, Tanith would never have
gone through Robert's bedside table looking for Nurofen –
and she would never have found the tapes. In a funny, homeopathic way the tapes did make her forget all about her
throbbing temples. But then since it was Robert and his
ongoing moodiness about Rosetta that had given her the
headache in the first place, it could be argued that he'd
brought it on himself. Maybe he even wanted her to find
them, but that was something for his own complicated
mental balance sheets of cause and effect, and not something she wanted to think about, sitting frozen on the bed,
listening to her own voice reeling off a list of cleaning products they needed for the bathroom.

Tanith sat with her back rigid, crushing the empty
Nurofen packet (one tablet left – Robert never kept loose
painkillers) in her sweating hands, feeling thoroughly
freaked out. It wasn't that he'd taped them having sex, or
something – that she could have dealt with, albeit in a pretty
disgusted way. But Robert seemed to have recorded some
pre-Sainsburys conversation – so random that she couldn't
even remember when it had been. Even Patrick had never
done anything as weird as this.

More than that, she couldn't get over how unlike herself
she sounded on the tape. She sounded like her *mother*.

'. . . More Jif, I don't know how we get through so much

when the bath always looks so filthy. Have you *ever* cleaned the bath?'

'Of course I have.' Robert's voice was slightly self-conscious, higher than normal. 'I clean it whenever I've used it.'

'Ye-ee–eah. Which is why there are always black pubes on the soap, I suppose?'

Tanith flinched at the harsh sound of her own disbelief and her scary obsession with getting brand-name products, rather than the supermarket stuff. She also had an annoying way of breathing, she now noticed.

'Tanith! I never—'

'No, no, no. If you say so. And have you been using the right sponge?'

'The right sponge . . .?'

'I mean *not* the red one.'

Tanith cringed at her tongue-clicking, and was relieved to hear herself laugh. Robert's uncertain, grown-up laugh followed, microseconds later. There was a pause on the tape in which she could hear the radio and the low whirr of the oven next to the kitchen table. It must have been a Sunday, since there was a very faint sound of church bells in the distance. Funny that she'd never really noticed them before.

She shot out her hand and stopped the tape, aware that her fingers were trembling.

Tanith came across surrealness most days, working with actors, and Robert wasn't exactly a run-of-the-mill boyfriend, but this was just odd. Why was he doing this? For what bizarre reason would anyone want to tape their girlfriend making a shopping list? It was the kind of freaky thing that serial killers did in made-for-TV mini-series. It would be one thing taping her making some secret confession or if he'd been trying to catch her out over . . . well, there wasn't anything to catch her out *about*. Tanith pressed her palms over her eyes, trying to calm herself down.

Was there something he could be trying to catch her out

about? She racked her brains and came up with nothing. And was it so weird? Had he just left the tape running by accident?

She ejected it from the machine. It was labelled with a date and the single initial T.

Freaky.

Absently, Tanith stared at the tape and took the remaining headache tablet, swallowing it with some blood-temperature Evian from Robert's side of the bed. He always kept mineral water by the bed. The metal ions in tap water, he claimed, hurt his fillings.

She flicked the cassette between her fingers, making the spools rattle like castanets, wondering at its anonymity, then gave in to temptation, and put it on again.

The conversation had moved on from cleaning products, she was pleased to note. In the background, the washing-machine revved up to the spin cycle and the ominous sounds of next-door's teenage son tuning up his cello began to penetrate.

'. . . Are you going to take your car in to be serviced this week?'

They must have been doing one of their diary realignments. Robert liked to sit down on Sunday morning, after they got back from the gym (him: violent circuit training; her: yoga), and make sure that all salient dates and arrangements were the same in each other's diary. Tanith didn't mind the secretarial overtones of this routine – she liked to be apprised of every eventuality too – but she consciously didn't tell any of her friends about it. Which, in itself, told her something about her relationship with Robert.

'I certainly am.' Robert's voice was a bit strangled. There was a series of clicks and rattles as he lined up his vitamin pills on the table. Tanith racked her brains to remember the conversation, but she couldn't. Then there was the sound of the table being jabbed with a finger and tea-cups rattling. Robert had obviously forgotten he was taping himself. 'And

I'm *not* going to let him rip me off with a recycled air filter. Like last time.'

Oh, no, it was all coming back now. Tanith felt the familiar tightening that spread across her chest whenever Robert did something which seriously annoyed her, and about which she couldn't criticize him because she did it herself. With a flick of her wrist she threw the Nurofen packet across the room, towards the bin. It fell in with a satisfying clatter. This must have been soon after she finished casting that rom-com set in Manchester, just after the last humungous row Robert had had with the garage down the road. The fact that Robert knew as much about the internal combustion engine as he did about the AHA content of her moisturizer didn't stop him from marching down to the garage and demanding to be led through the servicing process like Prince Charles witnessing a break-dancing demonstration.

Come to think of it, it didn't stop him telling her which moisturizer to get either.

A gusty sigh echoed through the speakers. Hers.

'Don't sigh at me, Tan! If people don't get to the bottom of things, that garage will be ripping you off next week, and some old lady the next . . .'

Tanith shut her eyes and eased her head back on to the pillows. After a day like today, being faced with impartial evidence of her middle-aged home-life was pretty much the last straw. And on this evidence, it was less 'comfortable old slipper' and more 'irritatingly tight impulse-buy heels'.

'Oh, don't. I'll go and speak to them.'

The washing-machine stopped and the beginning of endless lugubrious cello scales emerged through the silence from next door.

On the cassette Robert banged his cup down. Tanith was dismayed to realize that she could actually imagine his exact expression, despite not remembering the specific morning. 'No, they'll be even worse with you, when they see you're a woman. I'm going to tell them I'm from *Which Garage?* if they don't show me all the receipts this time.'

'Oh, shut *up*, Robert!' wailed Tanith in harmony with the Tanith on the tape, and pressed her palms against her face.

'No, no,' persisted the cassette Robert. 'I'll go and sort it out now.'

Tanith knew she should switch it off, but she couldn't. She couldn't put her finger on what was so compelling about listening to them squabble about nothing – but then she'd watched *Titanic* several times, each time hoping that the boat wouldn't actually sink.

The tape stopped suddenly and she stuck her hand out to turn it over.

It was a bit of a shock when rather than hitting the tape deck her fingers brushed against the wool of Robert's suit jacket.

'Rob!' she gasped, bouncing into a sitting position. 'You're back early!'

'As the actress said to the bishop. To the bishop's wife. Actress's husband. You know what I mean.'

They stared at each other trying to make that make sense, and then gave up. Tanith had long since abandoned her comedy instruction of Robert. He didn't get jokes. You were either born with comic timing or a love of accountancy. It was a mutually exclusive thing.

'What are you doing?' he demanded, with his customary lack of preamble.

Tanith tried to regain her initial sense of outraged indignation, but for some reason couldn't. Robert's face was stonily bland and defensive – an expression she'd seen before on all of the Mulligans, but to spectacular effect on Robert. Only the slight flaring of his nose gave away the simmering rage beneath.

'What does it look like? I'm listening to a tape of me running through my cleaning needs. I found it in your bedside drawer when I was looking for aspirin. And I could ask you what you were doing, taping me making shopping lists? What are you, some kind of psycho?'

'So it's OK to go through *drawers* now, is it?' spat Robert with unusual venom. His voice remained at conversational level, making the temper even more scary. 'Is *that* the kind of relationship we have?'

'Christ, you scare me! No, *listen* to what I'm saying. I was looking for aspirin and I found a tape you'd made of me – us – coordinating our diaries. And it completely freaked me out! It wasn't that you did it by accident, Robert, you even labelled the tape. Now, unless you're auditioning for some kind of soap opera, what kind of weird shit is that?'

Robert jabbed at the stereo and grabbed the tape out of it.

It occurred to Tanith – too late, as usual – that if only one of them had responded with a joke about stalking or something, it might not have escalated into the row that was now spreading and filling the room like mustard gas.

He stood and glared at her, half hiding the tape up his sleeve like a small boy. His eyes were black with rage and Tanith shook with the unexpected force of his anger.

'Don't ever go through my stuff again,' he said softly.

'Why? What else have you got?' she demanded, lured into filling the silence. She could hear her voice rising, and knew it was her panic speaking, and that she didn't mean half of it, but the words were streaming out of her mouth, borne along on the flood of tension pent up in her for days. 'Videos of me on the loo? Old pairs of knickers?'

Robert swore at her, whipped his arm round and hurled the tape into the laundry basket with terrifying force. Then he turned away and slammed his hands against the thick double-glazed windows. Tanith scrambled off the bed and headed for the door.

And to think that she'd always imagined that Patrick was too weird and screwed-up for her to deal with! Her pulse was banging in her neck. How could a man who looked so normal suddenly flip into these moments of hysteria? Which bit of his brain was missing?

She felt the sudden coolness in the hall as her eyes adjusted to the brighter light. The bin-bags she was meant to have taken out were still by the door.

'If you walk out of that door, then don't bother coming back!' Robert yelled from the bedroom.

'Oh, stop being such a *child*!' shouted Tanith. She pulled on her jacket. Stupid ultimatums. This wasn't the first time he'd issued them in a crisis but until now, on the rare occasions that he'd lost his temper, she'd always been calm enough to ignore them, talk him down. Tanith knew clearly enough that she should sit down and talk through whatever it was that had made him do this, but she wasn't sure, for once, that she'd know what do with what she found. She had too much background information now to imagine that there were issues she could deal with alone.

She had one hand on the lock, which was still sticking despite Robert's constant DIY efforts, when he appeared at the bedroom door.

'Don't go!'

She stopped. His broad shoulders were shaking and his face was red in blotches.

'Why?'

'Because I know it looks . . . weird and I want to explain.'

She raised her eyebrows. 'OK. Go on.'

'I made the tape because . . .' He sat down and put his head in his hands, running his fingers into his hair. When Robert was nervous or worried, Tanith had noted, he groomed himself like a small animal and this was exactly what he was doing now, rearranging his parting, smoothing down the rough curls at the front. She was annoyed at how maternal he made her feel when she knew she should be angry.

'When I was little,' he began, 'Dad gave me a radio cassette player for Christmas – they were quite new, at the time. We'd been away from home with Dad and Rosetta, on some bloody awful tour, but she'd insisted on coming home for Christmas. Total guilt trip. And Red was staying with us because Janette had thrown him out again so everyone was pretending nothing was wrong and making up this ridiculous Walt Disney Christmas for the kids. I must have been – what? Six? Five? It was when Greg and Pat still believed in Father Christmas, so Red sloped off to Midnight Mass with the au pair and we had to pretend to go to bed and . . .'

'Patrick still believed in Father Christmas? But wasn't he about . . . eight?'

Robert shot a look at her. 'I think he still believes in him now, doesn't he?'

'Sorry,' said Tanith, 'go on.'

Robert flicked the cassette in his fingers, making the spools rattle. Tanith realized he must have sneaked over to pick it out of the basket. He creased his brow the same way he did when he was making lines of figures add up, ordering the memories into lines of importance, dismissing fragments she didn't need to know. 'I remember it being a really cold night because Rosetta insisted we wore these ridiculous silk pyjamas she'd got in Japan for us. And there was no heating because no one had told Flower about paying bills while we were away and we'd been cut off. So when they thought we'd finally gone to sleep, Dad and Rosetta dragged all these presents in and left them all around the room – I remember they were having a row very quietly because Pat wanted to leave something for Santa's reindeer and Rosetta suggested a snowball and Red took her seriously and left a pile of coke or something on the fireplace, and Dad had to come in again and clear it up— Anyway . . .' Robert shook his head. '*Anyway*, he brought the tape recorder in and left the tape running in the machine while we opened our presents. He taped me and Pat arguing over some Action Man kit, playing with Greg, fighting over who got what . . .'

Robert looked up. There was a glassy tear swelling the bottom of each eye. Tanith recoiled in surprise at the childlike expression of pain on his face. 'It was a really sweet tape.'

'I bet,' she said softly and put her hand on his knee.

'I found it in a drawer about five years later, just after Dad left. It was so lonely without him in the house and all I could remember were the times when we'd fallen out – you know what it's like. You always think it's your fault. I was looking for some blank tapes to record the Top Forty and Rosetta always had heaps of cassettes in her room, so I thought she wouldn't miss a couple from her bedroom.'

'You went through her drawers?' asked Tanith, unable to stop herself.

'I went through her drawers.' Robert's face hardened a little. 'But then I was too young to realize what half the stuff was for, fortunately. It was always the first place we went to look for batteries, come to think of it.'

'Don't,' said Tanith.

'Both tapes were unlabelled, both half-way through, so I just put it on to check and there it was – Dad playing with my Action Man, laughing at the crap joke book I'd asked for, pretending to Pat that Santa must not have had time for his sherry, and that the snow on the mantelpiece must have come off the horses' hooves. It was all so *normal*. I mean, *normal*. Even Red was singing along with the carol service on the radio in the background. We sound like a family.' He bit his lip. 'I felt like I'd got a little piece of Dad back. I was so happy, I can't tell you how happy I was. *God*.'

'Have you still got the tape?' asked Tanith gently.

Robert smiled, but it was a pretty mirthless smile. 'I took it with me to boarding-school. And university. I didn't play it too much, because I didn't want to *learn* it, but I couldn't leave it at home.'

'And the other tape?' she asked, after a decent pause. 'Didn't you say there were two?'

Robert twisted up his face and began raking his hair again. 'Nothing gets past you, does it?'

'If you'd wanted it to, you wouldn't have mentioned it.'

Robert's expression hardened, and Tanith guessed it would have something to do with his mother. Something bad. 'Well, I wound through the other tape and it just seemed to have some guitar fiddling on it, so I saved the other and used it to tape the charts. You have to remember that most of the cassettes in the house had music on them – didn't mean it was any *good*. This just sounded like John or someone messing about with Red – nothing important. They used to punch out the little holes in the top if it was important. And this was a tape I found in Rosetta's room.'

Tanith noted how he still self-justified like a small child. His fringe was now flat on his forehead. 'So,' she said, 'what was on it? Demo tapes? You taped over *Sergeant Pepper*? Or was it the tape that proved conclusively that Rosetta was there when they recorded 'Get Back'?'

Robert looked up. His face was still wounded. 'To be totally honest with you, I don't know *what* was on that cassette. I was sitting in my bedroom with my radio all tuned in, waiting for the Top Ten and suddenly Rosetta was there, shrieking and wailing.' He bit his lip and shook his head, the memory still vivid on his face.

'I was *so* scared of her when she did her "bursting in" thing. We all were. I don't think she ever entered a room quietly. I remember she was wearing these high-heeled boots, covered in what looked like iridescent fish-scales, and her face was completely white. She looked as if she'd been exhumed. Come to think of it, she had just had Barney at the time, probably wasn't sleeping much. I remember thinking that she was just like the witch from *Chorlton and the Wheelies* – she could just pop up anywhere, any time, and scare the *shit* out of you. So she burst in, grabbed the tape and threw the radio across the room and broke it.'

'And what? Was it something special on the tape?'

He shrugged. 'Who knows? She did a bit of screaming – the usual, "You bastard ingrate children, you steal everything that's mine, it's the mother who's strangled by the bloody umbilical cord!" Etcetera etcetera – played a little bit of the tape, which was just the stoned wittering you always got on these things, burst into tears and yanked it out of the machine. Then hurled it across the room and stormed out. Then I heard the front door slam and Agnetha came in about an hour later to tell me Rosetta had run over Thor. Patrick's cat. He'd been sleeping under the car when she screeched off. She always did drive that Lotus like the petrol tank was on fire.'

'Oh my God,' breathed Tanith. There was so little you could usefully add to most of these childhood stories, without having a degree in child psychology. 'So what happened?'

'Oh, some pedigree Siamese thing turned up in a packing crate from Harrods about a week later. Shat all over the carpet and attacked Bonham, the Labrador Red gave me for my seventh birthday.' Robert's face softened. 'I wish you'd met Bonham. He was my best friend. He was the best dog in the world . . .'

'No, I meant about the *tape*. About you. And Rosetta.'

Robert closed his eyes and when he opened them, his face had resumed its habitual weary expression of handsome disdain. 'Well, she went off to the Priory for a few weeks. *Again*. The band had split up and Dad was off on tour with Red's new band at the time, so I didn't even tell him about it. Agnetha was terrified, wanted to go back to Sweden, but there were a couple of girls left over from the fan-club office, so they moved in. Ginny and Lindy. They were nice. Fancied Pat, naturally.'

'And she never said what was on it?'

Robert shook his head. 'I was just glad that I'd hidden the Christmas one under the bed. Course, it wasn't until ages later that it dawned on me that she never even missed *that*. Never even knew I'd got it. She's a selfish bitch through and through. Some women shouldn't be allowed to have kids.'

'You're very, very hard on your mother,' said Tanith wearily. 'You know, the more you tell me, the more I feel sorry for her. Why can't you let all this *go*?'

'In what way do you mean mother? Every time I needed affection as a kid, she would . . . pull away, like I'd mess up her clothes. That's when she was there. She's not *capable* of being a mother, Tanith. God! She's even scared of the *word*. And don't tell me she deserves another chance, because . . . it's too late now.'

Tanith got up and drew the curtains because she didn't know what to say. It was at moments like this that she wanted to throw her stuff in the car and run away too. There was just too much to mend here, too much to understand, and the more she learned, the more she felt implicated in the whole sorry mess. And she wasn't sure that she wanted to be. It wasn't getting engaged that dragged you into relationships, it was suddenly realizing you were fully conversant with all family hang-ups and feuds.

And yet with Robert, unlike Patrick, she couldn't walk away. She knew things weren't perfect between them, and that every day she spent there was setting their relationship in stone, but she couldn't bring herself to leave. Was it just resignation? Or was it fear of the responsibility that the perfect relationship would bring?

Tanith swallowed. 'So with all that in mind, why were you taping us making a shopping list?'

Robert paused and resumed his nervous grooming. 'Because it's only when it's all over that the little moments like that become important,' he said eventually. 'I didn't want a scrapbook full of pictures of my parents arriving at airports, or references in biographies – because that's what I've got. We don't have any little snaps – it's all David Bailey and Terence Donovan. Rosetta and us all naked in a pile of straw for Snowdon. I mean, come on! And I don't have many pictures of you and me together anyway. I wanted to have something small and real of us.'

'For when I go?' said Tanith in a small voice.

'Yes,' said Robert and turned to the wall.

Chapter Twenty-six

Chelsea, 1983

There had been no funny looks on the short walk from
the garage to her house, but Rosetta wryly put that
down to the fact that none of her Cheyne Walk neighbours
were likely readers of the tabloid newspapers. Still, she went
round to the back door all the same; she didn't want to face
the snappers if they were camping out on her doorstep, and
she didn't want to face herself if she was too old hat to war-
rant any.

Rosetta took a deep breath, hitched Barney higher up on
to her hip and pushed open the door with her shoulder. He
was warm and sleepy and didn't resist when she juggled him
with her keys and her overnight bag.

'We're back!' she called into the echoing hall, making her
voice as cheerful and normal as possible.

The house was silent, apart from the faint swishing of the
washing-machine in the kitchen.

Rosetta thanked God for her first lucky break in twenty-
four hours: that she'd probably managed to hit a solitary
minute when the phone wasn't ringing off the hook with
angry friends and persistent journalists. She assumed, from
the peace in the house, that Heidi, her latest au pair, had
taken Greg out to avoid it too. That gave her valuable recov-
ery time, even if the sheer sensation of being back in the
house again made her feel sick and ashamed of having run
away from it to begin with. Setting Barney down, Rosetta

strode quickly across the hall and pulled the telephone plug out of the socket, to be on the safe side.

There was no Brian, of course, waiting enraged by the door with a rolling-pin. He was in France, marshalling Red's new band, and had been for weeks now. They spoke every other day or so, to check that there were no problems with the boys and that he was taking his tablets, but to all intents and purposes they were two senior executives, running different offices of the same company. Affectionate, but no more. Barney had certainly been a surprise: an anniversary present, in a way, not unlike her cosmetic dentistry – intended to make her feel better about herself. Although, Rosetta reminded herself, there was nothing at all to stop Brian flying straight back and joining in the chorus of rage.

Behind her, Barney fell back on to his bottom with a soft thump, and she heard the skittering of claws as Bonham, Robert's corpulent black Labrador puppy, came trotting from the sitting-room out to welcome them. He nuzzled round her legs, suspiciously friendly. Rosetta wondered if he'd been sleeping on the sofa again, then realized she no longer cared.

'Do you think Bonham's hungry?' she said to Barney, making an effort to keep the everyday note in her voice, just in case Greg was lurking. Where the others happily drew as much attention as possible to their presence, Greg tended to lurk and pop up unexpectedly, like a reproachful little ghost.

'Barney's hungry!' Barney announced happily and Bonham licked his round face, from chin to forehead. Barney responded by grabbing the dog around the neck and clasping it to him like a long-lost brother, making affectionate cooing noises as he did so.

'Then we'll have some tea,' said Rosetta, stowing her overnight bag in the cupboard under the stairs. He didn't look like a child who had spent an unexpected night in a hotel with a runaway single parent, she thought, with a pang of gratitude for his amenable attitude to life. Of her four offspring, Barney was far and away the easiest: he didn't seem to expect anything other than unconditional devotion, and in return loved everything around him. She frequently found him putting balls of wool to bed, or tearfully consoling her embroidered cushions. Barney loved Rosetta, he loved Brian, he loved Bonham, he loved his bed, with exactly the same wide-eyed hippie fanaticism. Everyone loved Barney.

Rosetta wasn't unaware of the fact that he was the one child who'd never seen the inside of a tour-bus.

On the telephone table, a lurid papier mâché elephant brought back from a tour, was a pile of messages in Heidi's high school handwriting – Rosetta didn't want to look at them. There was some post as well, and the papers, but she didn't especially didn't want to see them either.

She sighed and realized that there wasn't much point in pretending everything was normal when it clearly wasn't.

Guiltily, Rosetta plugged the phone lead back in and immediately the phone rang. She looked round to make sure that Barney was occupied – he was carefully dunking a Pringle into Bonham's water bowl as if it were an avocado dip – and went up a couple of stairs then picked up the receiver through the banisters.

'Hello?' she said, in a faintly transatlantic voice so she could pass herself off as Heidi if it were a journalist.

'Rosetta?' said a firm little voice, and her heart banged in her chest. OK, so she was scared of her kids. But weren't all mothers, deep down?

'Oh, hello, Robert,' she replied. 'I was just about to call you, sweetheart. Talk about cosmic energy! How are you, darling?'

'Embarrassed. Ashamed. Humiliated. How are *you* feeling?'

Rosetta slumped down on the stairs and shut her eyes. So there was no point in trying to bluff it out then. At least she'd skipped the agony of steeling herself to call him. It was impossible to work out how to explain all this to an eleven-year-old because Robert wasn't *like* any eleven-year-

olds she'd read about in the childcare manuals. In three
terms at boarding-school, he had accelerated himself from an
amiable if mischievous little boy into furious adolescence
just as quickly as Patrick's natural introspection had turned
into worrying self-isolation. Where Patrick had vanished
into his own world, Robert had turned himself inside-out,
existing only to organize the rest of the school around him.
Both believed she had sent them away as some kind of punishment after The End's final tour, when nothing –
nothing! – could have been further from the truth.

'Would you like me to explain?' she asked defensively, 'or
have you already decided what you want to believe?'

'You can explain if you want,' sniffed Robert. 'It's not
like it's the first time, is it?'

Rosetta flinched. He had learned Brian's trick of using
disapproval as his hardest weapon. All the gutter press lies in
the world couldn't hurt her as much as the criticism in
Robert's voice.

'Well,' she began, imagining the lurid headlines in her
mind, 'apparently André, you remember – the hairdresser
that Anita was married to for a while?'

'No,' said Robert.

'You do, we used to go to his salon in Knightsbridge. You
shaved his dog.'

'Oh, yes,' said Robert. 'That slimy creep.'

Rosetta tried not to smile. He sounded just like Brian, but
it wasn't funny. 'Well, he's gone bankrupt and needed some
money, so he went to the papers and sold some old pictures
he had, of me and your father and Anita and Red . . . and
John. Really low-quality holiday snaps stuff, but . . .' she
took a deep breath, 'the paper doctored them to make them
look more incriminating than they really were.'

'I know,' said Robert. 'I'm looking at them now.'

'Robert!' Rosetta pressed her lips together. 'Tear them up,
darling. Throw the newspaper away.'

There was a pause. 'I can't. The boys in my house have

covered my locker in them. All I can see is you hanging out
of a bus upside down.' Another loaded pause. 'With no bra.
I beat them up.'

Rosetta felt like crying again, but squeezed her eyes shut
until the sob went back down her throat. 'Then ... then
take the stupid pictures down and leave them in the rubbish
bin where the boys can see. It's completely made-up, you
know. They must have got André drunk when they interviewed him, because most of it's lies. I mean, they weren't
even *on* those American tours, were they – immigration
wouldn't let Anita in with her drug convictions, and ...'

She trailed off, hearing the pleading in her own voice, and
closed her eyes. The teasing little phrases jumped out at her
in bold print between the paragraphs: *drunken orgies ...
wild parties ... innocent children.*

'Why didn't Dad's lawyers stop this?' demanded Robert.
'Couldn't they have stopped it?'

'They didn't know about it, darling,' said Rosetta. Now
that Sue refused to speak to her, Rosetta had no defender in
the press, especially with the band split up, and no legal
might of the record company behind her. While Brian had
moved into lower-profile, higher-return management, she
had started writing columns, appearing on the occasional
discussion panel – but she was still Rosetta Mulligan, schoolgirl groupie to the tabloids, and probably always would be.
Even now she was thirty-two and more dependent on sleep-
ing-pills than cocaine. 'None of us knew about it. I only
found out last night because an old friend tipped me off.'

'So where were you this morning?' Robert sounded suddenly close to tears. 'I've been trying to get hold of you all
day.'

'I was ... I was ...' Rosetta gripped the phone tighter.
There was no fancy way of dressing up the truth: she'd done
what she'd always taken pride in *not* doing – and run away.

She'd been trying to soothe Barney back to sleep after a
nightmare when the phone by her bed had rung at one

o'clock. For once Rosetta was glad Heidi hadn't picked up the extension. Karen, the old friend, was apologetic but muted, as if she could barely believe it herself. And through the paralysis of shock, Rosetta knew that the story would be much worse in her head until she saw what was actually printed – she had to see it.

Barney insisted on coming with her, so she'd put him into the back of her Lotus and they'd driven to King's Cross for the early editions, to see if it was true, that André – or Andrew, as she now felt entitled to call him – had dished up everything with colour pictures to illustrate. He had. And how! Rosetta stood on the chilly pavement and felt the cold go right through to her bones, as if her entire body was turning to ice, inside out, reading about John's 'squalid decline into heroin' and her own 'adulterous liaisons'. Even the smokescreen titbits she'd made up at the time stung, reminding her of how nothing used to hurt her, as long as no one knew about John. André couldn't possibly have known all this – Anita had dumped him way before most of it had happened – which made Rosetta wonder whether he'd had a secondary source. Like Sue.

Yet worst of all, worse than the sordid little nudges and winks, was that everything that had been glamorous and easy and charming now looked tired and cheap and has-been. And *over*.

Rosetta always kept a spare overnight bag in the car, in case Brian called her to fly out and deal with some problem on his tour. Barney was sleeping soundly – probably because he'd achieved her undivided attention – so she drove, heading out of town, away from anything that would remind her of the past, and turned the radio on, so Barney wouldn't hear her snuffling back the tears of self-loathing. When she woke the next morning in some anonymous roadside hotel chain, still in her clothes, with a vodka hangover, the paper was still there in her bag, and she realized that firstly, it hadn't been a horrible dream, and secondly, she'd have to warn Robert and Patrick.

But of course, by then it was too late to warn them – the paper was on the stands and in the shops.

At that moment, Rosetta despised herself more than she'd done in her life. All those months of trying to be a better mother, trying to put all that loose energy into the boys, trying to make herself 'normal' – and when it mattered? She knew she should have driven to the school and taken them out, explained everything with the modern honesty she always imagined would come so naturally. It was what they deserved, after everything she and Brian had dragged them through. There would have been a time when she would have taken *pride* in sitting them down and telling them the whole unvarnished truth, and all the beautiful, positive things that had come out of their unconventional arrangement.

But now she couldn't. She couldn't bear to give Robert yet another reason to distrust her. Without John, it was hard to see what good *had* come out of it, and she felt suddenly very weary, after the last few years struggling to carry on as normal with the centre of her world caved in. It isn't fair for them to see me like this, Rosetta told herself, and with her conscience still protesting, she took Barney to a park until he insisted that Bonham would need his tea too and they drove back to London.

'Where were you?' repeated Robert hotly, sensing he had her on the back foot.

'I was . . . out,' she said. There was no point lying to Robert. He always winkled the truth out in the end.

'Out. Very good.' He made a schoolboy noise of utter disgust which stung her more than words would. 'Well, then you've got no one to blame but yourself when Henderson phones.'

'Mr Henderson?' The headmaster, with whom Rosetta was virtually on first-name terms after repeated phone-calls about Robert's over-enthusiastic approach to contact sports. Her temples throbbed with lack of sleep. Had he seriously hurt the boys who had papered his locker? Red had shown

him how to throw a punch: ever the perfect godfather. As if
the school needed more proof of her maternal failures. 'Oh
no. What have you . . .?'

'Patrick's run away,' said Robert in a matter-of-fact tone
that shocked Rosetta. '*Again*. He hasn't taken his passport
though, so he can't have gone far. But this was his last warning, and he'll be expelled if they find out. So they might as
well kick me out too.'

Rosetta listened in mute horror. Robert and Patrick barely
tolerated each other at the best of times, but they clung
together fiercely in a crisis.

'So I've been *trying* to tell you that you might phone
Henderson and say that he's with you,' Robert went on.
'Or . . . I suppose you might want to go and find him.' Pause.
'Now you're *back*.'

'Robert!' She had no energy left for arguing. 'Thank you
for phoning to let me know,' she said weakly. 'I'm going to
get in the car right now and we'll find him together, OK?'

'Don't tell Dad, will you?' said Robert anxiously. 'I don't
want Patrick to get into trouble.'

'Well, I might have to, darling,' said Rosetta, although it
wasn't Brian's night for phoning, and she had no intention of
courting his attention and adding child mismanagement to
her list of failings. Not if she could find Patrick first.

She felt physically sick.

'I've got to go,' said Robert, 'I'm not meant to use the
phone, I'm gated.'

'I do love you, darling,' Rosetta said hurriedly. 'You know
that, don't you? No matter what it—'

'Yeah, yeah,' said Robert and hung up.

'Oh, *God*,' said Rosetta.

She put the phone down, and it rang again at once.
Automatically, she picked it up.

'Hello?' she said, immediately wishing she hadn't. It could
be the press, or, worse, Brian. Or, in a Satanic combo of
both, Sue.

Her heart throbbed with remorse. Or a scared Patrick, reverse-calling from some railway station, alone in a phone-box, nervously averting his big brown eyes from the strange man in the overcoat, lurking outside . . .

'Rosetta? It's Anita.'

As soon as she heard Anita's voice, a lead weight dropped into the pit of Rosetta's stomach. Anita never phoned unless there was a crisis. Either she was raging mad about the André revelations, or she had decided that Rosetta had sunk so low as to require support – although what kind of support Anita was likely to offer wasn't exactly reassuring.

Then she felt simultaneously relieved and panicked that it wasn't Patrick.

With one eye on Barney in the kitchen, Rosetta picked up the phone base and pulled it through the banisters. 'Anita,' she said. 'Jesus Christ. What happened to André? Has he really turned to religion? Or did he just run out of money?'

There was a snort on the other end and the sound of a lighter flicking. Anita hadn't felt the need to give up smoking and claimed that she owed her glacial cheekbones to twenty years of dragging dramatically on Gitanes. 'Boss-eyed little shit. *Andrew*, bloody *Andrew* Barnes from *Croydon*. Did you see he took a couple of years off himself and added them to us?'

'I care more that he implied I was not a natural Titian beauty,' Rosetta quipped automatically, then cringed at her own inability to be serious when it mattered.

'Well,' Anita's tone was frosty. Rosetta couldn't tell whether she was joking or not. 'He would know, *wouldn't* he?'

'I'm sorry?' Rosetta covered her eyes with her free hand.

'You have read the article, haven't you? Just in case you needed your memory refreshing? Or were you stoned when he trimmed your pubic hair into a butterfly shape?'

Rosetta peered through her fingers, to check Barney wasn't around. No, not Anita as well. 'You believe *that*?'

'Why not?'

'Why not? *Why not?*'

'And again – why not? There's a lot to assimilate.'

A long pause.

Rosetta fought back her anger, trying not to let it show in her voice. 'Because I thought *you of all people* didn't believe everything you read in the newspapers!'

'I *don't* believe what I read in the papers, on the whole,' snapped Anita defensively. 'But when your ex-husband writes an autobiography and you're not even the leading lady, it's rather difficult to know *who* to believe.'

'But you *know* it's all . . .' Rosetta's voice trailed off. What was the point in protesting if your best friend didn't even believe you? She could have pointed out that it was Anita, for God's sake, who had been the one railing against the possessive contradiction of marriage, but she hadn't the energy.

Rosetta gazed up at her reflection in the big mirror and was shocked by how small she looked. If Anita now couldn't tell the difference between the woman in the papers, the walking billboard for The End and Brian Mulligan and Anita's Boutique and The Hip Lifestyle You Wished You Had, then what chance did her sons have of telling the difference? It could only get worse from now on – once the papers had you down as someone they could target, that would be it. No wonder Patrick had run away. The bigger question was where would he have run *to*? And what on earth could she tell him when she found him?

Rosetta set her jaw. It was becoming glaringly obvious even to her that this might be more serious than she'd previously imagined. 'For Christ's sake, Anita, I would rather screw *you* than André!'

'I think he's covered that angle too, if you read the article properly.'

Rosetta flinched, and rubbed her eyes with her fingers. 'Look, can we have this argument later? Patrick has run away from school and I have to go and find him.'

'Because of this?'

'Yes. I mean, I think so. He has . . . lots of issues. Some with his father, actually. It isn't just me single-handedly ruining their lives.'

There was a pause. Another click of a lighter. 'Darling, it looks like your chickens are coming home to roost.'

'Bloody *hell*, Anita!' yelled Rosetta, forgetting temporarily about Barney in the kitchen. '*You* were there too! It wasn't just me, drinking and screwing on behalf of everyone! Just because it suits you all *now* to blame me for everything! Wouldn't it be nice if I had a drugs problem too, then you could really go to town?'

There was a click on the other end of the line, and the dialling tone cut in.

'Oh God,' Rosetta moaned into the crook of her arm.

The door slammed, heralding the return of Greg and Heidi, right on cue.

'Mummy! Mumm-ee-ee-ee-ee!' Greg's straining voice was unmistakable. He wasn't a natural shouter, unlike the others.

Rosetta wiped the mascara from where it had smudged under her eyes and blinked several times to get her eyes bright again.

'Darling!' she said, catching the bundled-up ball of duffel-coat and scarf as it cannoned into her legs. 'Darling, say Rosetta, not Mummy. I'm a person with a name, just like you. Not a mummy like everyone else.'

Behind her, Heidi the au pair appeared to be stuffing something back inside her embroidered bag, under the guise of removing her own scarf. It looked like a tabloid newspaper.

'You're back very late,' Rosetta said, over Greg's head. He was searching in his bag for something to show her, chattering to himself.

'It was, like, a really long pardy?' Heidi had come over from the San Fernando Valley in search of Glynn Masterson. Finding that Glynn was now tax-exiling in France, Heidi had appealed to Rosetta for a job and had subsequently joined the ranks of ex-groupies pushing infant Mulligans around the streets of Chelsea. Rosetta liked it that way – there was nothing like an afternoon with Greg or Barney to take the dewy sheen off a teenage temptress. Not that there was much to tempt around here any more.

'Miranda had this firework display?' Heidi continued. 'And it went on for hours? Which was cool because all the nannies got to have a chocolate fondue while they did, like, what are they? Sparklers?'

Rosetta knew this. Miranda's daddy did pyrotechnics for Def Leppard. Miranda saw about as much of him as Greg and Barney did of Brian. The longer the tour, the bigger the compensatory fireworks. She noticed that Heidi was too dis-creet to ask where she and Barney had been all night.

'The fireworks were ace!' exclaimed Greg, through a mouthful of birthday cake. 'They were a thousand feet high! In the shape of a space craft! And it took off in the garden! And Miranda's mum made us all Black Forest gateaux!'

'Rosetta, some of the mothers at the pardy were talking about the papers?' murmured Heidi. 'I haven't, like, read them, but I think you need to, like, channel those bad vibes into something positive before the house gets affected . . .'

Rosetta felt as if every wall was now collapsing in on her. Maternity, celebrity, domesticity, sanity. An animal desire to get out as far and as fast as possible rushed through her.

'Well, while you were out, I've had some very bad news about Patrick,' she said, addressing Heidi in as serious a voice as she could muster. 'Not now, darling,' she added, putting a hand on Greg's head as he attempted to show her the contents of his take-home bag, 'I'm talking to Heidi.'

'But I made it for—'

'Darling!' Rosetta clenched her fists in tight little balls.

Greg shot her a scalded look and slunk off into the kitchen, where Barney greeted him with a fistful of Pringles.

'I'm going to have to drive up to the boys' school,' she

said, getting more English as she went on, taking refuge in the 'concerned Chelsea mother' mask now forming a protective coating over her racing mind.

'Ewwww, neeewwww,' said Heidi, her rosebud mouth a circle of perfectly judged horror.

'Patrick has . . . has had an accident.' There was no need to tell her everything – she would only repeat it when Brian phoned from Paris and cause more of a scene. The whole point of her taking every other week off whatever tour he was doing to be with the kids was to keep domestic matters under reasonable control – or at least that's what they'd told each other in the beginning. Now Brian only seemed to want her to join him during school holidays when she could bring the boys with her.

In the kitchen, Greg was morosely helping himself to a glass of skimmed milk and lining his Shrinky Dink crisp packets up on the table. Barney looked unimpressed.

'Oh, Gaaad, Rosetta,' said Heidi. 'I . . .'

'So can you put Greg and Barney to bed and set the alarms? I don't know what time I'll be back.' Rosetta was already pulling on her long leather coat and searching for her boots. She kicked off the red slippers and they bounced underneath the papier mâché elephant.

'Is there anything I can . . .?' Heidi suddenly looked very childlike and vulnerable, and Rosetta wondered why she hadn't just given up the struggle with her conscience and got an ancient Norland nanny who would have brought discipline to the boys and at least made *her* feel young and fresh.

'Read Greg a bedtime story and explain that I had to go and sort out Patrick.' The zip was sticking on her boots and she nipped a tiny lump of flesh. 'Ow, *shit*.'

She looked up to see Greg's wary grey eyes level with hers and let out a gasp of shock.

'What?' she said, sounding more brusque than she meant to.

'Mummy— Rosetta, you said you would do my reading book tonight. You promised.'

'But I can't. I have to go out.' Damn. Rosetta pressed her tongue behind her front teeth to stop her teeth chattering. 'I have to go and see Patrick. He's not very well.'

'But *I'm* not very well,' protested Greg. 'Heidi said so. She said I'm damaged. And you were out last night too, I heard you go.'

Rosetta looked up sharply but Heidi was in the kitchen singing some ridiculous Captain Beefheart song to Barney and Bonham with the oven gloves draped over her head like ears. Irritatingly, she still looked like a Wrigley's gum advert.

'Did she? I don't think she meant that,' said Rosetta, more and more conscious, now the thought had lodged itself in her mind, of the dangers Patrick could be facing in his phone-box.

Greg said nothing, but carried on looking at her with Brian's eyes. When he was born, her mother had made a rare appearance at the expensive private hospital Brian had selected (no hippie road births for Rosetta, thank you), taken one look at the eerily placid bundle in the cot next to the bed and announced, 'He's been here before, you mark my words.' Brian had dismissed this as the ramblings of a middle-class woman suffering from terminal Madame de Farge Syndrome, but Rosetta had known precisely what she meant and had been tormented by it ever since.

'When can we go back on Dad's bus? I like the bus,' said Greg conversationally. 'I made you a painting, do you want to see it?'

Rosetta gave him a quick hug. 'Soon. When I get back. Darling, I really have to go and see Patrick. Now, give your book to Heidi and she'll do your reading.'

Greg backed off, scuffing his heels along the parquet floor, looking resigned.

Rosetta heard him muttering something about Patrick and

felt guilty. She handed him the takeaway leaflet. 'You can have whatever you want for supper?'

He sighed, spinning on one toe, and ran off to the kitchen, where he tackled Heidi round the legs so she stumbled into the dog basket, still singing.

Rosetta levered herself to her feet and grabbed her car keys from the glass bowl on the hall table.

'I'll be back as soon as I can!' she yelled, hoping she sounded more capable than she felt, and let herself out into the drizzle.

Rosetta drove too fast. She knew that. Her defence was that you couldn't drive a Lotus slowly, but tonight she wasn't really aware of driving at all. It wasn't a consolation the way it normally was, because she didn't really know where she was going, and she didn't have the first idea what she would do when she got there. But at least she was moving.

Unlike the rest of my life, she thought grimly, gripping the steering-wheel. The only point to my entire existence these days is the boys, and I can't even get that right.

She crept along in a traffic jam, the radio burbling in the background. Every pedestrian seemed to be looking into the car at her: the woman who slept with the whole band, who neglected her children, who thought she could get away with it. Rosetta had never felt so exposed, or so pointless. Seeing her life pinned out like that so even she had to be horrified by its flippancy – and no one to run to, and bury her head in shame. Did they think the occasional free dress and frequent air travel meant you didn't feel normal human emotions?

I only ever did what I thought was right, she raged in her head, *and my husband's just an old friend, the love of my life has gone, my best friend hates me and my children . . .*

One tear rolled down her cheek and Rosetta fought to stop herself crying. She imagined herself from outside the car and straightened her spine. It was too late for self-pity now. See how far that had got her: those hours spent trying to fill up the gap John had left with stupid articles and meetings, trying to make herself feel important again, when she should have been spending even more time with the boys.

She thought of Patrick and Robert, needing her to put everything right, like a proper mother would, and she felt hopelessly inadequate. How am I meant to help their hurt, she wondered wildly, when I don't know how to deal with my own? It's worse than not having a mother at all, this ridiculous nightmare of having a mother everyone can read about in the daily papers – a mother who *doesn't even really exist*.

Rosetta leaned back in her seat until she could see her face in the rear-view mirror. A scared and tired housewife with sluttily smudged mascara stared back at her. Too scared of her own past even to explain it to her own sons.

A car behind honked its horn as the traffic crept ahead.

It wasn't the first time hints of nasty gossip had appeared about her, but the defences weren't there any more. The longer she was just a Chelsea mum, the less of a front she had to put up against attacks like these. She didn't even recognize the woman they were talking about, and yet it stung her bitterly. And now they were bringing the children into it – that wasn't fair. It really wasn't *fair*. But then she'd made the rules, hadn't she? They hadn't asked to be paraded through airports.

Rosetta's hands slipped off the steering-wheel in defeat. She didn't want to drive on, because she had no idea how to find Patrick, much less explain herself to him. She couldn't turn back because she would only have to face it later. Again and again.

Rosetta chewed her lip and concentrated on Patrick. It isn't about you any more, she told herself harshly. It's too late to try to sell that traditional mother schtick to them, so you might as well stop beating yourself up about it. They don't believe it anyway. Maybe the best thing you can offer them now is to be a good friend, because then at least they might forgive you for the mistakes you made as a human being, where they can't ever forgive a mother for being so stupid and fallible. They're wise enough to understand.

That sounded reassuring, she thought, with a flush of surprise. It sounded right.

It sounded like something John might have said to her.

Rosetta blinked until her eyes cleared of tears and opened up the map on the passenger seat. She summoned up Patrick in her head, trying to feel where he might be. She even thought of Robert, and steeled herself to collect him first, so they could find Patrick together.

She turned up the radio and drove.

Chapter Twenty-seven

London, 2001

It had been another very long day and Tanith was beginning to think that all the sad journalists were right: there would never be an era like the sixties again, because there weren't any innocent people left to notice it.

She'd seen too many girls now to believe in it herself, some for the second or third time. None of them could have credibly existed any time out of the 1990s. Apart from the fact that, by maths alone, all her Amber candidates would have had to have been born well after punk came and went, well after John Lennon was shot – some even after Live Aid, for God's sake – none of them had the attitude she needed.

Or rather, they had plenty of Attitude, most of it Britney-flavoured, but it had all the authenticity of chewing-gum scraped off the underside of a table.

What Tanith was looking for (and even she now accepted that it was hopelessly fuzzy) was freshness, and confidence, and a refusal to accept less than the best. What she was *getting* was a lot of 'whaddevers' and more eye-rolling than the *Black and White Minstrel Show*. Amazing hair could be faked at the right hairdressers, and it was eye-opening what wardrobe could do, but attitude was acting and the whole key to finding the right Amber was a girl who *wasn't* stage school. In training, or in outlook.

Tanith eased off one of her shoes and wiggled her toes. There was a hole in her popsock and the exposed skin had turned black from the leather dye. She frowned at her scaly foot. She should really get a pedicure. Skipping regular beauty treatments was a bad sign in a relationship, like odd cracks appearing in the side of houses.

Tanith prised off the other shoe with her toes and wished that she could summon up some positive thoughts about Robert instead of falling into the Mulligan trap of constant comparison with one or more of his brothers. In the weeks when there were no mention of the others, their relationship bloomed, and she remembered why she'd moved in with this generous and affectionate man. Maybe that was the answer – to move away entirely?

There wasn't a knock at the door, so she couldn't decide whether she'd actually seen enough Ambers today, but before she could snap something about getting out, the girl had come in and was slouching across the room in a casual but hideously confident way Tanith had seen in a hundred coffee bars up and down the Fulham Road.

'Hello,' she said and without bothering to wait for a reply, settled herself on one of the chairs and folded one impossibly twig-like leg over the other. It was November and she wasn't wearing tights. But then her legs were perfect, and tanned the colour of milky tea. Her calves didn't seem to spread when she wrapped them round each other either.

Tanith sucked her teeth. None of this was immediately endearing.

'Hi, I'm Sophie, yeah? This where the auditions are happening?' drawled the girl. She pushed back the wave of blonde hair from her beautiful face, and it fell back immediately. She reminded Tanith of a palomino Sindy horse she'd had as a child, but this – she told herself quickly – wasn't necessarily a bad thing.

'Yes, it was,' said Tanith, trying not to let her annoyance override her professional judgement. 'About an hour ago.'

'I was in *school* an hour ago.'

You mean the *shops* were open an hour ago, thought

Tanith, but she merely raised an eyebrow and pretended to make a note of something on her A4 pad. The attitude wasn't too bad. The look was there. Her heart quickened. Maybe . . .

The girl raised an eyebrow back and Tanith was annoyed to notice that it was better shaped than her own. Threaded, no doubt.

'So, like, what do you want me to read?'

Tanith suppressed a strong desire to snap, 'You can *read*? Well, there's a start.'

There was a knock at the door and a momentary pause – again, not actually long enough for Tanith to say anything welcoming or otherwise – and then, to her surprise, Barney strolled in. He was dressed as if he was auditioning himself, for some manner of James Bond role, in a white shirt, caramel suede jacket and perfectly faded jeans. He was also sporting a pair of wire-rimmed glasses.

'Oh, hi, yeah,' he said without looking up, throwing the words casually in Tanith's approximate direction. He didn't take his eyes off Sophie the Pony Girl who now recrossed her legs like an indecisive flamingo. 'I'm acting in an agent-like capacity here, so I hope you don't mind if I sit in on . . .'

'So you're a teenage actress pimp now, are you?' said Tanith. She put on her scary black-framed glasses. They didn't have lenses in them, but she knew Barney's didn't either.

He looked up with an expression of polite confusion, and registered it was her behind the desk and not the hairy-faced theatre type he'd assumed it would be. A smile spread across his face. 'Oh, *Tanith*! I didn't realize it was one of *your* castings! Hey! What a nice surprise!'

Barney had the same kind of smile as Patrick. When it was genuine, it was like inhaling a glass of whisky. When it was fake, it was just scary – because it had exactly the same disorientating effect.

Today, to Tanith's astonishment, it seemed almost genuine.

She grinned back. A little light relief from Barney was exactly what she needed at the end of a long day.

Pony girl's calves flashed back and forth in a frenzy of leg-crossing.

'Do you two know each other?' she asked. It sounded more like an accusation than a question.

'Is that your audition piece?' asked Tanith in a friendly tone, nodding towards her plaiting legs.

'I beg your pardon?'

Tanith pretended to make some more notes and reflected privately that if Sophie was going to make a habit of getting uptight about women recognizing Barney, then those palomino legs were going to be plaiting like an electric may-pole every time they went out. She smiled to herself.

'Do you want me to read or not?' Sophie asked petulantly. 'Because I have another casting to go to tonight. And some other appointments.'

Tanith flicked an eyebrow up at Barney, despite herself, and in return he raised one corner of his wry mouth. It was hideously unprofessional, but she was coming to the end of her professional resources today, and seeing a face from her out-of-office life was disconcerting. And Sophie should be grateful for the practice – if she was one of Barney's blonde rota girls, then there would be a much more testing audition coming up in Cheyne Walk.

He didn't say anything, but there was a flicker of a pri-vate joke in his eyes, and suddenly Tanith had the distinct, and warm, impression of being included in an adult in-joke – which was incredible, because normally talking to Barney made her feel about a hundred and one, with no way back.

'Fine, well, then I don't want to waste any of your time,' she said to Sophie, and picked up her little Polaroid camera. 'Can I just take a couple of snaps?'

Instantly the girl's nose was pointed to the wall and the chin was raised exactly fourteen degrees. She really needs

Barney standing behind her, lifting up her tail and pointing to her pedigree, thought Tanith.

She clicked the shutter, feeling that the control of the interview was somehow slipping away from her, and caught the photo as it came out. She waved it thoughtfully, waiting for the colours to emerge and confirm what she was beginning to think, that maybe this could be the girl she was looking for.

And that, bizarrely, Barney seemed to be going out with the nearest thing to his own mother that she'd seen for months.

Barney raised an eyebrow, obviously trying to start a silent conversation, but Tanith steeled herself not to respond until she'd decided what to do with Pony Girl. It was odd enough seeing him here, without him starting to flirt with her as well.

Sophie's face floated into focus on the photo and stared accusingly out at her. The two-dimensional version was even more arresting than the real thing, thought Tanith: here was a girl who worked best on film. OK, so the colours were drab, but the cheekbones stood out like razor clams and the eyes were wide but challenging. Tanith felt the twist of excitement in her stomach that she always had when someone fell into the jigsaw hole and fitted.

She propped the photo on the window ledge to dry, next to the twenty-three other Ambers she'd seen today, and picked up the camera again. This casting was killing her, just in film costs. It would be good to draw a line under it. But not too soon. Never let the director think they're there, in case they're not. In case the director's changed and now wants someone shorter, or darker, or maler.

'And again . . .'

The long nose swung back round to face Tanith and pointed to the floor. The eyes squeezed shut, revealing carefully applied arches of butterscotch eyeshadow blended to perfection under the sleek brows.

Tanith paused, her finger on the button. 'Um, can you . . . open your eyes for me?'

The eyes did not open. Instead a cross huff of breath issued forth from the upper-class nostrils. 'You have to count to three, *then* I open them,' she said, as if this was how a hundred million people posed in front of Buckingham Palace. 'It looks more *natural*.'

Tanith wanted to laugh and looked over at Barney, who pulled an exact impression of Sophie's intended second pose: parted lips, wide eyes, a faun recently startled in the woods by a rabid crowd of faun-fanciers. She took a Polaroid of it and Barney laughed aloud, exposing endearing crooked teeth.

How unfair, thought Tanith. On Greg those would look geeky, and yet Greg has perfect teeth and gets no credit for them. On Robert they might be endearing, but his teeth are just as good, though no one knows because he rarely smiles in public. Barney needs his teeth done and it makes him cuter.

At the camera flash, Sophie's head shot up. Her beautifully highlighted blonde mane flowed in one silky mass, framing an expression of annoyance that would have stunned Jeremy Paxman into silence.

'Perfect,' said Tanith and pressed the button again.

'You were meant to count to *three*!' howled Sophie the Pony Girl, now looking more like a Home Counties Mare. 'That is *not* what I look like! I *demand* you take another one!'

'That's showbiz.' Tanith shrugged, dropped her camera into her bag under her desk, and tried not to examine too closely the rising instinct that, although this stroppy and beautiful cow was very probably the ideal Amber, she wanted to show her who was boss in front of Barney.

Tanith swigged the last mouthful of cold coffee out of the paper cup on her desk and dropped the cup in the bin. Suddenly, she just wanted to be at home with her feet in her foot spa and a big glass of wine on the go. Part of being a tough cookie was knowing when to stop. And now, she really wanted to stop.

But Sophie wasn't finished.

'Please?' The look of outrage had miraculously transformed to a charming smile and – Tanith's hand hesitated over her pencil case – was that a hint of self-deprecation in the blue eyes? 'I didn't mean to shout, but you know what it's like seeing horrible pictures of yourself. And when it's for a project that I want as much as this . . .'

Tanith prided herself on being pretty good at seeing through people, but this was something else. Even Barney was looking sympathetic and they *both* knew she was doing it to get her own way.

'It would only take a moment longer, and it would mean so much to me,' Sophie went on persuasively. 'I'll buy you another coffee on the way out if it would cheer you up. In fact, Barney could pop out and get you one now, while we're getting on with it. And you can tell me more about the film.'

Tanith looked at her, and wondered if she had any idea that this was the best audition piece she could be doing. She decided to give her ten minutes. It wasn't as if she was going home to anything more exciting than Robert simultaneously ploughing through Rosetta's accounts and a bottle of Glenmorangie, and her own hesitant attempts to draft the perfect letter to Patrick.

'Barney?' Tanith rested her chin on her steepled hands. 'You know how I take my coffee.'

She was pretty sure he didn't, but it rattled Sophie, who let the mask of pleasantness slip just a crack to let out a pissy expression of panic.

And Barney never let an opportunity pass of reminding his date how lucky she was to be with him for that particular moment.

'I do, indeed, sweetheart. Give me two minutes.'

With another flick of his eyebrows, he slipped out of the door.

'He's so adorable,' said Tanith, just before Sophie could say it.

'Isn't he?'

There was a stand-off silence, in which Tanith knew that Sophie was dying to ask how she knew him, but reluctant to expose her own hand, in case it was weaker.

'So, the film?' said Sophie, all brisk. 'What's it called?'

'Well,' said Tanith, scribbling down the hair flip on her notes as she spoke, 'there's no final title just yet. Or final team. But the funding's all there and there's a lot of buzz about it. Um,' she propped the Polaroid of Barney up on the phone, so Sophie couldn't see the huge brown eyes emerging sexily from the murky background, 'the film's set in London in the late sixties and it's a modern take on all those classic London movies, like *Georgie Girl* and *Billy Liar*, but a bit later. It's about a girl turning into a woman, growing up, going out, losing her innocence along with everyone else when The Beatles split up, learning about life . . .'

'So no plot then?' drawled Sophie, quick as a flash. She scrabbled in her bag for some Marlboro Lights and lit one.

Tanith noted that Sophie's lighter was a fake Cartier, liberally encrusted with Vegas rhinestones, and that the packet was not offered across the table.

She conceded a small shrug. 'Well, the script isn't quite finalized yet. There will be an element of improvisation in it, which is why it's so essential to cast exactly the right people.'

There was a pause.

'Oh, I'm *very* spontaneous,' said Sophie.

'I don't doubt it,' Tanith replied.

Barney's face sharpened into focus on the photograph. Like Rosetta, he was unfairly photogenic, radiating something above and beyond his physical good looks; as though he had another face that could only be seen through a lens.

Tanith shivered. And that was just without the toxic

charm. It was a good job she was going out with his brother. If anyone was the bastard son of a rock-star, why on earth didn't Robert imagine it was Barney?

Because she couldn't think of any more questions to ask that didn't involve quizzing Sophie about Barney and what he was like in real life, she gave her a bit of the script to read. It was Tanith's favourite section of the messy script she'd had so far – a scene in which Amber has a good old row with some rock musician who wants his turquoise love trinkets back to give to a different groupie. From the reading around that she'd started to do, Tanith suspected that it was lifted wholesale from *I'm With The Band* – or an old copy of *Smash Hits* – but it had a nice long section of monologue during which Tanith's time was her own. Repeated readings by increasingly earnest actorinas still hadn't dulled her enjoyment of it, and it was very, very easy to ditch girls within the first two minutes if they couldn't make 'I don't dig your heavy vibe, baby' sound like something a normal person might say in the course of conversation.

Her mind slid back to Patrick's letter, as it did several times an hour, even when she was concentrating on other things. If she did go to see Rosetta about the film (and as yet, she still didn't know how that conversation was meant to go), would she tell her about Patrick's letter? Would she tell her where her oldest son was? It had been one thing telling Patrick he needed to sort things out with his mother, but quite another thing to set her on his trail when he'd gone so far to get away from her. And yet there was no way Rosetta could start revealing all sorts of personal details about her life until she'd told Patrick, was there? She didn't have the right to throw open all sorts of secrets about *his* life without warning him first, even if he had effectively cut himself off from her to keep sane.

Tanith knew she had a responsibility to Patrick, and his privacy. And was it her fault Rosetta hadn't had a proper, honest relationship with her children?

'. . . But darling, you're the only real true soul-spirit I've found in this lifetime,' breathed Sophie with more enthusiasm than she'd mustered so far, and when Tanith's head snapped up in surprise she realized that it was because Barney had returned, balancing two cups of coffee, a copy of the *Independent* and a bunch of pink tulips.

'One full-fat cappuccino with an extra espresso shot.' He placed it carefully on the desk in front of Tanith, then balanced the complimentary chocolate square on the top. 'Have I come back at the right time?'

'Yes, Sophie's just finished.' Tanith resisted the temptation to throw the chocolate for Sophie to catch on her nose. She prised off the lid of the coffee and took a sip, switching off her laptop with the other hand.

'Office looks a bit dull, so I brought you these,' he said. 'Soph, be a sweetheart and stick these in some water while Tanith deboots her computer, or whatever it is you do when you knock off for the day.' He grinned at her.

Is he flirting with me to wind her up? wondered Tanith. Because, to her horror, it was hitting the mark. She tightened her stomach muscles as if that could make him less charming.

'Where's *my* coffee?' whined Sophie, in a voice that promised much more in reserve.

'Now, come on!' said Barney. He batted her affectionately on the head with the newspaper. 'You told me you were detoxing and you weren't going to let anything that wasn't a primary protein past your beestung lips, didn't you? Hmm?'

She screwed up the beestung lips and nodded sulkily.

'Well, then. I took that as a promise, despite my obvious disappointment. Are you all done?' he added, to Tanith, before either of the women could say anything in response.

'We are.' Tanith shut her laptop and put it in her bag.

'We *are*?' said Sophie, her almond eyes narrowing at Tanith.

'I'll give you a ring,' she replied, relieved to have regained control of the audition at last. 'You gave me your CV, didn't you?'

Sophie reached inside her expensive leather document wallet and produced a laser-printed document in a neon pink wallet. It looked like a promotional brochure for a very chi-chi warehouse development, with colour photos and all. 'No, I didn't,' she said, holding Tanith's gaze. 'But here it is.'

She turned to Barney and her manner melted. 'OK, Barns, all done.' She scrabbled in her bag for her Marlboro Lights and hooked an arm through his, tucking her hand into the back pocket of his jeans.

Tanith had a sharp insight into how invisible domestic servants must have felt.

'Are you ready to go then?' cooed Sophie into his ear. In her high boots, her glossy lips were almost level with it.

This girl is perfect, thought Tanith crossly. Damn it. No wonder Rosetta had no real female friends.

'You said you had other appointments after this,' said Barney, innocently.

'I *do*,' said Sophie. Her eyebrows stretched up and out, widening her blue eyes even more. She now looked as if she'd been sketched by Walt Disney, apart from the ciga-rette hanging out of her mouth.

'Well, off you go then.' He patted her on her perfect bottom. 'Give me a call, hey?'

'Barney! We were going to go to—' she hesitated, and Tanith pretended to check her Voicemail. 'Buy that *under-wear*,' she hissed.

'Hey, you don't want to ruin the surprise for me now, do you?' said Barney in a very agreeable tone. 'Biggest element of attack, you know. And to be honest, Soph, I don't think I could stand watching you model bra after bra in Peter Jones. You know what happened last time . . .'

Sophie's fish-eating grin suggested that she did.

'So why don't you run off and do your knicker-shopping and we'll meet up to review it tomorrow? How about that?'

Tanith cut a look from under her eyelashes while flipping pointlessly through her desk diary for tomorrow's appointments. Surely a true Amber would be able to force her boyfriend to go underwear-shopping with her?

Sophie was staring into Barney's amused eyes as hard and as meaningfully as she could, but there was something just too milk and bread in her Palomino make-up to break through Barney's Rosetta-reinforced defences. Tanith could almost see her decision to play harder to get.

'Fine,' she said. 'Well, I might see you tomorrow. It depends. Call me.'

'Good girl,' said Barney, slapping her on the arse again. 'See you soon.' Immediately, he turned back to Tanith and said, 'Tanith, I might be meeting Robert for a quick drink to talk about some new publishing rights Dad's found down the back of his Swiss sofa, so can I interest you in a glass of vino?'

Sophie looked aghast for one unguarded moment, then she strode out without a backward glance, blonde hair bouncing as she pointed her chin in the air with defiance.

Tanith stared at Barney, unable to believe he'd just done what he'd done.

'Glass of vino?' he repeated.

'Well, if you've just blown out company like that for me, how can I refuse?' said Tanith, and tightened her stomach muscles again, but Barney's amazing smile slipped underneath her defences. 'I'll just . . . get my things together.'

'What's that big grin for, hmm?' he said, perching on her desk, as she tried to recover her composure. 'The thought of a sneaky drink, *alone in London* without your boyfriend?'

'Don't flatter yourself.' Tanith allowed him to hold the door open for her. 'It's purely because I think I've cast the damn film at last.'

'Nice girl, Sophie,' said Barney as they walked down the busy street. It had started to spit with rain and the pedestrians were jostling to get to the Tube before the clouds opened.

'Shame about the brain. Still, not that she needs one with legs like that.'

'How did you know how I take my coffee?' asked Tanith, refusing to rise to the bait. 'I don't remember you buying coffee before.'

'I phoned Greg.'

'You phoned *Greg*?' Tanith tried not to let her face betray the intense flattery she felt.

'Well, *come on*. I assumed Robert wouldn't know. I bet you make the coffee for him, don't you? Anyway, he's always *far* too busy to talk. I heard from Rosetta you'd been out shopping with little Gregory, and it's the kind of thing he'd remember. He's like that. Gallant. Or is it that girls are still a novelty to him? Who knows.'

'Who knows indeed,' said Tanith, trying to sound mysterious. No wonder Barney pulled more often than the RAC, going to efforts like that. She wasn't going to tell him, but it was a very good cup of coffee. Whether that was because it *was* how she liked it, or because Barney had that knack of making you believe he'd made it special, she wasn't sure. She hoped he hadn't done it to try to put one over on Greg. 'But how come you'd call him to find out what kind of coffee I drink and yet you don't call him to take him out shopping?'

'Ah, family life. I don't spend as much time obsessing about it as they do. In fact, let's not go there. It's dull, sweetheart.'

'But Rosetta told you about . . . me taking Greg out?' she shot back at him. 'Shopping, I mean?'

Barney grinned and pushed his floppy fringe back off his face. 'Rosetta tells me everything, you know.'

'*Everything*?'

'More than enough, believe me.' There were traces of weariness in his eyes as he said it – or Tanith thought she could see weariness. She corrected herself: Barney, she knew, was a prime example of a charming man women liked to project sensitivity on to because they clearly had absolutely none, though they looked as though they should.

'What are these rights Brian's giving you?' she asked, to change the subject.

'Rights? Oh, sorry, that was a fib,' said Barney. He sipped his coffee. 'I just couldn't think of how to get rid of Sophie, and you know I hate to hurt these girls' feelings by saying I'm getting bored talking about their inner thigh measurements.'

'I don't believe you get bored by that.'

'Well, why talk about it, you know what I mean? You don't buy a Ferrari and then sit around *talking* about the engine, do you?'

Tanith laughed and gave him a gentle shove. 'You're so eighties, Barney. Such an unreconstructed cad.' Then it occurred to her that Robert was out at an evening of Japanese cinema at the National Film Theatre with a client and wouldn't be home until very late, so she could, in theory, be out as long as she liked – and a hot nervous flush of something shivered through her body.

Barney noticed her shiver and gave her a suggestive look, out of habit, putting a firm hand on the small of her back to steer her towards the busy pedestrian crossing.

Tanith was acutely conscious of the faint pressure of his hand. There was a danger about being out with Barney that she hadn't felt with Greg; the feeling that here the situation was more equal, and that made her more responsible for what happened. Or didn't.

You can't road test them *all*, she yelled at herself. They're not different models of the same car! Get a grip, woman!

But she said nothing. Best not to let him know she was on to him and his charm techniques.

'Listen,' he said on the other side of the road, stopping mid-stride as if it had just occurred to him. He put a hand on her arm. 'Do you want something to eat? There's a really good restaurant just opened near me and if we're going to have a drink, we might as well have something to eat.'

Tanith found herself nodding enthusiastically, and made herself slow down. 'That'd be good. I don't have much in the house anyway.' For some reason, she was unable to mention the fact that she knew Robert had a business meeting.

Barney gave her a grin of complicity and Tanith got the distinct impression that she might have picked the wrong model to test drive alone on a wet night.

Not surprisingly, Barney knew a very nice bar in Chelsea which had a happy-hour that stretched obligingly from 5pm to 8pm and waitresses dressed up as French tarts.

'Why are you so besieged with women?' Tanith asked, emboldened by two happy-hour tequilas. 'When your siblings are constantly moaning that they aren't?'

'Well, I don't know about that, they all seem to do all right with you,' said Barney, sliding a maraschino cherry off a cocktail stick with his teeth for maximum innuendo.

'I beg your pardon?' demanded Tanith.

'Sorry, sweetheart, didn't mean to sound *rude*,' he said apologetically. 'I *meant* you're a lovely, intelligent girl, and you've been kind enough to live with that stroppy arsehole Robert for over a year, as well as mad Patrick, who's much better off surrounded by sheep, if you ask me. And you even took Greg out shopping, so they're doing pretty well, I'd say, for a bunch of no-hopers. They just like complaining about it.'

'It's sympathy,' she said, burying her nose in her cocktail glass.

'Well, if they spent more time getting on with their lives, instead of running some kind of in-house football league of misery . . .' Barney's voice trailed off as a trio of blonde girls slid into the bar, and Tanith watched his eyes follow them across the room in the mirror.

'Don't *do* that,' she said. 'Not only is it very insulting to the lady you're with, it makes you look like an upmarket pimp on a recruitment drive.'

His gaze snapped back to her, and he gave her his special double-eye blink, the one that Greg had parodied so perfectly. 'Sorry, sweetheart. Again.'

It was very odd, having a proper conversation with Barney, thought Tanith, like being in a hall of mirrors.

'In fact, I don't know why they hold you up as an example,' she went on tartly. 'You date a string of women, usually several at a time, use them shamelessly, then once they start to get to know you, rather than dump them you just slip out of their lives like a . . . like a greased trout.' She frowned. These tequilas were pretty lethal.

'And what's wrong with that?' he asked, raising his hands ironically. He wasn't sounding nearly drunk enough for Tanith's liking.

'The fact that they're all small-scale models of Rosetta?' she replied in the same tone. 'Your mother?'

Barney's hands dropped and he picked up his drink. 'Now you're getting all scientific where you don't need to. I'm just looking for the right woman, OK? And there are a lot of them to sift through in London.' He drained the glass, caught the barman's attention and ordered another round. 'Sheesh, you clever girls are hard work, aren't you?'

Tanith couldn't help but smile. Written down, Barney's conversation would be truly appalling, yet there was something about the way he delivered his lounge-lizard lines with almost audible quotation marks that made it cheeky. She looked at him sideways, catching him raising his eyebrow at the tallest of the three blondes. He didn't take himself too seriously. That was it. Maybe he alone had learned the knack of playing a part and not being taken over by it.

'Are you always like this?' she asked. 'Even in your private, reflective moments?'

'Don't have them,' said Barney, sipping his drink. 'Unless you're making some shocking clever-girl suggestion about mirrors?' He arched the eyebrow at her.

'No, I am not,' said Tanith.

'Pity.'

She leaned back in her seat, pretending to scan the room in the mirror, but really so she could look at him without being seen.

'You're going to ask me something incredibly dull about my family now, aren't you?' he said, unexpectedly.

Tanith had been wondering how different Rosetta had been at home with him compared to the others, and was startled to hear him read her mind. Their eyes met in the mirror and she looked down. 'Er, no. No, not at all.'

Barney sighed. 'Look, just get it over with, then we can get on with enjoying this evening and pretending that we're having a very exciting clandestine affair. What did you want to know?'

'What Rosetta was like as a mother. When it was just you at home. Twenty words or less.'

It's research, Tanith told herself. I need to know for Robert.

He rolled his eyes. 'Oh, for God's . . . Listen, in spite of everything you may have heard, she was –' Barney tapped the table with his coaster, 'and I can't stress this enough – no better and certainly no worse than all the other leather-trouser stay-at-home mummies that did the school run in Chelsea, OK? That's why Robert has no time for me – I don't have the excuse of road-trauma, or post-divorce shock; it's always been me and Rosetta at home, and that's just the way I am. She didn't have boyfriends that I knew about, in fact I don't think she had *any* that I met. She was a bit loopy, and she used to walk around naked sometimes, and she always had her own ideas about what was suitable conver-sation for a seven-year-old boy, but there were no drug-crazed orgies while I was at home, I can assure you. More's the pity.'

'Lucky you,' said Tanith. 'The way Robert tells it, growing up on the road put him off drugs for life.'

'No, being the world's youngest pensioner did that, not

Rosetta. The worst thing she did, as far as I'm concerned . . .' He gave her an odd look. 'I can't believe you've even got me discussing this now. You should be charging for it.'

She shrugged. 'Maybe I am.'

He smiled wryly. 'Well, since we're getting it off our chests . . . I hated the way she's always different with all of us. Like she couldn't be herself. So we never knew where we were and that was . . . hard, sometimes. And when we're all together, to save confusion, she resorts to this near parody of a bad mother that Robert seems to have invented for her. God knows which version of herself she's going to choose to write about in her book.'

Tanith stared closely at Barney. His pretty face had gone very sad and hard around the eyes. With a jolt, she realized that she didn't know him at all, and yet she was encouraging him to tell her things that she wouldn't necessarily confide in the Samaritans. 'Why does he do that though?'

Barney shrugged. 'When it was just me at home, and Dad had left, and she had less and less to do, she just went to pieces a bit. She might have got drunk a few times, I don't know. There might have been discreet pills – all prescribed of course. She didn't have a lot of friends. Maybe she made some drunken phone-calls to Robert. Rosetta needs to have roles,' he explained. 'Otherwise she gets confused.'

'*She's* confused?' Tanith exploded, rather more emphatically than she'd have liked, had she been sober.

'I don't live my life within this big family myth, you know. And she's not as bad as Robert thinks, not really,' said Barney. 'I don't really understand why he has such a downer on her.'

'He likes things to be normal, and she's not.'

'Well . . .' Barney smiled to himself. 'There's normal and there's normal. Drama is normal in our house. When I was a kid, Rosetta used to get drunk with her friend Anita in her attic – normal – and then the two of them would get dressed up in Rosetta's old clothes – normal – which were Gucci

and Pucci and Quant.' He paused. '*Not* normal. And they'd
bring me up there with them and dress me up too.'

'Not normal!' said Tanith.

He looked down into his glass, which was empty. 'Can we
get out of here? I think happy-hour's just ended.'

They skipped supper, and walked in the direction of the
river, since the rain had stopped, and talked about anything
other than Rosetta; of all four Mulligan brothers, Tanith
decided, conscious of how impossible it was to judge them
individually, Barney was without doubt the easiest to talk to.

He had a way of listening, of repeating the last thing you'd
said to prove he'd been paying attention, and not immediately relating it back to his own experience the way Greg
did. Or challenging it, the way Robert did. Barney listened
and gave you that smile that reached his gorgeous eyes, and
responded with something interesting and witty. It must have
been all the practice he got at home, alone with an adoring
and demanding mother. Who sometimes walked around
naked.

Even if he had a paper bag on his head, Barney would still
pull because he knew how to talk to women.

The cocktails insulated them both against the chill in the
evening air as they strolled around Chelsea, chatting easily.
Tanith was relaxed almost to the point of forgetting he was
a Mulligan brother, or that he was actually five years
younger than she was. They discussed the films she'd worked
on, and the houses they walked past, and mutual friends,
until Tanith felt the first spot of rain touch her forehead, and
a mute shock of disappointment struck her, that now she'd
have to hail a passing taxi home and end the evening.

'Ah, I hope it's not going to rain again,' she said, and as
the words left her mouth, the grey sky opened and fat raindrops began to drench the pavement, splitting apart the
lights reflected in the river.

Barney laughed at the tipsy dismay on her face and

grabbed her hand. 'Come on, I know somewhere we can go!' he said, and started to jog off in the direction of the houses.

Tanith recognized the nearby streets as being at the other end of Cheyne Walk from Rosetta's and her heart sank still further at the prospect of being dragged in for an unexpected audience, but Barney's hand was firm in hers and she found herself jogging after him, though she didn't really know how she was managing it in her high-heeled boots on the greasy pavements.

Barney slipped down some side passages between houses, urging her on as if she were at a pony club point-to-point as her heels clicked like little hooves. Tanith could feel the rain slicking down her hair and making her mascara run, but she couldn't help laughing at the sheer stupidity of what she was doing.

I really must stop getting drunk with Robert's brothers, she thought.

Just as she was about to protest that enough was enough, Barney pulled her down an alleyway and arrived at some garages.

'I didn't know there were garages round here,' said Tanith, staggering a bit as she came to a halt.

'Can't leave the Porsche on the street, sweetheart,' said Barney. He was fiddling with his Swiss penknife, choosing a blade.

Tanith looked up into the sky, then shut her eyes and let the raindrops fall on her face. The rain wasn't slacking off but the air was fresher than she'd felt it for some time and it was nice. She felt pleasantly irresponsible. 'What the hell are you doing?' she said, surprised that she wasn't crosser.

'I'm breaking into a garage so we can get out of the wet,' replied Barney. 'Would you like to select a garage?'

Tanith stared at him. The cold was beginning to bite through her wet jacket, which she realized now wasn't as warm as she'd thought. 'You're going to burgle a garage?'

'OK, I'll choose for you. How about this one?' He started to pick the padlock on the nearest door.

Tanith folded her arms. 'Now, don't tell me there are no bars around here that we could have—'

'Oh, where's your sense of fun?' demanded Barney, and Tanith had to admit that it was unexpectedly exciting, to be breaking and entering in an area that almost certainly had twenty-four-hour police coverage. So what if Robert would go berserk if he knew what they were doing? It wasn't like –

'There!' Barney pulled off the padlock and rolled up the garage door, extending an arm. 'After you. But hurry up, it's pissing down.'

Inside it was dark but quite warm and Tanith, groping her way forward, knocked her shin against a chrome bumper.

She wasn't entirely surprised to feel Barney's arm slide round her waist to steady her as she lurched forward. It slipped down to caress the curve of her hip and then returned to explore her waist.

'No, I don't think so,' she said, before her body could come up with an alternative response.

The hand lingered, confident and firm, holding her upright. Tanith had read enough of Robert's bathroom magazines to know how sexy being seduced over the bonnet of a car would be.

For the bloke, if not for her.

'You're sure?' murmured Barney persuasively. His breath was hot on her cold ear.

'Yes,' squeaked Tanith, meaning, 'No, not sure at all.'

Barney sighed and switched on the lights. 'Fair enough.'

Tanith blinked in the sudden brightness and was impressed by a garage larger than some flats she'd looked at before she moved in with Robert. There were two cars parked in it; a new Golf GTI and, the one her tights were currently being ruined by, a beautiful cream sports-car. She looked closely at the badge on the bonnet. It was a Lotus. A Lotus Elan.

'*Barney*,' she said, turning to him with a smile on her lips.
'What?'

'When you said, break into a garage . . . why didn't you just use your keys?'

'I don't know what you mean.' He affected a look of hurt pride.

'Oh, come on.' Tanith got her compact out of her bag and started to repair the damage to her make-up so he wouldn't see how dark and dilated her pupils were. 'I know whose garage this is.'

'Do you, now?' said Barney, then gave up and towelled off his hair on a big yellow duster. 'Oh well. Suppose the hundred per cent strike rate had to end somewhere.'

'This works on most girls, does it?'

Barney searched in his pockets for his keys. 'Every time, sweetheart. The combination of the petty burglary, the romantic area, the sexy car . . .' He gave her his best puppy dog sigh. 'I should have known you're just too high-class to fall for it, but can you blame me for trying?'

'I'm flattered that you did.'

More than that, Tanith's conscience protested. *Did you see what you nearly did? Again? Is it horrible, realizing that you weren't quite the morally reliable person you thought you were?*

In self-defence she reminded her conscience that it wasn't *normal* to have the attention of so many good-looking men all at once.

At all, in fact.

At least she could make little mistakes and keep them buried. For a moment, she had real sympathy for Rosetta, surrounded by rock-stars and glamorous people who didn't run their love-lives according to any kind of recognizable high-street morality. Could Robert actually be right about his multiple paternity theory? A moment of weakness like this, under the guise of research or homage or drunken 'no one'll notice' delusion, that Rosetta thought she could keep secret under the cover of her marriage – but with the most permanent reminders of all?

'Fancy a lift home, then?' asked Barney. He bleeped the Golf open with his key-ring.

Tanith shook herself, trying to get back to her normal personality. 'Well, are you OK to drive?'

'I'm fine. You were the one knocking back the booze, honey.' He grinned. 'It looked like you really wanted to get drunk on your night off. Come on, get in.'

He could be much worse, thought Tanith, feeling chilly as the last traces of rebellion left her and the prospect of going home to an empty house and finding piles of dirty washing still strewn all over the bed marched back in their place. A few more minutes of flattering, non-parental company couldn't hurt.

She opened the passenger side door. There were CDs racked neatly in every possible space, Starbucks coffee cups in the footwell, and it smelled of mints. 'I assume this is Rosetta's?' she said. 'She doesn't mind you driving it?'

'No. As long as I don't breathe on the Lotus.' Barney got in and started the engine. 'None of us are allowed to touch that, it's a shrine to her lost youth, all parked up and out of petrol.'

'That's enough about Rosetta, thank you,' said Tanith. 'For some reason she's starting to feel more like an ex-girl-friend than a mother-in-law.'

Barney turned to her in all seriousness. 'You're the one bringing her up the whole time. Do you have some kind of a problem – with mothers in general maybe?'

'Barney,' said Tanith, wearily. 'Just drive me home, please.'

Chapter Twenty-eight

Clerkenwell, 2001

Robert had already got up and gone into work by the time Tanith's alarm went off, and she lay for a few moments in the warm bed, feeling the dent where his body had been and remembering what it was like to wake up alone in a bed that only she had slept in. She had been asleep long before he left his study last night and slipped into bed; so fast asleep she hadn't even been woken by his night-talking. Or maybe, she thought guiltily, he hadn't slept much. Tanith rolled over, trying to enjoy the space in the bed, but to her surprise she missed Robert's warm bulk and, finding no pleasure in dozing on alone, she got up.

He had left a note propped up against his new Porsche kettle (Robert was very feminine in his habit of comfort-shopping for kitchen appliances), apologizing for using up all the milk and reminding her that he was going to drop Rosetta's accounts off that evening, so wouldn't be back for supper.

Tanith stood and ate a piece of toast since she couldn't have cereal, looking at the note and feeling the cold tiles chill her bare feet. Energy was bubbling through her with a power she hadn't felt in months and she decided that today must be a new moon, because it felt like time to sort everything out.

She went straight into the office and faxed Sophie's CV to the director before she took her coat off, ignoring all Lily-Jo's bitching about what kind of actresses put publicity shots of themselves in bikinis and ski suits on the front of their CVs.

If Sophie didn't meet with the director's approval, there was always Lily-Jo, Tanith thought, watching her gesture meanly with her coffee-cup and cast wild aspersions about Sophie's Paris acting workshops. She could really see her in the scene in which Amber systematically destroyed the will to live of two photographers and a journalist.

'I mean, Jacques Le Coq, please! What is this, nineteen-seventy-two? Are you sure you've found the right one?' asked Lily-Jo, reaching the end of her tirade.

'There isn't *a* right one,' said Tanith. 'There are lots of right ones. It's up to them who they go for. Would you like me to fax your CV too? I'm going to be talking to the director this morning.'

Lily-Jo looked shifty and poured Tanith a cup of coffee from the machine. Tanith noticed that she was wearing a suit – albeit one with a very short skirt.

'Um, no, don't bother,' she said, with a winning smile. 'I've been having a period of career reassessment, and I'm not sure that acting is really the avenue I want to pursue.'

'You want my job,' said Tanith, taking the cup.

'Your *old* job,' Lily-Jo corrected her. 'And maybe I don't want to be an actress after seeing the way Frances talks about them.'

Tanith went over to her desk and flicked through her Rolodex to find the number of the Amber director. 'Frances is a lovely woman to work for, from an actor's point of view. Believe me, there are many worse casting directors.'

'No one likes to live knowing how disposable they are,' said Lily-Jo darkly. 'It's karma suicide.'

'Hello, can I speak to Marcus?' said Tanith. 'Yes, I'll hold.' She covered the mouthpiece. 'Lily? Can you make me some fresh coffee, please? And you're sure about . . .?'

'Very sure, thank you,' said Lily and disappeared into the kitchen with a pristine copy of *The Road Less Travelled*.

After some circular conversation about the remainder of the casting deadlines, Tanith eventually wheedled out the information she needed. No, the film was not a biography, but yes, the screenplay was written by someone around in the seventies. No, it was still being worked on with a team of established writers helping the author and yes, that author was Sue Morton-Thomas.

To which Tanith could add for herself that, yes, that was the sound of an axe being ground; no, Sue hadn't told Rosetta what she was up to when she commissioned that book; and probably, there was every chance she wanted to borrow bits of Rosetta's autobiography for the film. Or at the very least, use it as a cash-in project when the film came out.

Sophie and her giraffe-legs were apparently perfect and they would be arranging a meeting as soon as possible.

'Lily!' she yelled when she put the phone down. 'Lily, forget the coffee, darling! I'm going out!'

Tanith rang the bell with more confidence than she felt and adjusted her scarf so it looked more casual. She didn't buy into this whole idea of treating Rosetta like she was some combination of the Queen Mother and Coco Chanel, but even so, she'd felt a slight twinge of regret that she hadn't worn a better pair of shoes to work that morning.

She's just a *woman*, she thought to herself. Since when have people's reputations bothered you? Besides which, all this transferred hysteria only came from Robert.

And Greg.

And Patrick.

She's never been *directly* rude to you, Tanith reminded herself sternly. Although if she knew what you nearly did on her sports-car . . .

She shook herself and her blonde hair fell into her eyes. And you're about to do her a big favour. Maybe.

The door opened very quickly, and Tanith was mildly

surprised to see Rosetta had answered it herself. She was taller than she remembered, somehow more solid, and was evidently in the middle of baking as she had a spotless apron over her grey wool dress.

'Hello, Tanith,' she said with immaculately polite enthusiasm. 'How nice to see you.'

'Hello,' said Tanith, unsettled by the apron. 'I'm sorry to pop round without calling, but I, er . . . I wondered if I could have a word?'

'Of course,' said Rosetta and let her in.

It's as easy as that?

'Listen, I didn't meant to interrupt,' said Tanith, allowing Rosetta to shepherd her down a small flight of stairs into the vast kitchen.

The big central table was piled with flour and eggs and bowls and scales, three cookery books and tins. Tanith felt oddly disconcerted. Rosetta – in a kitchen?

They both stood and looked at the debris for a couple of seconds.

'I don't know,' said Rosetta. A smile twitched at the corner of her mouth. 'It's a bit late for me to learn to make bread at my age, don't you think? Especially when there's a fabulous bakery round the corner. Oh, sod it.' She untied her apron and pulled it carefully over the loose bun at the nape of her neck. 'It's a cycle I go through – every so often I try to acquire the skills that might have made me a better mother, you know? Baking, knitting, window-boxes . . .' She balled up the apron and threw it towards the stainless steel washing machine. 'But no matter how hard I try . . .'

'I don't hear any of them complaining about the lack of fresh bread rolls in their childhood,' said Tanith mildly.

'Let's go upstairs,' said Rosetta.

She led the way up the wide staircase to her big drawing-room and as Tanith followed her she noted for her own reference what a skill it was to be more relaxed than the other person. It immediately put them at their ease, and also at a disadvantage. It was Rosetta's composure, more than anything she said, that was so impressive, and she must have learned it from a master.

The last strong beams of winter afternoon sunshine were flooding the room, reflecting off the mirrors and framed photos until everything glittered like a child's musical box. Rosetta drew a couple of curtains across the long windows to stop the glare, turned on a table lamp and sank into the big velvet sofa like a cat, looking up at Tanith with an expectant smile.

Tanith chose a chair opposite and wondered why she was still so nervous, when Rosetta had been more than charming to her so far.

'So,' said Rosetta, in a friendly voice. 'What's to do? Are you having trouble with Robert? I wouldn't blame you if you were, but I'm afraid I don't know any instant cure.'

Tanith shaded her eyes from the sun. 'Well, I'm hoping he's going to go back to normal after he drops your accounts off tonight.'

'He's finished? Already?'

'He's been working on them every night for about ten days,' explained Tanith, 'usually until two or three in the morning. What he doesn't know about your bank details now . . .'

Rosetta gave her a funny look and sighed. 'Oh God, he's missed the point again, hasn't he? It wasn't just the ins and outs columns I wanted him to balance, you know. I had hoped . . . since Robert does tend to see things only in terms of straight lines of figures, it might give him a more realistic picture of . . . well, me. Via my finances, if that's possible.'

'I know,' said Tanith, 'I realize that. I think he does now. Sort of.' She cast her mind back to the final reckoning Robert had done. He had been very subdued last night, going through the files relating to the years Rosetta had been at home alone with Barney, and hadn't troubled the coffee-grinder at all. Lots of therapy fees, far fewer restaurant bills,

endless school fees – not much to support his favourite car-
icature of Rosetta the heartless party girl. 'I imagine he'll
want to . . . talk to you when he comes over with them
tonight.'

'That's why you're here now? The advance warning
party?'

Tanith nodded automatically, then shook her head.

There was something about Rosetta that you couldn't help
agreeing with. Unless you were Robert, in which case the
exact opposite was true. Barney's charm, again.

'Well, not really,' she said, trying to drag her own personality to the forefront of her mind. 'I thought you'd probably
want to see him on your own. I'm sure there's a lot of . . .
background detail to go through.'

'You're a very sensitive girl, aren't you?' remarked
Rosetta. She picked a clementine out of the stacked fruit
bowl and started to peel it with her short red nails. She put
the little scabs of peel on the glass table. 'Maybe too sensitive
for him.'

'Look, I don't really know how to broach this, and it
might not be any of my business,' Tanith began tentatively,
'but I thought you should know that I've been casting a film
for the last few months, and . . .' She frowned. It did sound
rather tenuous now she had to speak it aloud. 'And from
what Robert's told me, and Greg, it sounds as though Sue
Morton-Thomas is writing a film about you.'

'About me?' Rosetta's face broke out into a wide smile.
'Sue's writing a film about me? I doubt it, darling!' She
popped a segment of clementine in her mouth. 'I'll bet you
anything the heroine is a studious yet passionate journalist,
who starts out a plain Jane and, through the miracle of
slimming pills and hard work, ends up . . .' She caught the
expression on Tanith's face and stopped. 'She isn't, is she?
Oh dear. The heroine is a manipulative bitch who drains the
life out of others like so many glasses of champagne. Tell me,
does it end very badly?'

Tanith grimaced wryly and nodded. 'Sorry. Um, there are quite a few location shots in the Priory. And I haven't seen the whole script yet.'

'Classy.'

'I thought you should know. The end isn't finalized, I don't think,' said Tanith, hurriedly. 'But I was told specifically that any actress I found should be . . . I think, "comfortable with nudity" was the phrase they used. It, er, did cross my mind, as an outsider, that Sue might be wanting to use some material from your book, so . . .' Her voice trailed off.

Rosetta ate two more segments thoughtfully. Tanith thought she could make out a flicker of sadness behind her eyes, but the rest of her face remained calm, mildly amused.

'Darling, it's very sweet of you to come over to warn me, but if Sue's writing a film, I think she's got plenty of material of her own. More than enough. Clementine?' She offered the bowl over.

Tanith shook her head.

'No,' Rosetta went on, 'it's more likely that the crafty bitch is thinking of the tie-in possibilities when the film comes out. What a coup for her – to stitch me up in the film, and then make money out of the tell-all biography. *My Life With Rosetta* and then *My Life By Rosetta*. *God*.' She pulled the long pin out of her hair and shook out the coil, then messed it up with her hands, pushing it back off her face with a grimace. Immediately, she looked younger. 'They all make their money out of me, and that's the honest truth. Still, I suppose I can't complain, living here with all this. And they earned it.'

'How is it going, the book?' asked Tanith. 'It must be hard, knowing where to start.'

Rosetta nodded. 'It is hard. It's *very* hard, because when your whole life's been parading across the papers you forget what people know and what they don't. And what they know that isn't actually true. I have trouble remembering sometimes.'

It sounded good but Tanith bet she didn't. She bet Rosetta remembered every tiny slight, even if she didn't do anything about it right away.

'I've had a very ... very emotional couple of months,' Rosetta said, 'making myself see all sorts of things I've tried not to see for years, and it's *painful*, you know, realizing that you haven't always been the person you wanted to be. Or thought you were, with the benefit of hindsight. I suppose that's why I wanted the boys to help me – I needed to see myself through their eyes. And to do that, I *suppose*, I thought I needed to make them see me as just a woman, not some mythical mother figure. Course, I hadn't reckoned on quite how little they actually saw me as *any* kind of mother figure.'

'And have they been any help?'

'I'm not sure yet.'

There was a pause. Rosetta finished her clementine. 'I thought I'd seen the full scale of my failure as a mother, but I have a sinking suspicion that it was just the tip of the iceberg.' She made it sound flip, but Tanith could hear a hollowness in her voice, as if she didn't get the chance to confide very often. 'I just wanted them to see how much *fun* it was. But it didn't quite work out that way, did it?'

'There are a couple of things I wanted to give you,' said Tanith, reaching for her handbag. 'I wasn't sure you'd want them to go to the accountants with everything else.'

She took out a manila envelope and handed it to Rosetta, who opened it and slid out some bits of paper.

Tanith watched her, not sure whether she hadn't perhaps made a mistake, gone too far.

Rosetta looked at the first sheet of paper, an invoice from a private clinic, and screwed her eyes up tightly, as if someone had shone a bright light in them.

'I don't think Robert could work out what it was for,' said Tanith softly. 'I think he thought it was you.'

Rosetta shook her head. 'No, it wasn't for me.' She looked

up and tears were sparkling around the corners of her eyes like tiny Swarowski crystals. 'God, I haven't seen this in twenty years.' She swallowed and folded the page so she didn't have to see it. 'You know who it was for?'

Tanith had to lean forward to catch the whisper, but nodded. She'd been scrolling through the Internet while Robert had been sorting the accounts in his study. 'John?'

Rosetta wiped the tears out of the corner of her eyes and pressed her lips together. 'Yes, John. John's . . . hospital fees. He was a hopeless smack addict, you know. I mean, hopeless as in he just wasn't very good at it. He was too robust, and it got into his head more than into his body, if you know what I mean. By the end, he was so messed up that I think he wanted to punish himself more than anyone else could, and – added bonus – smack also put him to sleep so he didn't have to deal with all the things he felt bad about.' She sighed.

'Like you?'

'No, he never felt *bad* about me. He loved me too much to feel bad. But he knew it was wrong, and I suppose he pushed a lot of that on to other things.'

'Did he get through rehab?' asked Tanith and saw Rosetta's face register sharp pain like a slap.

But she still answered. 'Yes, he did, amazingly enough. He loved it. Loved the idea of repenting in a big group.' Rosetta laughed quietly. 'You know about his overdose in Dallas, when we cancelled the tour?'

Tanith nodded.

'Well, Brian flew him back on an emergency flight the same night, got him checked in and left him. I don't know what I did. I have a total blank about that. Anita told me later that she had taken me away, because I was acting like a zombie in front of the kids and Patrick started bedwetting again. She took me to Marrakech, apparently. And when I got back, Brian was in negotiation with Red about setting up a hands-off tour logistics agency, and John had done so well in rehab that he checked himself out.'

She went silent and Tanith waited for her to finish. When Rosetta said nothing more and reached for another clementine, Tanith couldn't help prompting. 'And?'

Rosetta started to peel, digging her short nails into the fruit and dragging the skin away. 'And nothing. He vanished. Of course I tried to look for him, but he'd disappeared. I became really obsessive about guitar auctions, in case any of his guitars came up, but they never did, and . . .' She stopped and put a piece of clementine in her mouth.

'Do you think he's still alive?' asked Tanith as kindly as she could.

'He had one guitar that he really loved,' said Rosetta softly. 'The old Gibson he had when he first came to London, the one he auditioned for the group with. It was red – cherry sunburst – the sexiest guitar I'd ever seen. He wouldn't let a guitar tech touch it, he loved it so much. And he left it behind.' She pressed her lips together. 'John could never have lived without music. If he was going away to start a new life, I know he'd have taken that guitar, but he left it behind. For me. It's in my room now, in a cupboard. I can't bear to look at it.'

'You must have loved him very much,' said Tanith, cringing immediately at the insufficiency of the words.

'John was the one *perfect* love of my life,' said Rosetta. 'I mean, I loved Brian too, but not the same way. You can love more than one person at once, I'm sure, but at different levels. The heart is a very stretchy one-size-fits-all garment. *However*, I think once in your life you meet someone that you fit with perfectly, and it's really up to you what you do with that. But . . .' She raised her eyebrows and looked at her hands.

'But?' prompted Tanith.

'But we just couldn't make it right in our heads.' Rosetta pulled a disbelieving face. 'It sounds so funny to say that, when everyone thinks of the Sixties as the great free love decade. Which isn't to say that we . . . stopped doing it. How could we? I was on the road with him for nine years on and off. On the road, I was John's, off the road, I was Brian's. You'd be amazed at how these things work out. But all the time it was happening, we couldn't ever square it with the kind of morality we wanted to believe we had, deep down, so when the papers all said I was a trollop and a hooker, I just let them, because it meant that I could be someone else in private and the papers wouldn't bother looking.' She snorted softly. 'I was embarrassingly naïve.'

'And Brian?'

Rosetta gave the invoice back to Tanith and raised her eyebrow. 'That invoice for John's medical treatment – have a look: whose name is it in?'

Tanith looked. 'Yours.'

'Mine, yes? Well, I was in Marrakech at the time, being spoon-fed yoghurt by Anita, darling. Brian paid that bill. But he made damn sure the invoice came to me, in my name, so I'd be reminded what I'd done. What the price to pay was. He could be very cruel like that.'

'But it must have been *impossible* for him, wasn't it?' demanded Tanith. 'Didn't he care that his wife was . . . That his wife loved someone else, someone he worked with, *lived* with?'

That was part of Robert's problem, she was sure – that Brian had never gone for Rosetta about John. And in his head, Robert, with his brutal sense of order and justice, was doing it for him, day in and day out, every time he saw her.

No wonder your sons are either hopelessly passive or manically manipulative in relationships, she wanted to scream.

Rosetta sighed. 'Oh, I don't think he minded as much as you'd think, not really. Darling, Brian's gay. Or bi, I'm not sure which he'd prefer to call it.'

Tanith's face froze. That she hadn't expected. '*Is* he?'

Rosetta nodded. 'Mmm. He loved John just like I did, only he never wanted to do anything about it. Just liked being near him while I did all the things he probably dreamed of doing. Not all bisexual men have limp wrists and like Shirley Bassey.'

'Do the boys know?'

She shook her head. 'Well, there's nothing *to* know. I know Brian – he's far too establishment to turn himself into Elton John at this stage of the game. I think he's more or less decided that it's all too messy, that side of life. He has his art collection and his management companies. It's funny, when you think about it.' Rosetta smiled, some of her archness restored. 'We would make a very good old married couple now – both worn out by love, looking for quiet companionship and someone to argue about the television with. Not so different from lots of couples in Esher, I'd say.'

The sun had set now, and the streetlights flickered on outside. Rosetta leaned over and switched on another table light, but didn't shut the curtains.

'I like to watch the evening set in,' she explained, gesturing towards the purpling sky with her long fingers. 'The sky reminds me of those mood stones, you remember? Or is that before your time? The ones that changed colour on your skin to tell you what mood you were in?'

'Do you ever think about getting back with Brian?' asked Tanith.

Rosetta shook her head. 'I like being on my own too much now. I have this lovely house, no one to tell me what to do, how much to spend on flowers . . . you know. It's nice.'

Tanith knew she was lying. The hollowness had crept back into her voice. 'What about someone else? You're *far* too young to be on your own.'

'Darling, I'm all used up,' laughed Rosetta. She fluffed up a cushion. 'I can't see the *point* in starting all over again, knowing I can't . . . knowing I can't have a love like that again. Besides, I've got my boys, haven't I, and they're enough to be going on with for emotional drama.'

Tanith gave her a searching look, unable to decide how

dangerous the ground was beneath her feet. Rosetta had let her say some pretty frank things, but discussing the boys was something else. But she had come here to be frank, she reminded herself, and what did *she* have to lose?

'I don't think that's necessarily a good thing,' she said, as neutrally as she could.

'And why do you think that, darling?'

'Because they're all in love with you, and since there's no man there to look after you, they all think they have to step into the breach. And they'll never leave, and you'll be stuck with them when they're forty, all complaining that they can't find the perfect woman.'

Tanith helped herself to a clementine to give herself something to occupy her hands. And because Rosetta couldn't hit a guest peeling an orange on her velvet sofa.

She studied Rosetta's face for signs of outrage, or indignation, but didn't find any. She just looked very sad and lonely, sitting curled up on her velvet throne.

'You know, you're not just sensitive, but clever too,' Rosetta said at last. 'You're probably right. We're not so dissimilar, are we, you and I? And that little Oprah theory would all work, too, if it wasn't for the fact that they think I'm utterly monstrous.'

'I don't know why they think that,' admitted Tanith. 'You seem perfectly reasonable to me. Unless you do it on purpose. So they don't see how scared of them you are.'

'Maybe I do,' Rosetta agreed. 'Would you believe I have never had this conversation in all these years? How interesting it's turning out to be.'

Tanith remembered something Robert had once said about Rosetta deliberately surrounding herself with less smart people, so she could always be the smartest. *That must have got so lonely*, she thought, with a pang of pity.

'Why didn't you explain all this to the boys?' asked Tanith. 'They're not so messed up that they wouldn't understand.'

'Well, I don't know. There's never really a good time for something like that. There was never a moment that felt right. And I was too proud to admit that I'd made a mistake and fucked it all up for them, *depriving* them of a father. Yes, I was scared of them. I *am* scared of them, especially Robert.' Rosetta picked at her nail varnish and smiled ruefully. 'True story – there was some early morning feature on TV-AM some time in the eighties, going on about how you could sue your parents in the States for not being good enough. Three hours later, I get a phone call from Julian, our lawyer, asking if I could come down to his offices and pick Robert up because he's trying to serve papers on me and Brian.'

'He's a very angry young man,' said Tanith, 'and it's *me* that has to deal with that anger, *all the time*. I don't know if I can . . .' She stopped herself. 'It's not easy, you know, especially when neither of us really understand where it's coming from. I wish you'd sort it out. I think only you can. You and him together.'

'Poor Robert.' Rosetta looked genuinely miserable. 'I must have been pumping guilt through the umbilical cord. He's been trying to make up for something ever since he came into this world, hasn't he? All my fault. I fucked that one up even *before* my dubious parenting came into play.'

'Guilt?' said Tanith, curiously. 'What do you mean?'

'Oh . . . do the dates!' Rosetta ran her hands through her hair. 'I thought I could, I don't know, *make up* for my terrible indiscretion to Brian by having a little girl – and he turned out to be Robert. And it didn't help anyway, as it turned out.'

'Make it up to Brian?' Tanith stared at her, afraid to get it wrong. 'You mean Patrick really *is* John's son?'

There was an affirmative pause.

'Oh, God. I thought that was just Robert being delusional,' said Tanith. 'Because he hated Patrick. Not because he was . . .'

'Of *course* he's John's son!' wailed Rosetta, finally losing her self-control. The years slipped off her face in the half-light now filling the room and Tanith could see a very young, very distressed woman, struggling to find words for a pain that gripped her whole body. 'That's why it breaks my *heart* that he's not here! I feel like I sent away the one person in the world who could make up for losing John, not intentionally, but because I didn't want him to suffer like his father had. *That* was the punishment for breaking rules and not being a good little housewife. Not losing John, not breaking up my marriage, not being humiliated in the newspapers . . .'

Tanith could see the pain etched on her face where there were never lines in the daylight.

'He was the result of my little bargain with the devil. I thought, if everyone was saying what a loose woman I was, why shouldn't I have the fun of being with John in return? I worked *so hard*. And for a while it worked out, but you can't split yourself up into multiple personalities for ever. In the end, I didn't even have *Patrick*,' Rosetta said, in a voice husky with pain. 'And neither of us had John.'

She hugged her knees up to her chest. 'Patrick used to run off all the time when he was little, but I always found him. The child psychologist said he only did it so I would come for him, but the older he got, the more I realized he did it because he couldn't live with us, any of us. Then when he left home and just never came back, a little bit of me stayed exactly where it was, just frozen there in time. Because if I could have made things work with Patrick, then there might have been some hope for everything else, and I kept going back there in my head, trying to see how I could have made things right, over and over again. I tried so hard not to have favourites, but how could he not be? And now he could be alive or dead, and the only way he can live is by cutting himself off from me.'

Tanith sat in silence, letting Rosetta's ragged breathing fill the room. She didn't know what to say, and certainly couldn't bear to mention her own secret knowledge of Patrick's whereabouts, in case it hurt Rosetta even more, but after a few seconds she couldn't bear the grief that was flooding across the room, and she slipped over to the sofa and put her arms around her.

Rosetta's body was surprisingly fragile, and Tanith could feel the sobs shaking her inside, and the effort she was making not to let them out.

What was more important – Patrick's independence and privacy, or Rosetta's sanity?

In the end, it wasn't hard to make the decision.

'Rosetta,' she said, 'I've got something else for you.' She took a folded piece of paper out of her bag and passed it to her.

Rosetta opened it and frowned, not recognizing the address written on it.

'That's where Patrick is,' Tanith explained. 'Go and see him. Tell him all this, explain. You need to.'

'But he doesn't want to see me,' said Rosetta. 'I can't force him.' She looked more closely at Tanith. 'And how do you know where he is?'

Tanith shook her head. 'It doesn't matter. He thinks he's sorted himself out, but he can't, not without talking to you. And there's no way you can begin to write your life story until you've worked out who you are when you're not pretending to be someone else.' She paused. 'Escapism – that's the really addictive thing, isn't it?'

'Yes,' said Rosetta. 'It is.'

There didn't seem to be anything else to say on the matter, for which Tanith was grateful, and they sat for a while, eventually quite comfortably, listening to the traffic along the Embankment and watching the police helicopters cut across the dark sky.

'Rosetta?' said Tanith, after a while. 'If I ask you something, will you give me an honest answer?'

Rosetta hesitated, then said, 'OK.' She braced herself. 'We'll call it book practice.'

'*Is* it you Paul McCartney's talking about on "Get Back"? You know, in the studio chat?'

Rosetta let out an unexpected and generous laugh that came from deep within her and echoed in the high-ceilinged room. 'Oh, Tanith, you're *too* funny! Is it me on the "Get Back" tapes!' She giggled to herself. 'Those "Get Back" sessions . . . God, I don't know.'

Tanith saw a glimmer of sadness cross her face, but it disappeared as soon as Rosetta tensed her jaw against it.

'There you go,' she went on, 'there's a perfectly honest answer: I don't know. I can *prove* nothing . . . But I will say no more than that.'

'So why do you put those girls through it if you don't know yourself?' demanded Tanith.

'Because . . .' Rosetta's face darkened and it looked for a moment as if her mood was about to turn sour. Then she dropped her gaze to a clutch of photographs on the table next to them and drew in a deep breath. 'Ah, come on,' she said. '*It's what they grew up with.* They may fight to look normal, but they're not really, inside. Robert still plays his drums when he's mad, doesn't he?'

Tanith had to agree with that. He'd spent a fortune soundproofing the cellar; it might have been cheaper to have analysed all the anger out in the first place, but she wasn't sure that that was possible.

'He wanted to be a drummer, like Red, when he was little, you know. And if a girl isn't tasteful enough to have all the Beatles albums, and not smart enough to be charming to a mother-in-law . . .?' Rosetta raised her eyebrows. 'Well. Easier for them to blame their bitch of a mother for pointing out her basic unsuitability than to realize for themselves when it's too late!' She smiled sadly. 'Always easier to blame their mother. It's the least I can do.'

'Well, I suppose if you didn't do it, they'd only devise ways of doing it to each other,' sighed Tanith. 'The one thing they all have in common is the ability to take great pleasure in tormenting the others. Anyone can see they're all the same blood, even if they don't believe it.'

She knew as soon as the words left her mouth that that was a niggle too far, and that in the warm thrill of this unexpected friendly moment she'd caught Rosetta off-guard and hurt her. Her face looked frozen with disappointment. Tanith wanted to take her words back immediately, but she knew she couldn't. There wasn't really any point.

'They still think that?' Rosetta's voice cracked. 'All different fathers, is that what Robert still says? Even now?'

Tanith nodded.

'God. He's a little shit. And while they believe that, there's a part of *me* that'll believe that too,' said Rosetta, half to herself. 'And then where am I?'

'Go to Patrick,' said Tanith. 'Talk to him, do it now. Tonight.'

Chapter Twenty-nine

Chelsea, 2001

Rosetta murmured enticing little words to her Lotus as she twisted the keys in the ignition and it started first time, roaring into life in the silent garage. She'd known it would, but a part of her was still grateful. Now wasn't the time to deal with the head-wrecking consequences of cars not starting, or other metaphorical downers which might act like the mutterings of black-clad elderly women on her precarious sense of purpose.

Rosetta hadn't been able to bring herself to drive her Elan since Brian had left for good; it reminded her too sharply of everything in her youth that used be right with no apparent effort or cost. The day their divorce came through in 1985, she drove it round Chelsea one last time and then parked it in the huge garage where his old Bristol used to be and pulled on the handbrake. She bought a new Golf GTI every other year, but she would happily have sold Barney into the white slave trade before she got rid of the Elan.

It was beautiful, she thought lovingly, running a hand around the slim steering-wheel. For a car that hadn't seen the streets of London for some years, it was immaculately well looked after. Greg – who assumed (wrongly) that he was going to get it in the great divvy-up of her stuff – came into the garage to turn the engine over every few months, although she wouldn't let him take it, and it had never known a winter without a sump heater warming its immaculate underside.

Like her, the car had aged well, and though unreliable now, it had been just as unreliable thirty years ago.

Rosetta inched her way out of the garage, which slid shut behind her electronically, and she turned left on to the deserted Embankment. Her stomach churned at the familiar smell of the leather and mints in the car, and with no one around so early in the morning, there was very little to tell her that she wasn't back in 1972, driving out to Hedley Grange to see John. Her hands felt so comfortable on the wheel that she couldn't believe it was, what? – fifteen years since she'd last driven this car.

She pushed her glasses up on her nose and peered at the road ahead; it was far too early for contact lenses. The Elan roared satisfyingly as she accelerated down the empty road, changing gear with a firm hand. The boys might think she knew nothing about cars but then there was so much about her that they didn't know, because their arrival had changed so much. It was amazing what you could absorb with little effort when you really loved something, and they'd never seen her blazing up the M1 with her hair flying out behind her. In the days when she drove properly. When she drove cars that didn't need to cope with baby seats in the back.

Besides, knowledge was power, she reminded herself, taking the long two-lane right-hand bend on a racing line, and Rosetta had never wanted to be one of those girls who sat like puddings on the hard shoulder, waiting for the AA to turn up, especially not in a car like this. She also had a lot of time on her hands surrounded by road crew, and you needed something to talk about with them, especially when you were trying to persuade them you were something more than just a groupie. Nev, in particular, had been so keen to explain things to her in the early days, possibly so she could drive the van home and he could drink with the lads . . .

She smiled nostalgically, then put those thoughts out of

her mind and concentrated on not scraping her wing on the double-parked cars.

Rosetta was travelling very light. The need to get in the car and on her way before she changed her mind had propelled her past the wardrobe, which she had already started to carve up for storage. She hadn't gone to bed after Robert left, just sorted through some of the accounts that were relevant and packed the rest in files. Then she'd gone round to Greg's in a taxi and left it waiting by the door while she picked up the box of her own photos from him. He hadn't expected to see her so late at night, but he was up anyway, going through his archive wedding pictures, he said, for some competition.

Barney wasn't there, though neither of them mentioned that.

Rosetta noted that Greg seemed unusually smart, more colourful, but she didn't say anything, in case he took it as a criticism.

He handed over the box of photos he'd picked out from her collection, initially with his eyes fixed on the ground. Then, as they both waited for the other to say something, listening to the rattling of the taxi engine, Greg muttered, 'Thanks,' and she hugged him tightly to her.

'When do you want the others?' he asked.

'Keep them for me,' she said. 'No, keep them for yourself. Take some out, any that you want, and keep them, will you?'

Greg nodded.

Rosetta wasn't sure, but as she turned to leave, she thought he was looking at her in a different way. An unguarded look she hadn't seen in ages.

On the passenger seat next to her was a tiny overnight bag which had more moisturizers in it than make-up, and in the foot well were two of the leather boxes. One full of photographs, one full of accounts.

Hope the ferry doesn't sink, she thought. Robert will go *mad* if I lose all this unphotocopied stuff.

Predictably, Robert hadn't been as easy as Greg. He'd been very angry – not just angry at her, but angry that she hadn't told him about how miserable she'd been. Angry at himself, angry with everything. At least he was fair in his anger, and thorough in his accounting. It was funny to think of Robert having sorted out what she'd ignored for so many years, condensing her messy life into his neat lines in a matter of weeks.

Rosetta grimaced wryly into her rear-view mirror as she changed lanes. There was something fully formed about that boy. When she thought of Robert, it was either as a red-faced squalling child, or a bossy, over-capable adult, who always seemed older than she was and made her feel irresponsible – a very Brian trait. Maybe that was why some devil in her made her behave so badly when she was with him.

And nothing really in between. No memories of where she could have changed things or made a difference. They hadn't managed to resolve much; her head was too full of starting with Patrick and smoothing her sons from the top down. But it was a start. She knew she had to get her life straight with Patrick first, before she could begin to untangle Robert. Maybe some drum lessons from Red would be a good start. Pick up where they left off. Red was looking for a new manager, now Brian was winding down.

Besides, Robert had Tanith.

Tanith.

Rosetta set her jaw and turned on the radio.

She drove fast and confidently and listened to the early morning breakfast programmes for truckers and night workers, only noticing the miles go by as the stations changed frequency and the radio automatically retuned itself. It was too early in the morning for the music stations to be playing any oldies that might make her nervous or nostalgic and once she'd heard one round of news, she didn't want to hear it all over again. She stopped for petrol on the way to

Holyhead and was pleased to see that the car got a few admiring glances from the truckers filling up, the long sleek lines gleaming exotically next to a lumpen Micra in the faint early morning light.

Other than that, Rosetta didn't want to stop again until she got to the ferry port. The clean and clear sense of calm in her stomach powered her on through county boundaries, and she felt light-headed with adventure, as if all the diary lines and boxes that squared off her days were vanishing, fading away, and time was just stretching out in a big blank sheet of paper, until she'd done the one thing she had to do.

When she got stuck in some rush-hour traffic, she called the ferry company on her mobile and booked herself on to the second crossing of the morning, priority parking and complimentary breakfast. Then she phoned the florist down the road and ordered a vast bunch of roses to go to Robert's house for Tanith, while she had her Visa card out. Then she listened to her messages at home, hoping that maybe Robert had phoned to see if she was OK, or if Barney had called to take her out for dinner. But there wasn't anything, and her battery died on her.

Rosetta was early for the ferry and she parked at the front of the car deck, where the Lotus nestled incongruously between a couple of Audi estates laden down with holiday packing. She slept fitfully for half an hour on a stylish but uncomfortable chair in the first class area and then walked around outside on the deck with a paper cup of coffee, letting the wind blow her hair around her face until it was stiff with sea salt. It wasn't that she was too wired to sleep; on the contrary, the strange sense of all-encompassing peace had overtaken her and, despite her aching arms and legs, the only thought in her mind was the road ahead, not what was at the end of it. She'd worked out the route the night before and had scrawled it on a large piece of paper so she could prop it up against the dashboard for reference, but somehow she didn't think she'd need it. Rosetta had a strong sense that she already knew where she was going. And she didn't let anything into her mind except the road ahead, the journey, the act of getting there.

It was eleven o'clock by the time they docked in Dun Laoghaire, twelve by the time Rosetta negotiated her way through the traffic chaos of Dublin and the sun was setting as she accelerated down the N6 out towards the west. She gave up on the radio, unsettled by the unfamiliar accents, and listened to the tapes still stuffed into the side pockets from the last time she'd taken the car out: Led Zeppelin, The Who, The Clash, anything but The End. And as she drove, time seemed to pass with the music, rather than with the distance she was travelling.

The broad yellow headlights picked out the very few cars racing in the opposite direction once she'd struggled through the Galway rush-hour, and though it was chilly outside, the heaters were working fine. As her mind ran like a train along the lyrics playing in the car, easing her back in time, Rosetta couldn't stop herself picturing Patrick, but like Robert, it was easier to see him in little snapshots: as a baby of six months, as a moody toddler of two, and most vividly, painfully, that blood-freezing moment backstage when she thought he'd overdosed on pills. At eight. Just before she found John.

'Oh, shit,' she said involuntarily and gripped the steering-wheel tight.

Rather than push the thought away, as she'd done for so long, she made herself face it, and it still made her heart twist with shame and guilt that the craven fear that John had been taken away from her was still more vivid than her horror that her own son might have overdosed. It was horrible to admit, just as it was horrible to admit that all memories of her sons tended to hang on memories of herself, but it was true. Every disaster seemed to involve a decision *she* had to make. Both accidents had felt like her fault, and as the years went by, she blamed herself savagely for not giving Patrick precedence in her panic. For not remembering *anything at all* that she said to the boys when John was in the hospital, before Anita took her away. What had she said before then? What horrible little seeds had she unwittingly planted? There were whole sections of their childhood that she couldn't tell them about, because she couldn't remember, and they were too young to have memories of their own.

But that's why you're doing this, she reminded herself sternly. A car coming towards her flashed its lights and she realized that she'd been driving with her lights on full beam. Guiltily, she dimmed them.

It started to rain at half past eight, just to stop her slipping into weary doziness. Rosetta had never known darkness like this: thick, black, smothering darkness, like the artificial night of a velvet airline eyemask. There was no ambient light from houses or streetlights as she roared further down the coast road, and only the occasional petrol station stood between the diminishing towns, the neon signs incongruously jolly and familiar in the deserted countryside.

Her headlights picked out the round carved slate bearing the village names as she passed through each little cluster of cottages, and she knew she must be getting nearer Patrick's house, since the English translations began to vanish and the Gaelic crept over.

An Spideal, Indreabhan, Ros an Mhil.

Fairy names.

Rosetta wound down her window to smell the musky peat smoke mingling with the rain outside, letting the drops of water fly on to her skin and wake her up. The air was so cool and clear she could feel it inside her throat and her lungs seemed to expand as she breathed it in.

For the first time in the journey, Rosetta's strange calmness was pierced by a fluttering of nerves in her stomach. She was

nearly here. The cottages were getting more and more isolated, with rocks and bracken stretching out the land
between each stone house, and she kept having to pull over
to consult the worryingly featureless map.

To begin with, Rosetta missed the turning off the main
road, and when she went back, she couldn't believe that it
was a road at all. The headlights lit up the boreen ahead of
her, a thin strip of tarmac between surging mounds of scabby
rock and marsh. In the distance were a couple of pinpricks of
light, maybe windows in a cottage. She slowed to a halt at
the mouth of the road, and started to say a prayer out of
long-dead habit, then stopped herself, and instead reached in
her handbag and pulled out a tape, which she slid into the
radio and turned up loud.

There were a few seconds of crackle, the background
noise of an informal recording session, then the icicle notes
of John's acoustic guitar broke through the silence and filled
the car.

Oh God, Rosetta thought bitterly, if there was ever a time
to kill myself, it would have to be listening to this. Because
hearing him play doesn't make me want to live another
minute, knowing that I can't have that happiness ever again,
and that I was so wrong to have it in the first place.

She ran her hand over the mouth of the tape player, feeling the hot metal where tapes had been revolving all day, and
thought of how close Robert had come to recording over
this, her last memory of John, the only personal thing she
was able to keep from the mass of group photos and stupid,
impersonal fan-club mugs.

She closed her eyes as he started to sing. Hot tears
brimmed around the edges of her eyelids.

'You have the sweetest crooked smile,' sang John, 'but
you only smile for me.'

Rosetta cupped her hands around her face, wishing she
could fool her brain into thinking they were his long fingers,
one more time.

'You have another smile for them, the one that they all see, but your heart is in that crooked smile, in private, for me.'

She let the pain engulf her for a self-indulgent moment, then, with a supreme effort, she opened her eyes and stared down the road ahead, down the boreen to Patrick's cottage.

Hold on to all the feeling in your head right now, and show it to Patrick, she told herself. *Make him see exactly where he came from and why he can't run away, pretending all of that isn't part of him. And if I can't make him understand why I did what I did, trying to keep for him what his father couldn't have, and why it went wrong and how much I wanted to make it all better, then . . .*

She took a deep breath.

. . . then I won't tell any of it at all. Not even to put Sue right.

Then Rosetta turned up the radio as loud as it would go and put her foot down and flew down the narrow road, hearing the engine roar like a plane in the silence of the night.

There was only one cottage along the track and she knew it must be the right one. It was set back from the road by a little lake, small, with a slate roof, and the moonlight picked out the whitewash. Pale light shone out of the two visible windows, deep set into the walls. Outside was a huge fairy ring of stones, covered in moss and planted with rusty bracken.

She pulled up next to an old Alfa Romeo and turned off the engine. It ticked in the quietness.

Nice car, she noted as she got out, pleased that Patrick showed a bit of style, even in the wilderness.

She walked to the door, feeling every stone through the thin soles of her driving shoes. Rosetta's heart was hammering so hard she could almost see the blood pumping in her wrists. She stared at them for a moment, then with a flash of her old defiance, she knocked on the door before she could think twice.

There wasn't an immediate answer.

He must have heard me coming, she thought. How ridiculous. What does he think that car was, the Garda coming for him?

She stamped her feet, suddenly aware of the penetrating coldness of the air.

The door edged open and she stopped breathing.

Patrick looked back at her with an enigmatic expression on his face, his dark auburn hair curling around his ears, faint gingery stubble prickling his chin. He could have lived alone in the wilds of Ireland all his life.

He's so beautiful, thought Rosetta painfully.

'Rosetta,' he said, as if it was no surprise to see her there. 'I thought it would be either you or Tanith. But I guessed it would be you.' His voice had taken on a faint Irish lilt over the calm English vowels.

'Nope, I came. Is that why you went so far away?' she asked, joking. 'To see how far I'd come?'

He said nothing, but opened the door wider and swung his hand inward, inviting her inside.

All of a sudden, she couldn't move, didn't want to speak for fear of saying the wrong thing.

'Will you come *in*,' he said again, more gently, and she stepped over the raised step, suddenly feeling worn out by the drive and aware of a buzzing in her head where the engine note had been until now.

The cottage was small but warm inside, with a peat fire burning in an open hearth, filling the room with an earthy sweetness. Books were piled everywhere, and a couple of tatty bodhrans were propped up by the table, a guitar left flat on a chair and a little basket of whistles by the fire. It was odd to find a room full of life in such a deserted setting, thought Rosetta. It looked as though half the village had just left after a trad music session. She felt unusually awkward, and gauche.

'Will you have a drink?' asked Patrick. 'I was just about

to . . .' He indicated a half-full bottle of whisky on the dresser.

She nodded, trying to shuffle her thoughts into order like a pack of cards. When she tried to think where to start, nothing would come. Is there any point starting at the beginning, she wondered, when he already knows half the story? It's like unravelling knitting. Too many kinks.

'I –' she began.

'No, drink that first,' said Patrick, offering her a glass. 'Then talk.'

Rosetta sipped the whisky gratefully. It was disorientating seeing Patrick here with his shadowy stubble and long hair, looking so much like a man, not the child he always was in her mind. She had to remind herself that he was thirty. Older than John had been. Older than she ever thought of herself being.

They sat at the table, and didn't speak until their glasses were empty. The fire crackled and shifted.

Then Rosetta said, very simply, 'I came to say I'm sorry. I was sorry the whole time underneath, and that's why . . . I know it must have seemed otherwise, when you thought I was putting everything else in front of you, but I've always loved you – too much, probably.' She pressed her lips together, before she said too much and spoiled it.

Patrick set his glass down, and hesitated a moment.

Rosetta shut her eyes, not knowing whether she could bear to have him speak to her in that gentle, agonizing tone of patient reason John had driven her mad with, always reasoning away exactly what she needed to hear most. She didn't know what she had left if Patrick said it was too late.

Patrick said nothing, but stood up and took a step towards the fireplace. Then he turned, walked quickly back, and put his arms around his mother. 'Please stop being so hard on yourself, Rosetta. I know. I didn't used to understand, but I do now. I understand it all.'

'But how *can* you?' She leaned her forehead into his chest.

'My whole life was based on a lie and I didn't even know what to believe *myself* and now I'm trying to set it all right it's only making everything *worse* and . . . God! I didn't come here to cry at you.' She tried to pull herself together. 'I was going to be so *brave* . . . and take responsibility for my actions . . .'

Patrick put his hands on her shoulders and pushed her gently away from him so he could see her tear-stained, sorry face. Her hair hung in thick pale-gold curtains around her bowed head, hiding her eyes.

'Rosetta,' he murmured, 'I said I *understood*. And you have to stop carrying this around like some sort of cross. You were fine. I wasn't going to sit around and wait for you to sort my life out, then blame you for my problems. I'm not like that. This is *my* life, not yours. Not Robert's, or Dad's or anyone else's. That's why I had to go away and find things out for myself.'

Rosetta held her breath and looked up at him fearfully. What had he found out?

'Look, OK . . . this . . . isn't my cottage,' he said gently.

'Didn't you have enough money to buy one?' she asked quickly. She stood up, wiping away the smeared mascara. 'Because you have a trust, you know, with royalties and . . .'

'Rosetta,' Patrick smiled, then the smile vanished from his face, as if he wasn't quite sure if he was doing the right thing. 'This . . . cottage belongs to a friend of mine.'

There was a movement from the kitchen and a million thoughts whipped through Rosetta's brain – a female friend? A wife? A gay lover? An older woman mother-substitute?

Suddenly she felt like an intruder; what right, after all, did she have to march in here and expect a tearful reunion? All she had was her apologies, and an explanation, if he wanted to hear it. If she didn't get it out now, she might never be able to.

'Patrick, I've made a lot of mistakes, but every mistake I

made was because I was *in love*,' she said firmly, 'and I've come to believe, too late, that counts for a lot.'

Patrick held up a hand, but she wouldn't stop.

'No, I *need* to tell you this,' she insisted and got up to pace around, so she wouldn't have to look him in the eye. 'When I was eighteen I had the one big love of my lifetime, and I should have had the guts to grab that chance, instead of pretending to be someone else, to make everyone else but me happy. I thought I was putting myself last, out of some weird, misguided moral logic, when I was really just . . .' She turned and caught sight of someone in the kitchen doorway and put a hand to her mouth.

Patrick groaned. 'Not now! My mother's finally being honest with me and you come and spoil it all! God!' But his voice didn't sound angry.

Rosetta grabbed hold of the chair to stop herself falling, because standing in the doorway to the kitchen, still lean, but now grey like an Irish wolfhound, was John O'Hara.

He had a dishcloth in his hands, and his face was wind-tanned with outdoor work where it used to be pale with late nights in the studio, but he was smiling and his shy smile hadn't changed at all.

Rosetta wondered wildly whether she was having another vision.

'Ah, still on with the old religion, I see. "Though they be punished in the sight of man, yet is their hope full of immortality . . ."' he said.

'"And having been a little chastised, they shall be greatly rewarded." The Wisdom of Solomon,' repeated Rosetta automatically. Her arms and legs felt full of sparking energy, as though she could run for miles and miles, and she was suddenly scared that she wasn't going to pass whatever test this was. Then she realized that she'd already taken the test, and that John was still smiling. And she was still there, and so was he.

'The Wisdom of . . .' She smiled with her mouth closed, in

case the sob in her throat came bubbling out. 'You sancti-
monious bastard.'

'Old people today,' said Patrick, and finished his drink in
one. Then he discreetly slipped out of the room, taking his
guitar with him.

Rosetta's heart felt like a balloon swelling up in her chest,
and sheer happiness lifted her out of her body until she felt
as if she was hovering above the ground with the power of
her joy; a wave of feeling that she'd taken for granted for so
long, and resigned herself to never feeling again.

She couldn't move or truly believe that the moment was
real, until John crossed the kitchen in a long stride and gathered her up in his arms, pushing her face into the bony
hollow of his neck, cradling the back of her head with his
broad hand.

'Let's start again at the beginning,' he murmured, stroking
her hair. 'You're allowed to start again, right up until the last
moment, you know.'

'OK,' said Rosetta, and she felt a huge invisible weight lift
off her shoulders that she didn't have to say anything clev-
erer than that, and he kissed her.

Chapter Thirty

London, 2001

'What is it that's so hard to understand about speed limits?' demanded Robert. 'They are *there* . . . to *protect* you. I mean, God! There should be an instant disqualification law for people who can't grasp that. And if they're using a phone at the same time they should have their car confiscated.' He handed his coat to the cloakroom attendant with a quick smile, and carried on again immediately. 'I might write to that idiot of an MP of ours. See what he thinks about my London driving test idea. If you can't work out how to get round Hyde Park Corner, you should-n't –'

'Calm down, Robert,' said Tanith heavily. It had been a long journey, with him dispensing 'advice' on how she should reorder her office at the same time as offering a running commentary on the road legality of the vehicles around them. Rosetta leaving the country hadn't lessened his quest to organize London. Quite the contrary.

'I am calm.'

She looked at him as he helped her off with her jacket. He was calm too. In fact, he looked positively luminous with joy. She could almost see him dictating the letter to the local council in his head.

Tanith felt a deep sense of resignation sweep over her in a paralysing wave and had to force herself to shake it off.

'And if people actually read the Highway Code, they

would understand that rules are there to *protect* you . . .' He
was away again, but this time she wasn't listening.

Tanith picked up a glass of orange juice from a passing
waitress and gazed round the room, which was crammed
with people standing in little knots, chatting earnestly and
knocking back the white wine, others walking in a slow
circle, pausing to examine the huge black and white photographs on the wall.

The title of the exhibition was 'The Wedding Planner:
Lifting the Veil on The Big Day', illustrated on the invite and
on the huge board by the door by a picture of a gangling
teenage bridesmaid forlornly tweaking the petals off a ger-
bera while the famous Carolyn Mackenzie bore down on her
with a clipboard and a fiendishly cheerful expression. The
pictures were meant to represent 'an antidote to the saccha-
rine traditions of wedding photography', so much so that
some of the brides who hadn't agreed picture clearance
(Tanith assumed) had black *Readers' Wives* boxes over their
eyes, which only added to the incongruity of seeing them
falling over headstones, or trying to get out of be-ribboned
Ford Fiestas. But the exhibition was really about the one
constant factor in all the photographs: the tall and impecca-
bly dressed figure of Carolyn, who hovered in the
background (and sometimes the foreground) of each like a
beady-eyed wedding policeman.

Tanith looked around to see if she could spot her in the
crowd, and if so, whether she could push her in the direction
of Robert. From what Greg had told her, they of all people
were a match made in heaven.

Her eye fell on Greg, who was standing in the centre of
the noisy hubbub, looking bemused but delighted. Three
women were talking animatedly to him and he was, naturally, blushing, but Tanith was pleased to note that he didn't
seem as embarrassed as he did normally. He even seemed to
be giving it some of the old Barney eyebrow here and there.

'Maggie's done really well to get so many people along to

a private view of a mediocre unknown photographer,' said Robert, breaking off from his road safety lecture to grab a glass of wine. 'S'pose they've all come to see if there are any candid shots of your charming mother-in-law.'

'Oh, I think you're wrong there,' said Tanith, determined not to snap at him. 'Greg *is* well known in his own right. And if anything I suppose all his clients from the past year have turned up to see if they feature in the exhibition.'

Robert grunted. 'Good idea to hold it in a smallish room, anyway. Above a pub.'

'I'm going to talk to Greg,' said Tanith through gritted teeth, and swept off.

It took her a little while to reach him in the mass of people. As she waded slowly through the human quicksand she could hear him talking about his day rate and his 'inspiration' and other unusually professional terms. She waved over someone's head and was gratified to see Greg's face light up as he waved back, inadvertently spilling the drink of one of the women next to him all down her dress.

She was also gratified to see he was wearing his dove-grey cashmere jumper and a decent pair of trousers.

'Greg!' she said, and kissed his cheek.

In return he gave her a mute hug, reaching out an arm and squeezing her into his chest. Tanith got a brief blast of wine fumes in her ear and conceded that she and Robert *were* an hour late and that he'd probably opened the first bottle of champagne when he started hanging the pictures.

'You're Tanith, aren't you?' said the middle-sized of the women, inspecting her closely.

'Maggie, Tanith,' said Greg, happily. 'Tanith, Maggith. I mean, Maggie.'

'Great exhibition,' said Tanith, shaking Maggie's hot little hand. She had the distinct impression that she was being sized up.

'Total surprise to me!' said Greg. 'I had no idea what she was up to! I thought she only wanted the negs to do some kind of new filing system. Turns out she was planning all this!' He threw out an expansive hand and narrowly missed smacking the girl on his other side in the face.

Both of them exchanged glances and slunk off together towards the bar. Greg didn't notice them leaving.

'You really didn't know?' asked Tanith. 'With all this great material?'

Maggie adopted a long-suffering expression. 'Oh, you know what he's like. Refused *outright* to enter the Wedding Photographer of the Year, so I had to do something . . . I had an instinct about it, do you know what I mean?' Her face went fierce. 'And I couldn't let him screw it up.'

'Didn't it cost a fortune to put on?' asked Tanith, looking round at the huge prints, framed elegantly in black ash. 'It's . . . very impressive. Little wedding albums wouldn't do *any* of this justice. Is someone sponsoring it?'

Maggie seemed surprised that she'd asked. 'Oh, I phoned Rosetta.'

'You phoned *Rosetta*?' Tanith was conscious that she was talking entirely in stunned questions, like one of Barney's SW3 girlie friends.

'And she sent Maggie a cheque,' said Greg. He couldn't seem to make up his mind whether he was annoyed or not.

Tanith looked at Maggie with approval. But then why shouldn't she phone Rosetta? After all, she was Greg's mother. Any sentient person would assume she'd *want* to help.

And she had.

'Anyway,' Maggie took a large gulp of her wine, 'she could have all the cash back if she wanted it – we've sold seven prints already. And Carolyn wants some. She's going to come and talk to you later about it. For her office, she said.'

'Embarrassment,' explained Greg. 'Damage limitation.'

Maggie let out a howl of frustration and poked Greg in the stomach. 'No! Because they're *good*. Carolyn's been really nice about it, actually. Really supportive. Still, I suppose it's all publicity for her.' She looked up at Greg from beneath her eyelashes. 'I think Carolyn likes you.'

'Please tell me that's not a psychic definite,' said Greg.

Maggie twirled a strand of hair round her finger and jerked her head towards the nearest photograph, in which Carolyn had been caught offguard, smiling into the camera with an unexpectedly emotional grin. There might even have been a tear in her eye. Or a fly, or something. Carolyn didn't seem to smile like that at any of her brides, or their mothers, or even their fathers, and without one of her elaborate hats she looked much younger and almost approachable.

Tanith thought it was typical of Greg to make sure there was one nice picture of Carolyn in amongst all the dragonish display.

'Greg, why don't you show me round?' she asked. 'Show me the best ones?'

'OK.' Greg gave his glass to Maggie. 'Can you get me another, Mags? From the . . . *special bottle*, behind the bar.' He winked, in what he imagined was a subtle manner. As his right eye closed, his mouth opened all by itself.

Maggie winked back the same.

Tanith noticed Barney appear at the door. Immediately the knots of people nearest him unravelled so the girls could get a better look.

'And I think that's my brother arriving,' Greg went on, 'so you might want to go over and give him your phone number now, save yourself a trip later. Give him Tanith's as well.'

'Maybe I don't want his phone number,' said Maggie defiantly. 'Maybe his aura isn't . . . as nice as yours.'

'Mags, you're drunk now, but in the morning you'll be sober,' said Greg. 'And you'll wish you'd slipped him your mobile.'

Maggie looked as if she were about to say something, but changed her mind, and disappeared into the crowd.

'And maybe I don't want to give Barney my phone number either,' said Tanith as Greg steered her towards the photographs.

'Why not? It's years since Robert hung him over the banisters by his heels. I'd quite like to see that again.'

'It's got nothing to do with Robert,' said Tanith, trying to keep her voice light, although in her mind she was shrieking and banging her hands on the front of her brain.

Greg didn't hear her above the general chatter even though she was squashed right up against the back of his head as they moved slowly through the crowds. She said, right into his ear, 'You've had your hair cut, haven't you?' and saw the tips of his ears turn red.

'Yes, I have. Look, this is my one of my favourites,' he said, stopping at a photograph in the corner.

It was a huge family group shot, and a second, or possibly third marriage going on the array of kids that clustered around the bride and groom. Greg had sat the parents on a bench and made the children balance as best they could on what space was left; the result was that every face was creased with laughter, apart from the one requisite sulky teenager at the back and a small child with a black letterbox of a wailing mouth who had obviously just been scooped up by an older sibling.

'Sweet,' said Tanith. 'Looks like a lovely day out.'

'It was.' Greg took a little step back and tipped his head to one side. 'What I love about it is that they're totally different kids, but – look at them. You can just tell they're related, that they all live together in one big madhouse.'

Tanith looked and he had a point. There was a certain similarity about the children that went beyond eye colour or noses. It was more of a spirit that linked them together, if that wasn't too hippie-ish.

'Was it a third marriage?' she asked. 'Nice that all their kids wanted to come along.'

Greg shot a sideways look at her. 'It was a first marriage,

actually. I mean, they'd been together for years. But these are their foster kids.'

Tanith processed this information in silence, embarrassed at her own assumptions about 'normal' families. You should know better by now, she told herself.

'I like it because when I sat down and did the prints it made me realize a lot of things about my own family,' Greg explained. 'All that shit about Patrick not being Dad's son, and Robert trying to write *me* off as some one-night-stand with a roadie. It's actually irrelevant in the end.'

'Robert said *that*?' Tanith's heart sank. She looked over the crowd to see whether he was in chastising distance: Robert was at the bar, holding forth to some waitress about the temperature of the wine from what she could see.

'Oh, it was at the end of a very bad row,' Greg conceded. 'I used to lie awake at night, wondering whether I was some-one else's son, and whether that was why I didn't like my brothers. It was like an excuse, you know, for not getting on with them. But you can't live like that when it's what you *go through* together that counts, and for all her very many flaws, at least Rosetta went through it all with us, and we should give her more credit for sticking with it, even if she quite obviously didn't want to sometimes. Well, that's what I think, anyway. Like it or not, we're all related and I per-sonally can't be bothered with what a DNA test would say. Not now. We have to move on, don't we?'

'Will you read the book? What if she comes out with things even Robert hasn't thought about?' asked Tanith as they moved slowly towards the next photograph: a close-up shot of Carolyn's face as a couple made their vows. Framed by a pair of out-of-focus mothers both pressing hankies to their eyes to stop the mascara smearing as tears cascaded down their cheeks, Carolyn was achieving the impressive facial contortion of glancing down at the tiny watch on her wrist while her salmon-pink mouth carried on smiling at the bride.

'Funny you should mention that,' said Greg. 'I had a phone-call from Rosetta this morning.'

'To wish you luck?'

'Yes, actually, yes, it was.' Greg pulled a face to express his extreme surprise. 'She sounded like she was on drugs. Kept wandering off mid-sentence and just . . . *giggling* at me. Saying how happy she was in Ireland.' He mimicked Rosetta's throaty drawl: '"La, la, la, sea air, la, la, la, real sense of self, la, la, la, found the meaning of life, la, la, la." And I don't know how she *can* be so euphoric when she wouldn't even tell me where to send her post on to. There are catalogues and invitations and everything building up at home. Six months' worth of contact lenses. Apparently she's put her deadline back and is starting all over again with the book.'

'I didn't know she *had* started.'

'Well, no, me neither. But she was wittering on about using Robert's accounts as a starting point, of all things. Sort of "debts paid, monies owing", she said. I have no idea what she means.'

'I hope she's not going to do a complete hatchet job,' said Tanith darkly, thinking of Sue Morton-Thomas and the film script.

'No, not at all. Far from it.' Greg helped himself from a tray of mini-quiches as it went past at shoulder-height and gave one to Tanith. 'She says she was wrong to write about other people when it should all be about her. Bloody typical, but I suppose that's a good sign.'

'Well, being a bit selfish for once doesn't seem to have done you any harm,' said Tanith. 'It's great to see The Quiet One doing a solo gig.'

Greg flushed and shuffled his feet for a second or two then made a conscious effort not to and pulled his head back, without, Tanith noted, having to do an impression of Barney in the process.

She smiled at him and felt her stomach pulse. *No*, she thought. *Remember what you promised yourself.*

'We're having a party tonight, me and Barney,' he said. 'After everyone leaves here. Will you come?'

'Oh, yeah? So while the cat's in Ireland, the mouse will trash her house and drink her single malt, is that it?'

'*No!* We're having it at my flat. Not Rosetta's.' Greg looked mildly scandalized. 'That would be *sick*, trying to pull in my own mother's house. I'm not eighteen any more. And besides, she's probably got CCTV everywhere.'

Tanith decided not to tell him about Barney and the garage. There were Freudian overtones to that which she wasn't dwelling on.

'Can you come?' he repeated hopefully.

'I can't,' she said. 'Sorry, I, er . . . I've got quite a lot on at work. The film's almost done and I need to write some letters. I told you about my boss leaving to go to America, didn't I? And Robert's not . . . Well, I think Robert's very tired after all those accounts.'

Greg moved slowly on to the next picture and stood in front of it. There was a little yellow sticker in the lower corner, which meant that someone liked it enough to have bought it already: Carolyn running for cover in a sudden shower, roaring into a walkie-talkie while consoling a distressed but still beautiful Italian-looking bride. The ever-present clipboard was held over the bride's head to keep her elaborate floral headdress from getting wet and Carolyn's face was as thunderous as the sky.

'I like to think she's on the phone to God in that picture, yelling at him to turn the weather down,' said Greg. He paused and then added, 'Listen, I don't want to get involved, and don't think I'm . . . um, but please don't let Robert make you into someone else. You're the casting director, not him.'

Tanith put her empty glass on a passing tray and picked up a new one. She didn't want to catch his eye, and wasn't unaware of the irony of Greg looking directly at her, while she stared at her feet and blushed. 'I won't,' she mumbled.

'That's not like you,' said Greg.

Tanith looked up. 'No, it's not, you're right.'

It was uncanny how he could pick up thought-waves like that, she thought; presumably Greg never needed to be told when a groom was going to be late. Ever since her long conversation with Rosetta, Tanith had had several nightmares in which she was being pressed to death in a shrinking room, and she knew it was to do with Robert. The trouble was, she didn't know how she could get out, and leave herself room to come back again. Robert didn't work like that, she knew.

They had come round to the table where a dark-haired friend of Maggie's was taking notes and dealing with offers for the pictures.

'Oh, yeah, Greg,' she said, as they passed. 'There's a parcel for you. Came by courier.' She reached under the table and pulled out a box. 'It's from your mother.'

'Oh, this'll be it,' said Greg, rubbing his hands. 'The big dramatic present that will explain everything. What do you think it'll be?' he asked Tanith as he slit the tape with a knife. 'The DNA test results? Her real photograph albums? A cassette tape with her last will and testament on it?' He scrabbled in the polystyrene chips. 'That would be so Rosetta – a cross between Agatha Christie and *Dynasty*.' His hand emerged with a Jiffy bag, with a piece of paper wrapped round it.

Greg slipped the paper out from underneath the elastic band and read out the note.

'"Dear Greg, Good luck tonight – you deserve all the success in the world. Now you can stop being an observer and join in for a change. Please can you pass this on to Tanith. R xxx."' Greg frowned and turned the paper over to see if there was something written on the back, but there wasn't.

'Funny,' said Greg. 'Well, not funny at all, come to think of it. It's for you.'

He handed her a Jiffy bag with 'Tanith' scrawled on the front in black marker pen.

'Careful, she's not above anthrax,' said Greg, as Tanith pulled the staples out. 'No, I'm joking. She wouldn't waste good cocaine, just to scare you.'

'Not tonight, Josephine, OK?' said Tanith and felt inside the bag. Inside was a painted box and an envelope. Inside the box was a set of keys on a VW key-ring: the keys to Rosetta's Golf, the one Barney had driven her home in a few nights' ago.

Tanith ignored that memory and opened the envelope. There was a note in Rosetta's urgent, looping handwriting, with no address or number on the paper. She had written:

Dear Tanith,

Take the Golf and drive as far away as you can, for as long as you like. Maps in the glove compartment. The key to a woman's sanity is knowing when to leave, and when to come back. You're not running away as long as you're going somewhere, even if you don't get there for a long time.

I'm no relationship expert, darling, but I will say this: if the wind changes, your face can stick like that. Apologies for talking like a fortune cookie – am in a rush!

With every best wish, from Rosetta.

Tanith clutched the keys in her hand until she could feel the metal ridges digging into her palm, and gazed around the busy room, letting the conflicting impulses in her head come to a natural balance without interference from her or her conscience.

Eventually, they did, with a satisfying click.

'Greg,' she said casually, 'did you drive here?'

He nodded. 'Yeah, my car's outside. Did you want a lift back? Barney came in Rosetta's Golf, but I might just leave the Beetle here and go with him, since I'm a bit . . .'

'Pissed,' said Maggie, returning with two pint glasses full of champagne.

'OK, so I'm a bit pissed.' The broad smile returned to Greg's face as Maggie pulled a stray yellow sticker off his jumper. 'Hooray! I'm pissed at my own exhibition! Rock 'n' roll!'

'Don't drink all of that,' Maggie reminded him as she handed him his pint glass, 'not until you've done your speech.'

Greg looked aghast.

'Don't worry, here's one I made earlier.' Maggie produced a sheet of A4 and tucked it into his pocket. 'And yes, there are lots of references to me and your mother.'

Greg frantically searched for somewhere to put his drink down so he could check exactly what those references were.

Rosetta was right, thought Tanith: it was time to go. The rest she could decide later.

'I need a breath of fresh air,' she said, flapping at her hot face. 'See you in a moment.'

'Soon!' said Greg. 'Don't miss my speech.'

'It's spectacular,' Maggie added drily.

'I bet,' said Tanith and gave Greg an impulsive kiss on the cheek. He smelled rather nice, of aftershave and champagne.

'Later?' he asked hopefully.

'Maybe.' Tanith smiled and edged her way out through the crush, pausing when she heard Robert's voice stridently enumerating the reasons why those who didn't have personal pension plans deserved to live out their old age in specially converted Butlins' holiday camps.

She hovered there for a second, and then pushed out on to the landing and ran down the stairs to the cool air of the street below.

Rosetta's Golf was parked under a lamp-post and all the lights flashed on and off when she unlocked it, welcoming her to drive it away, just like an advert.

Tanith slipped behind the wheel, adjusted the seat from where Barney's long legs had last sat in it, and started the engine, enjoying the chills of exhilaration running up her forearms. She checked in the glove compartment, and yes, there were maps. Including one of Ireland.

With a wry smile, Tanith reapplied her lipstick in the rear-view mirror, found first gear and turned on the radio. It was playing a song she'd heard somewhere before.